PASSIONATE CHALLENGE

"Who is he?" Garner demanded, his voice deep and resonant with need. He burned to know and yet dreaded to learn.

"Who?" The feel of his fingertips sliding across her cheek made it impossible for Whitney to think.

"Your man . . ."

"Now, Major"—she tried valiantly to summon that old Daniels flippancy—"what would I want with a man?"

It was as provocative a challenge as a woman had ever laid at a man's feet, and Garner Townsend was not a man to walk away from a challenge, however fraught with peril.

"This . . ." He cradled her face in one hand as the other slipped around her waist, drawing her fully against his lean body. Her hands came up against his chest, but could summon no force to resist him. He was going to kiss her again, she realized, and she was going to let him. . . .

"Captivating . . . Enchanting . . . Charming . . . Delightful. All these adjectives apply to Betina Krahn! A Leading Lady of Love and Laughter."

Kathe Robin
ROMANTIC TIMES

"Brimming with a wonderful sense of humor . . . *Love's Brazen Fire* has an innovative plot and is enhanced by endearing, charismatic characters."

Carol and Melanie Leone
AFFAIRE de COEUR

DANGEROUS GAMES   (0-7860-0270-0, $4.99)
by Amanda Scott

When Nicholas Barrington, eldest son of the Earl of Ul-
combe, first met Melissa Seacort, the desperation he
sensed beneath her well-bred beauty haunted him. He
didn't realize how desperate Melissa really was . . . until
he found her again at a Newmarket gambling club—being auctioned off by her father to the highest bidder. So,
Nick bought himself a wife. With a villain hot on their
heels, and a fortune and their lives at stake, they would
gamble everything on the most dangerous game of all:
love.

A TOUCH OF PARADISE   (0-7860-0271-9, $4.99)
by Alexa Smart

As a confidence man and scam runner in 1880s America,
Malcolm Northrup has amassed a fortune. Now, posing
as the eminent Sir John Abbot—scholar, and possible
discoverer of the lost continent of Atlantis—he's taking
his act on the road with a lecture tour, seeking funds for
a scientific experiment he has no intention of making.
But scholar Halia Davenport is determined to accompany
Malcolm on his "expedition" . . . even if she must kidnap
him!

*Available wherever paperbacks are sold, or order direct from the
Publisher. Send cover price plus 50¢ per copy for mailing and
handling to Penguin USA, P.O. Box 999, c/o Dept. 17109,
Bergenfield, NJ 07621. Residents of New York and Tennessee must
include sales tax. DO NOT SEND CASH.*

LOVE'S
BRAZEN FIRE

Betina Krahn

Zebra Books
Kensington Publishing Corp.

http://www.zebrabooks.com

ZEBRA BOOKS are published by

Kensington Publishing Corp.
850 Third Avenue
New York, NY 10022

First Printing: December, 1989
10 9 8 7 6 5 4 3

Printed in the United States of America

One

October, 1794
Westmoreland County, Pennsylvania

"Come on, Whit . . . give it to me. . . ."

There was only a hitch in Whitney Daniels's fluid stride as she moved along the well-disguised forest path. She was careful not to disturb the early fallen leaves with the toes of her boots, and she gently batted away overhanging branches so there would be no broken twigs to mark their passage through the woods. Continuing down the trail, she cast a quick glance from under the brim of her old felt hat at the muscular young man who strode beside her. Whitney had learned at her pa's knee how to tell when a man was serious about striking a bargain . . . and Charlie didn't show any of the usual signs.

"Well . . . whadda ye say, Whit?" Charlie Dunbar was watching her long, muscular legs work beneath the soft deerskin of her man's breeches. He was beginning to heat seriously in the warmth of the early afternoon sun, but Whitney Daniels didn't seem to be the slightest bit warmer than when they'd started.

"I'll . . . chop an' split a cord o' wood for the winter . . . off'n our best stand of timber."

"No." Whitney responded casually, then stopped, searching the twiggy herbs on the forest floor. "Help me look for some teaberry, Charlie. I located some along the other trail two days past."

"Mebee a bolt of cloth . . . flowered . . . fer dresses? I brung some back wi' me fer Ma and the girls when I come back from th' fort."

She responded with determined absence of attention, stooping to sift through the herbaceous growth at her feet, looking for the rounded leaves of the sweet, pungent herb she loved to chew.

"Did ye hear me, Whit?" Charlie squatted beside her on his heels and dipped his head to catch her gaze in his. Golden-flecked green eyes, the color of the impending riot of autumn around them, swept over him in a conquering wave, then casually resumed their search for teaberry. "A whole bolt of flowered cloth . . . fer dresses," he prodded.

"I hate dresses, Charlie." She scowled at him and rose, adamantly concentrating on looking for her treat. Charlie rose beside her and stepped closer, blocking her line of sight. He was bigger than she'd remembered, and just now his plain, homespun shirt was only half buttoned and his hairy chest was damp and glistening. The cumulative impact of his nearness and his blatant heat and maleness confused Whitney. She whirled and struck off down the path again, shoving her hands into her breeches pockets.

"You bucks have the best end of it when it comes to clothes, Charlie. Breeches and boots . . . you don't even have to wear a shirt when you're workin' if you don't want to. Dresses——" She shuddered for effect and, as Charlie caught up with her, she launched into a treatise on the bondage imposed by female dress: "They're intolerable. Why, do you have any idea of just what and how much gals have to put on and cinch up underneath one of those proper dresses? Why, it's purely stultifying, that's what it is. A body can scarcely manage to move in the wretched things. Bone corsets and corset covers and shifts and petticoats. Yard after yard, layer after layer of heavy homespun—and starch! Ugh! Chafing and rubbing——" She realized Charlie had stopped again a few paces back, and turned to see what had halted him.

He was staring at her with a discomforting glint in his eye that said he was well acquainted with what gals wore under their dresses . . . chafing and rubbing . . .

"Are you coming with me or are you just going to stand there all day?" She pivoted and strode off down the path with a new furrow in her brow.

Charlie watched the womanly sway of her nicely shaped buttocks and had to agree that it would be a shame to bury the sight of them beneath layers of muslin and homespun. But on another level, it might be good to watch her in skirts, since he was already privy to the knowledge of just what curvy delights would lie beneath them.

The look in Charlie's eyes remained in Whitney's mind as she walked along, and it bothered her more as she thought of it. He hadn't been acting the same since he came back to the valley a fortnight ago from his three years of soldiering at Fort Pitt. They'd been friends, rivals, and companions before he went off to serve in the army. He'd adventured a bit, it was said, and likely that included a bit of adventuring in the ways of women. Such doings probably changed a body, she realized.

"All right." Charlie's energetic stride soon caught up with her. "I just brought in a brood from one of the sows marked as mine. Might be at least six good shoats—"

"Got all the pigs we can use," Whitney said flatly.

"Whit-ney," he groaned, pulling her back by the arm so that she faced him. Her heart-shaped face lighted with a pure enchantment of a smile. It took a moment for him to realize that she wasn't looking at him, but past him.

"There it is!" She pulled her arm away, then climbed gingerly over several scraggly bushes to reach a small patch of the glossy, low-growing leaves. She pulled several and started to pop one into her mouth, then suddenly remembered the mission of this trek through the woods. "Guess I'll have to wait till after the beer," she murmured, stuffing the leaves into her pocket. She rejoined Charlie on the path, visually scouring the area around her, committing it to memory. "Help me remember this place, Charlie. That's the nicest patch of teaberry I've seen in a long time."

"Whit—"

But she was off again, and when he caught up with her and took her by the arm this time, it was only to be cautioned. "Shhhh! We're getting close, and if you don't want your tail shot off, you'd best hush and let me give the signal."

While he decided how or even whether to protest, she led him on through the emerging colors of autumn in western Pennsylvania. The canopy of leaves was still thick above them, though now edged with gold and yellow and brown, and the shade-loving ferns and herbs were still abundant among the growth on the forest floor. It was Indian summer; the sun was warm and the ground was still damp and fragrant from recent rains. But the cool kiss of the breeze and the musk of new-fallen leaves bespoke the coming end of another cycle of life and preparation for the oncoming bleakness of winter.

They were soon scrambling down an incline that dropped gently toward a deepening ravine. Charlie tried to help Whitney down the last rugged step or two, but she wrested away as if she didn't want the help.

They climbed over and around weathered boulders and past jagged outcroppings of sandstone that had been exposed to the elements, and they began to descend toward the mouth of the ravine. It was a purposefully torturous path, chosen to dissuade unwelcome visitors from the secluded clearing where Whitney's pa, Blackstone Daniels, had secreted his great copper-pot still.

Whitney's pa, like most of the folk in the valley, farmed corn and rye and barley. But if asked to name his trade, he would identify himself with the activity that gave him the most pride and earned him the most gain: distilling.

The folk who farmed the bottomlands of the rugged western part of Pennsylvania faced all the hardships common to farmers everywhere; drought, pestilence, spoilage, floods, and disease. But they faced one additional hardship not shared by their counterparts along the eastern coast: isolation. Even if they withstood the capricious elements of nature to urge good crops from that stubborn earth, there was still the overwhelming problem of how to transport those crops to markets in the East. The cost of driving grain wagons over the intervening hills and the labor involved in such an undertaking was staggering. So, with the ingenuity born of necessity, and characteristic of the proud Scots-Irish who had settled the region, the farmers had learned to convert their surplus grains into a far more lucrative and more portable commodity—whiskey.

Of all the small distillers in Westmoreland County, Blackstone

Daniels was the acknowledged best. He had both the senses and the soul for distilling fine Irish-style whiskey. It was a pure gift, some folks said. For miles around they brought him their precious surplus grain for making into his marvelously refined brew. And just now, with harvest nearly complete, Black Daniels's still was in full production.

Whitney stopped near the mouth of the ravine, waving Charlie to a halt behind her. Cupping her hands to her mouth, she made a convincing imitation of a whippoorwill, then poised, tensed with expectation, until she heard it returned. She flashed a quick grin at Charlie as she proceeded with a good bit less stealth.

The clearing was actually the broadened end of the ravine, sheltered on two sides by sheer sandstone cliffs that were topped by thick brush and trees. On the floor of the clearing were a hastily erected lean-to, a stack of empty casks, a mound of bags of surplus grains, and a makeshift stone hearth bearing a great contraption that resembled two pudgy copper kettles stacked one on top of the other. From the top of the fused and enclosed kettles came a pipelike copper spout with several odd turns and kinks in it. The contraption was Black Daniels's pride and joy.

"Uncle Julius, Uncle Ballard!" Whitney called in greeting as she reached the edge of the clearing. She grinned at the two grizzled old men who were tending her pa's "makin's" in his absence.

"Thar ye be! Stay right thar, gal." White-haired Uncle Julius pointed a weathered finger at her and hitched up from his seat on an overturned keg. They'd obviously been waiting for her. Both the stooped-shouldered Julius and wiry, bristled Uncle Ballard hurried over to a huge oak barrel and lifted its wooden lid, fanning the contents with it to send an unseen vapor toward Whitney. It was a ritual they'd enacted too many times to even count. Charlie Dunbar, Uncle Julius, and Uncle Ballard all watched intently as Whitney braced and closed her eyes, breathing deeply several times to analyze the pungent smell. It filled her head, her lungs, and seeped into her blood. And at every point of contact it was judged against years of experience with the rash, potent bouquet of newly fermented grain.

She shivered visibly. Her eyes opened and her mouth turned up at the corners.

"It's good," she pronounced. "But I'll have to taste it to know just how good."

"Yer pa alwuz knows jus' from the smell, from twenty paces out," Julius chided with a twinkle in his aged eye, and beckoned her forward. "When'll he be back? Ye heared anythin' about the meetin's?"

"Nothing yet. I don't expect him back for another week or two." Whitney strolled forward and beckoned Charlie along with her. "You're stuck with me, Uncle Julius. And I always *taste* first."

That she did. They had expected she would. Through the years the two old uncles had helped Black Daniels with his still; they knew his routines, his habits, and his superstitions about brewing and distilling. And through the years, they had watched Black Daniels's little daughter, the way she trailed Black like a worshipful shadow, the way she absorbed his speech and manner and knowledge like thirsty ground. Black had proudly tutored her quick reason and acute senses, and wryly indulged her quixotic spirit. Now, in Black's absence, they'd sent for Whitney Daniels to come and judge the brew. For they knew that Whitney Daniels had inherited her father's gifts, every one of them.

Julius squinted and began casting around him for the long-handled copper dipper that was used for tasting. "Whar be that dipper, Ballard? Ye had it jus' this mornin' . . ."

Uncle Ballard looked confused, scratched his head, and, as Julius grumbled and searched, he began to cast around himself. He ambled around kegs and the cold remains of their breakfast fire, and finally into the lean-to, where he spotted it in the water bucket and hauled it up with a flourish.

Whitney took the dipper solemnly, wiped the water from it on her sleeve, and plunged it with great ceremony down into the barrel of "distiller's beer." One slow swirl beneath the pungent, foamy mass that floated at the top of the barrel, and she raised the dipper to her nose, inhaling the tangy, fermented aroma. Her eyes narrowed in concentration as she skimmed the remains of the foam from the liquid with the side of her hand, just as Black Daniels had taught her. While the others watched and searched the nuances of her expression, she lifted the brew and took a goodly sip, swirling it about in her mouth.

Then she turned and spat, inhaling through pursed lips, judging every minute part of every sensation. Tingling occurred on the edges of her tongue, and little tendrils of warmth radiated through her cheeks and palate. There was a jagged almost-sweetness in her mouth and a clear-vapored redolence filled her head and lungs. It was wonderful!

"Pure *ambrosia,*" she announced her judgment, her clear, fine-featured face breaking into a smile of joy. Uncle Julius and Uncle Ballard weren't exactly sure what ambrosia was, but Black Daniels sometimes talked that way and they could tell from the pleasure on Whit's face that it was good. They whooped that they'd known all along it was a great batch of brew, and they danced around, clasping both Whitney and each other in great, bearlike hugs of glee.

Immediately, they set about skimming and transferring the precious "beer" into the bottom half of the still. Charlie proved valuable in the hefting and pouring, and Uncle Ballard set about laying his special even-burning fire under the great pot. While Julius and Ballard positioned and sealed the copper still, Charlie split an extra bit of wood for the fire and Whitney restacked it near the makeshift hearth.

Uncle Julius watched Whitney's lithe young body as she moved about the clearing, stooping, lifting, and stacking. It took her long enough, the old man mused, but she'd filled out right womanly in the last two years—straight, broad shoulders, a small waist, and a nicely rounded bottom. And precious little of her womanliness was disguised by the soft deerskin breeches, heavy belt, and loose homespun shirts she always wore. Just then she straightened and arched backward, hands at the small of her back, unwittingly thrusting full, hard-tipped breasts against her plain shirt so that they were clearly outlined. Uncle Julius sighed at this reminder of the passage of time and looked away . . . just in time to catch sight of a sweaty Charlie Dunbar leaning on his ax handle, taking in the same sight. Uncle Julius scowled deeply, reading the lay of the young buck's interest in the reddening of his face.

They all stood together, sometime later, watching for the first drops of the clear, potent whiskey to issue from the end of the pipe. It was a proud and solemn moment that prompted Uncle Julius to whisper reverently: "If'n only old Black wuz here . . ."

"No, Pa's where he needs must be, Uncle Julius." Whitney spoke resolutely and crossed her arms over her chest. "If he can just keep a proper rein on his temper . . . he's got to speak for us distillers, to help Mr. Gallatin make those federals see how unjust their cursed taxes on stills and spirits are. He has to show them we won't be bullied and coerced into handin' over our precious freedoms. Maybe those fat congressmen have forgotten how dearly they were bought, but we haven't . . . and I'll wager General George hasn't forgotten either. He'll listen. Pa fought long and hard for those freedoms; took two British balls himself back in the War of Independence. He's already paid for our freedom with his very blood and he shouldn't have to pay for that war a second time by surrendering up his livelihood to satisfy those federals' piles of debts. It's not right." Her voice dropped to a husky pulse of determination. "And by the raging Sons of Thunder, we won't stand for it."

"Naw sir, we won't." Uncle Julius lifted his shrunken chin, stirred to patriotic fervor.

The sentiments were familiar, and were almost universally shared in the western counties of Pennsylvania. The new federal government of the United States had lurched from crisis to crisis, beleaguered by power-hungry internal factions and beset by nagging debts carried over from the War of Independence. The brilliant and aristocratic Alexander Hamilton proposed a solution that had been used by rulers since ancient times: tax that which folk loved best, yet could subsist without—spirits. The harassed Congress passed what became known as "the Act," levying a substantial tax on both distilled liquors and the stills that produced them. And the tax was payable only in cash money; something that hardly existed in the rugged hill country of western Pennsylvania, where whiskey itself had become the preferred currency.

The sturdy Scots-Irish farmers found the meager profits from their whiskey now claimed in entirety by the hungry federal excise tax collectors. They who had fought with such distinction and bravery in the war for independence now found the personal and economic freedoms they had fought for annulled by the stroke of a bureaucrat's quill. It was an outrage. And they had pledged to resist that unholy tax just as they had pledged to uphold their fledgling country—with everything in them.

Resistance to the tax had been passive, almost playful, at first: hiding stills, confusing and outwitting the collectors of revenue who came into the remote valleys to establish excise offices. But the collectors learned, and with each humiliation became more determined to succeed in their commissions. Resistance hardened and deepened as each successive meeting with government officials offered hope, only to have it crushed in the next wave of political maneuverings in Philadelphia. In raw frustration the farmer-distillers had finally taken up arms and were now poised on the edge of a full, armed rebellion. President George Washington himself was rumored to be on his way, with federalized state militia, to quell the resistance.

With the weight of such an uncertain future on their minds, Whitney and the old uncles and Charlie Dunbar watched and collected those precious first few drops of new whiskey. Whitney sampled them and declared they'd be as fine as any to come out of the Daniels still, given a bit of "barrel time." Then, using a recipe that was locked deep in her very senses of smell and taste, she evaluated the grains from the burlap bags stowed around the camp, tasted the clear water from the nearby spring, and helped Julius and Ballard set a new batch of mash to fermenting.

Carrying water, splitting wood, tasting, and mixing grain, the afternoon slipped by quickly. She located the lowering sun through the gold and russet leaves, gave each of the old uncles a brief hug, then struck off for home with Charlie Dunbar trailing behind.

Uncle Julius and Uncle Ballard stood in the descending quiet, watching Whitney and Charlie as they picked their way up the rocky ravine. The casual tightening of Whitney's breeches across her lush young bottom drew Uncle Julius's eye again. He crossed his bony arms over his chest and scratched his salt and pepper whiskers.

"Black oughten'ta let that gal strut about like that . . . in them breeches," he declared. "She be filled out right womanly now. Just ain't fittin'."

Uncle Ballard cast a look of consternation at his brother, then at Whitney's nubile form. His age-grayed eyes widened. Nodding, he echoed, "Ain't fittin'."

As soon as they were on level ground and striding along the unmarked path once more, Whitney recalled her teaberry and fished in her pocket to produce one of the fragrant leaves and pop it into her mouth. Charlie saw the little shiver of pleasure that coursed through her as she chewed, and took a deep breath to renew his attempt at bargaining. The heat of his exertions in the long afternoon had baked his resolve like a brick in an oven. "Well, whadda ye say, Whit?"

Whitney walked on a few paces, then, realizing he'd stopped, turned to face him with her hands on her waist and an impatient look. But the determined set of his husky shoulders and square jaw surprised her, and she looked immediately to his familiar brown eyes. And there it was: that acquisitive glint, that light of yearning in his eyes, which was the unmistakable first sign of a dead-earnest bit of bargaining.

"Don't be ridiculous, Charlie." She turned and shoved her hands into her pockets as she walked, feeling oddly aware of Charlie's eyes on her homespun shirt.

"What'll ye take, Whit?" he demanded as he caught up with her again. His breath came faster, and there was an edge of determination to his voice that skewered Whitney's attention. It was the second sign. In striking a proper bargain, a fellow always tried to get the owner to state what he thought his goods or services were worth. Whitney swallowed uneasily. She'd thought he wasn't serious, had taken his wheedling and bargaining as a variation on the old taunts and the games they used to play. But that look and that question said he was getting serious now and she didn't like it. Not one bit.

"Don't need a thing, Charlie . . . don't *want* a thing either."

"Well, if'n ye *were* dealin' . . . would it be a whole winter's wood or my next foal, or what?" he persisted, following her as she deliberately abandoned the easy, leaf-littered ground to climb onto a low sandstone ledge and walk along the rocks.

"I'm not dealin', Charlie, and there's no good in discussing it further." She was wishing with all her heart that she hadn't let Charlie talk her into coming along. He surged past her on top of that jutting rill, and as the narrow ledge came to an end, jumped down onto the soft leaf bed and turned to her with his arms raised.

"Come on, Whit."

She couldn't tell exactly what he was urging her to do, accept his help getting down from the ledge or accept one of his several offers. When she hesitated, he grabbed her by the waist and his heavily muscled arms flexed and lowered her easily to the ground beside him. Then his brawny hands refused to leave her waist and drew her stiff body close to his as he searched her flushed face beneath the rim of her hat.

"I jus' ain't found the right trade yet, have I?" he insisted, looming big and hard and heated against her.

"Don't be . . . absurd." She grasped his wrists and pushed them away as she jerked back. It was downright disconcerting, the way her heart was beginning to thud in her chest. "I'm *not* dealing and I don't want to talk about it anymore. What's gotten into you, Charlie? We used to be friends, good friends. We used to hunt and fish and wrestle . . . like . . . you recall that time on Little Bear Creek, when we decided it was time for Hal Dobson to learn to swim?" Her face lit with a mischievous grin. "Lord! Remember how I swam out into the deepest spot in the pool—"

"I don't want to remember, Whitney Daniels." Charlie set his square fists at his waist and stared at her with that discomforting determination in his gaze. She knew that look. He was going mulish on her. "That was then . . . this be now. And there ain't nothin' on God's green earth that don't have its price."

Whitney felt his assertion like a slap of cold water. The alarm that Charlie's single-minded heat had failed to produce in her was now generated by his reversion to that primal and inescapable philosophy. *Everything had its price.* The good Lord knew that was the truth. It was the code she and her people lived by in their cashless society. There wasn't anything a body wouldn't surrender up if the trade was right. She turned and struck off down the path, feeling roundly irritated that he'd throw her own ethic in her teeth to serve his ends. She'd probably underestimated him, and that irritated her too.

"I swear, that army put some queer notions in your head," she growled, feeling a bit relieved as he fell into step beside her. But a minute later her anxiety was booted again.

"It ain't like ye can keep it forever," he proclaimed, watching the hint of a jiggle beneath her shirt as she stalked along. "Sooner or later somebody'll get it. Might as well be me."

"No." Her volume rose slightly.

"Dammit!" He jerked her back by the arm. "Just what makes your blessed virtue so almighty precious? Half the gals in the valley been flickin' their skirts at me since I got back." He straightened, goaded by the heat of his own complaints, and released her arm with a show of disdain. "You ain't nothin' special, Whitney Daniels."

Whitney stopped, stock-still. That was the third sign of dead-to-rights bargaining. A fellow always pointed up the flaws, the undesirable characteristics of the thing he wanted, angling to keep the cost down by belying his own interest in it. Whitney was relieved to recognize this tactic, for it gave her the logical edge she needed.

"Exactly. I hate dresses, I ride wrong, and I drink in Harvey Dedham's tavern every chance I get. I'm not the least bit womanly, Charlie Dunbar. You can have near any gal in the valley. What in holy heaven would you want to bed me for?" She turned her head and blew the chewed teaberry leaf from her mouth for a masculine bit of emphasis as she finished. Her eyes were blazing and her chest was heaving, bringing the hard tips of her breasts against her shirt.

It struck Charlie, for the first time, that she really meant it. She honestly didn't understand what about her had changed and caused such a change in the way he treated her.

"God, Whit, it ain't got nothin' to do with ridin' nor drinkin' nor wearin' dresses. Don' ye know that? Ye went and filled out proper whilst I was gone . . . uppers and lowers." He swept the air with his hand to indicate her body, and suffered another excruciating wave of heat all through him. He clenched his jaw as he mastered it. "Ye got smooth skin and a purty face—I swear, Whit, I'll make it fine for ye. I'm good at it. All the gals 'round Fort Pitt say so . . ." He went to put his hands on her shoulders, and she lurched back, her eyes spitting sparks.

"No." She breathed her reply through clenched jaws and stomped off down the trail, trying to swallow the confusion that had settled in her throat.

"Lord, Whit—I want to be the one—th' first—" He jolted into motion after her. "I'll teach you how it's done . . . real slow and easy. God, Whit, it feels so good . . . and with you . . ." He groaned in frustration. "Don' ye want to know what it feels like?"

"No!" She kept a quick, even pace as she began to calculate just how much farther they had to go to reach the main wagon road. But the prime fruit of her calculation was anxiety, for the road was still some distance away, over two rock-strewn ridges. And Charlie was building fast toward the fourth and final stage of negotiations . . . offer and counteroffer. She didn't want his bargain no matter what he offered, and she could tell by the ruddy glow on his face and half-bare chest that he was determined to strike a deal then and there. Why hadn't she seen this coming?

"I ain't a skinflinty man, Whit." Watching her sleek legs working and her full young breasts heaving had inspired Charlie to take an entirely new tack with his persuasions. "I'll e'en give ye a taste of it to help ye make up yer mind—" And before she knew what was happening, he pulled her into his arms, clamping her fast against his taut body.

"Charl—" She gasped, just as his mouth came down on hers. His lips were as hard as the rest of him at first, but, amazingly, they seemed to soften as she stilled. He dragged his lips over hers, turning and pressing and mashing them around, as though he hadn't quite found the right spot somehow. Then came the crowning indignity—his tongue thrusting, seeking entrance through her clamped lips.

Her eyes widened. She knew what this was; she'd heard the young bucks' low, desultory laughter about which gals had allowed them to "do the French" with them. That was back in the days when they still welcomed her into their midst as an equal.

"No!" She exploded in his arms, shoving back with enough

force to surprise and break his hold on her. She jolted away, trying to swallow, trying valiantly to muster that famed Daniels gift for talking her way into, or *out of,* most anything. It seemed to have totally deserted her.

"Come on, Whit . . . *Whitney.*" Charlie's chest was heaving just like hers. "You liked it . . . say you did."

"I did not," she squeaked, humiliated by her constricting throat and cracking voice. "It was like kissing Uncle Ballard." It was true; she felt the same uneasiness, the same roiling, stomach-turning sense of wrong she imagined would accompany such a kiss from one of the old uncles—or from her own brother if she'd had one.

In the instant it took Charlie to digest that little morsel, she turned on her boot heel and made straight for the crest of the first ridge, at a very fast clip. She heard him tromping up behind her and braced for another round.

"My stallion, Bearcat, he's yours. You always wanted him."

"Keep him!" She managed a glance at his flinty jaw and ruddy face. His fists were balled at his sides and a distended vein was now visible in his temple. She recognized that vein and it boded ill.

"Dammit, I'll throw in our little roan mare—"

"No."

"Then, them bottom acres my pa left me . . . twenty prime acres, Whit—"

"No. I said *no!"* Fingers of dread were crawling up her spine at the way things were escalating.

"Hell's fire, Whitney Daniels, you are the cussedest female!" He labored along beside her, stewing in the steamy silence.

"All right," he ground out, forced by his own brash cravings into playing his trump card. He made a lunge for her hand and jerked her to a straining halt.

"Stop it, Charlie—"

"I'll marry ye, Whit. I'll hop o'er the broom with ye, then I'll marry ye proper, soon as the ridin' preacher comes through." When she tugged frantically on her hand, he demonstrated his superior strength by using it to drag her a bit closer.

"I don't want to get married." She scrambled for better footing, straining away and twisting her arm in his grip. "I don't want to bed you, Charlie. You're like a brother to me . . . it wouldn't be right."

"It *is* right, dammit," he growled, snatching her other arm and using it to pull her against him. "Who else in the whole damned valley would mate and marry ye and make a proper wife outta ye?"

As his mouth lowered toward hers, she read the determination in his dusky face, and old feelings, old responses, burst free inside her. Lightning quick, she hauled back and smacked him in the nose with her fist. His head snapped and his arms dropped as he reeled back. She pulled away, eyes wide, as shocked as he was by the fierceness of her reaction.

"Whit-ney—"

With a dazed look he reached up to feel his nose, and she took advantage of his disbelief to bolt toward the ridge. Over fallen branches, around tree trunks, dodging boulders and low-hanging limbs, she ran. She knew these woods like the back of her hand: each hollow and rill, each major outcropping of rock, each lightning-charred hulk of a tree. Her anger quickly dissolved in the heady excitement of the chase. She'd run from Charlie before, just like this; pell-mell through the forest, with him churning furious behind her. She always won. And she'd win this time . . . see if she didn't!

Charlie tore through the woods behind her, his muscular frame churning, closing the distance between them. The sensations were familiar for him as well, but the intervening years of experience and the promise of victory's hot reward spurred him to greater craftiness than ever before. Thus, when he saw her crest the first ridge and start down the other side, he knew exactly where she was headed, and knew also that she was about to lose—for the first time in her life.

Blood roared in Whitney's head. Her lungs were burning, her throat was dry, fire was shooting down her legs. She hadn't run like this since Charlie left, over three years ago and—Lord!—how it hurt! The pain distracted her momentarily from her frantic instant-by-instant course corrections, and she suddenly found herself flying and scrambling down a wooded slope, toward another rock-filled ravine.

A misstep—she'd miscalculated: This was the Dutchman's run . . . a stream-cut ravine that deepened sharply until it came to the place where the one-time stream had mysteriously ducked underground, smack beneath a massive wall of rock. She'd be trapped there. Cutting a scrambling path across the leaf-covered slope, she fixed her eyes on the far side of the ridge and gritted her teeth, willing her screaming legs to work. Behind her, she could hear Charlie gaining on her, and it stung her to greater effort.

But the die was cast; her misstep had cost her precious energy and time. Without similar drawbacks, Charlie was soon within arm's reach. He grabbed Whitney by her shirt, and the resulting collision as she snapped and whirled sent them crashing onto the leaf-slippery slope . . . with Charlie on top. He wrestled her onto her back, holding her clawing hands at bay as he panted and growled at her. She tried to bring her knee up between his legs as he sprawled over her. But he caught her booted foot with his leg and pinned it down as well.

"D-damn you . . . Charlie . . . you can't . . . do this!" she spat out, jerking and twisting her shoulders, refusing to surrender. "If Pa doesn't kill you . . . I swear I will!"

"Not hardly, Whit," he panted. But he realized she meant it, for she'd cursed at him. It made him pause. The Danielses never cursed; they had too much pride in their fancy range of words to stoop to such. "I'm gonna marry ye, Whit . . . make whiskey and babies wi' ye . . ."

"Like bloody hell you are—" She whipped her head to one side, and before he realized it she had dragged his wrist near her face and opened her mouth.

"Oh, no." He quickly countered her move and pushed her wrists wide. "No biting." Whitney Daniels was a dirty fighter, he suddenly remembered, and it stayed him momentarily.

She saw him staring at her mouth and realized he was deciding whether to try to kiss her again. "Oh, I'll bite, all right," she vowed.

Charlie's eyes narrowed as he struggled with the rebellious curves beneath him. "I wanted to love you proper," he panted, "but I don't have to kiss ye—" He flexed upward, arching his back so that he could reach the front of her shirt, and he sank his teeth into the buttoned edge of the coarse fabric. He jerked his head violently and there was a horrifying rip.

Two

Cooling breezes flirted with the painted leaves of the trees that overhung the main road into Rapture Valley, allowing the late afternoon sunlight to dance blithely about the columns of soldiers moving four abreast along it. In truth, the road was little more than a winding path along Little Bear Creek, and just now, the width of that wretched trail was trying the patience of a troop of sweaty, footsore troops and their unwilling commander.

The Ninth Regular Maryland Militia, or at least this contingent of it, was clad in heavy woolen coats of varying shades of blue, and in breeches that were motley versions of white. Most wore dilapidated boots, some wore plain work shoes, all wore some version of a low-crowned, broad-brimmed felt hat. All carried blankets rolled lengthwise and wrapped diagonally across their bodies, as well as muskets, powder and shot, and their own food and kit. Dirty, worn, and surly, they'd been on the march for three long weeks through harsh mountainous terrain. They'd been barked at by sergeants, alternately boiled and frozen inside their uniforms, and aggravated roundly by flies and fleas. They'd been sorely beset by disdain, dysentery, and lack of decent food—in short, they were not a force to be trifled with.

At their head rode a rail-straight major on a magnificent roan horse. He wore a pristine officer's uniform that was exquisitely tailored to his long, well-muscled body. His blue coat sported a double row of gold buttons and gold braided epaulets. Precisely fitted breeches hugged his manly loins, and an elegant cockaded tricorne, and tall, expensive boots fitted with businesslike silver spurs finished the effect. Though visibly better off than the foot-soldiers he led, he, too, had weathered exposure, hunger, and deprivation. And while his men had blisters on their feet, he bore his in infinitely more annoying places . . . and in stern, aristocratic silence.

Major Garner Townsend raised himself in his gentlemanly saddle and twisted about to inspect his column of men through narrowed eyes. He saw them struggling to maintain formation against the encroaching trees and brush along the road, and his jaw flexed.

"Lieutenant!" he barked, turning back. The junior officer spurred his mount and came alongside. "We're not here to battle the damned trees. Break down formation . . . two abreast."

As his order was relayed back through the column, there was an audible murmur of relief and a palpable change in the muffled tramping of feet. The lieutenant turned back to his commander's chiseled scowl with a sense of dread.

"No word from the scouts," Major Townsend observed testily. "They *do* know enough to report back before attempting any action on their own?"

"Yes, Major," the boyish-faced lieutenant answered smartly. "I can't speak for Benson, but Kingery and Wallace are our best scouts, sir. If there's an illegal still or other activity out there, be assured, they'll nose it out."

"They'd better." Garner Townsend cast a hard look at his junior officer, who was, in fact, three years his senior. His eyes drifted over the lieutenant's dull blue coat and worn boots and gloves, clear marks of the fellow's station in life. In this hastily conscripted "watermelon army," as it was called derisively, a man's social rank and economic status followed him, often to his detriment.

"We're not leaving here, Lieutenant, until this rats' nest is cleared out." He saw the flicker in Lieutenant Brooks's face and looked ahead again, setting his patrician jaw. "None of us wants to be here, Lieutenant, cut off from the real thrust of action, thrashing about in this filthy, miserable creek bed. We're ordered in to hunt down petty miscreants and dirt-grubbing churls as though they were some grave threat to national survival. It's absurd, all of it." Then a rare urge to aristocratic candor seized him.

"I have no earthly idea why you've been sentenced to such

duty, Lieutenant. But your sins must have been heinous indeed to merit this exile . . . under me."

Exile, it was indeed. Major Garner Townsend was an officer of the Massachusetts militia, and since no troops had been mustered and federalized in Massachusetts, he was technically an officer without a command on this campaign into the wilderness. His own call-up had been something of a surprise to him; it came in the form of an official communiqué from the secretary of the army himself. He soon learned that his politically ambitious father had engineered the summons in order to have Townsend present and active at the scene of the first major test of the new federal government's civil authority.

However, his father and the secretary of the army had thoughtlessly neglected to provide him with an actual command of any sort. Arriving at the muster, he was summarily assigned to the Maryland Division and was passed down the chain of command, to lodge like a stone in the craw of one Colonel Oliver Gaspar, who previous to military service had been a merchant of modest means and a rabidly self-made man. Gaspar took one look at the handsome and aristocratic Major Garner Townsend and assigned him an insultingly paltry command of thirty-six men and only one junior officer.

"Three damnable weeks," Townsend growled half to himself, "slogging through wilderness, only to have that pettifogging shopkeeper order me into the tail end of nowhere."

" 'The environs of some of the leaders of the rebel element,' he said, sir," the lieutenant said, braving a terse reminder.

"And likely a 'hotbed of treasonous dissent.' " Townsend's carved mouth curled on one end. "Look about you, Lieutenant." He waved an authoritative hand. "Indisputably a hotbed. Of *fleas.*"

"Resisting lawful tax, committing mayhem on lawfully appointed collectors . . . scalping and tarring and burning . . ."

"It's a paltry civil order action, no more. And precious few laurels are ever handed out for such duty, however honorably acquitted." Townsend wiped his face with a fine linen handkerchief and resettled his braid-trimmed tricorne on his dark, queued hair, the fashionably cropped curls falling around his face. Looking at the placid stream and gently rolling hills around him, he exhaled harshly and forced himself to calm.

"For this grave duty, Lieutenant, I spent five grueling years at the Royal Military Academy in England." He snorted a self-deprecating laugh that brought a surprised look from his junior officer. "This may be the major military action of my lifetime . . . and I'm stuck away up some cursed hollow."

The irony of Garner Townsend's position was not lost on him. By both training and experience he was vastly better qualified than most of the officers in this expeditionary force. But his outstanding qualifications had been nullified by the very political maneuverings and favoritism that were meant to benefit him. A petty bit of class-bred resentment had relegated him to military oblivion.

But Townsends were known for wresting a bit of fortune from even the most unpromising of circumstances. His family's rise to fortune had all begun when a forebear was sold out of an English jail into an indenture on a sugar plantation in the West Indies. Since that time, the Townsends of Boston had in one way or another been involved in the lucrative manufacture and import of rum. Garner Townsend was determined that if his larcenous forbear could rise above serfdom to found a rum-trading empire, he could find a way to wrench a few wretched military honors from a belittling assignment. His face set with determination. He was going to find Rapture Valley's elusive stills and hoard of secreted liquor and he was going to parlay them into—

"Majur!" came a call from the top of the wooded slope far to the right. A blue-clad soldier came hurtling down the incline toward them, battling to retain his footing in the dry leaves.

Townsend's raised arm halted the column, and he waved his lieutenant forward with him as he reined aside to meet his scout. The paunchy fellow was puffing violently as he skidded to a halt next to his commander's mount.

"Commotion—" he huffed and gasped, flinging a finger behind him, "in th' woods . . . half a mile off. Two fellers, mebee more . . . couldn't see it all."

Townsend swung his long frame down from his horse in one sleek movement, and by the time his boots touched the ground, he'd already decided his course of action. "Brooks, stay with the column." He handed his reins to the lieutenant and hung his hat on the pommel of his saddle. "I'll take Benson here—it is Benson, is it not?" he shot at the breathless scout, who nodded. Townsend scoured the column of men behind him. His eyes fell on the craggy-faced Sergeant Laxault, with the voice like grating gravel. He pointed to the man and beckoned him forward. "And the sergeant. I'll check it out myself. No sense alerting these rebels by a greater show of force until we find out what they're up to." He removed his pistol from his saddlebag and stuffed it into the side of his sash, issuing one last command for his junior officer, "Stay alert, Brooks."

"Lead out." Major Townsend waved his scout ahead and struck off through the woods behind him at a lope. The middle-aged scout's report was pathetically vague—"two fellers" and "commotion." But in truth, Garner Townsend would have seized any report as an excuse to uncoil from his mount and plunge into action. After weeks of gentlemanly restraint in the face of sometimes agonizing provocation, he was burning inside for a bit of violence to purge the frustration in his blood. He needed a fight, and not a damned gentlemanly duel either. None of that "ten paces—show no emotion—turn and fire." He needed to bash and wrestle and struggle and *win*.

They ran through the woods, down the first ridge and up the other side, where turnip-faced Benson raised his hand and slowed, slamming himself against the side of a huge old shagbark hickory. Townsend and Sergeant Laxault quickly followed his lead, ducking behind trees and reading in Benson's hand movements that the "commotion" they sought was just over the crest of the rise. After a moment's recovery, Townsend waved his scout forward, and the soldier executed a crouching run and a flopping dive onto the ground on top of the narrow ridge. Townsend winced at the accompanying noise.

After a moment of silence, the major waved his sergeant forward and joined him, running at a crouch and coming to rest beside the beleaguered scout. Benson was craning his neck, scowling, and now rose fully onto his elbows, fingering his musket nervously.

"Where are they?" Townsend whispered.

Benson looked a bit bewildered when he turned to his commander. "I reckon they be gone, Majur. They wuz right here, I swear. They wuz moving thataway." He pointed off down the hollow. "Mebee they run off—"

Townsend sagged, frustration now a rolling boil in the middle of him. He scoured the hollow for traces of passage, and discerned a disturbance in the leaf litter toward the bottom of the hollow. It was small, but to his experienced gaze it laid a clear direction to follow.

"We'll track them." He pushed up to his knees and rose, waving the others up. "Spread out, but stay within sight. And listen."

They began to move again, the rustle of their progress mostly covered by the shoosh and rattle of dry leaves overhead. Moving along the hollow, muscles coiled, senses thundering in the quiet, they paused periodically behind trees to listen. It was a few minutes before the first sounds came, muffled, brushing by their ears on the wind, then whisked away. With greater stealth Townsend motioned them on and they zigged and zagged from tree to tree.

Voices, Townsend realized. They were angry. Strife among thieves, he snorted as he flattened and edged his shoulders around a tree trunk to scour the gentle slope before him.

There they were, two men half buried in a leafy depression, grappling and snarling in obvious combat. There was no further need for stealth. Townsend bellowed his order: "Seize them!"

Laxault got there first, brandishing his musket and shouting at the two to break it off. But they were so engrossed in bucking, gouging, and thrashing that his demand was drowned in the roar of their conflict. When Townsend skidded to a halt beside the sergeant, he was incensed to find his booming order for them to halt ignored also.

"Get them up, dammit!" He seized Laxault's musket and waved him in with an angry swipe of the hand. Benson and the sergeant grasped the big fellow on top and hauled him to his feet. The muscular young buck only now seemed to come aware of what was happening to him, and began to thrash violently.

"Lemme go—dammit—" The fellow's face was dusky and his eyes fairly bulged. His flailing gained him freedom on Benson's side and he turned on the sergeant, swinging wildly and finally connecting. He staggered free, only to lunge, bearlike, at the sergeant again.

Townsend was moving into the fray, when he realized the other fellow was scrambling to his feet, weaving and staggering about. He whirled, throwing down the musket he was holding and barking, "Stay where you are, boy!"

But in an instant he realized the lad was turning to go. In that heartbeat's delay, things moved as if immersed in molasses. An undefinable something about the lad speared Garner Townsend's attention. The moment he bolted for the safety of the forest, Townsend bolted after him.

The boy ran pell-mell through the woods ahead of him, twisting, dodging trees and branches with the practiced grace of a fleeing deer. Townsend followed doggedly, his long, muscular legs and well-honed endurance bringing him closer and closer. Through twiggy thickets and drying fern beds they charged, scrambling up eroding banks, grasping at branches for help in climbing. The boy seemed to know every twist and turn in the place, and twice Townsend found himself stumbling and lurching over hidden rocks the boy had dodged or leapt across as though they didn't exist.

His heart was pounding, his throat was burning, and his booted legs suddenly felt leaden. His elegant coat weighed down his broad shoulders and his sword kept banging against his legs and catching on things as he ran. His braided collar became strangling and his fashionably slim breeches were fiendishly confining. Sweat trickled down his temples, ran down his neck . . . he was being stewed in his own juices! Each stumble, each knock, each hot, aching stride fanned the fires of determination in him. Townsends didn't quit. Townsends turned adversity into profit. Townsends—

Then, miraculously, the underbrush gave way beneath a thicket of tall pines. On the comparatively level ground, the major finally overtook his quarry. The lad heard him coming and made the classic runners' error, glancing back over his shoulder. He banged against the snags of old branches and recoiled in a desperate lunge for the edge of the pines, where there was a thick

undergrowth of drying ferns. The major gathered his strength
for a final spurt of speed and launched himself at the lad just as
they reached that lush undergrowth.

The collision sent them crashing together down an incline,
scrambling and tumbling until they came to rest in a low spot,
surrounded on all sides by a pallet of soft lady ferns.

The world spun wildly and Townsend shook his head to clear
it. A movement beneath him sent a galvanic charge through him,
and he grasped the lad's arm with steely fingers and levered his full
weight onto his captive. The youth was facedown beneath him, gasping for breath just as he was. The lad's hat had been knocked off,
and when he raised his head, he found himself staring at a tangled
mass of hair . . . very long hair . . . half pinned up.

Confusion shot through him as he raised himself on one arm
and turned the lad over. Resistance eased and the lad was on his
back—with nails bared and springing straight for Townsend's
face.

"Oh, no, you little bastard—" The major caught those wrists
just as they reached his face, and he forced them out to the sides,
pinning them to the ground. He found himself staring into big
green eyes littered with gold sparks, set in a furious red face. He
braced, gathering perceptions frantically, sending his eyes down
over the body that wriggled beneath him. They caught on a great
rip in that shirtfront and froze. Another quick vision of that rip
flashed in his memory—the sight of that flapping tear in her
shirtfront as she'd risen from beneath that hulking brute.

That was what had snagged his attention—that glint of pale,
rounded flesh.

She. It shot through him like a lightning bolt, and his eyes
fixed on smooth, creamy skin visible through the torn shirt . . .
curving skin . . . the side of a soft, warm mound of flesh.

"Let me *go,*" she demanded, panting hoarsely. Then her defiant
wriggle, meant to punctuate her demand, ended his aching sus-
pense. The fabric caught on a gold button on his chest and slid
back, baring a taut, rosy bud of a nipple atop a sleek, well-
rounded breast. She watched his eyes widen by degrees and began to struggle again. "Don't you touch me!"

But mentally he was already touching her . . . everywhere. His rattled senses gradually admitted more of her; the slim strength of her wrists in his grasp, the husky timbre of her voice, the narrow curve of her waist. She suddenly went still beneath him, and he dragged his burning eyes from the sight of her bared breast up the slim column of her throat to her glowing face as it was framed in a jumble of gingery, brown-blond hair.

"Who are you?" he rasped. Her warm, panting breath and the expectation of an answer drew his eyes to her mouth. Her lips were full; the top one arched into firm-bordered peaks, while the lower one swept a grand, voluptuous arc. Some involuntary instinct lowered his head toward them until he realized it and halted. But he was close enough to feel her breath on his face, close enough to be bathed in a strange, spicy fragrance that seemed to be coming from her parted lips.

"Let me up!" she ordered.

"Not until I have some answers, wench." He drew his head back, hoping to escape that alluring scent, and finding that it came with him. "Who are you, and what in hell are you doing out here in the woods"—his hammered-steel eyes raked her ruined shirtfront—"dressed like that?"

The defiant tension of her fine-boned jaw was her only response.

"Out for a bit of slap and tickle, were we?" he prodded nastily, only to find himself roused by his own taunt and shockingly aware of the softness of her against his hard loins.

"No." Her eyes shimmered as they fixed unseeingly on the gold braid on his shoulder.

"Talk," he commanded with a squeeze of her wrists.

"If you hadn't come, he'd have—" She bit off her words and sank her teeth hard into that velvety bottom lip.

The ache of unaccustomed exertion now focused in his loins. The sight of her biting that delectable lip sent a wave of unexpected hunger through him. Suddenly, all he could think of was that he wanted to make her stop, wanted to part those teeth, to taste that velvety flesh himself, to salve that crimson slit with strokes of his tongue. The heat from his wild run was turning his body to steam inside his heavy uniform, and some of it condensed to trickle like fingers down his neck and between his braced shoulder blades.

Without warning, his body revolted against the harsh strictures of deprivation and discipline. Need and consequence locked in mortal combat, leaving heat and hunger ranging free. All that mattered was the pounding of his blood in his head and the driving urge to spend his heat within a soft, receptive frame. The frustration of weeks of restraint lay coiled inside him, aching for release. And he lowered his head.

She lay still for an instant as his lips covered hers, then she came to life and began to struggle. He followed her movements instinctively and let the combined weight of his big body and her own fatigue subdue her. When she lay perfectly still beneath him, he eased and absorbed the delicious resilience and the spicy sweetness of her mouth. Tilting his head to fit his parted lips against hers more intimately, he massaged her savaged lips, coaxing, willing her to respond.

Her mouth slowly yielded its promised softness even as the rest of her lay tensed and wary beneath him. And he began to stroke that moist, fragrant velvet with the tip of his tongue, exploring the sleek inner borders of her lips ever so gently. Wave after wave of stunning sensation broke over him, trickling through his hard body to concentrate fluid warmth wherever their bodies met.

He risked freeing her wrists to cradle her head in his hands, exploring the shape of her ears, the sleek texture of her damp skin, the surprising softness of her gingery hair. When his tongue touched the tip of hers, he felt her startle, and his hands tightened subtly to forbid resistance until she relaxed, accepting his sinuous strokes, then tentatively returning them. Her movements were untutored and exploratory, and when he withdrew even her breath stilled.

Her thickly lashed green eyes had a dazed look about them when they opened. The languor of preparation was invading her face, her very body, transforming the heat of the chase into the heat of response.

"Who are you?" he whispered against her mouth, then pressed his lips over hers with aching gentleness. Her helpless response was to lift her chin, encouraging that entrancing pressure against her mouth. And he granted her silent request and kissed her deeply again.

Whitney Daniels had never felt anything like it, never even imagined anything like it . . . the feel of his lips on hers, the tantalizing intimacy of a man's tongue touching hers. She was totally unprepared for the overwhelming sweetness of sharing her mouth or of receiving such a personal touch. Then his hand drifted from tracing those hypnotizing patterns on her face to her breast, and she was equally unprepared for the budding excitement that bloomed there as he caressed her. Sensations seemed to collect and intensify in the tip of her breast in response to those shocking toyings.

"Never mind who you are." His voice penetrated the blur of her senses. "Maybe it's better this way." His words lodged in her mind and she tumbled them about like a kitten would a sock of catnip, feeling through her fascination that the real meaning of them eluded her. He braced, flexed, and pushed back onto his knees, rising like a colossus astride her lower legs.

Cooling autumn air replaced him against her bare breast and heated face, and with it came a sobering draft of reason. The sight of his blue uniform with its gold buttons and elegant gold braiding shocked her; he was a soldier, the uniform said. Logic supplied the rest; a *federal* soldier. She watched, reeling, as his lean, muscular fingers began to work those glittering buttons on his chest. One by one, they twirled and gave.

"I'll soon know all about you that's worth knowing, wench," Garner Townsend murmured huskily, his eyes silvering with heat. The last button released and he grasped the edges of his coat to peel it back. The coat was halfway down his arms when the wench pushed up onto her arms and slowly drew one leg up from between his braced thighs . . . and then she *kicked—Oh, God!—like a bloody mule!*

"AGHHH!!"

All his bodily processes stopped . . . breath, sensation, blood flow. . . . He contracted violently around the blinding pain in his loins, holding himself and toppling over. He saw the wench scrambling up, staring at him, and he tried to grab her. But she was already out of reach, backing away, then wheeling and running.

He gritted his teeth and closed his eyes as he sank to the ground and waited for the sickening waves of pain to subside. The little witch knew exactly where to kick. Dammit—he could be ruined for life!

But his heart resumed beating, his blood began to course again, and the searing patches of light that filled his vision gradually faded. He gulped air and gritted his teeth as the world righted itself. His control finally exerted itself over all but the worst pain, and he pushed up to a sitting position.

He was in one piece; he'd survive. No permanent damage done, he hoped. But it would take something akin to herculean fortitude for him to sit his horse when he got back to . . . *his men* . . . he'd forgotten all about them, forgotten all about his bloody mission. Give him a curvy bit of flesh within a mile of his highly reactive loins and he forgot time, forgot duty, forgot his own last name. Dammit—even here in the bloody wretched wilderness!

Chagrin poured over him, scalding his male pride. His face, his neck, even his ears began to burn. He staggered to his feet, swayed, took a deep breath, and began to walk in the direction from which he'd come, thanking God for a decent sense of direction. At least he wouldn't be lost out here.

Each step jarred both his pride and his body. He afforded his body some relief by affecting a slightly straddled, stiff-legged gait. But there was no relief for his seething pride. With every step his anger grew, fueling his determination to take this miserable assignment in hand and wring some credit—and perhaps a bit of vengeance from it. He was going to go through this enclave of treasonous rabble like a dose of salts, and in the process was going to find that curvy little piece with the legs like a mule. Soon she'd regret ever laying eyes—or anything else—on Garner Townsend.

By the time Garner crested that final ridge and paused to straighten, his double-breasted coat front was flapping, and twigs and pieces of leaves still clung to his gentlemanly sleeves and breeches. Benson and Laxault were exactly where he'd left them, and they'd managed to subdue the miscreant they pulled off *her*. Lord—he growled mentally—they should have given the poor bastard a hand instead of trouncing him. He was probably the one in the greater danger.

"Did ye git 'im, Majur?" Benson jumped up from his seat on the ground, staring at his commander's disheveled state in some perplexity.

Their gaping looks made him look down and he buttoned his blue officer's coat with brisk, angry movements as he came forward.

"I learned all I needed to know. He's the one we need to interrogate." He gestured to Charlie, who was pushing up from the ground, shaking his head groggily. "Get him up on his feet and back to the column. I want to find this ditchwater settlement and secure a bivouac before dark."

"Aye, sir." And "Yessir." Laxault and Benson hauled Charlie Dunbar to his feet and prodded him into motion with their muskets. And as they trailed their hard-nosed commander back to their unit, they exchanged heated looks and silently dared each other to tell him that he had a bit of lady fern stuck in his hair.

Three

Whitney reached the broad, tree-rimmed clearing of her family farmstead and headed straight for the log and planking barn, throwing herself against the side of it. She clasped her heaving middle and gasped for breath. Her lungs were burning, her stomach was cramping, her head was pounding, and there were ominous dark blotches swirling in her vision. She turned her back against the rough planks and pushed her legs out in front of her, bracing to stay upright.

After a moment, she dragged in a deep breath and crept to the corner of the barn. Scouring the side yard and the gardens around the two-story log house for some sign of Aunt Kate, she finally spotted a familiar bonnet, just visible through the remnants of the pole beans in the far garden.

It wasn't too difficult to slip from the barn to the arbor to the kitchen door at the rear of the house without being noticed; she'd done it dozens of times. She was soon through the dark, fragrant kitchen with its stone hearth and sturdy oak table and racks of pots and crocks, and on her way through the keeping room, with its strange mixture of frontier primitive and imported French furnishings. Hand over hand, she pulled herself up the rough-hewn stairway, thinking what a mixed blessing it was to live in the only house in Rapture Valley that had one.

It took a full minute for her to swallow her heart back into place as she leaned back against the door when she reached her room. Sweat trickled down her sides, and matted hair clung to her neck and forehead. She removed what was left of her shirt and held it out to examine its tellingly placed rip with trembling hands. Charlie. With his *teeth* . . . like some bloody barbarian!

She slid down the door as the impact of what had happened that afternoon crashed in on her. She'd nearly been . . . and *twice!* Her green eyes widened as the sights and sounds flashed through her mind again. But, in truth it wasn't Charlie's square, bullish face and barrellike chest that rose up inside her. It was that other face, that second chase, that *soldier.*

Soldiers. She straightened onto her own two feet. It was true, then, about the federals sending in troops to enforce *the Act.* And Pa and several men of the valley were still off at the meeting. Sweet Jehoshaphat—she prayed it was still just a meeting and not bloody warfare by now. Pa probably wouldn't be home for a while. She swallowed hard. Maybe not for a very long while . . .

"No," she declared tightly. "He'll come home." She cast a desperate look around her safe little room under the eaves and wished she could be there at her pa's side. But she knew she had responsibilities here. And with the soldiers come . . .

She pulled a clean shirt from an oak trunk and poured water into a china basin. She stripped off green-stained breeches, tossing them into a pile on the floor.

But as she scrubbed her face and throat vigorously with the rough, soapy cloth, she found that her lips were tender, and that they tingled strangely as she rubbed them. She scowled, concentrating on the feeling, and touched them with her fingers. There was a disconcerting itch welling up beneath the tingling, an odd, pleasurable sort of feeling. And when her fingertips pressed harder against her lips, she felt a surprising surge of warmth through her cheeks. Her eyes widened, then narrowed.

Her Scots-Irish temper billowed up from beneath those mysterious feelings. It was what she'd felt when that *soldier* kissed her.

She growled from low in her throat and licked her lips vigorously. It didn't help. Alarmed, she raked her teeth over her upper and lower lips . . . and only made it worse. Even the slightest pressure seemed to make her crave more. She growled and rubbed her mouth hard with the back of her hand, trying to obliterate the alarming perceptions.

Seizing the soap in one hand and the wet cloth in the other, she covered the rest of her body with angry efficiency. But when the soap raked the rosy nipple of her breast, she felt a shocking flash of pleasure radiating through the firm mound. She froze, her eyes widening as she looked down and watched the nipple drawing up, tightening before her very eyes. What was happening to it, to her? Swallowing hard, she raised the soap and drew it slowly over the nubbly berry that was forming at the tip of her breast. The soap fell on the planking floor with a loud bang. That same tantalizing half-itch, half-tingle she had felt in her lips now lodged in the sensitive tips of her breasts.

Thunderstruck, she slowly brought both hands up and rubbed her fingertips experimentally back and forth over her taut, expectant nipples. Swirling eddies of sensation surged and curled through her, lapping at unacknowledged centers of pleasure embedded deep within her body. Her legs went weak and she felt all fluid and wriggly inside. Her fingers cupped and curled over her breasts, tightening. A hot, moist wave of pleasure swept her from head to toe. She stared at her breasts in shock. Suddenly her hands became *his* hands, and bold, stunning sensations of pleasure coursed through her as memory and perception were enjoined. It was exactly the same as when that soldier had . . .

The wretch! He'd done something to her, caused those shocking feelings to linger in her body, bedeviling her like this! She gritted her teeth and picked up the soap, flushing those strange, tingling wonders from her body with a blast of anger.

This was all Charlie's fault, he'd started it all, him and his wretched *bargaining!*

But in truth, it wasn't Charlie's bald-faced bargaining for her virtue that angered her. She'd been raised to believe that *everything* was fair game for an honest bit of bargaining, including that most personal and intimate of services. After all, that's what most of the marriages she knew were: a "proper bargain" struck betwixt a buck and a gal, where each dealt and traded to get their needs and wants satisfied. Most marriages in Rapture Valley had begun with just such heated negotiations.

No, it was the fact that Charlie wanted her virtue at all that angered her. And mystified her. Since he had come back from the army, he'd spent a great deal of time studying the changes she'd reluctantly undergone in his absence. When he looked at her now, he just saw those bumps and bulges on her body that branded her as hopelessly female . . . and vulnerable in special and sometimes humiliating ways.

Until today, it had still been her lingering hope, a vestige of childhood's wistful logic, that if she ignored the changes in her body, they would someday go away. But nature had already prolonged her childhood well past the norm, and now seemed bent on recouping lost time by inflicting womanly attributes on her with a vengeance.

At fourteen, when most of the young gals in the valley were budding and filling out and casting sheep's eyes at the young bucks, Whitney had still had the shape of a young lad: broadening shoulders, long, gangly legs, slim hips, and a flat chest. She still strutted and swaggered and challenged local bucks in the manly frontier exertions of riding, running, and wrestling . . . and generally beat them. Then at the ripe old age of fifteen, she began to "bust out all over," as she had dismally put it. "Blooming," her aunt Kate called it. Whatever it was called, it made her shirt-fronts bulge and her breeches bind and made the young bucks back off from her company as if she had a bad case of the cooties.

She had breasts now, healthy sized ones, too, she'd learned from surreptitious comparisons. Her waist had suddenly begun to shrink, and her hips rounded and mounded alarmingly. And something had happened to her straightforward gait. Her bottom rocked and swayed annoyingly when she stretched out to cover ground. It was all faintly embarrassing, having her body up and change on her like that. And so she had ignored it as much as possible . . . until today.

"Spit and roast you, Charlie Dunbar," she growled, blaming him for this unholy rebellion of her bodily responses. But she stopped in the midst of rinsing, stilled by the realization: "No . . . not Charlie."

She hadn't felt anything except angry when Charlie fell on top of her and pressed her lips and tried to pry her mouth open with his tongue. And when he had reached through her ripped shirt for her breast, it was just a humiliating invasion of privacy, a typically and absurdly male flaunting of power. It wasn't anything like when *he* touched her there and sent trickles of warmth and quivers of pleasure through her. She'd never felt anything like that in her life . . . and prayed desperately that she'd never feel anything like it again.

Washing her hair took considerably longer than she anticipated. With her wet hair wrapped in a towel, she shoved into a clean pair of breeches and was just buttoning her shirt when three sharp raps came at her door.

"Whitney?" Her aunt Kate's voice had the imperious tone that demanded immediate answer. "Whitney Daniels, are you in there?"

"Yes, Aunt Kate, I was just . . . freshening up a bit." Whitney winced, realizing her thoughtless honesty only opened her to a raft of questions. She was known to wash and scrub her person when the necessity arose, but she'd never voluntarily "freshened up" in her life. She hurried to the door and jerked it open with a purposefully dazzling grin on her heart-shaped face. "Sweet Moses—I completely forgot the time, Aunt Kate—" She slipped by into the narrow passage and would have quickly been halfway down the stairs if Aunt Kate hadn't had the reflexes of a timber rattler.

"Here you are, ready for evening cookfire, and here I am, late with it, and we're purely starving, the both of us—"

She found herself nose to nose with Aunt Kate's stern, blue-eyed suspicion and gave it one last, valiant try. "I'll have a fire going quick as a dog'll lick a dish." She tried to duck around Kate Morrison's rail-straight form and found her way blocked again.

"You washed your hair." It was an accusation. Aunt Kate's eyes narrowed at the same time and by the same amount that Whitney's widened and rolled to catch a surprise glimpse of the towel on her head.

"So I did." Whitney managed a look that was impossibly bright and innocent.

"Where were you this afternoon?" Aunt Kate cocked her head and crossed her arms under her full bosom.

"Out—walking." Whitney faded back into her room and busied herself removing the towel from her head and taking a brush to her jumbled hair. "I'll just do a quick plait, then I'll get the wood and water——"

"Walking where?" Kate followed her inside, scrutinizing her fresh-scrubbed skin, her clean breeches and shirt. She stepped close to Whitney and sniffed pointedly several times. There was the faint scent of teaberry on her niece's breath, but none of the rash, vaporous undercurrent of raw whiskey that often accompanied it. "The still. You were out at Blackstone's still, weren't you?"

"I was out for a walk, Aunt Kate." Whitney was a master of the technique of the artful half-truth. "Gloriful heaven, the colors that are comin' on. 'Even Solomon in all his glory was not arrayed like one of these.' "

"Now, stop that!" Kate demanded irritably. She hated it when Whitney or Blackstone Daniels quoted Scripture like that. Just rolling it off their glib tongues, innocent as you please. "You know you're not supposed to be thrashing about in the woods by yourself, Whitney Daniels. It's not seemly. Or safe."

"But I wasn't by myself." Whitney managed to seem completely absorbed in her hair tangles. She didn't stop to think how it would sound when she revealed: "Charlie was with me."

"D-Dunbar?" Kate choked. "You went out into the woods with Charlie Dunbar? Good Lord, Whitney." Her horror over this new development eclipsed her ire at Whitney's continuing involvement in the operation of the still.

"Well, you said I wasn't to go out alone anymore." Whitney defended herself with no small pang of guilt, "So I took Charlie."

Aunt Kate sputtered, then seemed to find her tongue again. "Charlie Dunbar is no mere stripling, Whitney Daniels. He's a man . . . with a man's . . . urges. And he's strong as a bull. Why, if he were to decide. . . . He could . . ."

It took all of Whitney's control and most of her considerable guile to face her aunt Kate with convincing nonchalance. Everything she'd been through that afternoon validated her aunt's fears in the most emphatic way possible. A moment later, separate relief poured covertly through two sets of limbs.

"Plant your bottom on that stool, young lady." Kate thrust a genteel but authoritative finger at the three-legged stool near the washstand.

Whitney obeyed and surrendered the brush to Aunt Kate's practiced hands. She could tell by the curt, tugging strokes of the brush that she was in for a lecture, and she could guess what about.

"It's not like you haven't been warned." Her aunt's finely featured face tightened as she worked. "You're not a child, Whitney Daniels. You know the straight of things where men are concerned. I've told you what men are like." She took a deep preparatory breath, and Whitney braced.

" 'Bucks,' as you call them, all have a raging tempest in their gut and an unholy taint in their blood. It makes them prone to fits of heat and disagreeable tempers . . . and ludicrous demonstrations of their brute strength. And it makes them crave certain . . . fleshly indulgences . . . the satisfaction of which requires them to seek out the association of low, immoral women. . . ."

"Delilahs," Whitney supplied. She'd heard this part before.

"Exactly." Both Kate's tone and posture tightened. *"Delilahs* . . . women born to tempt and betray and lure men from their rightful duty and decent conduct. Men get that fever in their blood and the heat just purely melts their spines, and their brains along with it. They forget everything they've ever learned: decency, honor, trustworthiness. All they know is they have to satisfy that craving fever no matter what the cost, no matter whom it hurts. Just like Samson craved Delilah, even knowing she was bad clear through." She began to plait Whitney's hair with the intensity of a funeral preacher. "There are two kinds of women in this world, Whitney Daniels: Delilahs and decent women. But there's only *one* kind of man. They're all Samsons . . . all just waiting for a Delilah to come along."

Whitney nodded, more in understanding than agreement. She'd heard her aunt Kate's summary of the world of men before, several times, and it never failed to make her a bit uncomfortable.

Oddly enough, proper, upstanding Aunt Kate didn't hold much with "all that 'Bible business.' " She declared she'd started to read the Good Book straight through once, in her formative years, and was so offended by all the begetting and slaughtering that she never made it past the Book of Judges. There was one story that seemed to stick in her mind, however, one story that seemed to her to contain a cogent and incontrovertible truth for womankind: Samson and Delilah. And though she never talked about it, Whitney had guessed that somewhere in her prior life, probably in her life as Mrs. Clayton Morrison, there was a Samson who'd succumbed to a Delilah.

Now just past thirty years old, Kate Morrison had come to live with Whitney and Blackstone Daniels upon the death of her husband, nearly five years before. She was the younger sister of Whitney's deceased mother and, lacking children of her own, had decided to devote herself to raising her sister's motherless daughter. When she arrived, with her wagonload of elegant furniture and her fine lady-dresses, she was appalled to find a meager two-room cabin and a wild, gangling colt of a girl, who at thirteen was appallingly accomplished in sundry male vices. She immediately set about transforming both their house and their lives.

The log cabin was slowly extended into a two-story house with two real glass windows and hand-split planking and whitewash added to the interior. Kate Morrison made few concessions to the hardships of their frontier setting. A proper house was a proper house, she maintained, and decent standards of living and behavior had to be upheld regardless of location. Unfortunately, those standards also included a rather trying set of expectations for her brother-in-law and niece.

Single-handedly she had set about regularizing their quixotic home life, no mean feat with a pair whose prime axioms in life were: "Good enough" and "Everything has its price." She instituted household routines, provided for improved nutrition and hygiene, and insisted on what she termed "civilized decorum" in her presence. "In her presence" became the operative term in the new Daniels household; for what her aunt Kate didn't see, she couldn't disallow. Thus, Whitney's unconventional life of rambling about at her pa's side continued, covertly, for another two years, until nature itself added impetus to Kate's insistence that Whitney's "buckish" behavior be curtailed.

But now it seemed that what nature and her aunt Kate together had failed to accomplish, Charlie Dunbar and a nameless federal soldier with hot, silvery eyes and a mysterious, lingering touch had managed to achieve. Sitting on the stool, having her aunt Kate put finishing touches on her thick braid, Whitney suddenly felt her entire universe rising in unison and shifting one seat to the right.

Everything in the world as she knew it seemed to be changing somehow, her relationships, her outlook, even her awareness of her own body. A slow-building feeling of dread crept through her. The pure and inescapable fact was that in spite of all her determination and efforts to forestall it, she had turned into a woman.

The only question was: which kind?

Through the rest of the evening Whitney immersed herself in work and miscellaneous talk aimed at staving off Aunt Kate's too-close-to-the-mark suspicions and her own discomforting thoughts. They dispensed with the cookfire, settling for a cold supper, then set their hands to mundane evening tasks like milking, shelling dried beans, and stringing onions for hanging in the smokehouse.

The autumn evenings were growing quite cool in the valley, and Whitney laid a fire in the keeping-room hearth and lit the oil lamp. Kate settled on her quilt-covered French settee, near the fire, and picked up her tin-rimmed spectacles and needlework. Whitney purposefully took down the flintlock musket that hung above the mantel and began to clean it.

All through supper and chores, Whitney's mind had been racing, returning over and over to the soldiers that had invaded Rapture Valley. Sooner or later, they were bound to learn of her pa's distilling operations and come looking for his still and his cache of spirits. And after this afternoon, she realized dismally, there would be at least one among their number who would be ill disposed toward believing any denials she and Kate might make. She watched Aunt Kate surreptitiously, and tried to decide whether to risk raising still more questions by telling her about the federal soldiers.

"Whitney . . ." Kate peered over her spectacles. The sight of Whitney's tapered hands working knowledgeably with a firearm had produced a determined knot in her brow. She'd been doing a bit of watching and thinking herself. "I want those breeches. All of your breeches, in fact."

"Why, Aunt Kate!"

"And your boots. And I want them now." Kate lowered her embroidery hoop and glared solidly at Whitney.

"M-my b-boots? And b-breeches? But, Aunt Kate, they won't fit you at all." Whitney's eyes got that impossible wide and innocent look that never failed to infuriate Kate. It was the hallmark of Daniels guile.

"Don't be absurd, Whitney." Kate's chin came up to a familiar, no-nonsense angle. "I want those breeches."

"Well . . . you know I'm exceedingly partial to them, Aunt Kate." She rose, rubbing her hands down her thighs, having the disturbing feeling she was about to be boxed further into that "womanly" corner.

"And exceedingly indecent *in* them. They're too small and too revealing . . . and they give you far too much license of thought and movement." They both knew the latter was exactly the reason Whitney clung to them so tenaciously.

"But I'm not indecent, Aunt Kate." Whitney managed to look a little shocked as she scrambled mentally to rescue both her mode of dress and her freedom. "I'm just comfortable. Like you always say: a decent woman's known by deeds, not by fancy trappings. You'll recall, I did try that corset and those skirts you made me. Didn't take to them at all. Felt all trussed up, like a pork rump ready for the spit. Just goes to prove the righteous wisdom in that old saw: one shoe will not fit all feet. Why, I tell you, Aunt Kate, once you get used to the slide of soft deerskin against your bu—"

"Boots, Whitney . . . and breeches!" Kate pushed up from her seat with a furious scowl and pointed demandingly to the spot where she stood. "And none of that slippery Daniels talk of yours will change my mind. It's time you began to dress and act like a proper young woman."

"B-but what'll I wear climbin' up in the loft to pitch down a bag of oats, or muckin' out barn stalls, or hitchin' up the oxen for plowin'? I've purely got to have my boots, Aunt Kate—why, even you have a pair of old boots for when the mud gets ass—ankle deep."

"Whitney!"

"I don't see the sense of it, Aunt Kate, I surely don't." Finding practicality falling short, Whitney scrambled yet again and instinctively reverted to the familiar and reassuring ground of down-and-out bargaining. "But I'm nothing if not dutiful. And as such, I'm willing to trade my breeches for those torturous skirts . . . on Sabbath. And I'll sit, properly trussed up, and read the Good Book and not spit or scratch—"

"You will not wear skirts just on the Sabbath, young lady." Kate stalked forward, her expressive eyes snapping. "You'll wear them every day."

"And get not a stroke of work done?" Whitney made the most of a properly horrified expression. "But who'll feed the stock and carry wood and roust broody hens up in the trees? Why, that would be a purely mortal sacrifice, Aunt Kate. We can't possibly spare me more than one day a week."

"You'll learn to work in skirts, in time. And there's no better way to get used to them than to plunge in and wear them every day."

"Every day? But I'd positively suffocate, being stuffed into the wretched things more than one day a week. A body has to ease into these things, Aunt Kate, or the shock of suddenly being encumbered and lashed in could bring on some dread bodily complaint." She was watching Kate's eyes intensely and saw the flame in them flicker . . . just as she'd hoped it would.

"Every single day, Whitney Daniels." Kate stiffened her back and tucked her chin, bracing for what she knew in her very bones was about to happen.

"No more than two days a week."

"Every day . . . but, keep the boots for chores."

"Plus one pair of breeches, and I'll wear skirts two days a week after dinner and all day on the Sabbath."

"Every day," Kate demanded stubbornly. But she was feeeling the pull of Whitney's glowing, autumn-fire eyes and couldn't stop herself from adding, "After chores and all day on Sabbath."

"No corset."

"Yes, a corset. Proper womanly dress."

"Every day of the week . . ." Whitney countered, "after supper and all day on Sabbath. But *no* corset."

They stood nearly nose to nose, neither flinching nor batting an eye. But in the end, Whitney's worldly apprenticeship in "dealing," under the charismatic, smooth-talking Blackstone Daniels, gave her the edge. A slow, stunning mischief of a grin cast irresistible, green-eyed charm around her like a net, and Kate Morrison's proper matronly resistance was swept up in it. It was the final and most devastating weapon in the Daniels's considerable arsenal of persuasion . . . a grin that was a final gambit and a claim of triumph all in one. It was the ultimate seduction and there wasn't a body alive, regardless of age or sex, who was known to resist it when a Daniels turned it on full force.

"At supper *every day."* Kate reddened and scowled at her own gullibility. She hated the way Blackstone and Whitney sucked her into the blessed bargaining again and again, and hated even more the way she always seemed to come out on the short end of things. "And all day on Sabbath." When Whitney's eyebrows rose expectantly, she found herself adding: "And no corset."

"Done!" Whitney slapped her thigh with her palm, her face aglow, her forest-green eyes littered with flecks of gold. She flashed a brilliant smile as she started for the stairs. "Now that we're agreed, I guess there's no need to surrender up my breeches, is there? Oh"—she paused and looked at Aunt Kate with infuriating sincerity—"are you retiring now too, Aunt Kate? I could bank the fire and light you a candle."

Kate drew her chin back farther, and the dent in her brow deepened. Her lips moved, but no sound issued from them. Lord—how she hated it when Whitney nimble-toed around her, then got all earnest and helpful.

"No!"

Whitney collapsed back against the door for a second time that day, feeling as though she'd run yet another frenzied race for her very life. In the quiet darkness, her heart was beating in her ears, her breathing was ragged. The euphoria that always accompanied the final escalation of striking a deal drained all too quickly, and she was left feeling winded and strangely unsettled. She pulled off her boots and felt her way through the familiar darkness to collapse, facedown, on her large mahogany bed.

A moment later she rolled over onto her back and stared up at the ghostly tracings formed by the lace of the elegant crocheted canopy above her. As her eyes adjusted to the moonlight coming through the wavery glass of the window, she could make out the slanting sweep of the roof just beyond the lace. She turned her head to search out the familiar shapes of her room: the lumbering oak chest-of-drawers, the graceful washstand with its marble top glowing eerily in the moonlight, the three-legged stool, and the linen closet. How could everything else seem so unchanged?

She was going to have to wear skirts now, every day; for whatever else they did, the Danielses always kept their word. She sighed heavily and stared up into the crochetwork again, wondering how she would manage to clamber down the rocky ravine to the still in skirts when the old uncles sent for her. The thought of being encumbered and weighed down by those layers and layers of itchy homespun was depressing indeed. Still, she'd managed to dilute her womanly confinement, to restrict it to the evening hours for the time being.

The look on her aunt Kate's face when she realized she'd been into "dealing" again had been purely priceless. Poor Aunt Kate; she never quite seemed prepared for the verbal sleights of hand that came as easily as breathing to Whitney and her pa. In the dimness, Whitney's mouth drew into a fetching grin. At least that hadn't changed.

The realization swept over Whitney like a life-giving tide. Her gift of gab, her unerring instinct for striking a bargain . . . that was still intact, that hadn't changed. She fairly melted into the feather bed with relief. She was still Blackstone Daniels's smooth-dealing, easy-talking protégé . . . even if she did have to put up with the uncertainties of womanhood and the indignity of skirts.

Four

The next morning dawned bright, the lacy frost covering the earth soon melting into a cool, dewy blanket. Whitney was up and about at first light, wearing her precious boots and breeches while tending to her chores. Her mood was determined and her step was light, belying the troubled night she'd spent.

The darkness and quiet of her bed had conjured harrowing images in her mind of confrontations between the valley folk and federal soldiers. But her anxieties condensed and focused alarmingly on the image of one soldier in particular. Dark hair with curls . . . she remembered that much. And she recalled lips that were bold and intriguingly curved, rimmed with distinctive borders. Strange that she should recall his mouth so well . . .

It was some time before she had succeeded in banishing them and managed finally to wrest some sleep from the echoes of womanly awakening that had filled the hollow night.

Midmorning, as the biweekly wash was in progress in the rear yard, there was a flurry of dust and thudding feet up the cart path toward the house. Both Whitney and her aunt Kate paused over the huge black wash kettle to see ten-year-old Robbie Dedham churning toward them at a dead run. They exchanged surprised looks and hurried to meet him.

"Wh-Whit—" he gasped when she caught him in her arms. He slumped against her, heaving and gulping for air. It was obvious he'd run the entire mile and a half from his pa's tavern in the little settlement at the crux of the valley.

"What is it, Robbie? What's happened?" Alarm shot up Whitney's spine, and before he could regain the power of speech, she had a horrible feeling she already knew what the first words out of his mouth would be.

"S-s-sol-diers! Lots—" He gulped and, realizing he was held in a female embrace, wriggled and shoved until he stood on his own feet again. "They got the tavern all hemmed in, Whit. They's a boodle of 'em! They's moved right in . . . goin' through Pa's kegs fer th' certificates and marks—" It all came running out as he shoved his damp hair back from his red face with a grimy little hand. "Didn' find nothin', tho. Pa snuck me out . . . sent me to fetch you—"

"Soldiers?" Kate met Whitney's gaze, paling, clearly alarmed by the news.

Several different reactions registered on Whitney's clear, oval face, but none of them was even close to surprise. Indignation, pride, determination: all were some part of the heat that rose up in her and made the golden flecks in her eyes glow like sparks. But there was something else rising within her too: a bit of dread.

The realization stung. Never before had she let a man, whether uncle or buck, keep her from doing what she had to do. And she certainly couldn't let one humiliating encounter with a soldier interfere with her call to duty now. The sparks in her eyes merged into a decisive glint, and she started for the path at a brisk clip.

"Whitney? Where are you going?" Kate would have gone after her, but the sound of water sizzling in fire brought her up short. She whirled to find the huge black kettle of clothes and water boiling over furiously, and jolted back to her chore, reaching for the wooden clothes paddle. "Don't you *do* anything, Whitney Daniels!"

But Whitney's mind was as set as her shoulders. Her hands balled into fists as she stretched her booted legs to cover ground along Little Bear Creek. She was headed for the tiny settlement of Rapture. She was going to see this federal menace for herself, to find its leader and serve notice that they'd get nothing out of the folk of Rapture Valley. No taxes, no whiskey . . . and no stills.

Most of Rapture's people lived on farmsteads bordering the rich little stream that flowed through the center of the valley. But a few who plied necessary trades had collected at a convenient wide bend in the creek to establish a settlement of sorts. "Uncle"

Harvey Dedham ran a trading post and tavern, which served as the social and commercial hub of the valley; Uncle Sam Durant did a bit of grain milling, with a bit of lumbering and carpentry work on the side; and lean, stringy Uncle Radnor Dennis ran a forge and doubled as local barber and surgeon. There were a few other cabins, belonging mostly to widows who'd been left with broods of children, and had had to move into the settlement for protection. They found sustenance in Rapture's tightly knit community by bartering their sundry homesteading skills for the necessities of life, while they cast about for another husband.

Just now, with several of the valley men off at the "meet" with Black Daniels, Rapture boasted a true rarity in frontier life, a populace that held a slight female majority. And it was into that defenseless community that breeches-clad Whitney Daniels strode, determined to help balance the scales of gender and power.

"Whit-ney!" Someone called her name from down the cart path to the left of the road. By the time she paused and turned, she recognized the voice as well as the plump, graying form hurtling toward her in a flurry of dust and young, unshod feet.

"Aunt Sarah." Whitney scowled, watching Charlie Dunbar's mother hurrying down the path with three of Charlie's younger brothers scrambling around her.

"Whit!" Aunt Sarah huffed, holding her hands to her heart and stumbling to a halt in Whitney's arms. "Whit! They gots my Charlie—"

"Who got—" Whitney frowned, thrust Aunt Sarah's round form back gently, and dipped in order to see her face. The anguish there enabled her to make the dread connection. "The soldiers? *They* got Charlie?"

Sarah Dunbar nodded, frantically trying to recover her voice, and then to be heard above the babble of her offspring. "He didn' come home last night. I wondert . . . but, 'cause he wuz with you last, I didn' worry none. Figgered you two must've struck a bargain—"

Whitney flamed and turned her troubled green gaze aside, listening to Charlie's mother with one ear and to her own thoughts with the other. *Noah's knees!* She'd forgotten all about Charlie—

or about her last glimpse of Charlie—thrashing and bashing against gun-wielding federal soldiers. Her own fate and its disturbing aftermath had completely driven it from her mind. But then, Charlie was so big and strong—and she had been so angry with him—it never occurred to her to be worried about his safety.

"Harvey Dedham sent word just a bit ago—" Aunt Sarah's round face began to pucker, and a sob caught in her throat as she finished. Her soulful brown eyes were wells of misery, and her chin quivered like a scolded child's. There wasn't a body alive who could match Aunt Sarah Dunbar for sheer, gut-wrenching pathos. "Them sol-jurs got 'im." She clutched Whitney's hands desperately as the tears began to roll. "Whit—they got 'im in *chains.*"

"Chains?" Whitney drew the word in on a breath. "Charlie in *chains?*"

"Oh, Whit, ye gotta do somethin', *please,*" Sarah wailed. "Charlie—he's the man o' the house since my Earl passed away back last June."

The injustice of it shot a blast of angry heat through Whitney's blood. The federals took their precious liquid currency, took their means of making more, and took their very land when they didn't have anything else left to take. And now they stooped to taking poor widows' sons away from them. Charlie in chains—it was just too much!

She straightened as she stared at Aunt Sarah's pleading look and thought of Uncle Harvey Dedham's desperate summons. They were looking to her for help. In a pinch, they always turned to Black Daniels . . . Black always seemed to know what to do. Now, in Black's absence, they turned to his unusual daughter to see them through. She raised her chin and squared her broad shoulders as the weight of their trust settled on her. These were her people, her family, her valley. She wouldn't let them down.

"Come on, Aunt Sarah."

The residents of Rapture Valley's little settlement saw her coming from the slits in their oilskin-covered windows and heaved audible sighs of relief. Just seeing Whitney Daniels striding their way was tantamount to watching the biblical David picking up stones. They could tell from the set of her stride and the gleam in her eye that she was dead set on a course straight for their Goliath.

Dedham's tavern was set between the smithy and the mill on one end of an oval forest clearing that extended along the banks of Little Bear Creek. Its two-story log and stone structure towered over the other cabins, visually underscoring the tavern's place as the center of the community. The second story housed the burgeoning Dedham family and provided two sleeping rooms for hire for whenever outsiders ventured into Rapture Valley. The first floor, with its thick stone walls, puncheon floor, and huge, friendly hearth, was part tavern, part village hall, and part trading floor for the brisk business of barter that sustained the valley. Apparently, the soldiers had been clever enough to recognize the strategic importance of Dedham's tavern in Rapture Valley, and had seized it straightaway.

She slowed as she traversed the hard-packed dirt of the clearing. At her back she could feel and hear the gathering of bodies. Rotund Aunt Sarah and Charlie's little brothers bustled along behind her, joined by Uncle Radnor and his three oldest children, ancient Uncle Ferrel Dobson, the widow Frieda Delbarton and her brood of strapping young bucks, who never seemed to be far from the voluptuous widow May Donner. Each time a curtain twitched or an oilskin dropped back into place, more bodies emerged from the cabins and added to their number.

Halfway across the clearing, she paused and set her hands to her waist, scrutinizing the men tromping purposefully back and forth outside the tavern. They shouldered wicked-looking muskets and wore rumpled blue coats and broad-brimmed hats that were pulled down tightly over grizzled and sullen-looking faces. Whitney frowned as she studied them. Somehow, they weren't quite what she had expected. Where were the radiant blue uniforms and all the flashy gold braid?

Behind the tavern, an encampment was visible in the grassy clearing leading down to the river. Whispers and clucks and murmurs of indignant agreement rose as her folk peered at her thoughtful expression, then followed the trail of her gaze to the outpost of federal tax enforcement. When she crossed her arms, narrowed her eyes, and stalked ten paces to the right for a better view, they lowered their brows, crossed their arms, and followed along. The enclave of federal oppression proved to be a field of blotchy canvas tents clustered around several campfires that still wheezed smoke from the morning's cooking. Here and there guards could be seen at the edges of the clearing, cradling guns and nursing fierce scowls.

She'd seen all she needed to see. It was every bit as bad as she'd feared it would be. She took a deep breath, stuck her thumbs in her belt, and headed for the front door of the tavern with her Daniels audacity firmly in place. As they neared the patrolling knots of soldiers, her following began to straggle and dwindle in her wake, spreading itself into a wary phalanx across the clearing behind her. If an explosion occurred, their uneasy glances said to each other, it wouldn't do to be too close.

Five paces from the open tavern door, a grizzled form bearing dirty gold stripes on its sleeve suddenly inserted itself into her path, blocking the way. She jerked to a halt just in time to keep from crashing nosefirst, into a pair of callused hands that held a musket at a martial slant across a burly wall of a chest. Her eyes climbed that steely barrel to a weathered snarl set below two dull-glowing coals of eyes, and she had to fight a constriction in her throat.

"Jus' whar do ye think yer goin'?" came on a low growl that sounded like river gravel grinding underfoot. The big fellow's bristled jaw didn't move when he spoke, and his thick torso seemed to swell before her very eyes.

"Just . . . into the tavern." Whitney managed to distance herself a few inches while giving the appearance of just straightening. Then she took a deliberate half-step back, put her weight on one leg and her hands on her waist, a stance that all of Rapture's inhabitants recognized as being part of the Daniels repertoire of "dealin' " postures.

"A body's still entitled to wet his whistle, isn't he? I mean, there isn't anything in *the Act* that prevents a fellow from takin' a nip in a decent, law-abidin' public house, is there?" She forced her chin upward at a defiant angle, but found her cheeks heating as the big soldier looked her up and down with a brash, knowing curl to his mouth.

"Ye don' look like any 'feller' I ever seen."

"Trust me," Whitney shot back, summoning all her native sense of authority, "you haven't seen anything yet. Who's in charge here, sir? I want to see him . . . *now.*"

"Wellll," Sergeant Laxault drawled, "that be the majur, I reckon—"

"The *major.* Fine. I want to see him."

A wrangle of raised voices suddenly rolled out the tavern door. Whitney reacted to the noise with a start, and the sergeant braced and tightened his grip on his musket. She feinted one direction, then ducked deftly around him the other way and made it to the doorway before she realized the voices were coming her way and stopped halfway in. In the dim, musky interior she could make out diminutive Uncle Harvey over near the bar, nose to nose with a hulking blue-clad figure. They were arguing, fingers stabbing, arms flailing, and every valiant step Uncle Harvey made toward the door was matched by tall, determined boots. Alarm shot through her as the wide blue shoulders towering over Uncle Harvey flexed irritably and she glimpsed the unmistakable glint of gold. She squinted, forcing her eyes to speed their adjustment from the brightness outside, and dread rose in her at the sight of elegant gold braid and loosely curled dark hair. . . .

"—nothin' in yer cursed Act what says I gotta feed fed'ral troops!" Uncle Harvey's genial round face was purpled and puffed like a boiled beet, and his neck had all but disappeared into his shirt collar.

"I have written authorization—the military order of the President of the United States—to requisition foodstuffs and ration stores." The tall soldier thrust a document he was holding by a death grip into Harvey's face. "And by God, you'll surrender them up or I'll see you clapped in irons!" His deep, rolling storm of a voice sent a cold rain of recognition lashing over Whitney.

"I don't got to do anythin' of the kind. Just you wait'll—" Uncle Harvey caught a glimpse of Whitney in the doorway, jerked away from the confrontation, and turned to her with angry relief. "Gal! Thank God yer here."

Whitney could see Uncle Harvey's mouth working, and she heard the rumble of his hot complaints. But the sense of his words was utterly lost to her. The soldier had turned on her, his fists clenched, his tall, broad-shouldered frame coiled, vibrating with unspent ire.

Whitney stiffened, finding herself unexpectedly face-to-face with her pursuer of the day before, and scrambling to regain her equilibrium. Everything about him assaulted her senses at once, demanded comparison with paling memory. Those soft, wavelike curls, those broad shoulders with their gleaming gold braid—he was so tall, so big, standing up. She'd never imagined . . .

In the charged silence she could see his face tightening, his feathery brows lowering, his bold, memorable mouth lifting contemptuously at one corner.

"You!" His gray-blue eyes became steel as they dropped pointedly to her shirtfront, then drifted lower to her narrow waist and the graceful flare of her hips. His straight, finely chiseled nose curled in derision as he boldly retraced that visual path upward in a way that made Whitney feel heat rising in her body with it.

"You!" she countered, her face flaming with the turmoil his insolent visual inspection created in her. A heartbeat later, she squelched her chagrin, and, along with it, all dread of consequences from the devastating maneuver she had performed the day before in self-defense. After all, she hadn't done anything wrong, just defended herself in the most effective manner possible. One look at his powerful bearing and she knew the arrogant churl probably hadn't divulged the disastrous outcome of their encounter or revealed the nature of his "injury." What could he possibly do to her here, in front of half of Rapture and all these soldiers?

"I might have known I'd find *you* here, haranguing and oppressing decent, honest folk."

"You tell 'im, gal." Uncle Harvey scowled, a bit confused by the flash of recognition between them. "Tell 'im I ain't got to lodge nobody I don't want to. And I ain't got to 'sell' nobody food I don't want to."

"I'll go one better, Uncle Harvey." She lifted a defiant half-smile to the innkeeper and, while her gaze fixed meaningfully on her erstwhile abuser, she strode into the tavern with a swagger. The door behind her filled with curious heads. "I'll tell it to his commander . . . *the major.* That and a few *other* things . . ."

The tall, dark rogue stalked one step closer, a vengeful smile transforming his bronze features into an unpleasant blend of raw command and refined hauteur. He sent a lean, graceful hand to tap the gold braid on his collar and shoulder, and when he spoke, his cultured tones drove straight into Whitney's middle.

"I am the major."

Years of training in the emotional sleight-of-hand that successful bartering required were all that saved her from a humiliating display of dismay. He was the *major? He* was in charge? She held her breath even as she held her ground, and the only outward sign of her inner turmoil was the narrowing of her glowing green eyes.

"Major Townsend . . . of the *Boston Townsends.*" He wielded the announcement as if it were a sickle meant to reap a harvest of awe, or obedience. "Attached to the Ninth Maryland *Militia.*" He said the last word as though it fouled his mouth. And his display of distaste shortly broadened. "I've been sent into this godforsaken hollow to uncover and destroy all illegal liquor operations and to arrest those participating in this treasonous trade at *all* levels. I intend to do exactly that."

The pronouncement produced a wave of murmuring from the heads crowded into the doorway, and his gaze swung pointedly to Uncle Harvey. "Failure to cooperate with my lawfully constituted authority may rightly be seen as abetting this whiskey insurrection, and dealt with severely.

"I paid my tax." Uncle Harvey colored and drew his neck in defensively. "I got the certificates fer the marks on m'barrels. You seen 'em with yer own eyes."

"Suspicious certificates," the major charged nastily, "more than a year old. I don't believe for a minute you haven't sold off even one whole barrel of that hell-broth in the past year." He cast a sneering glance about him. "Dead drunk is the only way this pest hole could possibly be endured for that long." He set his lean, long-fingered hands at his waist and thrust his shoulders forward to drive home his point: "My men need *food,* Dedham, and I'll have food and liquor rations for them, and I'll have them *now.* Or you'll have serious trouble on your hands."

"You can't come marchin' in here, pillagin' and plunderin' honest folk, takin' what little means we got."

"It's *not* plundering, it's commerce, pure and simple. I've said you'll receive notes redeemable in hard coin at the army paymaster in Pittsburgh. You'll be paid full well in U.S. currency for the swill you serve."

"Currency?" Whitney pulled her chin back with an incredulous look at Uncle Harvey. "He wants to give you *cash money* for food and whiskey?"

"I've told the fool so several times." Townsend snorted contemptuously and settled back on one leg, feeling thoroughly vindicated by his civil offer and grudgingly glad he'd restrained his impulse to lay hands on Whitney the instant he'd laid eyes on her again. Restraint was a well-known Townsend virtue.

"Well, if that's not the silliest thing I ever heard," she murmured, staring at Uncle Harvey and shaking her head in sheer disbelief. The initial shock of seeing her "soldier" again, of learning he was the one in command of the federal force was fading. Her inner control was returning, and close on its heels came her cat-quick Daniels cunning.

"See there, Dedham?" he sneered, savoring the irony of *her* championing his logic. "The voice of reason."

"Money for food?" She laughed softly, realizing the major had taken her comments for support of his arrogant demands. Her coolly derisive gaze swung from Uncle Harvey to the tall major. He was so arrogantly "eastern" and high-handed, it was a wonder to behold. Money for food. Only an easterner would stoop to such dealings. There was something purely indecent about the very idea!

"Now what would Uncle Harvey here want with *money?"* she asked in a voice still husky with amusement. "He can't eat it or wear it, can't plow or plant with it . . . and it surely won't keep him dry."

Townsend twitched, and reddened furiously at her insolence.

"In Rapture," she said, taking advantage of his speechlessness to continue, "a man trades honest sweat for his bread. Just like the Almighty decreed he should: 'In the sweat of thy face shalt thou eat bread'—the Book of Genesis. Whether he puts his sweat into the soil itself or trades the fruits of it to his neighbor, a fellow earns his bread by it in Rapture Valley. We've got no use for money. Whatever else is needful is procured by good, honest *trading*."

"Barter." The major's nostrils flared and his lips curled as though that word soiled them too.

"Exactly." Whitney broke into a devilish crook of a smile. "If you need food, then you need to work at strikin' the proper bargain, Major." There was a hot bit of mischief in her eyes as they flitted over his manly form with the same raw evaluation that he had turned on her moments before. So the jack-a-dandy major thought bartering was beneath him, did he?

"Well now, Major." She leaned back on one leg and set her hands at her waist in a parody of his arrogant stance. "The harvest has been dismal and dismayin' this year . . . food is purely scarce all around. Isn't that right, Uncle Harvey?" Harvey's jaw loosened, then shut as he caught that familiar look in Whitney's eye.

"Ohhhh, dismal an' dismayin'," he echoed, nodding earnestly.

"Food and whiskey ration for all those hungry men"—Whitney shook her head with mock gravity—"it'd purely *deplete* Uncle Harvey's already beset and beleaguered winter stores. Isn't that right, Uncle Harvey?"

"Bee-leegered an' bee-set," Uncle Harvey nodded again, wide eyed.

"So you'd just as well put your paper promises back in your pocket, Major, and do a bit of honest tradin' instead." She looked his rigid frame up and down pointedly. He looked like a man just itchin' for a lesson in bargaining. "Now, what have you got to trade that's worth the great hardship you're looking to inflict upon Uncle Harvey here?"

That drew muffled snickers from the heads that filled the doorway, including some belonging to blue-clad shoulders. Red was seeping up Major Townsend's neck, and his skin and jaw tightened the way a man's does when he's feeling twinges of pain. He shot a burning glare at *her,* then at their leering audience.

"That's enough—"

"Horses?" Whitney was just settling into stride and growing rather fond of her game. "You could use a few good horses, couldn't you, Uncle Harv?"

"No horses, dammit," he snarled, his hands slamming down his sides, where they fell into fists.

"From what I seen, they gots only two," Harvey offered.

"Two horses?" Whitney's disbelief struck the major in a very vulnerable place.

"We're infantry, dammit, not bloody dragoons." He stalked toward her, his wide shoulders like a moving wall, his face an irritable mask.

"No horses? Oh, that's a pity." Whitney's green eyes widened as he advanced, and she began to retreat toward the door at the same deliberate pace. She had him riled now, right where she wanted him. It was an established fact that a fellow couldn't think or bargain worth piddle when he was all wrought up and furious.

"Well, then, what else do you have? Blankets? You could use some good, tight-woven blankets, right, Uncle Harvey?"

"Uh—blankets. Sure—" Uncle Harvey nodded, watching the major growing inside his coat, hardening as he closed in on Whitney.

"No bloody blankets!" The major backed her right into those curious heads in the doorway, scattering them back into the clearing.

He forced her straight out the door, into the bright sunlight, and into the plain sight of Rapture's collected citizenry and his own puzzled and glowering men. This part of Maryland's rough and sometimes disreputable Ninth Militia had never seen their commander show anything more than cool disdain, no matter what the provocation. They melted back, glued to the sight of his rising passions. A path into the clearing opened among the crowd as the major forced Whitney back, hulking over her, burning with urges to bash and thrash.

"No blankets either? How about boots?" From the corner of her eye she saw the sly grins on her people's faces and the lurid curiosity on the soldiers'. Her eyes danced wickedly down his braced and combative form to his long, muscular legs. "Lord, you do have splendid boots, Major. The finest I've ever seen."

A wave of jocular agreement greeted her judgment. "But I'm not sure they'd feed a whole regiment."

"Dammit—" The major was quivering with raging heat, and that was the only word he could seem to summon.

"No boots?" A taunting little grin escaped to tug at the corners of her mouth in spite of her.

"No!" he roared, relieved to find at least one other syllable within his command.

"Well, it doesn't appear you've got much anybody'd want, Major." She came to a dead stop, beaming all the infuriating innocence of a beguiling Daniels smile. The hidden meaning in her assessment was meant to push him over the edge.

He stopped, molten beneath his stonelike exterior. For a minute she wasn't sure she'd succeeded, so she decided to add: "Of course, if your men were of a mind to work for their suppers . . . felling trees, pulling stumps, splitting winter wood. There's always a place at a Rapture Valley table for a pair of diligent hands."

"Dammit!" His reflexes were as quick as lightning and his lean, muscular hands closing on her upper arms had the same nerve-burning electrical jolt. A wave of shocking mutters went through the spectators. "No horses, no blankets, no bloody bartering . . . my men *have* work to do, you understand?"

"Wait!" Whitney braced in his hands, rocked by the galvanic impact of his touch and scrambling to maintain her margin of advantage. "Maybe there *is* something . . ."

Her continuing gambits in the face of his physical threat stunned him, and he halted for an instant. Just what in hell did he have to do to daunt the little witch?

"Your buttons." She brought her hands up, braced, and with one finger plinked an elegant gold button so that it rattled back and forth on his hard chest. "If they're real gold—"

Inside that staid military coat, inside that hard military body, the vibrations of that rattling button were suddenly echoing through his flesh and descending. In horror he watched that slender finger reach out again and felt the same devastating reverberations reaching deep into his loins. *Oh, God.* That molten heat was draining from his head, his shoulders, his coiled arms . . . right into his wretched loins. Here, in front of—

"They *are* real, aren't they?" She stared up into his heat-bronzed face, glimpsing a flicker of uncertainty that the "trader" in her read fluently.

His tongue seemed bolted to the roof of his mouth as he fought the excruciating waves of feeling. She was saying something . . . those clear forest-green eyes littered with flecks of gold, those soft, velvety lips, bending in a coquette's curve . . . then she was bending her head, coming toward his chest . . . her lips parting . . .

Whitney's teeth closed on one gold button, and she felt the soft metal give gratifyingly as she clamped down hard, purposefully distorting and flattening the hollow fastening. She drew back with a flush in her cheeks and a challenging gleam in her eye.

"Now, those"—for some reason she had to swallow to finish it—"might be worth a week's provender. Mighty nice buttons, Major."

Townsend looked down his chest to the squashed button and froze, choked and suspended between disbelief and eruption. His button! *The little witch bit his blasted button!*

Peals of laughter erupted all around, setting off the impending explosion inside him. He clamped down on her arms savagely, giving her a nasty shake.

"You little witch." He released her forcefully and she stumbled back two steps. "And *you*"—he whirled—"all of you—don't think you've won anything with this absurd display—except *enmity*."

The jovial taunt of an instant past now stuck fast in every throat, and a quivering silence reigned. The major towered above them, black with wrath and deadly potent. He turned on Uncle Harvey's paling face with molten-silver eyes and a determination that was chilling.

"You'll supply my men with food, and myself and my lieutenant with quarters." He stabbed a burning glare back at Whitney and shook the crumpled parchment in his hand. "And you'll do it for paper promises, or I'll shut down your miserable establishment altogether. And the rest of you"—his arm swept over the stunned crowd—"will cooperate fully with our searches and investigations. We'll find the illegal liquor you have hidden and we'll find your secreted stills one way or the other. And if you interfere"—he turned, white-eyed, on Whitney—"you'll find yourselves in chains, the lot of you!"

Whitney stiffened, her face aflame. She'd never seen such deep, pulsating hostility in a human being in her life. He meant it—he'd put them in ch— "Chains?" She dragged it in on a breath, remembering, and lifted an angry chin to the major. "You've already got Charlie Dunbar in chains somewhere, and he's done nothing—nothing at all."

"If you're referring to your little playmate of yesterday"—he towered over her, his face radiating heat like an iron forge—"he's exactly where he deserves to be. And he'll stay there until we're through questioning him. By the time we're through"—his voice lowered to a menacing rasp—"he'll tell us everything he knows."

"Charlie?" she snorted contemptuously. "Charlie doesn't know anything about stills or secreted liquor! He's just a plain farmer . . . and sole support of his ma, Aunt Sarah, and his six younger brothers and sisters! She's worried sick about him and will likely starve this winter unless he finishes corn harvest."

"Oh, *please,* yer honor," came a choked voice from behind the jostling crowd. Aunt Sarah Dunbar shoved through to the front, clutching her heaving bosom with one hand and reaching for the major's impeccable sleeve with the other. "Please, let me see m'boy."

Townsend shook off Aunt Sarah's hand. "He's a prisoner and he'll stay a prisoner for as long as illegal stills continue to produce that gut-rotting swill in this valley." Then he turned on Rapture's horrified inhabitants. "The sooner you deliver up the criminals among you, the sooner we'll be gone and you can get back to . . . whatever it is you do in this godforsaken sty. And you"—he jabbed a finger at Whitney—"you'd better stay out of my way."

When he whirled to make for the tavern, he found himself facing half a dozen of his own men, their faces dark as they took in Aunt Sarah's dramatic tears.

"What are you gawking at?" the major demanded, jerking his

coat down into place as though straightening his rumpled dignity as well. His thundering order snapped their fascination with Aunt Sarah and sent them lumbering to obey.

"Back to your posts!"

Five

Rapture's citizens suffered the major's parting blast, then turned from the confrontation in front of the tavern in shock. They watched Whitney spin on her heel and head for the far end of the clearing, and followed instinctively. They always looked to a Daniels in times of trouble, and, Lord knew, they certainly had a passel of trouble now. Their minds were full of the lean, hardened faces of the soldiers, and of the angry force of the soldiers' aristocratic commander. The full impact of their stubborn opposition to the tax on their stills and whiskey was finally brought home to them.

When they neared the edge of the clearing, Whitney paused and turned aside sharply, heading for the side yard of buxom May Donner's cabin. With nervous glances back over their shoulders, Rapture's folk followed, reading in her destination a very sensible desire to be out of sight of the tavern.

She sought out one of several tree stumps in the grassy yard and plopped down on it, her cheeks flushed like blushing apples and her eyes stormy. She was feeling a jumble of strange new feelings: anger, frustration, and not a little humiliation at the way the major had overridden her clever manipulations with raw anger at the end. He'd effectively nullified all the embarrassment of the mortifying little exchanges she'd put him through. Nobody had ever turned the tables so effectively on her before, even if it had been done with brute force.

Aunt Sarah and the others wandered about, their minds buzzing, and slowly settled themselves, uncles and aunts, bucks, gals, and children, so they could all watch Whitney.

"Whaddo we do, Whit?" Old Uncle Ferrel Dobson finally

raised his shrunken chin and age-faded eyes from a nearby stump in bewilderment.

What indeed? Whitney took a long breath and drummed her fingertips on her thigh, a sure sign she was thinking. Her eyes shifted and darted as though scrutinizing some mental tableau.

"That thar major." Uncle Radnor rubbed his stubbled chin with a soot-stained smithy's hand. "He acts like he swallered an iron poker an' can't stoop to—"

"Hell's fahr," Uncle Ferrel broke in, "e'en his own men look like they hate 'is guts."

"Got breeches made o' iron, he has," buxom May Donner declared with a righteous nod.

"An' got iron fer a heart as well." Aunt Sarah started to pucker up again and was soon gathered against May Donner's ample bosom, drawing looks of pale envy from the four strapping Delbarton bucks. "That man's made of iron." The heart-rending sounds of her weeping and the sympathetic chirps and trills of birds were all that could be heard in the small clearing.

The Iron Major. Whitney's eyes narrowed in agreement. Today he certainly did seem made of iron, and flint and ice and all manner of hard, unyielding things. But then a tide of confusion surged inside her. Yesterday parts of him had been surprisingly soft, incredibly gentle and rousing. Where Charlie had pawed, he had stroked. What Charlie had commanded, he had coaxed . . . ohhh, so effectively. When the insight struck her, she reeled on her seat; if he was made of iron, it certainly wasn't solid all the way through. Somewhere inside him there was something . . . more human. And if human, then capable of being "bargained."

"He's not made of iron," she announced, snapping rod-straight on her seat with her heart thumping harder. "He's mortal flesh, like any other man." They all came to attention as she came to life before their eyes. "And if he's a mortal man, he's got a man's mortal wants and weaknesses. All men have them, even him." A very Daniels glow crept over her heart-shaped face.

"Everything has its price. What we have to do is find *his,* and use it to get rid of him before he finds Pa's still and the whiskey we've got stored away."

The onlookers stared at one another in relief, drawing confidence from Whitney's contagious determination. They focused on every flicker of her expressive eyes, knowing they were watching a wonder at work. Then suddenly her lithe body relaxed and her fetching face lit with a crafty grin they'd all come to know and appreciate.

"I need to know everything about him . . . *everything*. His habits, his druthers, his daily routines—there has to be something he wants." She snapped her fingers in sudden inspiration. "Robbie"—she looked around quickly—"where's Robbie Dedham?"

"Here I am, Whit!" He popped up from his seat on the ground behind her and hurried to her side.

"He'll be staying in your pa's tavern—likely, sleeping in your very bed. Can you do it? Can you keep an eye on him and tell me everything you learn?"

"Shur can!"

"Good." She tousled his hair and sent him off with a swat on the behind, only to call him back a second later. "Better tell your pa to let his barrels run dry," she advised in a conspiratorial tone. "Can't risk filling them up again with the major sleeping overhead and lurking about." Catching her meaning, he nodded, and left at a run.

She collected the concentration of the other eager eyes with an upraised finger. "Now, I guess you heard; harvest has been 'dismal and dismaying' this year. That means crops and foodstuffs for trading are in shamefully short supply . . . just like liquor will be in a day or two, when Uncle Harvey's barrels run dry." She wriggled forward on her seat and they drew closer with nods of understanding and smiles creeping over their faces. They were in good hands, all right.

"Now—the hungrier a soldier is, the harder it is for him to hear orders. Pa learned that in his days at Valley Forge with old General George. And I suppose that extends to being thirsty too. After a fellow gets so hungry, so thirsty, he just quits hearing orders at all." Her expression was deviousness distilled. "I'm proposing that we interfere with the federal soldiers' hearing, a bit. It'll buy us a bit of time while we learn what it will take to bargain the major out of Rapture Valley. Even the Iron Major will have a hard time tracking down stills and whiskey and arresting folks single-handed . . . and hungry."

There were murmurs aplenty as the folk caught the thrust of what they were being asked to do. They agreed and began to lay plans and strategies for hiding the recently harvested abundance of their fields. It was thirsty work, and soon May Donner produced an earthen jug filled with the best whiskey made, Daniels whiskey. They passed it around, savoring the clean tang and the full, warm vapors.

Whitney took a swallow and closed her eyes to trap the sheer delight of it inside for a minute longer. That rare taste, that full-flavored redolence, reminded her of all they stood to lose if she was wrong. But she wasn't wrong; she could feel it in her bones. And in sundry other parts of her as well.

"I need to know what they're up to and who they question. And you'll have to bring or send me word about where they search so we can move Pa's still. I don't think it would be a particularly good idea to mention *Daniels* whiskey, or the fact that it's my pa who does our distilling." Mentioning her pa made her realize how much she missed him. She rose with a sigh, realizing they'd all been absent from view long, enough. "It's time we got back to our usual chores."

"And my Charlie?" Aunt Sarah pushed herself up and went to Whitney's side with a doleful plea. *"Please.* I got to see my Charlie—to see if'n he's all right."

Whitney paused, chewed the inner corner of her lip, and then grinned. "I need a pie, Aunt Sarah. One of your special ones . . . apple . . . with cinnamon."

When Aunt Sarah stammered and looked puzzled, Whitney laughed that lush Whitney Daniels laugh.

"No . . . better make it *two.*"

Late that afternoon Whitney and Aunt Sarah Dunbar appeared in the settlement clearing, headed straight for the soldiers' camp at the rear of Dedham's Tavern. In each pair of hands was a tin, filled with a selection of delicious pies, and in their wake was an aroma so potent and so tantalizing that it drew folk from their houses all along their route. The soldiers on a desultory patrol in front of the tavern door caught wind of it and came to immediate attention, locating the source and elbowing each other. The guards posted at the edge of the camp came stalking around their assigned perimeters to meet the incursion of "locals," and as they came, their eyes widened and their steps quickened.

The two soldiers jolted to a halt on the path, blocking the way into the federals' camp. They sniffed and stared and shifted their muskets from hand to hand nervously. Belligerence, contempt, harassment, even armed resistance; they'd experienced them all during their passage through frontier towns and villages, and were equipped to withstand such adversity. But pie-bearing females! They had no earthly idea what was expected of them in a case like this. And their confusion was shortly to grow worse.

"Gentlemen"—Whitney turned her smile on them—"we've come to beg a boon of you. Aunt Sarah here"—she nodded to little Aunt Sarah, whose motherly suffering was plain to behold—"her heart's next to breakin' from not seeing her beloved son, who, we understand, is being detained in your camp. Now, I've tried to explain to Aunt Sarah that you're men of honor and duty bound to see justice done, and that you're undoubtedly seein' to her Charlie's needs, as men of integrity would. But she's pining and woeful in the extreme, and achin' like only a mother can, to see with her own two eyes that her Charlie is all right."

The smooth, lulling flood of Whitney's words and the seductive aroma of fruit pies were too much for the bone-weary foot soldiers, drawn from the ranks of Maryland's impoverished, to resist. Whitney could see capitulation written all over their faces before she was even half finished.

"She's fearful he won't get fed properly. You know how mothers are. I told her *two* pies were too much for one fellow to eat by himself, but she wouldn't listen."

"Will ye let me see my Charlie?" Aunt Sarah's chin quivered with exquisite subtlety.

The soldiers swallowed hard, their eyes fixed on the pies, two whole pies, that their prisoner probably wouldn't be able to eat all by himself. "Wull"—one cast a desperate look at the other—

"they ain't packin' weapuns . . . jus' pies. Where'd be the harm, Ned?"

"Bless you." Tears rose up in Aunt Sarah's eyes. "You're a good boy." She reached up to pat the lanky one's cheek with motherly license. "I bet yer ma is worried sick about you." And as they started down the path toward the tents, she clinched their resolve with, "You look a bit lean, son. How long's it been since ye had a slip o' pie?"

They found Charlie lounging on the ground at the base of a large oak tree on the far side of the camp. Two guards slouched nearby, shaving the bark from sticks with their knives to pass the time. Charlie was in chains all right, good-sized ones that linked the shackles on his feet to the base of the tree. He wore a bored, petulant look, but otherwise seemed hale and unharmed. He scrambled to his feet when he saw them, and when he saw the pies, he began to grin.

Aunt Sarah thrust her pie into the lanky soldier's hands with orders for him to share it with Ned and the other guards and sailed straight into Charlie's bearlike hug. There was some weeping, some questioning, some assuring, and, as the soldiers hurried to cut their pie, lifting it out on their fingers, Charlie sat down on a nearby root to stuff himself with his favorite treat.

At the very moment his camp was being invaded by pie, Garner Townsend was responding to a knock at the door of his room on the second floor of Dedham's Inn. He called permission to enter and found himself staring at his new "personal aide," recruited from among the men by Lieutenant Brooks. There stood the paunchy erstwhile scout, Benson. Townsend crossed his arms and looked the frazzled, earnest-faced fellow up and down. Uniform too small, boots too big, musket a corroding mess; there was damned little of the soldier in Benson. He was even overage.

"You," Townsend huffed long-sufferingly. "Why you?" It was meant rhetorically, but Benson, not used to hearing questions nobody was expected to answer, did just that.

"Well, sir, Majur"—he shifted from one outsized boot to the other—"I guess 'cause I wuz a barber oncet. An' I done tailorin' and boot-blackin' and used to help my ma with the warsh. An' because I cain't keep up too good on them patrols—"

"Enough." Townsend's hand shot up to halt him. "It's perfectly clear to me, Benson." He was simply the most expendable man in the unit—probably in any unit, Townsend sighed inwardly. "You'll see to my laundry and linen, sharpen my razor, polish my boots, brush my coat, and see to the necessaries." He said this last with a wave to the chamber pot and washbasin. "If there's mending, you'll do it, and you'll see that the lieutenant's and my meals are delivered up here on a tray from the kitchen of this establishment. Do you think you can manage all that?"

"Ohhh, yes sir, Majur." Benson's round eyes suddenly lit with understanding. "Ye be needin' a gentlemun's gentlemun, then." When Townsend looked surprised, he inhaled proudly and explained, "I been one o'them, too."

The pride in the fellow's face made Townsend bite back his sarcastic demand for the identity of the poor wretch who'd employed him. He proceeded to acquaint the fellow with his kit and routines, then handed over his boots for a good cleaning and a polish.

"I'll need them tonight when I take out the evening patrol," he explained. "Lieutenant Brooks and I are trading off patrols; he takes the early patrol, I take the late. It's my expectation we'll have a better chance of nabbing these criminals at night, when they think they're safe under cover of darkness."

Benson settled himself on the floor with rags, polish, and boot brush, and a loud groan filled the room. He looked up, red-faced, into Townsend's puzzled glare. "Don' mind me, Majur. That were jus' my belly talkin'."

Townsend closed his eyes, and his jaw flexed as if he were still suffering some lingering pain from the morning's unthinkable episode. Bargaining . . . for food. It was pathetic, the depths to which humans could sink when cut off from the normal decencies of regular commerce. With no cash money available, they were reduced to squabbling and *bartering*. Well, he wasn't going to be sucked into it, wheedling and haggling like a fishwife.

He clasped his hands behind his back and began to pace in his stocking feet. "We're all hungry, Benson, and tired. But I won't allow a minor annoyance like scarce provisions to jeopardize this mission. If there's food in this valley, I'll have it, by damn. And I'll have the stills and liquor and the wretched criminals themselves along with it!"

"Criminals?" Benson paused with his brush on the boot and frowned. "I didn' see no criminals, Majur. Jus' old men and green lads an' widder wimmen . . . an' that young gal, that frisky one."

Townsend tightened, realizing that Benson simply echoed the thoughts going through many of his men's heads since they'd arrived in Rapture Valley. "We're here to enforce the law, Benson, to uphold rightly established authority. Whether you realize it or not, we're engaged in a desperate struggle here, the forces of justice and order against the reign of chaos and anarchy. When the good of a people demands the passage of laws, then men have a duty to obey them, and we Townsends have a duty to enforce them on everyone equally. And I'll succeed in enforcing this law, restoring order . . . even here."

"How's that, Majur?" Benson was utterly captivated by his commander's stirring summary of their mission. Why, if his mates-in-arms could only hear this—

"Townsends always succeed, whatever the challenge. It's in our nature, bred in our very bones. We turn adversity into triumph, we Townsends. It's our . . . destiny." He clamped his wrists behind him and paced even harder.

His destiny . . . and his father's *command*. In the lengthening silence, his determined pace slowed as he stared into memory, reliving the moment just six weeks before, when he'd received that command. He'd answered a summons to his father's study in the heart of their fashionable Boston residence, to be handed a communiqué from the secretary of the army, without a word. As he read his call to military duty, his graying, rail-straight father had given him a hard look of appraisal, then turned to watch the rain fall on the window. No words were spoken; none were necessary. The expectation was clear; he was to bring home some achievement or honor to serve as political grist. Serving under President Washington in the campaign to put down a "whiskey revolt" in the western provinces was to be his contri-

bution to the family laurels . . . and just perhaps his final re-
demption as well.

And nothing, *nothing* was going to interfere with it. Not an
assignment to a ragged, undisciplined troop of foot soldiers
drawn from the gutters of humanity, not a lack of food and clothing and rest, and certainly not a sly, tart-tongued little witch who
dressed like a ragamuffin and kicked like a mule. His tender
nether parts began to throb slightly at the reminder, and heat rose
under his strong cheekbones and crept into his ears. The infuriating little tart with the big green eyes and the lush, pouty lips
had just succeeded in wriggling into his thoughts again.

The rhythmic shushing of the boot brush on leather imitated
the quickening of his blood. He stood, braced, feeling the remnants of the tidal wave of arousal he'd suffered earlier that day.
He tried telling himself it was coincidence: he'd been wrought
up or angry both times he'd seen her. And her being the irksome,
she-devil sort, it was probably natural she'd get under his skin
when he was already hot and agitated.

But the sight of her standing in the tavern doorway, with her
gingery hair lit from behind as if it were a tarnished halo, seized
his mind. He had stood there like a tongue-tied schoolboy, staring—staring, hell!—*absorbing* her with his eyes. And all he
could think as he searched for the remembered shape of her ripe,
succulent breasts beneath her clothes was "Fresh shirt."

Even now his body was fairly vibrating, thinking of it, and of
the way her mouth had looked moments later . . . open, velvety,
inviting, as it came toward him just before she bit his damned
button. He went taut as a bowstring and flushed with fresh humiliation. A bloody frontal assault. And he hadn't had the presence of mind to put up a single shred of resistance. The brazen
little witch! He was going to see her repaid for it, stroke for
stroke, humiliation for humiliation. He'd make her regret tan-
gling with a Townsend.

He paced to the window and pulled the open shutters a bit
wider. He leaned against the sill, surveying the encampment below and taking a deep breath of renewed determination. The sunlight was going, he realized; Lieutenant Brooks would be back
soon with his patrol. He should have rested that afternoon while

he had the chance; he'd likely be up half the night, thrashing through the woods.

His eye caught on a knot of figures near the trees at the far edge of the tents, in the vicinity of his prisoner. He straightened and scowled, searching them. A white shirt, deerskin breeches, and a wide black belt, *Lord*. It was her; the recognition poured through him like hot sparks, followed by disbelief. How dare she invade his bloody camp to consort with a known suspect? And his own men were just standing there, not doing a thing about it.

"Dammit!" He made straight for the door and remembered only at the last minute that he was in shirt-sleeves. He snatched up his coat and shoved into it. At the bottom of the stairs, the cold, uneven feel of the puncheon floor made him halt and look down at his stocking feet in dismay. He was back up the stairs in a flash and snatching his boots from Benson's puzzled hands. Now beyond dignity and decorum, he hopped up and down, storklike, on one leg as he pulled on his boots. A moment later he was flying down the stairs a second time, his coat flapping and his face burning.

Whitney and Charlie stood a few paces apart from Aunt Sarah and the others. Her thumbs were tucked in her belt and she shoveled dirt back and forth with the toes of her boots, his arms were crossed and he watched her shapely legs move with a wistful expression.

"I . . . I'm sorry about this, Charlie," she admitted. "It's hard . . . seeing you in chains."

"It is?" He grinned halfheartedly. "Well, that's somethin' anyway."

"They didn't beat you, or anything, did they?" She looked up into his sturdy, familiar face and his earnest brown eyes and felt perfectly horrible.

"Naw, they jus' give me a poke or two with a gun butt." His mouth quirked up on one end. "Ye don' have to worry, Whit. I won't say nothin', if'n they do beat me."

"I know. You're a good friend, Charlie Dunbar." The last part seemed to stick on something in her throat, and she had to lower her eyes again. The part she'd left unspoken was resonant on the air between them. A good friend was what he would always be. But the days of their wild camaraderie and volatile competition were gone now, splintered by their separate destinies as a man and a woman. For the first time in their lives they were silent with each other.

"Well, mebee I could bring m'Charlie a bit o' food now and again, when we can spare it." Aunt Sarah's voice brought them back to more current matters. She was smiling at the men who sprawled on the grass by her feet, licking their fingers for the fourth time. Freckled Ned and lanky Albert, the sentries they'd pulled from their duties minutes before, were quick to speak up.

"Well, you jus' come along, ma'am." Albert got to his feet, nodding his head respectfully. "We be pleased to have ye—"

"The hell we will!" came their commander's booming voice, bringing the rest to their feet as though they were attached to strings. They all turned to find the major bearing down on them with a stony face and an angry stride. "Just what in hell are *they* doing here, soldier?"

When Albert stammered and looked around for help, Ned blanched and scooped up an empty pie tin to hold it out to his commander as though in explanation. He soon saw the error of his action and it drooped in his hand.

"What the devil is *that,* soldier?" Townsend glowered fiercely, sending the young soldier reeling back a pace.

"A . . . p-pie t-tin, sir."

"I can see that, numskull. What the hell's it doing here?"

"Th-they brung it fer the pris'ner." Ned waved weakly at Aunt Sarah, who had scuttled back toward Whitney's protective embrace.

Townsend's eyes narrowed first on Aunt Sarah and then on Whitney. He turned back to snarl at Ned and Albert. "You've abandoned your posts, a court-martial offense. Surrender your weapons and confine yourselves to your tent. You'll face discipline at reveille tomorrow morning before the full company. *Move!*"

They grimly handed over their muskets to Charlie's guards and exited their commander's wrath at a run. He watched them go, then turned on Whitney with a glint in his eye.

"Aunt Sarah was worried that Charlie wasn't dead or tortured." She seized the initiative, pushing Aunt Sarah behind her. "So we came to see for ourselves. And, expecting that you wouldn't have had the decency to feed him, she brought him a bit of food."

"You've invaded my camp, lured my men from their rightful duty, and expect me to believe your little sortie was motivated by motherly concern?" He was fighting the way his eyes were drawn to her shirtfront again and his face reddened in chagrin that was a fair imitation of fury.

"You have no right to hold him here." Whitney stalked closer, planting her fists on her waist. The move thrust hard-tipped breasts against the front of her shirt and made the opening gap between buttons. "It's a pure travesty of justice. He's done absolutely nothing to be arrested for."

"I should think *you* of all people would understand just how much of a menace he can be," the major sneered with a slow, insinuating look down her body. Instantly, he regretted it, for his comment had brought the confrontation down to purely personal terms and his look at her body brought him alarming reminders of just how personal he'd been with her himself.

"What happened was between Charlie and me." Whitney found herself reddening under his bold stare. "And it has nothing to do with taxes or whiskey or anything else you might be interested in."

"Then what were you doing out in the woods with him in the first place?" Townsend demanded. It sounded strikingly personal, and he was dismayed to find a sizable personal curiosity about the answer lurking beneath it.

"I don't have to answer that," she said, stalking closer, so close she could begin to feel the heat radiating from his tall, muscular frame. "I'm not under suspicion here."

"Aren't you, wench? Whatever gave you that idea? In fact"— the insight poured a measure of heat through him—"you're a prime suspect, out rambling about in the woods in men's clothes, in suspicious company. And you've an insolent, defiant nature and an unbridled tongue, which makes you just the sort to rouse this common rabble against lawfully constituted authority."

As he spoke, Whitney's eyes widened in spite of herself. He

was too blessed close to the mark . . . *and* too blessed close to
her body. For some reason, her gaze was coming unfocused everywhere but on his fascinating lips. Then it slid helplessly downward over the hard planes of his cheeks to his corded neck and
finally to the half-buttoned shirt beneath his gaping coat front.
His bare chest was visible . . . black, curly hair. And his skin was
so smooth, so hard, and it gave off wave after wave of heat . . .
Lord! She rallied to produce one last spark of defiance.

"Well, arrest me, then, if I'm so desperate and dangerous,"
she challenged. "Put *me* in chains and let Charlie go."

His hands closed on her shoulders and he drew her toward
him before she could counter it. Their bodies were now inches
apart, sharing the same lightning surge of sensation.

Her in chains. God. If he only could. Images of cold iron and
soft flesh suddenly galvanized him: to have her, keep her, tame
her as he had that first time. To feel her lush mouth opening
under his, to hold those firm young breasts and feel himself
wedged in her softness—

"Don't tempt me, wench." His shimmering silver eyes con-
veyed a deeper, sensual level of warning.

Charlie, Aunt Sarah, and Charlie's two guards stared, openmouthed, at them. Whitney and the major were clasped together
and yet braced apart, chests heaving, eyes locked and glowing,
until hoofbeats and the appearance of a horse intruded on the
charged flow between them.

"Major!" Lieutenant Brooks reined up and dismounted hur-
riedly, alarmed by the volatile scene.

The sound of his rank jarred him back from the brink of sheer
catastrophe. He released Whitney with embarrassed force.

"Stay away from this camp, wench," he warned.

Whitney blinked and began grasping at words. "His family
has a right to see him—"

"You're not family, wench. If I catch you in this camp again,
I'll slap you in chains, so help me."

"But Aunt Sarah . . . she's his mother." She was scrambling,
trying to boot her mind back to full operation. "What will it take
to . . . ? She'd be willing to feed him every day." She cast a quick
look at Aunt Sarah, who nodded eagerly.

Bargaining again, he realized. His face grew a shade darker.

"And you can set the time and the place she sees him," she blurted out irritably, breaking her own long-standing rule of bargaining: Never up an offer until you have a definite rejection. "What do you say, Major?"

"No."

"You—" She took herself in hand. This was bargaining pure and simple. This was no place for feelings. "You drive a hard bargain, Major. Then . . . we'd be willing to feed Charlie and his guards. That's *three* less mouths you'd have to feed." He stood watching her, his nose curled as though he were smelling something distasteful, and she added with unraveling calm: "With food scarce like it is, you won't get a better offer. Aunt Sarah here is a marvel of a cook."

There was a crackling silence as Townsend looked from her to Aunt Sarah's desperate clinging to her son's arm, and then to the intense faces of his own men, some resentful, some prodding him to take the deal. Lord, how he hated this. There was only one way to end this wretched impasse without looking like a bloody tyrant.

"If she feeds him every day"—he struggled to be logical, wishing he could sound more mercenary—"it takes a burden from my own men and frees them up for more important duties."

"Ohhh, thank ye—" Aunt Sarah came forward with a chin-quivering gratitude, and Townsend braced, backing her off with a glare. Whitney scooped up the pie tins, thrust them into Aunt Sarah's hands, and led her off with a glare at her gentlemanly adversary.

Charlie watched Townsend observe the sway of Whitney's bottom as she left, and his broad brow furrowed. He suffered a momentary twinge of sympathy for the gentlemanly major, who obviously wanted Whitney Daniels's delectable little body too. But there was a major difference in their situations, Charlie realized with unwelcome insight; Whitney Daniels wanted the major back. That was what all that clutching and staring and trembling was about. The minute the major had set hands to her, she'd gone all trembly in the knees. Only a fellow who was familiar with and fond of Whit's shapely legs would have caught it.

Charlie watched the major conferring with his lieutenant and laying down orders and assessed him anew, as competition. His tall, refined good looks were formidable, his fancy uniform and cultured speech were probably fascinating. But he had a healthy dose of arrogance and raw, uncloaked contempt for frontier folk and their ways. And Whitney had a greater than normal share of pride, and a fierce love of both independence and her pa's way of life. Whatever their cravings; Whitney and the major were sworn enemies. The thought sent Charlie back to his regular spot, lounging under the tree on his back with a very smug smile on his face.

Garner Townsend came to stand over his prisoner minutes later, his hands set on his waist and smoke in his gray eyes. "What the hell *were* you doing out in the woods with her, Dunbar?"

Charlie pushed up onto his elbow with a ghost of a smile. "What would any buck be doin' out in the woods wi' her, Major?"

Townsend flinched privately. He'd asked for that. "You could have been checking on a liquor cache, or operating a still."

Charlie just laughed a very insinuating laugh and lay back, tucking his arms behind his head for a pillow. "Ye know, Major, yer right about one thing: she's a real talker. Once she gets goin'—I swear—she can talk a dog down off'n a meat wagon." His taunting grin broadened. "But if ye'll take a bit o' wisdom from me, ye'd do well to show more caution, up close to her like that. She kicks. *And* she bites."

The sudden flaming of Townsend's face was hidden by the closing shadows. Involuntarily his eyes dropped to his coat front, and one squashed button. His hand closed around it as Charlie's words rumbled about in the hollow inside his chest. *She kicked;* nobody knew that better than him! And she bit; *Lord, how she could bite!* As he turned to go, he managed to realize Charlie was saying something else and collected part of it.

"—aniels is a dirty fighter."

But through the bewildering steam in his senses, it took a while to register. He was halfway back to the inn before it struck him; he finally knew her name.

Whiskey Daniels.

Six

Whiskey Daniels.

Dear God. He was in more trouble than he knew. There was no question, the long-dormant beast inside him was rearing its ugly head again. This last confrontation with her had confirmed his worst fears. The throbbing blood, the flash-in-the-pan fever, the irascible temper, the impaired judgment—the warning signs were unmistakable. His single flaw, his old malady, his great weakness was uncoiled in the depths of him, he could feel it in his bones . . . and in sundry other parts of himself as well.

It wasn't lust, not precisely. He knew how to take fleshly pleasures in discreet, gentlemanly fashion when the dire need arose. This was something altogether different. This was a consuming, gut-rending, uncontrollable desire for a whole woman, a *specific* woman. It was an exhilarating madness of fascination and possession and arousal. And for Garner Townsend it spelled catastrophe.

He entered the tavern and made for his room, fighting a sense of panic with everything in him. He was older now, more experienced, wiser. And he was in charge. He could control these troublesome urges and he could see to it that temptation was kept at a distance. He could see that Whiskey Daniels was—

Whiskey Daniels. What the hell kind of father would name his daughter after that hell-broth they cooked up in this crude outpost of humanity? He stopped dead, halfway up the creaking stairs. A father who was deeply involved in brewing and distilling that hell-broth, he realized, and who was damned proud of it.

It was as though someone dumped an icy bucket of water over his head. That was why she was so prominent in the opposition to him and his mission. She was part of it, or at least her family was. Either way, she was involved, he was sure of it. He took two more steps and stopped, seeing her again as she stood in the tavern doorway, her hair aglow, her green eyes flashing, her soft lips parted. . . .

Whiskey Daniels. And the beast was rising again. Lord, why did it have to be her?

Early the next evening, Whitney strolled into Dedham's Tavern, still wearing her breeches and boots. It was past suppertime and by all rights she should have been in skirts. But she needed to check with her informants in the settlement, and she wasn't about to risk confronting the major while dressed like a female. She'd already spoken with Uncle Radnor and Aunt Frieda Delbarton and had come to the tavern to collect Robbie Dedham's report.

The lanterns burned cheerily in the tavern and the air was filled with traces of woodsmoke and the pungent tang of ale and whiskey. She removed her coat and hung it on a peg near the door, surveying the evening's trade. The Delbarton bucks were playing cards in their usual place near the door, Uncle Ferrel and Uncle Radnor were now baking their shins by the fire, and a dozen or so soldiers were lined up by Uncle Harvey's planking bar, drawing their liquor rations. She greeted the locals broadly as she watched the soldiers process through the line then plant themselves at the long planking tables to nurse their rations in the tavern's warmth. When the bar was free, she sidled up to it and ordered, "A good strong pull of it, Uncle Harvey."

"I don't give it away," Uncle Harvey answered with his stock response. His eyes were twinkling.

"Well, perhaps you ought to." She launched into her trader's gambit of devaluing the desired object. "That barrel isn't quite up to your usual stuff, Uncle. A bit rashy . . . and weak, watery underpinnings. I wouldn't give more than a handful of oats for it."

The soldiers were watching, she could feel their eyes on her back. She laughed that low, intriguing Whitney Daniels laugh and took her drink from Uncle Harvey and downed it with a conspiring sparkle in her eye. She plunked her tin cup down on the bar for another drink, offering, "A whole strip of side pork, Uncle Harvey."

She drank her second drink with a flourish and decided to sit a hand of cards with the Delbartons before slipping out to talk with Robbie. They got into their usual row over who was cheating and the Delbartons, as usual, banded together to declare Whitney the culprit. They demanded retribution and she bargained them down to an exhibition of her ability to balance a plate on end, on her chin. By the time she rose, laughing, to comply with their demand, every eye in the tavern was on her.

She had to start over twice; she was seized by fits of laughter that had a bold, mischievous quality to them that was utterly contagious. Soon soldiers' shoulders were shaking and they were making bets among themselves as to whether she could actually do it. And it took only a challenging look from a Delbarton to broaden their betting, soldiers versus locals now. They all held their breath as she tried a third and final time. And when she did it, two precious twists of tobacco changed hands and several soldiers' smiles disappeared.

"Now, that's hardly right, Mike Delbarton." She grinned at the strapping blond buck who'd just won himself a month's pipe fodder. "A fair trade's one thing, but I believe you took unfair advantage of the gentleman. Give him a chance to win it back." And so she found herself pitted against gravel-voiced Sergeant Laxault, representing the federal militia, in a "blink-off."

A place was made at the long planking table and rules were agreed upon. Whitney and the sergeant faced each other across the table with their chins propped on their hands. At the order to go, they opened their eyes and began to stare at each other, daring each other to be the first to blink. The wheeze and pop of the fire in the great hearth marked the lengthening passage of time.

Major Townsend had been watching the entire spectacle from the darkened stairs, and was alarmed at the dangerous spirit of camaraderie that was developing between his men and these locals, spearheaded by the irksome Whiskey Daniels. He stalked to the table, and his men, made nervous by his presence, fell back to give him access. He stood at the sergeant's right shoulder, scrutinizing the proceedings, trying to decide whether to break up the absurd contest. But a certain petty vengeance made him want to give Laxault a chance to win back his tobacco, and a certain unwelcome feeling in his gut made him seize the chance to stare at Whiskey Daniels.

The major's monolithic presence cast a shadow over Whitney's face, and in her peripheral vision she was surprised to see two gold coat buttons and the very snug fit of a breeches flap. And they stayed there, those buttons and those provocatively bulged breeches, working on her concentration and producing heat in her smooth cheeks. She had intended to let the soldiers win some of the tobacco back, but the longer he stayed, the more heated and itchy and the less charitable she felt. She bore it as long as she could, then slowly her enchanting face began to light with the infamous Daniels grin, a final gambit and fatally charming declaration of triumph all in one. It was a low thing to do to a fellow in a fair contest, but she honestly couldn't take any more.

The leathery sergeant blinked. And a second later, as hoots and catcalls descended on him, he reddened furiously and blustered, somewhat confused by his loss. But the major knew exactly what had happened, and it infuriated him to a fever pitch.

"Uncle Harvey!" she called. "A drink for the sergeant here." Then she turned and seemed surprised to find the major standing so near. "Oh, and one for the major too."

"No, thank you." Townsend declined through clenched jaws.

"Well, it's the least I can do, Major, in light of the heartwarming generosity of your men."

"No, thank you." He started to move off, but was slowed by the press of his own men around the table.

"Well, perhaps the gentlemanly major just dislikes *common whiskey.*" Her assertion quivered on the air like a javelin, then struck. "Harvey here can't afford fancy Jamaican rum, nor that pricey New England cork. And after he pays those outrageous liquor taxes, he has no money left for *fine French wines.* But, perhaps you'd take a draught of ale or cider with us, Major . . . to be sociable." She had risen as she spoke and now faced him across the table, her face glowing with challenge.

"I said, no thank you. That means I don't want a drink of any sort."

"With us, you mean." She seized the chance to drive his aristocratic airs like a wedge of confusion into his men. "You don't wish to drink with the likes of foot soldiers and poor dirt farmers." The hit produced a tremor of raw anger in him. He jerked back across the table toward her, eyes narrowed and face dusky.

"No. What that means is, I don't drink alcohol of any sort. And I'm not about to take it up to please the likes of you."

"Don't drink? Anything?" She pulled back, genuinely shocked by his pronouncement. And from the looks on their faces, she realized his men were equally surprised. "Why, that's . . . you mean not even breakfast ale?"

"No." His face was burning as he straightened and pulled his coat down, refusing to meet the questioning looks of his men as he turned to order: "Back to camp, Sergeant, now. Get them bedded down. We have a patrol to mount before sunrise."

Not a soldier moved; few even blinked as the order died away. Their commander was an abstainer. A gentleman and now a damned *abstainer* to boot! The looks of horror on the gal's and the locals' faces were all that was required to complete their humiliation. They looked at each other and at their crusty sergeant in disbelief.

Seething now, Townsend turned on Whitney and the Delbartons. "And you—you'll stay away from my men, do you hear? All of you. I'll not have you bleeding them of what few possessions they own with your sleight-of-hand tricks and bets. From now on the tavern will be closed to locals every evening during the dispensing of rations. Do you hear that, Dedham?"

Uncle Harvey sputtered and muttered, before surrendering with an "I hear."

"And you"—he turned to punch a finger at Whitney—"do you hear? Or shall I repeat it?"

She blazed, furious with the vengeful smirk on his face and with the way he rolled his wide shoulders as though shaking off possible contamination from contact with her and her kind. It just wasn't in the constitution of a Daniels to give anybody the last word.

"I heard, *Major Samson.*"

He was already three steps toward the stairs when he turned back, just as she knew he would. He felt his men turning back too, to take in the final salvos between them.

"Perhaps all that whiskey has already fuddled your brain, witch. The name is *Townsend,* Major Townsend."

"Is that so?" She cast a wickedly sweet smile at their audience, then turned it fully on him. "Well, it's understandable, me mistaking you for a Samson. You *do* have the *jawbone of an ass.*"

Townsend flinched visibly as choked laughter erupted around the tavern. Whitney cast him a wicked smile, snatched up her coat, and sailed out.

"I want to know where she lives." The major demanded of Uncle Harvey the next afternoon. There was no need to explain who was meant.

The major had returned from his fruitless predawn scouring of the countryside, dropped into his bed for four tortured hours, and risen in a particularly disagreeable humor. Then he'd scraped his face raw with an ice-cold shave and descended the stairs to face a breakfast of cold beans, greased liberally with fatback, and two unsalted biscuits.

"You must be mad." He had pushed it away with a snarl of disgust. "I'll have two eggs, boiled, and some decent bread."

"Got no eggs. You et my last hen last night, Major." Uncle Harvey had drawn in his neck so that he resembled a resentful turnip.

"Then I'll just have *coffee.*"

"Got no coffee neither. Ye drunk th' last, last night."

"Dammit."

The hungry, hot-under-the-collar major had risen and stalked out to his men's camp to get them ready to continue the search for liquor, stills, and distillers.

All morning long, as they searched the cabins and outbuildings of the settlement itself, he had found himself looking for something, an ill-defined but nagging something that produced a coiling of anticipation in his gut and made him surly indeed when he didn't find it. And it wasn't until he sat down to his dinner of leftover beans and caught sight of his squashed button that he realized just what it was he had expected, but failed to find. *Her.*

"Near a mile down the road, then cut left on the path by th' oak stump with a 'B' cut in it." Uncle Harvey answered reluctantly, hoping the revelation didn't bring trouble down on Whitney and her Aunt Kate.

" 'B'?" The major scowled. "I understood her name was Daniels."

" 'B' stands fer 'Black.' " Uncle Harvey snorted defensively. "Wouldn't do no good to put a 'D' on it, now, would it? That could be anybody in Rapture . . . Delbarton or Dobson or Dunbar or Donner or Dedham."

"Good God." The major straightened, only now realizing why he'd had such difficulty keeping the identities of these motley inhabitants straight.

"We all be fam'ly," Harvey declared with stubborn pride.

"You mean to say this entire valley is related by blood?"

"Nooo"—Uncle Harvey looked at him as if he were a bit daft—"by *al-phy-bet.*"

The major exploded out of the tavern, heading for the smithy where his horse was stabled. And shortly he was leading a grim-faced contingent of the Maryland Ninth down the main river road. He was spoiling for a good fight, and the heat in his blood conjured Whiskey Daniels strong in his mind.

Whitney was repairing a bit of harness in the pole shed that leaned against the barn, when Kate hurried up from the garden, her skirts billowing and her bonnet flapping. An instant later, the cause of her uncharacteristic, agitated behavior appeared around the corner of the barn, following her. Soldiers.

Whitney ducked out of the shed and came face-to-face with *him* as he sat arrogantly upon his great roan horse, his gold braid and his tall boots gleaming. Her face heated and her eyes sparked as she felt his gaze slide over her and fix on the piece of leather in her hands and the stain it had left on her fingers. He dismounted with flagrant grace and handed his reins to his tight-lipped sergeant.

"What are you doing here?" Whitney tossed the harness back into the floor of the shed and stepped in front of Kate, clamping her work-stained hands on the sides of her breeches-clad thighs.

"I am doing my duty, madam." He pointedly ignored Whitney, choosing instead to address her aunt Kate. The rank appraisal of his flinty gray eyes was soon transferred to the rambling two-story log house, the sturdy barn, and the drying gardens near the house. "I am here to search for contraband liquor and stills, and those who harbor them. I advise you to cooperate with my men. If you have nothing to hide, you have nothing to fear. I assume there is a *man* of the house?"

"How dare you come—" Whitney lurched forward, only to have Aunt Kate grab her by the arm. A half-instant later, Whitney was grateful for Kate's restraining presence; the cool little smile that never left the corners of the major's eyes said he would love nothing more than to see her lose control. She suddenly understood; she'd earned this little visit last night when she humiliated him in the tavern.

"My brother-in-law, Blackstone, isn't here just now." Aunt Kate drew herself up regally. "I am Kathryn Morrison, Whitney's aunt."

"Whitney?" He turned a focused gaze on Whitney's braced, resentful form, letting his eyes fall with provocative leisure to the rise and fall of her breasts, then to her narrow waist. He felt an unreasoning trickle of disappointment that her name was a legitimate one after all, however unusual. *Whitney.* Somehow "Whiskey" had seemed more fitting . . . and forbidden.

"Where is this Blackstone?"

"He's . . . well, not expected. He's gone. . . ." Aunt Kate faltered under Whitney's warning look. Thank heaven they'd purged the premises of whiskey!

"To Pittsburgh," the major finished smoothly, "with the other men of the valley . . . the other *distillers.*" And before they could refute his incisive conclusion, he turned to his men with eyes narrowing. "You, you, and you." He waved three soldiers into the barn with hard authority. "It has to be here somewhere. Start with the barn and that shed. Check every barrel, box, loose board, and suspicious bucket."

"Now, see here—" Kate voiced, realizing the full scope of what was about to occur. "You can't just go through our—"

"Like a dose of salts." He declared with a vengeful smirk. "Sergeant, bring two men and come with me." He made a martial pivot and struck off for the house itself. He was halfway to the kitchen door at the rear of the house when Whitney and Aunt Kate ran after them.

Whitney reached the house first, her every instinct roused in response to his fierce, determined presence. But as she spread herself across the kitchen door, it was the trader instinct in her that surfaced first. "Just where do you think you're going?" she demanded.

"Inside." Intending a smug bit of intimidation, he lowered his face toward hers. It was a grave mistake. His lips began to part of their own volition and his head filled with a blast of warmth that was tainted with a strange spiciness. The effect was potent indeed. He jerked up and grabbed her by the waist to set her aside bodily.

But Whitney had a viselike hold on the door frame, had her boots wedged in the corners, and managed to resist being hauled aside. "If you want to search, you'll have to pay for the privilege," she ground out, huddling back into the doorway, unwittingly drawing him closer to her in a tug-of-war over her waist. "Nothing is free, Major. Folk in Rapture learn that early on in life."

They were nearly nose to nose, faces heating, breathing harder.

"Don't be absurd." He straightened, ripping his hands from her waist as if she had scorched him.

"Damages." She scrambled for a bargaining position as she caught a glimpse of his men's uncertain faces. "There'll be damages. Why, just look at them." She jerked her head contemptuously toward his grimy, grizzled minions. "That ham-handed lot will likely wreck the place. Vile, wanton destruction that'll set all Rapture dead against you. And they'll soon hear of it clear in Pittsburgh, see if they don't!"

He went rigid, feeling his men's eyes questioning him, feeling his blood and reason both heating to intolerable levels. He couldn't think of a suitably nasty retort.

"Just compensation, Major," she prodded, wondering if his hesitation was a harbinger of victory.

"Dammit."

With that ambiguous expletive he snatched her out of the doorway and barged inside, followed by his three men, a red-faced Whitney, and a rather ashen Aunt Kate.

"Check the flour barrels," he ordered, surveying the comfortable kitchen gruffly and giving the planking floor a stomp with his heel. "And test the floor for loose planks . . . and the larder and foodstuffs. Leave no bag or vessel unchecked. No telling where they hide the stuff."

The horror on Kate's face deepened as the soldiers unsheathed their long knives and began stabbing through barrels and splitting open bags of potatoes and turnips. She flew furiously from one small disaster to another, ordering them to leave things alone, or at least use more care. More than once she smacked a clumsy hand as the scruffy, wooden-fingered soldiers invaded the cupboard to plow through her precious glazed china dishes, and rifled through her linen trunk. They thumped and dumped, overturned the woodbox, and clattered carelessly through the kettles and cooking irons.

Everything came to a sudden halt when one soldier called out that he'd found something on top of the cupboard. Into their burning glares he lowered it, a black cherry pie. Every eye fixed, every muscle froze for a moment, focused on that tin mounded with golden crust.

"Damn." The sergeant's raspy voice finally broke the silence. *"Pie."* And at the word, every man in the room felt his mouth watering violently.

"Damn suspicious pie, I'd say, Sergeant." The major waved the soldier carrying it over to the table and relieved him of his knife. Two whisks of his blade cut it into fourths and, over Kate's gasps and moans of frustration, he lifted one piece out. He opened his aristocratic mouth and, with a meaningful glance at Whitney, devoured a third of it in one bite. A shudder of raw pleasure went through him and, lacking deterence, his men dug out the remaining pieces and wolfed them down, groaning gustily.

The major's eyes closed in concentration on the way the succulent cherries squished between his teeth and the sugary juices bathed his tongue. He opened his eyes and found himself staring straight into Whitney Daniels's ripe cherry lips.

"*Damages,* Major." She crossed her arms angrily, drawing her coarse shirt tight over her breasts.

He squashed a quiver in his loins and made himself swallow that last bite. He swung away and was halfway through the next doorway, waving his men after him and snarling, "What's in here?"

They invaded the tranquillity of Kate's precious keeping room and set about lifting and examining and overturning things while the major strolled about the room. He tossed aside the quilt that covered the French settee and ran his supple fingers over its silk brocade. Then he examined the delicate carving of the French writing desk, and evaluated the wrought iron chandelier hanging in the center of the room.

Kate rescued a blown-glass lamp globe from one quarry-faced fellow and her sewing basket from another, appealing indignantly to the major, who paused, leaning back on one leg, inspecting Kate as baldly as though she were part of the furnishings.

"*Something* in Rapture must be prosperous indeed. Where did all this come from?"

"It's mine." The harried Kate drew herself up formidably, cradling a painted Dutch figurine against her bosom, daring anyone to set hands on it, or on her. "I brought these things with me from Allentown when my husband died and I came west to see to Whitney's upbringing."

"So you're the agency responsible for the niceties of her behavior," the major charged as though it were a criminal offense. Flicking a taunting glance at Whitney, he savored this bit of revenge for the spectacle she'd made of him yesterday. The little invasion was proving more entertaining than he'd expected, if less productive. He pointed to the stairs. "What's up there?"

Before they could intervene, he was mounting them.

"How dare you—" Whitney was after him in a flash, trailed by Aunt Kate and the burly Sergeant Laxault. When he ducked into her room at the top of the stairs, she burst past him to take a hot-eyed stand in the middle of her room. "Get out."

"Yours?" Scanning the chamber with casual contempt, he was struck by the unnerving blend of the primitive and the elegant in the little room. It was utterly like her, he realized; an intriguing mix of beauty and coarseness, the splendid and the common. He sidestepped her to saunter about, poking and examining things. One aristocratic hand feathered a touch across the smooth marble of the washstand and one arrogant boot pried open the lid of the oak trunk. Ignoring her indrawn breath and wordless ventings of ire, he fished around in the contents and came up with a thin muslin chemise, dangling it on one finger.

"Give me that!" She snatched it from him and clasped it protectively against her chest, flaming.

"It can't be yours—you never wear one," he taunted in a vile, throaty whisper.

"Are you quite satisfi—finished?"

"Not quite, wench." He turned toward the bed with its crocheted canopy, soft quilt coverlet, and plump down pillows. Whitney inserted herself between him and the bed, as though trying to shield it from him. In the dim light of the small window, she was flushed, appealing, outlined by the frame of her unexpectedly elegant bed. In one hot movement his eyes stripped her shoulders bare, loosened her gingery hair . . .

This was where she slept. Images of her lying warm and languorous with sleep swirled through his taut body, tightening his belly, curling his fingers into restraining fists. The strange, spicy spirals of her warm breath floated upward, mocking his control, entwining about his resolve. Soft bed, soft flesh . . .

He was here, in her room, beside her—she managed the distracted realization. For the last three nights she'd lain in her bed, haunted by images of him, by whispers of the passion he'd roused in her. Now he'd invaded her room in the flesh . . . those long, corded columns of his legs, those broad, encompassing shoulders, those molten silver eyes. She'd never exorcise him from her bed now, she groaned privately; his potent male presence would be indelibly etched into its vulnerable confines. Hard eyes, hard muscles . . .

They stood beside her soft bed in the hazy light, their bodies close, their gazes drawn together. Tension came alive on the air around them, drawing throaty mutters of confusion from the doorway.

Kate Morrison watched them standing beside the bed, chests heaving, bodies coiled with raw excitement. The heat of their confrontation fanned across Kate's face in a blast of sensuality that dried her eyes and squeezed at her throat. Alarm rose in her, but could find no outlet in the charged atmosphere.

"There ain't nothin' acrosst the way, Majur." Laxault thrust through the bodies in the doorway to growl his report. It was like a lightning crack, releasing the hot potential between them.

The major took a reeling step backward. Lord. She'd done it to him again. He wheeled and was down the stairs in a flash, trailed by his gawking men, his crimson-faced adversary, and her stunned aunt. Charging irritably out into the side yard, he spotted the spring house, and ordered his men to give it a thorough search. He was aching for a bit of evidence, an excuse.

"Lookit here, Majur." Laxault emerged moments later with a wicked grin, holding up a heavy earthen jug.

"That's not liquor!" Aunt Kate protested as Whitney flew down the steps and ducked into the spring house to defend their food stores from pilferage.

The major snatched the jug, uncorked it with a spiteful glare, and inhaled a huge whiff of hard cider. Ire grew to replace his disappointment, and he declared that it would have to be checked for alcohol content back at Dedham's Tavern. Above Aunt Kate's furious sputters, he ordered Laxault to confiscate the lot.

He moved on to the barn, where the contingent that had searched the area earnestly reported no contraband to be found in the shed, the barn, or the gardens. The major's eyes grazed their bulging pockets, detecting telltale litter of purloined oats and dried onion skins stuck to the nearby fabric. And a few men had developed strange round growths under their coats . . . suspiciously pumpkin-sized.

Whitney saw it too. The chill of the spring house had drained the heat from her fevered senses, and she was in control again, determined to set the major back on his fancy heels a bit. His men's covert filching provided the perfect opening.

"Well, they've filled their pockets handily, Major." She planted herself before him with her hands on her hips and her chin raised. "Pillaging and plundering innocent folk. Just like you high-handed federals—*stealin'*. We demand just compensation for the damage inflicted upon us in the name of the U.S. government."

"Don't be absurd, wench." He turned away, but found his path blocked by his own men as they crowded closer to watch expectantly what transpired between their commander and this feisty little gal, Their looks prodded him to look to their pride as fighting men, to take no sass from the wench. He turned back. "You've sustained no damages; indeed, my men have shown admirable restraint in the face of grave provocation."

"Pie, Major." She rounded to face him again with a knowing glint in her eye. "And six full jugs of fine cider, close to forty gallons, and God knows what else they've stuffed their pockets with. And there's the monumental task of setting things to rights again. Aunt Kate's time and anguish alone are worth ten-dollars—*federal money*."

"Ten d—" He choked, feeling red creeping up his ears and dread creeping up his stiff neck. That insolent tilt of her head was back, and her voice had a clear, confident ring that he was beginning to recognize in the marrow of his bones . . . *bargaining*.

"A dollar a jug for the cider, and another dollar for the pie. That makes seventeen dollars, Major. Reparations, I believe, that's what they call it in wartime."

"Reparations, hell!" Warning rumbled through him at the spread of a challenging smile on her face.

"And we won't take your paper promises, Major," she declared evenly, reading the nuances of his shimmering eyes and aristocratic features with a keen trader's eye. He was bracing for something, and she wasn't about to disappoint him. "Now what have you—"

Her eyes flitted over him and her heart-shaped face flushed

with the pleasure of discovery. She grabbed a long knife from the nearest soldier's belt and severed one of the major's gleaming buttons, mid-chest, with one neat stroke.

"That ought to do it." She handed the soldier back his knife by the hilt and held the button up for an instant's appraisal before stuffing it into her pocket. "Seventeen-dollar buttons, Major." Her green eyes had borrowed a glitter from the gold. "Mighty nice."

He stared, thunderstruck, at the tuft of thread where his button had been, and his entire body began to quake with rage. His head jerked up. His eyes glowed white-hot. His fiber was frayed to mere strings; he was within a half-breath of trouncing her . . . female or not. He'd never been so close to a total rupture of control in his life.

"Assault on a duly constituted officer of the U.S. government is a treasonous offense," he rasped, his voice dredged from the deepest, most primitive regions of his being. His stark anger melted her taunting smile and silenced the muffled snorts and guffaws from his men. He turned on them, seeming to grow before their very eyes, and snarled, "Fall in!"

Whitney watched the major as he mounted his horse and led his soldiers off, bearing away their winter cider. The magnitude of his fury had poured through her like hot lead, solidifying in her limbs to forbid movement.

"Assault . . . treasonous offense . . ." echoed in her head. It was more than a statement; it was a vow made to them both. The next time she provoked and humiliated him before his men, he'd slap her in chains, and there was no one to say him nay.

It was a wonder he hadn't done it already. The thought circled meaningfully in her mind. She'd incensed and exasperated him, outraged and defied him with small, infuriating encroachments on his dignity and his self-control. And he'd threatened and bullied her, menaced and outmuscled her with devastating explosions of brute force and male dominance. And yet when they came together minutes before, they both had grown hot and silent and very still. And she always felt those swirling liquid sensations in the core of her that seemed to dissolve her mental processes.

It was a pure "womanly" response he provoked in her, she reasoned, something she wasn't quite prepared to handle. It was probably a bad sign.

A very bad sign indeed, her aunt Kate was thinking as she watched Whitney's concentration produce an unmistakable womanly glow in her cold-polished face. She, too, was recalling that stunning confrontation beside Whitney's bed, and she was dreading the implications of what she'd witnessed. She couldn't have picked a worse time to insist that Whitney begin acting like a woman.

Seven

The Iron Major honestly didn't use liquor. It was a genuine disappointment to Whitney. What kind of man wouldn't take at least a sociable tilt now and again? And he didn't use tobacco. And according to the frisky May Donner, he had no use for voluptuous widows either.

Over the following two days, Whitney collected these and quite a few other tidbits about her prime adversary. Robbie Dedham reported solemnly that the major's boots didn't stink, that he owned four very fine shirts with mother-of-pearl buttons, that he wrote left-handed, and that he shaved shirtless every morning. Uncle Harvey observed that his "guest" did not care much for "leather britches" beans nor the fatty salt pork that flavored them, that he carried his own salt and a pepper grinder in his kit, and that, in the absence of coffee and tea, he insisted on drinking only preboiled water. The major was punctual about rising and retiring, saw to his horse before he saw to himself, and liked his boots polished to a high sheen, none of which revealed a particularly useful vice or vulnerability in him.

There had to be something the man wanted besides the complete destruction of the whiskey trade in the valley. There had to be *something* that could persuade him to abandon his pursuit of Rapture's elusive stills. Every man had his price; it was an established fact.

Whitney admonished her people to watch more closely, and soon learned that he permitted little gambling in his camp and never participated in games of chance himself. She sighed when she heard this: another promising vice dispensed with. With each report it seemed another of the seven deadly sins was eliminated: lust, drunkenness, gluttony, greed.

Sloth didn't seem to be one of his deficits either. He personally led half the soldiers' daily sorties into the woods, looking for stills and signs of illegal activity. Otherwise, he devoted himself to systematically searching out and questioning nearly all of Rapture's inhabitants, using fancy words that had them scratching their heads by the time he was through.

In short, he proved the very model of decency, diligence, and decorum. In both word and deed he upheld an infuriatingly inconvenient philosophy of "moderation in all things." The only thing even close to an excess in him seemed to be his penchant for using his own last name, *Townsend,* in conversation at least three times a day, especially when giving orders or lecturing poor Uncle Harvey. Apparently he was rather impressed with his family's status and expected everyone else to be properly awed as well.

"It's not much to go on," Whitney admitted wanly to a small assembly of Rapture's folk, "but it smacks of pride. And as the Good Book says: 'Pride goeth before destruction, and an haughty spirit before a fall'—the Book of Proverbs."

The only problem was, it didn't "goeth" quickly enough. Daily, the folk brought Whitney word of searches drawing ever closer to their main cache of liquor and Black Daniels's current still site. Fortunately, the major proved to be a methodical man, given to orderly methods of dividing up territory for searching. Whitney donned her breeches late at night, when Uncle Julius and Uncle Ballard sent for her, and slipped out of the house to help them move the still, always to a spot the soldiers had searched the day before.

Such strenuous nightly activity took a toll on her daily energy and concentration, and more than once Aunt Kate's eyes narrowed suspiciously on her fatigued form. Her whole life was being consumed by her covert battle with the Iron Major. Things would be so much simpler if he were just the normal, temptation-prone sort.

What did the wretched man want?

* * *

Four days into the occupation of Rapture Valley, Uncle Harvey's barrels went bone dry.

"Well, then—buy more, dammit," the major steamed as he personally rechecked the notched depth-stick that was used to test the barrels. "My men have to have rations of spirits."

"Cain't, Major. Don't have no cash money—only your paper." Diminutive Uncle Harvey just managed not to flinch when the major leaned over him. "Them fellers over at Greensburg got to have cash money fer their whiskey, 'cause they gotta pay cash money fer their tax."

"Then go to Pittsburgh and get your blessed money and *then* buy more!"

"I ain't never been to Pittsburgh." Uncle Harvey seemed genuinely horrified at the prospect of leaving Rapture Valley. "An' anyway it'd take at least a week or two." He watched the major glower and grind internally and finally surrender with a *"Dammit."*

The very next evening, Uncle Harvey had yet another bit of bad news for the tenacious major and reluctantly sought him out as he made his routine evening inspection of the camp.

"What do you mean, no food?" The major stalked across the trampled grass at the far edge of camp to tower over the little innkeeper again. Uncle Harvey was getting a crick in his neck from the frequency of such unnerving encounters.

"Well, not quite no food yet, Major. But we got precious little. So I thought ye'd be wantin' to reduce them rations to stretch it a bit."

The major insisted on seeing for himself, and was given a doleful tour of the tavern's kitchen and smokehouse. He stomped back out to his camp with the sight of the meager flour in the bottom of a barrel burning in his mind. "Then barter or bargain or whatever it is you do, and get more."

"I already tried, Major," Uncle Harvey protested, shooting a sweaty look at Charlie Dunbar, who lounged nearby. He had no wish to join Charlie in shackles, no matter how good the food was. "Nobody's got much to trade, an' they don't want no paper money for what little they got. I be taxin' my neighbors sorely to take in my own child'rn to feed, the way it is." The major flamed at the innkeeper's left-handed revelation of just how earnest the shortages were; he was sending his own children out to neighbors to be fed.

"Then I'll have my lieutenant pay a call on these residents, to persuade them they can part with some of their food."

"He won't get nothin' neither." Charlie Dunbar snorted a laugh. "That lew-ten-ant of yers, he's got city boy writ all over 'im. They won't trade him nothin'."

"Who the hell asked you?" The major wheeled on him.

Charlie's smug look had a patronizing air about it. "Majur, what you need's a born trader, somebody who can swap th' spurs off'n a rooster."

"And I suppose *you're* just the man?" The major sneered.

"Naw, not me, Majur." Charlie's blocky face took on a wicked glow. "I'm a pris'ner, remember? Ye need th' best. Ye need Whit Daniels. Why, she can swap sheep straight outta their wool . . . and, I hear tell, th' buttons right off'n a stuffed shirt."

The major twitched and, in spite of himself, glared down at the empty buttonhole on his chest. Raw pride roared to flame inside him, and soon Charlie was repenting his vengeful gibe beneath new bindings and a rag stuffed into his mouth.

But the boy-faced Lieutenant Brooks, being no trader, was no more successful than Uncle Harvey had been, and that very night the Ninth Maryland Militia went on half rations. The major and the lieutenant, in an unexpected move, began to take meals outside with their men, making it clear they shared the deprivation and intended to set an example of duty and determination under hardship. The men's eyes widened at the sight of the major eating his handful of watery beans and meager biscuit sop, just like they did. But it didn't assuage the emptiness in their bellies or improve their mood.

By dinner the next day they were grating on each other's hunger-bared nerves, and by nightfall they were bristling at each other like porcupines. Their misery was seriously aggravated by the sight of Charlie Dunbar, lounging indolently beneath his tree, stuffing himself with crusty johnnycakes and leftover slices of pie that had been brought to the edge of the camp by various of the locals in Aunt Sarah's name. There was considerable snarling and wrangling over who would be assigned to guard him, and the only way Sergeant Laxault could prevent mayhem among the men was to rotate the assignment, so that each soldier would have the chance to fill his belly every few days.

It was into that volatile state of affairs that Aunt Sarah Dunbar, with the help of a younger son, carried a pot of venison stew and a big pan of warm biscuits. Behind her, in spite of the major's prejudice against locals in camp, swayed the curvy May Donner, bearing two apple pies. As they trod that central path, soldiers rose up in their wake, following the beckoning aromas like rats would the Pied Piper. Hungry faces ringed them as they fed their charges. The men pressed closer as it became clear there was more to eat than Charlie and his two guards could manage.

Aunt Sarah turned nervously to them, and the hunger in their faces melted her motherly heart. She began to hand out biscuits, then offered them the stew to "sop" in. May cut her pies in small wedges and distributed them as far as they would go. And when the flurry of feeding was over, Aunt Sarah murmured, "It be hard . . . managin' without m'Charlie at home. If ye gets too hongry, Ned," she patted his cheek fondly, "ye can come, mebee split me some wood . . . fer a bit of supper?"

"I—I'll come tomorrow morn', ma'am," Ned answered eagerly.

"Me too? I can split wood like a fork o' lightnin'!" lanky Albert declared, searching her with an expression of raw hope. And when Aunt Sarah sighed and nodded acceptance, a bolt of excitement went through the rest.

"I reckon I could use a bit o' help . . ." May Donner inserted into the rumble, and instantly had a dozen volunteers. Everyone was more than willing to split curvy May Donner's wood. She finally selected two soldiers who looked up to the task, the biggest and strongest among them, and the others muttered and growled disappointment.

"Ain't there anybody else who could use a bit o' work done?" came a frustrated voice from the back.

"I been plowin' since I wuz knee high, an' done butcherin' too," came another.

A storm of useful skills assailed them, and Aunt Sarah finally managed to raise a trembling hand to gain quiet enough to say, "I can ask around. With some o' the men gone, most o' us need th' help."

And so it was that come the next morning at sunrise various residents of the Rapture settlement and the valley beyond appeared at the edge of the major's camp to take home with them soldiers who were willing to work for their food. The soldiers pushed back from their big, hearty breakfasts, satisfied, not knowing they had Whitney Daniels to thank for their opportunity. And the residents of Rapture viewed their mounting woodpiles and reshingled sheds and new-harvested corn with equal satisfaction, breathing prayers of thanks for that uncanny Daniels "trader instinct" for creating a need in folks . . . then making them pay well to satisfy it.

The major and the lieutenant, of course, knew nothing of the burgeoning arrangement between their men and the local folk. The soldiers, exhibiting the innate craftiness of hungry men, saw to it that word of such opportunities was passed quietly. With the major and the lieutenant frequently on patrol and dropping from hunger and exhaustion into sleep the minute they returned, it was relatively easy to carry on undetected. And when the rigors of their bartered work made them tired, and interfered with the thoroughness on patrol, the major and his lieutenant were apt to put it down to hunger and deprivation . . . and overlook it.

"Shore hope we don' haveta move agin soon," Uncle Julius said, sitting on a log in a tiny clearing in the forest, scowling into his cup in the gloomy dampness of the predawn hours.

Across the smoldering remains of fire, grizzled Uncle Ballard was nodding off, and beside him Whitney Daniels was staring similarly into her tin cup. They'd spent a good part of the night sealing and transporting their last batch of whiskey to safe storage and were all totally exhausted. The cup of fine Daniels whiskey they'd shared was for soothing their aching muscles as much as for providing warmth in the misty night air.

"Well, we outwitted them this far, we can outwit them a bit longer. The major's men are fast losing their enthusiasm for arresting distillers," Whitney observed thoughtfully. "Now, if we could only find some way to dim the major's enthusiasm . . ."

They sat in silence awhile longer, then Uncle Julius slapped his bony knee and declared, "We'd best git ye home, gal. I'll see ye partway."

"I'm not going home; I'm staying with Aunt Sarah tonight. Aunt Kate's getting suspicious. You don't have to go, Uncle Julius . . . your knees . . ."

"Don't be yawpin' about m'knees, gal. Everbody knows I wuz bred part mule."

Whitney smiled tiredly, and soon they were moving through the forest, their eyes fighting the rising mist for familiar landmarks and sure footing on the descending slopes. When they neared the Dunbar farmstead, Uncle Julius left her, and she proceeded through the graying woods toward the main road on her own. Her hands were shoved into her coat pockets, her shoulders were slouched as she lifted her head and glimpsed the road just ahead. She was bone weary, and concentrating wholly on her direction and on the bed she would soon share with Charlie's little sister.

A branch snapped, and there was shouting and a charging rush all around her. Rough hands seized her from every direction, and she struggled mightily as she recognized her assailants.

Soldiers!

A harsh voice rang out above the snarls and grunts around her and above her own virulent protests. The frenzied motion and countermotion slowed and paused in a heaving silence.

"Well, well." The major's voice had a nasty ring of triumph as he stared down at the rigid, defiant form of his prisoner. "What have we—"

"You let me go." The sight of him, looming big and fierce out of the foggy gloom, was daunting in the extreme. Fatigue and the last traces of the whiskey's effects left her few words to battle with. "This is . . . an outrage. Assaulting a young woman in plain sight."

When she raised her chin, recognition rained through the major like an exploding can of shot. Distillers, whiskey rebels, tax evaders, and sneak-thieves he would have expected, even welcomed at this ungodly hour of the morning. But Whiskey Daniels, tousled, flushed, and defiant, was something he wasn't quite prepared for.

"Young, perhaps." He managed a healthy sneer, leaning back in his saddle to distance himself. Every numbed and aching muscle, every strained sinew in his exhausted body was coming to life at the mere fact of her presence. It was mildly alarming. "But not much of a woman. What in hell are you doing out in the woods in the dead of night, witch?"

"I was . . . checking traps," she answered with all the convincing half-truth she could muster. Checking the soldiers' traps . . . and avoiding them, she told herself.

"Is that so?" His gaze raked her coat, her wet boots, her rumpled hair, and he felt an unreasoning twinge of relief that burly Charlie Dunbar was still in chains. Acting on raw impulse, he turned to his sergeant. "Sergeant Laxault, take the men on into camp. I'll question Daniels myself as I take her home."

Soon Whitney found herself standing alone with the Iron Major at the side of the narrow road, and her heart began to thud. His grip on her arm was fierce, and his eyes on her were cool and silvery.

Garner Townsend found himself holding Whitney Daniels while his blood coursed faster, and knew he'd taken complete leave of his senses. It was sheer folly to set hands to the little witch; every time he touched her, she wreaked some form of mayhem on him. His grip on his mount's reins and on her arm both tightened.

"Come on, wench." He turned her down the road toward the Daniels farmstead.

"No." She dug her boot heels in to resist him and wrested her arm back and forth. "I'm not going home—I'm staying the night at Aunt Sarah's."

"The hell you are." He reeled her close enough to feel the

warmth of her, to smell the whiskey on her breath. "You've spent the night with someone else already, witch. Who? Who the hell were you out in the woods with?"

"I told you," she snapped, realizing he thought she'd been out with some buck in the woods. But indignation gave way to a strange mixture of anger and relief. If he thought that, then he still didn't suspect her connection to Rapture Valley's major distilling operation. "I was out checking traps . . . *alone.*"

"I don't believe that for an instant," he growled, feeling the steam in his blood seeping into other parts of his chilled anatomy. His hand on her tightened, his pulse quickened. Beneath his fingers she felt soft, so damnably soft and warm in the cold morning.

"I don't care what you believe, Major." She swallowed, finding it hard to speak against the squeezing in her throat. The warmth radiating from his wide shoulders was seductive, melting her defiance. Her head was beginning to waffle strangely as his eyes became patches of dawn sky with morning stars rising in them.

"You've been drinking . . . whiskey." Even as he said it, he was breathing it in, absorbing it into his blood. It was a smell he associated with the rough company of men, with fighting and bold revelry, with camaraderie and challenge. It was a scent that brought his blood up and started his muscles coiling with expectation. Somehow it was fitting that "Whiskey" Daniels smelled that way, for in every sense she was his adversary. She boldly challenged both his duty and skill as a soldier and his personal control as a man. And with the warning of that last beleaguered bit of logic resounding in his head, he still drew her closer to his stirring body.

"It was a cold night, Major." She fought for control of her senses, trying to resist the sensual effects of his touch, knowing she was unable to counter his superior physical strength. But her eyes sought the bold curve of his mouth, and her fingertips itched to touch the dark curl that lapped his temple. Unintentionally, her voice softened. "A nip of good whiskey warms the blood. . . ."

"Your blood is already warm enough, wench," he uttered, losing to the urge to drag his fingertips across her cheek and down her straight nose with the tiny dent in the end. Lord, she was soft . . . every bit as smooth and satiny as he remembered. Dunbar was right. What else would a man be doing out in the woods with wild, sensual little Whiskey Daniels?

"Who is he?" he demanded, his voice deep and resonant with need. He burned to know and yet dreaded to learn. "He's a distiller, isn't he?"

"Who?" The feel of his fingertips sliding onto her lips disrupted her logical processes momentarily.

"Your man."

"Now, Major"—she swallowed against the squeezing in her throat and tried valiantly to summon that old Daniels flippancy— "what would I want with a man?"

It was as provocative a challenge as a woman had ever laid at a man's feet, and Garner Townsend was not a man to walk away from a challenge, however fraught with peril.

"This . . ." He cradled her face in one hand, tilting it up as the other slipped around her waist, drawing her fully against his hardening frame. Her hands came up against his chest, but could summon no force to resist him. He was going to kiss her again, she realized; his head was bending, his bold, expressive lips were parting.

And she was going to let him, he realized, watching the way her velvety lips parted and her head tilted instinctively to receive him.

This was what each of them had recalled during those seething encounters at the inn and in the camp. This was what both had felt echoing through them every time they faced each other. Every steamy look, every crackling silence, every angry charge and countercharge, challenged them to test the memory of the startling pleasures they had stumbled upon that first afternoon.

She tingled with anticipation, then the wonder of his mouth on hers poured warmth through her again. His lips caressed and coaxed hers wider, and his tongue traced the pliant opening with slow, hypnotizing strokes. A noise that was part pleasure, part distress escaped her throat when his tongue found the tip of hers and traced luscious circles around it. Her arms slid weakly down his chest and seemed to catch at his waist. It took so little effort to send them curling around his lean middle.

Her movement drew a moan from deep in his throat and his arms flexed, crushing her against his chest as he probed the sweet, steamy recesses of her mouth. She opened to him, savoring the sleek contours of his tongue with hers, exploring the sensation of the slow, intimate dueling.

The trembling of his braced legs finally registered in Garner Townsend's senses, and he opened his eyes to find himself standing in the middle of that weedy road, clasping Whiskey Daniels to him as though he intended to take her on the very spot—standing up. In his dangerously hot state, he wouldn't release her, not when her curves were pressing against him, filling the aching hollows that memory and desire had carved into his body. He began to move, carrying her back into the trees with the force of his body against hers.

Wrapped in his strong arms and immersed in a steamy sea of sensation, Whitney didn't protest as she was swept backward. She came to rest against a tree trunk, and he came to rest against her, pinning her there with his hard weight. Her arms wriggled uncertainly between them, and he pulled them up, directing them around his neck as his head lowered to join their mouths again. Her fingers slid wonderingly up the side of his muscular neck, above the sinuous gold braid, to invade the tangle of his loosely curled hair. It felt curiously like a child's, wrapping silkily around her fingers, returning her caresses.

The splendor of his kisses deepened, then lowered to her throat and the side of her neck, sending a wanton need for more radiating under her skin in all directions. Her nipples were tightening against her shirtfront, and a familiar burning tingle congregated in the sensitive tips of her breasts. Recent experience had taught her there was only one way to assuage that divine torture. She wriggled closer to him, pressing her hardening breasts against him through her coat. As if he understood and shared her desire, he traced her shape with his hands, working his way around her shoulders and waist to her front. His lean fingers slipped between them and he quickly released the bone buttons to invade the light wool of her coat.

His whole body trembled with eagerness as he claimed the generous, hard-tipped mounds of her breasts with sure, caressing motion. She moaned and arched to meet him, imploring a firmer touch, seeking a deeper pleasure. The barrier of her shirt was freed from her belt, and the cool hardness of his fingers slid beneath it and over her nipples; their velvety peaks were soon pebble hard from the gentle, rhythmic friction of his thumbs. Frissons of excitement raced along her nerves, and she felt his body quiver against hers, resonant with pleasure.

Whitney couldn't breathe, couldn't think. All her senses were engulfed in the new currents of desire swirling through her. His caresses seemed to reach inside her with a physical presence, stirring the potent liquid of her womanly response. Nothing mattered but the hard feel of him around her and the curiously sweet communion of his mouth on hers.

When his knee slipped between her thighs, she yielded, allowing him to nudge her legs apart. His arms moved to clasp her bottom and lift her against the bulging hardness of his arousal. Smooth, arching thrusts of his hips rubbed his hardened shaft against her womanly center, sending jagged flashes of pleasure radiating upward through her. The brilliance of sensation momentarily overwhelmed both her perception and her response.

Through the fiery turmoil in his own blood, Garner Townsend felt her sharp intake of breath and the rigid tremors of her body against his. It registered in him as surprise; and it somehow startled him. Awareness of his body's position and intensity began to surface through the dense steam in his head.

His legs were bent and braced to support them both, his body was coiled, his arms were flexed, and his hands were splayed, clasping her bottom possessively. Blood drummed frantically in his head, and its dangerous cadence echoed like thunder in his loins. He had to lose himself, spend himself in Whiskey Daniels's lush little body. It was so close, that softness, that moist, beckoning heat . . . just a snatch of fabric between them. . . . He could take her here, now.

His passion-glazed eyes focused slowly on the wet, fallen leaves at their feet, and that cold riot of color, made brilliant by the morning dew, registered in more than just his gaze.

A creeping paralysis of reality gripped him. He must be mad, roused to such a state that he was ready to take her on the cold, wet ground . . . as if he were some damned heaving animal.

Whitney felt the confusion in his response. She opened her eyes to marvel at the shadowed planes of his cheeks, the feathery grace of his arched brows, and the spare, geometric sweep of his muscular jaw. Wrapped in the web of sensation he'd spun about her, she caught his hands as they released her and guided them beneath her shirt again, rippling as they closed on her warm flesh.

He shivered, and the change in him telegraphed a warning through her. His eyes changed even as she watched, chilling to a cold shimmer as he recoiled from his complete abandonment of self, and from knowledge of the one who'd caused it.

"God."

The raw power in that single syllable rumbled through her with devastating effect. His face drained and his hands withdrew from her shirt, falling into fists at his sides. He stalked backward, looking gray and granitelike.

"You!" He finally summoned the power of speech, jabbing an impotent finger at her as raw frustration choked off the rest of his verbal capacity. Something about the little witch seemed to lock his speech mechanisms. When he did finally manage another word, it turned out to be the very eloquent, *"Dammit!"*

Whitney watched his disgust, his horror at finding himself entangled bodily with her again. She made no move to right her dangling shirtfront or straighten the coat he'd peeled back from her shoulders in his eagerness to savor her womanly shape. She honestly couldn't move; the sweet languor of her muscles was turning to shame-filled weakness.

How could he kiss her like that, touch her like that, then just back away?

How could she just stand there, looking so sensual and appealing, he groaned . . . so damned defenseless? His aching loins, spurring him toward all manner of wild, irrational behavior . . . like taking her back into his arms and kissing that bewildered frown from her brow, and filling his hands with her silky breasts and filling her frame with the full measure of his passion for her.

"Dammit—" he ground out again, gesturing furiously to her

disarranged clothing. "Will you—" He stopped, then lurched at her, intent on remedying her disheveled state himself, to remove both reminder and temptation.

But when his hands lifted her shirt to stuff it back into her belt, the sensation was too keen, too much like his actions of minutes ago and too lacking in those same tender motives. She stumbled aside, finally stung to life by his anger.

"Don't you—" she choked out, finding her voice too thick to continue. She had to battle a squeezing in her throat and a frightening prickle at the backs of her eyes as she wadded her shirt quickly into her breeches. Everything was blurring and it was suddenly hard to get her breath. Lord! She couldn't let him get the best of her like this. What was happening to her? She swallowed desperately. "Don't touch me again—I swear—you'll regret it."

"I already regret it," he growled.

She bolted for the road with her eyes and her heart on fire. He'd stripped her of every defense she could claim, leaving only the tender, painful responses of a newly exposed and very vulnerable young woman.

"Dammit," he gritted through clenched teeth, lurching after her. He overtook her at the edge of the trees and snagged her wrist as she dodged to escape him. She snapped back toward him, wheeled, and dug her heels in.

But he bested her protests to pull her closer. They wrestled briefly then the force drained from her resistance and they both slowed. His grip eased, shifting to her shoulders, and she turned her face as far from him as possible. He could see delicate muscles working in her clamped jaw, and knew she was trying to control her feelings. He wanted to speak, but found that his vocabulary had utterly deserted him once again.

"What do you want from me?" Whitney demanded quietly without looking at him.

The question drove into his gut like one of Laxault's meaty fists. He'd just participated in a humiliating demonstration of exactly what he wanted from her. And he could still taste the strange, potent spiciness of her mouth, could still feel the provocative press of her breasts against his ribs.

"I need answers."

"I don't like the way you ask questions . . . with your hands," she said softly.

It was the most potent indictment possible of his lack of self-control. He'd known she was suspect in this whiskey business, and instead of quizzing her properly, he'd violated every precept of an officer's code of honor to set hands to her every time he'd seen her. *He'd asked his questions with his hands.*

Dunbar was right. She did have a way with words.

He released her wrists as he reached for her chin, turning her flushed face to him with much gentler fingers. "Who were you with, Whiskey?"

"Whiskey?" She paused, glancing up through the filter of her long lashes, stunned by his taunt. She didn't even hear the part about the stills. He hated whiskey, considered it low and crude. And Whiskey was his name for her now. A cruel little jest on her name that clearly spoke his contempt for her, even after he'd . . . Maybe he really was made of iron all the way through.

But she certainly wasn't. Just now her newly vulnerable body was aching all over and something big and heavy was sitting on her heart, making each beat more painful than the last. Darting around him, she started for Aunt Sarah's.

He caught up again, facing her and slowing so that she had to slow as well. This time there was no question, only a tight, troubled look in his striking gray-blue eyes. That look tugged at her chin the way his hands couldn't. And finally her burning eyes lifted.

"You kissed me," she charged softly. The huskiness of her voice masked a wealth of turmoil.

"I . . . didn't mean to . . ." It sounded awful in his own ears too. *Didn't want to,* it said, and *didn't value it either.* He shuddered through the outraged flailing of his conscience. He didn't try to stop her when she struck off around him again, but he did match her surprisingly brisk stride.

God, he was in chaos inside. He couldn't think straight! Desperately, he retreated into the cool, conquering dignity of the Townsend persona that straightened his spine and stiffened his face. As a Townsend, he could deal with anything, face any challenge, command any situation.

"It was . . . a deplorable lapse . . . unbefitting an officer or a Townsend." He stopped when she stopped, and when she looked up at him with that bruised look to the jewellike green of her eyes, he felt his insides going molten again.

"Then you cursed at me." Her chin trembled ever so slightly and the dark centers of her eyes pulsed with ill-concealed hurt.

"I . . . apologize . . ."

"I don't want your apology." She held her shoulders very straight and tried not to blink so that the moisture in her eyes wouldn't run down her cheeks. "I just want you to go away. Take your men and go back to Boston. My people have never done anything to you." Her voice cracked, and she stopped. Her gaze dropped to his rich blue coat front that was missing one elegant gold button, and her throat closed entirely.

His hand came up, drawn by the quivering pulse at the base of her throat, and he drew the backs of his knuckles gently across her cheek. Whitney felt that tender stroke like a lash across her opened heart and quivered, closing her eyes. She could feel his stormy gaze on her, could feel the heat of him flooding into her again. Please . . . not again . . .

That steely gentleness withdrew, and she braced instinctively for what she knew must follow.

"Dammit!"

Suddenly his broad shoulder was ramming into her middle and she was being hoisted bodily. She jerked and flailed, gasped for breath as he carried her to his horse and transferred her from his shoulder to lie across the pommel of his saddle. Facedown, she dangled and flopped humiliatingly, snarling biblically inspired threats connecting Job's boils and certain sensitive parts of *his* anatomy.

"Don't you move!" he thundered, mounting in an instant and resettling her vulnerable bottom over his hard knees as he gave his horse the spur.

Blood pooled in her head and everything careened and roared around her as the hard saddle and his hard knees pounded against her ribs from below. And just when she thought she would burst, the motion came to a thudding halt and he peeled her from his legs and slid her off into the dirt like a bag of turnips. She staggered, scarcely able to breathe or to walk, fighting the humiliating tangle of her hair to see where she was.

His tall boots with their spurs, a flash of roan flank, an expensive stirrup; they came into focus briefly as the blood drained from her vision. Then they shot into motion and were gone.

She blinked and gasped in the billowing dust, unable to expel her breath. Wheeling, she recognized the nearby cabin, the barn, and the sheds that nestled on the creek bank. He'd dumped her square in the Dunbars' dusty yard.

She ducked into their small barn, holding her abused middle in her hands and praying no one had witnessed her ignominious arrival. Every step up the pole ladder was sheer torture to her pummeled ribs and abdominal muscles. But when she climbed onto the planking loft in the rafters and collapsed onto the fragrant hay, her misery actually seemed to worsen.

Every bone in her body had been jarred loose. But she felt disconnected in more than just her joints; her actions and responses were confused and frighteningly unreliable. As she wiped a stray lock of hair back from her face, she felt the gentleness of his touch again in the brush of her own hand. A second later she felt a cold burning trickle down her cheeks. An awful, hurtful swelling began in her chest, crowding her lungs, making it hard to breathe again.

Crying. Lord above, she hadn't cried since she was ten years old. Now he'd kissed her and cursed at her and made her cry. *The wretch.* He was doing things to her, making her feel things that disrupted her easy flow through the world around her. It was a little frightening, and a lot humiliating.

When he had moved close to her, her lips began to tingle and her skin came alive beneath her softly molded deerskin and raspy homespun. Oh! There it was again—the torturous, quivery feeling beneath her skin and in her womanly parts. Suddenly she could feel the lingering press of his body against hers and the gentle rubbing of his fingers over her nipples. The tactile memory of his warm hands smoldered in her bare breasts, and his chest-deep moans rumbled through her body again.

His hands . . . his moans . . . the thought captured her imagination. The arrogant, self-righteous major had behaved just as badly as she had, wriggling and touching and invading her very clothes to do shocking things to her! He'd kissed her and touched her bare—

Oh, no. She closed her eyes, but the realization wouldn't go away. That dusky heat in his face, that hot gleam in his eye . . . the way he invaded her mouth and rubbed his swollen self against her. All this time she'd had her people watching him, trying to learn what he wanted.

And all along, the one thing the Iron Major wanted in Rapture Valley was her.

Garner Townsend was halfway to the settlement before he slowed his horse to a walk and wrenched his thoughts from the vision of her curvy bottom, her lush lower lip, her crystal-green eyes.

Good God, she was the most infuriating, most unthinkable, most inappropriate female ever put on this earth—

And extraordinary, a small voice interjected. Extraordinary, he admitted with a snarl.

And appealing. Too damned appealing, he agreed nastily.

And he kicked his mount into motion again, making for the heart of Rapture at a gallop. He handed his horse over to Uncle Radnor at the smithy's without the usual reminder to rub him down thoroughly, and stalked straight to the tavern without seeing two of his men and Aunt Harriet Delaney scurrying to separate as they made their way back to her farmstead to begin their day's work. He blew through the tavern door and into his small room on the second floor, ripping off his coat and wrestling with his emerging feelings.

She was by turns insolent and innocent, defiant and delectable, but always unpredictable. She wheedled and bargained shamelessly, as if she *enjoyed* it, and she talked like a cross between a tent preacher and a snake-oil peddler. She was brash and reckless, wore skin-tight breeches, and drank whiskey like a man. She swaggered when she walked and chased about the countryside all night in the company of men.

How many men, he wanted to know. Which men? Who? And did she kiss them back, her mouth soft and pliant beneath theirs, opening to them, yielding them that lush, spicy heat that clung to their senses long after she was gone?

He groaned and stumbled facedown onto the straw-filled ticking of the bed that couldn't quite contain all of his long frame. His mind filled with colors . . . brilliant sea-green, ripe-cherry red, burnished gold-brown ginger . . . like the tarnished halo of her hair. A tarnished halo . . . a perfect image to describe her. There was an odd sense of goodness in her reckless vibrance, a bizarre virtue in the honesty and openness with which she eschewed feminine constraints.

She was the very antithesis of everything a woman should be, and yet he was drawn to plunge himself into the tempestuous warmth of her unthinkable appealing being. She roused the man in him like no other woman ever had—not Amanda, not Chloe—

Amanda . . . Chloe . . . his very blood stopped. Just thinking those names always pounded his priorities back into their sternly regulated order, and this time it booted his entire being onto harsh new planes of determination. Suddenly the tawdry, pathetic mush of his previous thoughts appalled him. Good God.

He had a duty to perform here; ambition to satisfy. What in hell was he doing rutting about in the woods with some rebellious, half-savage tart? He was letting her interfere with his clearly defined duty. He shuddered and turned onto his back, staring up at the open rafters. Confusion coiled in his stomach again. It was the beast inside him, his fatal weakness.

Twice before, women had wreaked havoc in his life. Twice he'd been tempted and betrayed. Twice he'd been forced to face his family's horror, to bear the intolerable shame of disgracing the Townsend name and honor . . . in debacles involving women. Only now, after years of harsh, sober diligence and iron-clad propriety, was he on the verge of earning back his family's respect and his rightful place in the distinguished Townsend Companies. And nothing, he vowed grimly, nothing was going to interfere with that.

Eight

"If you have any trouble requisitioning those supplies from the locals," Townsend said, referencing the paper he'd shoved into his lieutenant's hands the instant the fellow walked through the door, "then haul Dunbar's arse out to the front of the tavern and lash him, standing up, to that damnable 'liberty pole.' And leave him there under guard all night! I'm through pussyfooting with this lot. They'll soon see I mean business!" He jerked his second glove on and tugged his loose coat front down with an air of finality. "And while you're at it, you can start rounding up those Delbarton dullards for questioning about the source of that pole. It's a damned affront to the nation . . . a call to treasonous rebellion."

He paused, pressing the corners of his eyes to assuage a low throbbing in his head, and saw on the backs of his eyelids the twenty-foot liberty pole that had been raised in the clearing in the dead of the night just past. It was a fresh-peeled pine trunk, sunk three or four feet into the ground to stabilize it, and adorned with a crudely carved: LIB-R-TE. It was a familiar silent protest against the Act, against the tax, and against the federal presence in Rapture Valley. During their march west, they'd encountered a dozen such poles along their route, all appearing mysteriously overnight, on common ground. And no local ever seemed to have the faintest idea where they'd come from.

More infuriating than the pole itself was the fact that not one of his men seemed to have noticed the noise and commotion that must have accompanied raising the hellish thing. It was an alarming indication of just how drastically the grinding adversities of constant hunger and constant antagonism had worn them down.

"Are the men ready for patrol?" The major turned with a dark look at his silent junior officer and found him rather pale, looking quite sickly in fact.

"I—I hardly think so, sir. There's been . . ." The haggard lieutenant swallowed hard and screwed his courage to the hilt. "It's that cider, sir. They got into it a-and . . ."

"Cider? What cid—" Townsend twitched, drawing the only conclusion possible. "The cider we confiscated?"

Brooks nodded warily, stepping back, bracing for a full explosion. The major didn't disappoint him.

"Dammit! Who gave them—how did they—?" When Brooks spread his palms and braved a shrugging denial, the major tore from the room to see for himself. Shortly he was stalking through the camp, his temper flaring, his shoulder muscles knotted into aching lumps, his hands knotted into itching fists.

The men of the Maryland Ninth were sprawled everywhere, limp as noodles and just about as sensible. The earthen jugs they'd drained littered the central path, obviously empty. The men lay in tangled heaps around their smoky campfires, their tents, and tree trunks. The Iron Major stomped about the camp, bellowing at them and giving their inert bodies furious prods with his boot. A few managed to rouse, one or two to grin drunkenly, one, totally insensible wretch to actually offer him a snort. None made it up past their knees, and one poor fellow was actually found facedown in the cold-running creek. The major grabbed him by his belt and the scruff of the neck and pulled him back onto the bank, snarling that if he weren't already dead, he'd soon wish he were.

"All this"—he turned on Brooks, wild-eyed and quaking with fury—"from a few damned jugs of cider?"

"They had empty bellies, Major." Brooks massaged his own hollow middle. "And they're bone tired and sore. It went straight to their heads. We hadn't checked it for content, but it must have been strong stuff. Once they got started, they just couldn't . . . please, Major—" But the dusky rage in his commander's face made him choke back a plea for clemency.

The major towered, black with wrath and burning with frustration. He had a job to do; they all did. They were sent in to uphold the law, to enforce order and stability . . . and look at them. Drunk as David's sow, the surly, disreputable lot of them. Not only did he have to fight those cursed distillers and the stubborn locals that supported them, but now he had to battle his own men's baser impulses to make them perform their sworn duty. If he had only been assigned a gentlemanly troop of dragoons he'd have had this viper's nest cleared out in three bloody days!

He turned on his heel and strode for the smithy, a painful heat in the bottom of his own empty belly. He saddled his horse himself and rode off at a gallop, following the main road blindly, burning off some of the angry energy that made him feel like he might fly apart at the seams at any moment.

He rode hard, into the dusky evening, freeing his tangled feelings and frustrations, bending low over the powerful animal beneath him. Together they raced and jumped and dodged, merged in escape from the oppression of duty and expectation.

When much of his tension and energy were spent, the major found himself near Little Bear Creek and dismounted to give his horse a drink and a rest. As he stood there, straddling the boulders imbedded in the bottom of the creek, his own fatigue and thirst turned his thoughts back to his men again. They were tired and sore and hungry. Too many of them had been conscripted into an army bent on a cause they neither understood nor cared much about. They'd endured deprivation and hunger and contempt— sometimes even his own. There was probably no true malice in their drunken spree, and no intentional mutiny. They'd simply seized a bit of comfort where they could find it.

He knelt on the rocks and drank from the clear stream himself, then led his mount back to the road that trailed through the heart of Rapture Valley. The evening was quiet and in the lowering light he walked, absorbing the sounds; the rustle of dry leaves, the dull thud of hooves, the whooshing of the nearby creek.

Minutes later he found himself standing before a tree stump at the site where a now-familiar path joined the road. His eyes traced the crudely cut "B" in the chiseled stump, and his guts tightened. Without conscious effort he'd located the path leading to *her* home. He was instantly stung by the irony of his force of men lying drunk and disabled from the very brew they'd confiscated as a punishment to her. Even when he won a round with Whiskey Daniels, he never quite seemed to win. He was nettled sharply by that admission. The sight of the liberty pole flashed into his mind again.

He jammed his boot into the stirrup and bounded up into his saddle, his jaw and shoulders set. And when he applied his heels, his horse sprang into motion . . . headed straight for the Daniels farmstead.

Kate Morrison was carrying a basket of potatoes up from the spring house when the sound of hooves pounding up the path halted her on the top step. In the murky evening light she made out glowing patches of gold braid on a dark, spectral form and knew instantly who approached. She suppressed a shiver at the determined wall of his shoulders and the completeness of his command over the huge horse. The great roan pounded to a halt at her feet, and she had the distinct impression that the animal had stopped exactly where he'd willed it to just short of running her down. Her heart began to beat frantically as he dismounted and faced her with a pull at his elegant hat.

"Madam."

"Major." She acknowledged him with a terse nod and raised her chin a notch. "What do you want with us?"

Excellent question, a sardonic little voice in him prodded.

"I want to see your niece, Whiskey." Heaven knew that was the truth. "I have certain . . . questions to put to her."

"My niece's name is *Whitney,* sir." Kate Morrison's authority and breeding asserted itself naturally. In the rising light of the full moon, she saw his mouth quirk up tauntingly, as if to say he knew Whitney's name well enough. And he still chose to call her Whiskey. The implications of that particular appellation were clear and unnerving. "I cannot think what possible answers she might give you that you are not quite capable of discovering on your own."

The major straightened, his light eyes piercing the dimness.

"Still, it may save me precious time to speak with her, Madam. If it would not inconvenience you."

Kate felt her face heating at the overpowering aura he exuded; he was so totally, so ruthlessly male that he set even her impervious heart quivering. And it was clear he suspected Whitney's involvement in the local whiskey trade. Why else would he make such a telling play on her name? But what did he know . . . and, more important, what did he intend to do with his knowledge?

"This way, sir," she said, releasing the breath she had been holding in as she decided. They entered the fragrant, fire-warmed kitchen and found Whitney lifting a fresh pan of biscuits from the Dutch oven built into the side of the hearth.

"We have a visitor, Whitney," Kate said with meaningful calm as she shed her shawl and relieved the major of his hat.

Whitney turned straight into the major's steely gaze and nearly dropped the pan of biscuits. Everything in the room stilled temporarily, down to the wheeze of the fire and the beating of Whitney's heart. He filled the kitchen with his male presence, and in a breath he filled Whitney as well. That soft, curly hair, that sensual set to his mouth, the wide expanse of his shoulders . . .

The major's eyes drifted from the golden mounds in the pan she held to the pale, creamy mounds that her low-cut bodice revealed. And his mouth watered violently on both counts. She was wearing a dress. It was the first time he'd seen her in womanly guise, with her hair piled up on her head. He swallowed hard, sending the heat that was building in him to his eyes, to keep it from settling in his loins.

Whitney recovered enough to hear the explanation her aunt Kate made about the major wanting to question her. Even through her vibrating senses, she collected the strain in her aunt's voice and the peculiar emphasis of wording that warned of the major's intent. She felt his eyes on her dress, on her liberally bared skin and flushed, embarrassed at being caught looking so "womanly." Somehow she felt it gave him an edge in their covert battle, and she vowed that her appearance was all he would find womanly . . . and susceptible.

By the time they were ready to sit down to eat, Whitney's control was returning and the major's was unraveling. He had watched the sway of her skirts, tortured by the imaginings of the movements of her rounded buttocks and her lithe, muscular legs beneath them. And while he struggled to blunt the effect of the provocative fit of her bulging bodice, the delicious aromas of meat and fresh-baked bread assailed his defenses on another, very vulnerable level. He was in turmoil inside; his mood had gone from cool and taunting to heated and surly. He was mad— stark, raving mad—to have come here!

"If it would not be misconstrued, sir"—Kate faced him as Whitney and she sat down to eat—"we would offer you supper with us."

"Oh, Aunt Kate"—Whitney exuded that Daniels brand of innocence—"such an offer could be seen as an attempt to compromise the major's ethics. But do be seated, Major. You can question me while *I* eat." She smiled sweetly as she waved him to a seat across the table from her.

He managed to sit, and Whitney noted with satisfaction that he gripped his thighs tightly with his hands. She spooned the heavenly smelling beef stew into her mouth and, feeling his eyes hard on her, made a subtle spectacle of savoring it. Those light, flaky biscuits were soon spread with pale, creamy butter and layered with sweet fried apples. She bit into them with lurid pleasure, licking some of the melted butter from her glistening lips. The major watched the darting of her tongue with predatory intensity, swallowing hard, feeling his righteous ethos sliding into a cauldron of roiling desires. His face grew dusky, his jaw clamped, and his eyes silvered. Whitney firmly hoped he was squirming inside.

He was. He was also suffering an alarming melting sensation up his spine . . . that was creeping into his brain. To counter the effect, he sat straighter and tried desperately to recall his reason for coming here. Questions, he recalled. Ask some damned questions, for heaven's sake, any questions!

"To what do you attribute the meager harvest this year, Mrs. Morrison?"

"A plague of vermin," Whitney said before Kate could answer. There was dangerous insolence in her tone as she brazened:

"Blue locust. They've been known to strip a valley clean, left unchecked."

The major stared hard at her, fighting the watering in his mouth to answer her challenge. "And would those vermin be the sort that strip the limbs and bark from a pine tree, transport it to the center of a settlement, and sink it four feet into the ground? That sort of vermin?"

"Please, Major—" Kate stiffened, darting a panicky look between Whitney and the handsome federal.

"A liberty pole sprang up in the clearing overnight. What do you know about it?"

"A liberty pole?" Whitney's eyes grew wide. The Delbartons had been talking about making one for almost a week, ever since some of the soldiers started splitting May Donner's wood. "Why, nothing, Major."

"Where were *you* last night?" He gripped the edge of the table as he awaited her response. An involuntary flicker in her eyes told him she'd caught the emphasis in his statement . . . and the taunt behind it.

"Why, here, at home, with Aunt Kate." Whitney flicked an instinctive look at her aunt, betraying a concern the major read too fluently.

"And the night before?"

"Here, as usu—"

"No—" Kate corrected her. "The night before last you were at Aunt Sarah's, remember?" Then she turned on the major to drive home a point. "With some of the men gone and some *in chains,* the womenfolk don't feel safe . . . with *soldiers* prowling about the countryside at night. Charlie Dunbar's mother sometimes asks Whitney to stay with her." Her indignation was so ladylike and so adamant that it was undoubtedly genuine. She obviously knew nothing of Whitney's nightly exploits.

"Of course"—Whitney tightened, driving daggers of double meaning at him—"how could I have forgotten?"

"Heavens—" Kate sucked in a breath at the sparks being exchanged across the table. She had to do something. "This is absurd. Major, we've never let a body leave the Daniels table unfilled. Ethics or no, you must have a bite to eat." As she rose anxiously to fetch a plate of food, the major's eyes crinkled knowingly at the corners.

"Liar." He hurled it quietly, dredging the bottom of his register and volume.

Whitney felt blood bursting against her liberally exposed skin. How dare he invade her own home to taunt her with their wretched encounter of yesterday morning? Her womanly feelings were too new, too tender, not to be rasped by his callous behavior.

"Never mind, Aunt Kate. The major is just leaving." She pushed up and flung her finger toward the door. He didn't move at first, and she strode to the pegs beside the door and held his hat out to him. And a moment later she punctuated her nonverbal command by opening the door and thrusting it wide.

His boots smacked the floor as he rose, and in three long strides he was at the door, jerking his hat from her hands. He stared down at her, his chest heaving, feeling the strange physical pull in his chest that he'd come to associate with her alone. As he pivoted and ducked out the door, he snagged her by the wrist and pulled her outside with him.

"Stop." She tried to dig in her heels as he pulled her across the cold, moonlit yard. Her heart convulsed at the wicked glow of the look he turned on her.

"Come with me, wench," he ordered in a husky voice that lowered meaningfully, "unless you'd rather your aunt heard what I have to say."

A chill went through her as heat was drawn from her limbs to fuel the sparks in her eyes. She allowed herself to be dragged along toward the barn and the horse she could see tied by the corral railing.

"I want some answers, wench." He halted by the corner of the barn, out of sight of the house, and threw his fancy hat onto the dusty ground beside them.

"Asking questions with your hands again, Major?" She raised her wrist, still captive in his steely fingers. But she had no time to enjoy the spark she struck in his silver eyes.

"No hands."

Even as he dropped her wrist, his body was in motion, looming, crowding her, forcing her back toward the wall of the barn. When she banged into the weathered boards, his fists shot to the wall on either side of her, imprisoning her shoulders. A wordless sputter of protest died on her lips. She was trapped on three sides by his hard-muscled body, surrounded by his heat. And he hadn't touched her, not with his hands.

"You know where the stills are, don't you? That's where you were the other night . . . out at a still, drinking whiskey."

"N-no." She braced, feeling he invaded the very air she breathed.

"Don't lie to me. I know your man is a distiller. Who is he? Where is he? You can't go on protecting him." He was larger, more dangerous than she'd ever seen him, and more determined. Despite what had happened between them, or because of it, he still believed she met a buck in the woods at night.

Everything about him screamed for caution: the uncompromising strength of his hard body, the arrogant beauty of his face in the unearthly light, the force of his assault on her reason. And all that fevered warning was doomed by a single shiver of feeling that vibrated in her. For some reason, she didn't want him to go on believing that about her.

"It's not my man," she murmured softly, "it's my pa."

"Your pa," he echoed, absorbing it, letting it wash through him with an unexpected wave of relief. "And only your pa?"

She found her throat tightening and simply nodded. The glitter in his eyes muted to a sensual glow, and his braced arms on either side of her were bending, bringing him closer by torturous degrees.

"You mean, there's just one still?" He rescued his gaze from her parted lips and found himself losing it again in the shimmering pools of her eyes.

"Just one."

"You know I'll find it sooner or later . . . and him as well." His body tightened in expectation, rebelling against the confirmation of his tight-fitting reason and against the tyranny of duty and ambition. "It'll go easier on him if you cooperate . . . tell me where he is."

"He's in Pittsburgh. You already know that." Her thoughts

were tripping over one another. She couldn't feel her limits any-more, couldn't know whether she was telling him too much. Everything was beginning to blur around her and in her . . . everything but him.

"Is he really in Pittsburgh?" For some reason, when she nod-ded with that wondering glow in her eyes, he believed her. "But if he's in Pittsburgh, then someone else has to be running the still."

Whitney stood very still, scarcely breathing, her body alive to his presence as she watched him draw the only conclusion pos-sible.

Her. He swallowed that bit of information and found it went down hard. Lord—she wore a man's clothes, drank whiskey like a man, stayed out all night, and her pa was the valley's main distiller. Why should it surprise him to learn *she* was a distiller too? He realized that was the one thing he *hadn't* wanted to hear. A brief, violent struggle ensued for control of his response . . . and Garner triumphed over Townsend.

"I don't want to hurt you, wench."

His eyes raked her pale skin, her seductive shape, her delicate features. And the longing he'd suppressed and tried to banish slammed through him with gale force. His fevered body closed on hers as his head lowered and his senses opened. He lifted his hands from the wall beside her, and they hovered briefly at her shoulders. But he smacked his palms back against the rough wall with a fierce murmur.

"No hands."

When he hesitated to join their mouths fully, hovering ago-nizingly, she ran the tip of her tongue over her lips and in the process, stroked his in irresistible invitation. His mouth closed over hers, taking her lips boldly, claiming the sleek wet satin of her mouth as though it were his birthright, his destined posses-sion. And she opened to him, yielding him the response that only he commanded in her.

Her arms slid around his waist and crept up the center pillars of his muscular back as he pressed tight against her. She rose up to meet the urgency of his kiss and to satisfy her tortured need for the feel of his body against her. Her dress constrained her body in ways that mimicked the hard embrace he withheld. The press of her clothes became strangely erotic, like the feel of his hands caressing her. She rippled against him, rubbing the deliciously imprisoned mounds of her breasts up and down his ribs.

Assured by the molding of her body against him, his mouth gentled, then grew adventuresome, roaming her temples, the line of her jaw, the hollow of her throat. He nuzzled the satiny swell of her breasts and showers of sparks rained through her, lodging in her sensitive nipples and the cleft between her legs, burning, then muting to a tingling warmth. Her hands came up to glide over the intriguing planes of his face, and to savor the broadness, the hardness of his shoulders. They brushed the cool glow of his officers' braid, and her eyes opened, fixing on it, getting lost in its sinuous curves. It was cool, unresponsive under the touch of her fingers, unlike the warm, vital flesh of his neck beside it.

And yet it was a part of him; the insight chilled and solidified some part of her melted logic. Very much a part of him. She cast that awful onslaught of reason aside, wanting him the way a woman wants the man who awakens her. Tantalized by the memory of his body thrusting rhythmically against her flesh, she trembled with desire for that as well, and for what she knew would follow. And the realization finally filled her: she wanted the Iron Major just as much as he wanted her.

For the first time in her life, she truly wanted to be a woman. And she wanted a woman's "bargain" with a man. With every pulse of her trader's blood, she knew that with the Iron Major, it would be paradise.

"What will you take, Major?" she murmured against his neck, sending small molten spirals beneath his skin. A long, bone-melting kiss later, she surfaced again, fighting to regain her meager foothold in sanity. "It has to be a proper bargain . . . we have to 'settle' first. Tell me what you want."

"You know what I want, wench," he growled from deep in his throat, and his body undulated along the length of hers, arching and caressing her. She moaned softly and buried her face in his coat front, meeting his thrusting body, luxuriating in the reined power inside him. Yes, she realized dizzily, she knew what he wanted.

"But we have to agree to a bargain," she whispered into his chest, into his heart.

Bargain. The second time she said it, it registered in his passion-fogged mind. His first reaction was simple confusion. His second, spreading through him like a stain of betrayal, was alarm. A bargain? He went still against her, and one ragged breath later the lusty swell of his body, thrust against hers, shocked him. The impact of her words and the driving intent of his body burst through his consciousness, exploding like military flares, illuminating the dark recesses of his unthinkable desires.

"When we bed, it has to be a proper bargain. What will you give?" she prompted breathily. And when he focused on her face, his congealing reason threatened to melt away beneath him again. Her eyes were shimmering pools of desire, her lips were swollen, her face glowed in the moonlight as though she were some goddess of temptation.

His gut contracted sharply around the core of need burning in the middle of him. And with each passing heartbeat, the Townsend in him recovered lost ground. *A bargain.* He quivered, not wanting to believe his ears. She wanted to bargain him with her body . . . bribe him with her own tempting flesh? He went rigid in her embrace and dragged his hands down the splintery barn wall into fists. Anger welled within him, alloyed with lingering desire.

She had assaulted him, made him a laughingstock before his own men, tricked and finagled and "bargained" him. And now she was shamelessly wheedling and bartering her own body to get him to pull his men out of Rapture, to get him to slink back to Boston empty-handed and in disgrace.

"I want the liquor," he rasped, finding that each word ripped vital connections in the middle of him, isolating that core of desire in his center. "And the stills, and the lawbreakers."

It was happening again . . . the coldness, the angry withdrawal. Whitney was stunned. Her arms slid down his rigid sides as she searched the changes in his face, felt the leashed trembling of his body. He wanted the distillers, he said. Was that to be part of the bargain between them? His price for loving her? When the question formed in her heart, it formed on her lips as well.

"Including me?"

Lord, there it was. The one question he'd avoided, the reason he'd not allowed himself to think she was really involved. Was he really capable of arresting her? Every time he was near her he went completely out of control, disgraced himself, compromised his mission. Even now, catching disturbing glimpses of vulnerability in her eyes, he was seized by an unholy urge to gather her against him.

"A *bargain?*" he snarled, panicking at the mess she'd made of his manly determination and making himself ignore the shock in her face. She was a deceiver, a dissembler without peer. It was his flaw, his weakness that made him imagine something as absurd as hurt in her. She was a soul-wrecking piece of temptation, nothing more.

"Wheedling and bartering. Your charms for a strategic military withdrawal, is that the bargain you expected? You really thought you could rut and wriggle your way out of what you and the rest of your lot have coming? You conniving little Jezebel."

He took two steps back, shaking. "Well, you've gotten nothing for your base, tawdry bit of bargaining except trouble. I, on the other hand, now know exactly who to watch. And I'll catch you, wench . . . you and your whole gang of traitors."

Whitney watched, horror-struck, as he raked her with a look of contempt, retrieved his hat, and bolted onto his horse. A moment later she was standing in a swirl of dust, choked, unable to breathe. Hurt rampaged inside her.

He thought she'd been offering her body in payment for his withdrawing his men from their search? The irony of it sickened her physically as the full ramifications of it bore in on her. If only she'd been so clever! He was the sworn enemy of her pa and her people and she'd sought a bedding bargain with him, would have given herself to him in loving. Her womanly desires had overridden her duty, her responsibilities—everything of value to her. When his lips closed over hers, she forgot everything except the blinding pleasures of his kiss and his caress. Where was her trader instinct? And where was her pride?

She shook her head and closed her eyes, hearing those last cruel words rumbling about in her head. Now he knew who to watch . . . who to catch. He'd gotten exactly what he came for—

information. And under his expert kisses—Lord!—he hadn't even stooped to caressing her! He'd let her own desires do his foul work for him. She felt the ache of need that lingered in her and recalled the way she sought him with her body, eagerly, without shame. Shame now filled her from head to toe, crushing the budding womanliness of her heart.

She'd betrayed her pa, and likely her people, into his hands. A Jezebel, he'd called her. Maybe he was right. She'd cast years of love and loyalty aside for a few moments of pleasure—

Holding herself together with her arms around her waist, she made her way to a bench at the side of the house and collapsed. The squeezing around her heart was unbearable. A Jezebel.

The thought froze in her mind. For a moment she sat suspended between the crush of shame and the countering swell of stubborn Daniels pride. She slowly straightened on the bench, the pain in her heart now challenged by reason. Blood flowed back into her limbs.

"Not a Jezebel," she murmured, feeling all the world taking on a new order. In her Daniels heart, another of life's haunting puzzles was suddenly solved. She wasn't a Jezebel; she was a *Delilah.*

There were two kinds of women in the world, Aunt Kate had always said; decent women and Delilahs. The summary had always made Whitney a bit nervous, afraid she'd hear that fateful judgment pronounced upon her someday. Deep within, she had feared that her dislike of skirts and her shunning of customary femininity made her a prime candidate for the category Aunt Kate disdained so: Delilahs.

Now the reality she had dreaded had finally arrived. She drew a taut breath and waited, probing, exploring it. But out of the ashes of expectation rose a surprising feeling of relief, a sense of self discovered. She'd tried the "decent" way, had opened her womanly heart to a man and tried to strike an honest bargain. And look what it had gotten her. Hurt, humiliation, tears. Ugh! The Delilah in Whitney Daniels would never have been so stupid as to try to deal forthrightly with the likes of—

Major Samson. That's what she'd called him, in angry jest. Little had she understood the revealing nature of her taunt.

Every man was a Samson, Aunt Kate said. And that included
Major Garner Townsend, whether he liked it or not. He had that
fever in his blood, just like Charlie and the other bucks. That
was what made him kiss her and touch her and turn all hot and
lustful when they were together, just pure *Samson fever.* It had
nothing to do with her, she realized with shame in her heart.
He'd have undoubtedly done the same with any Delilah, nothing
personal to it at all. It happened exactly like Aunt Kate said,
she realized, swallowing the bitterness in her throat. The proud
and self-righteous Iron Major, that paragon of abstinence and
federal virtue, was just a Samson after all, waiting for a Delilah
to come along.

"Whitney?" Kate found her a minute later, sitting on the
bench, her back straight, her eyes glowing strangely in the silvery
light. "Heavens, Whitney, it's freezing out here." She slipped her
thick shawl around Whitney's shoulders, making room for Whitney in it. "Are you all right?" She settled on the bench beside
her niece. "The major, he didn't . . . *do* anything . . . ?"

"Him?" Whitney felt the welcome warmth of her aunt's embrace and purged the last of her qualms in another of her artful
half-truths. "He's too fine to soil his hands with the likes of us."

Of all men, smug, self-righteous Major Townsend deserved a
Delilah. And he'd certainly found one.

Nine

The very next morning, Whitney broke her long-standing habit of late to bed, as late as possible to rise; she was awake and about at the very first rays of dawn. And when she came downstairs to help with breakfast chores, she was dressed in her green woolen dress, and wearing a much-dreaded corset beneath. Her aunt stood in the middle of the kitchen with her arms limp at her sides and stared, slack-jawed. Whitney greeted her with a sweet smile, put on a shawl, and seized the milking bucket. Kate watched her crossing the yard, headed for the barn, and her eyes widened on the determined sway of the proper green skirts. Whitney's overnight conversion to the rigors of womanliness was alarming in the extreme, for it didn't take a Gypsy palm reader to know what had prompted it.

It was that major and whatever had passed between Whitney and him in the darkened yard last night. Kate's stomach did a slow turn. The handsome, arrogant major was obviously of good family and high social position, and with his stunning good looks was undoubtedly a man of the world. Just the sort to dazzle and disgrace a spirited but inexperienced young girl like Whitney. Nothing in Whitney's life or associations in this tightly knit frontier community could have prepared her for the smooth treachery and carnal opportunism of the well-bred gentry.

The sudden remembrance of the sight of them standing by Whitney's bed, roused and trembling with restrained desire, booted Kate's anxiety to intense new levels. Whitney was a good and decent girl with a tender heart, for all her buckish ways. It would be partly her fault if the major took advantage of Whitney,

Kate realized. Her, with all her insistence on ladylike behavior and praise of society folk and their ways . . .

A mile and a half away, in his room on the second floor of Dedham's cozy tavern, the Iron Major was breaking his long-standing habit of early to bed, early to rise. He lay sprawled, facedown, on his too-short bed, having failed to remove even his dusty boots before collapsing on it. Midmorning, Benson braved his commander's lair to bring him a bowl of watery oat porridge and found him dead to the world. At Benson's discreet cough, Townsend came alive, springing up, wild-eyed, with a disoriented snarl.

Seeing that it was just Benson, he dragged his hands down over his reddened eyes and tight face. He flinched and pulled his hands away to glare at them. Benson sidled over warily for a look and let out a sinking whistle.

"Wheeeoooo. Them's some nasty splinters, Majur. Lucky I done a bit of surgury now an' agin."

And shortly the Iron Major was having several rather painful reminders of his latest encounter with Whiskey Daniels plucked from beneath his skin. Fiendishly appropriate, he snarled, trying not to flinch when Benson dug in with his knife point. Under his skin. God. Some depraved minion of fate was having a regular horse laugh over it, to be sure. His hands were full of splinters from the damnable barn wall! This was what he got from trying to keep his hands *off* Whiskey Daniels. Imagine what horrible fate awaited if he ever actually . . .

His eyes closed. It didn't bear thinking about.

By midday the major was shaved and dressed and stalking through his camp, surveying the damage done by the damnable Daniels cider. His men were moving slowly, as though their heads might topple from their shoulders, but were otherwise intact. Seeming eager to appease his wrath, they scurried to implement his commands. Despite their pounding heads and furry mouths, they were soon pulling down and chopping up the wretched liberty pole and cleaning the camp, even digging the new latrines he'd ordered. If their commander was willing to let bygones be bygones, then they'd not grumble against their luck.

The major called Laxault to him and sent the sergeant and two of his long-suffering men out to the Daniels farmstead with orders to stay hidden and see everything. They were to follow "the wench" wherever she went and report back regularly. He watched them slip into the woods and smiled a tight, vengeful smile. He was going to see the little Jezebel got a bit more than she'd "bargained" for.

Things were quiet in the camp that afternoon and that evening. The morning's driving sense of urgency was transformed into an uneasy sense of expectation. The relief the men felt at not being punished for their drunken spree was short-lived. By evening they were back to their surly, uncooperative selves, nursing their shovel-sore arms and backs and staring, disgruntled, into their watery beans. And the next morning, when Aunt Harriet Delaney appeared covertly at the edge of camp, seeking a willing worker or two, she had quite a few hungry volunteers.

The second morning, Whitney appeared again in skirts and went about her chores with a pleasant mien and an infuriating helpfulness to her manner. Kate watched her with an unnerving feeling that something was simmering within her. Occasionally Whitney would stop in the middle of something, like feeding hens or churning, and her head would tilt and her eyes would take on a speculative glint as they perused some distant vision. Kate knew the signs: a Daniels at work.

When Whitney came in to dinner she announced, "Well, there are three of them."

"Three what?" Kate asked, straightening over her stew kettle at the hearth and pushed the swing-iron back over the coals with a wooden spoon. She turned to find a dangerous sparkle in her niece's eyes.

"Three soldiers, watching the house and barn. They've been there all day." Blackstone Daniels's crafty smile lit his daughter's similar features. "I expect they're good and hungry, Aunt Kate.

They'd probably appreciate a bit of that stew and a hot cup of coffee."

Kate couldn't suppress a grin and felt a slide of relief in the middle of her. No doubt that was what had had Whitney so preoccupied. Trust Whitney to know everything that was happening around them. And trust a Daniels to find a way to kill an enemy . . . with kindness.

In truth there was a good bit more on Whitney's mind: the future of Rapture Valley, her pa's imminent return, and the potentially catastrophic admissions she'd made under the major's treacherous questioning techniques. What would happen when Black Daniels came back to Rapture and found the place awash in federals who were just waiting to entrap him? Whatever else Blackstone Daniels was, he was passionate about the causes he believed in, and not the least bit timid about trouble. When her pa came back to the valley, he'd be set on a collision course with the Iron Major. If she was responsible for betraying her pa's distilling activities, then she'd just have to see the damage undone. She'd have to get rid of the major before Pa came home.

There was the "Daniels" way and the "Delilah" way. . . .

"Majur, she ain't been nowhere." Laxault made his report the next evening, trying not to show just how underhanded he felt. She couldn't have been anywhere, he rationalized, 'cause she brought him and his men food three times a day and otherwise was in plain sight, doing chores, or in the house.

"And just where the hell is she now, while you're standing here palavering, Sergeant?" the major demanded, rising from his seat at the tavern table and planting his fists on his waist.

"Why, she's right outside, Majur . . . in camp. Bro't a blanket to that Dunbar buck. I figur'd it'd be time fer me to be makin' a repor—"

"Dammit." The major tore from the tavern, and was halfway down the path to his camp before he pulled his haste and his temper back under control. He slowed and stiffened his spine, searching for the annoying deerskin breeches and boyish boots. But it was skirts that caught his eye, green woolen skirts and the burnished glint of gingery hair in an unbound girlish fall. He faltered slightly. He hadn't expected to see her like this . . . womanly. He'd half convinced himself the incident of the other night had been a dream, a very disturbing dream.

Whitney was just bidding Charlie good-bye, when she caught sight of the major bearing down on them like a runaway freight-wagon. Taking a deep breath, she turned to face his ire and perform her solemn duty.

"Just what in hell are you doing here?" he demanded, stopping a prudent four feet away. It wasn't quite as intimidating, he knew, but it was certainly safer. "I ordered you to stay out of this camp." His eyes drifted irritably to the creamy flesh visible above her overlapped shawl.

"It's getting colder, Major," she answered in a level tone. "Since you're so intent on keeping poor Charlie, here, chained to a tree, in the cruel elements, I thought it only right that he have an extra blanket." It was said with a straight face, but she couldn't help flicker a pointed look at the pile of blankets stacked on the exposed roots of the tree where Charlie was tied. Apparently everybody in Rapture was concerned for Charlie's warmth, just as they were solicitous of his belly, which had broadened noticeably in the idleness of captivity. The major followed her gaze and felt the goad in it.

"Dammit, I want you out of my camp now! This instant!" he roared.

"You certainly are given to swearing, Major. Makes a body wonder just what kind of people raised you."

"Out!" he growled, stalking forward, threat visible in every line of his body. She backed away, along the path, though with a noticeable lack of quailing. And when they were out of Charlie's earshot, she stopped, causing the major to jerk to an abrupt halt to keep from running her down. A quick look around assured they were not likely to be overheard, though they were being watched from several quarters.

"I want you out of Rapture Valley. We all do." Her voice was low and earnest and her eyes glittered like emeralds. "And you obviously want to succeed in your mission here. I have a proposition, Major."

"Don't be absurd," he growled, feeling a warning prickle rising in his neck. "I've made it perfectly clear I'll have nothing to do with either you or your wretched bargains." He was unnerved by her calm demeanor and the chilled look in her lovely eyes.

"You can't have our still or our distillers, Major." She raised her chin to a well-known trading angle, outwardly ignoring his declaration of disinterest. Inwardly she quivered as his caustic words sank deep into her womanly heart. "But I'm here to offer you the liquor, every last drop. And I can assure you, there's quite enough to make a regular triumph of the military maneuvers you've been conducting in the countryside night after night. It's yours, Major, providing you take it and leave the valley the very next day, without looking back."

Her shawl slipped from one shoulder as she crossed her arms beneath her bosom, but she gave no indication she'd felt it. Her eyes were intense on his reaction. Derision flashed through his eyes first, an urge to sneer and berate both her and her "bargain." But before it blossomed into full reaction, the true scope of the opportunity dawned in his heated mind and he began to realize what it involved.

What it involved, Whitney knew, was the accomplishment of his ambitions in Rapture . . . in a way that both preserved his precious pride and made a mockery of it at the same time. His victory was being handed to him, and she couldn't say whether she wished to see him take it or refuse it. Some part of her wanted to see him abase those arrogant, self-righteous principles of his; another part wanted to see him turn it down, wanted to make him uphold his male honor at the expense of his ambition. That's what this was ultimately about, she realized, pride and honor. She held her breath. Had she found the arrogant major's price or not?

Red crept up his neck into his ears and infused his cheeks, then his forehead and scalp. She was offering them *both* a way out, a bargain that would give him something to take back to Boston and would preserve her people and their capacity to produce their brew. A sure catch, a bird in the hand, albeit a partial prize, had at the behest of insolent, irksome Whiskey Daniels.

He wanted nothing more than to shake the dust of this wretched place from his expensive boots. The temptation was monstrous.

Dammit! She was doing it to him again. Temptation was exactly what this was, another little bit of Jezebel barter. Barter, hell! It was an out-and-out bribe! She was trying to lure him into betraying his duty and his honor as an officer and a gentleman.

"No." He took a step forward, bringing himself close enough to brush her skirts. "I won't take your little bargain, witch. I'll have it all, the liquor, the still, and the distillers, or I'll have nothing at all. Contrary to the popular wisdom of this warped little hamlet, there are some things that don't have a price, some things that cannot be bartered or bargained. And you, you pretentious little Jezebel, *have just encountered one."* His eyes narrowed furiously, and he took another step, forcing her back.

Whitney tightened visibly at his use of that particular name for her, but her well-steeled nerve stayed her first response. She drew her shoulders back. "No deal?"

"No deal," he sneered quietly. The unexpected calm of her response and her silent appraisal of him stole some of his pleasure in refusing. She wasn't nearly angry enough, nor outraged enough, to suit him.

"You'll be sorry, Major."

She turned with a swirl to her skirts and was soon out of his camp, making her way across the clearing toward the road home. Her thoughts roiled with confusion on all but one point: the Iron Major honestly couldn't be bought. It was positively infuriating for a girl whose life's philosophy was based on the premise that everything had its price.

"Well, you tried the *Daniels* way," she ground out furiously as she reached the main road. A flame was struck in the backs of her eyes. "A plain, honest bargain of mutual benefit to both parties. And he refused it. What happens now is on his own head. He's driven you to it."

Garner Townsend watched the deep, knowing gleam that crept into her eyes as she uttered her last threat and walked away. And he couldn't take his eyes from the sway of her skirts until she faded from sight across the clearing. Something was wrong; she took it far too well, as though she'd half expected . . . He stiffened as a chill raced up his spine and raised goose flesh on his skin. The way she'd looked at him, the icy, controlled tone of her voice. He swallowed hard and whispered the truth that rumbled through him: "Hell hath no fury like a woman scorned." And Whiskey Daniels was known for being a dirty fighter.

He turned and walked, unseeing, back the way he'd come. And in precious few steps he was nearly nose to nose with Charlie Dunbar, who was standing, his legs braced, his brawny arms crossed over his chest.

"I saw ye talkin' wi' Whit, Majur." Charlie's face bore an obviously false geniality. "I swear, that gal could talk the breeches off'n a bishop." He sobered instantly, his voice dropping, his eyes becoming glowing coals of resentment.

"Did she talk yours off, Majur?"

The major twitched. "Unless you want another night in ropes, you'll keep a rein on your tongue, Dunbar."

"Did ye make a bargain wi' 'er, Majur?" Charlie jolted forward as far as his shackles would allow, lowering his arms and hardening into a thick wall. Something in the intensity of his reaction made Townsend realize it was not a bargain over whiskey or stills he was concerned about.

"A bargain?" he said, feeling heat rising into his face as her offer came rushing back to him. Her body . . . was that the kind of bargain he meant? How would Dunbar know about tha— "Good God, you mean *that* kind of bargain? Do you barter *that,* too, in this unspeakable pest hole?"

"We bargain fair and square fer everythin' in Rapture. Here, when a man wants a gal, he strikes a proper bargain wi' her. Sets out what he wants an' what he'll give, an' whether he'll marry 'er or not. Settles it all up front, straight and honest." Charlie's voice dropped to a raw demand. "Did ye bargain an' bed 'er, Majur?"

God. Dunbar even used the same words. "Proper bargain," "what he'll give," and "settle." Townsend managed a convincing look of contempt after a telling silence.

"Both she and bartered pleasure are a bit too crude for my tastes, Dunbar. The crudity, the unthinkable immorality of it—"

"Yer eastern city ways ain't no better," Charlie asserted, evaluating the arrogant man before him. Coiled muscles, tight face, surly temper; he sure didn't act like a man who'd pleasured himself in a woman's arms recently. In fact, Charlie's envy eased enough to permit a bit of insight; he exhibited every symptom of raw sexual frustration known to man. Charlie recrossed his arms and eased his stance. "I hear tell, back east, ye buy an' sell women fer cash money."

"Perhaps in the gutters, Dunbar, but not among civiliz—"

"Dower-tries . . . or somethin' like that," Charlie charged, and watched the major lose some of his starch. Then he was back to his original point with a warning look. "Whit Daniels is mine, Majur. I'm gonna make a proper bargain wi' her e'en if I have to marry 'er. An' I want to be her first."

Some of the heightened color in Townsend's face drained. "Do you mean to say that half-tamed termagant is a . . . a . . ."

"She ain't never had it," Charlie announced flatly. "Ain't never struck a proper bargain with nobody. An' I'm gonna be her first."

Townsend felt himself going liquid inside and affected an air of disdain to hide it. *A proper bargain.* She said it had to be a "proper bargain" between them. She'd been bargaining, all right. But not for his *withdrawal* . . . for his—

"God."

"I'm gonna make 'er a bargain," Charlie boasted smugly.

Townsend eyed him with a blunt assessment of carnal competition. "You mean like the kind you tried that day we plucked you from her in the woods? That kind of bargain? Then look to your health, Dunbar. I believe it was you that said she kicks and bites."

"She won' be kickin' nor bitin' by th' time we're through." Charlie tightened. "She'll be purrin' like a cat. I'll be makin' her a *paradise bargain* for sure—"

"What in hell's a paradise bargain?"

"It's th' kind o' deal ever' trader hunts for. A deal so sweet"— Charlie smiled a carnal, knowing smile—"that it could get ye past St. Peter at the pearly gates if'n yer name weren't in his book. A born trader like Whit, she'll know one when she feels it." His low, insinuating laugh raked Townsend's skin like steel claws.

The major pivoted on his heel and strode for the inn, his back straight and his entire being in upheaval. She was untouched territory. Every step jarred the knowledge deeper into his gut. Lord, it was so improbable and so paradoxical and Dunbar was so adamant . . . it had to be true. He groaned audibly; it had been so damned much easier thinking she was a loose little trollop.

He reached his room and stood in its dim, shuttered confines, near a total eruption of self. She'd been bargaining, all right . . . for his loving. Whatever else her motives, she had wanted him as a man. It was in every quiver of her untried body, every gasp of surprise, every sweet, hesitant motion against him. And she'd bargained, or tried to, in accordance with her people's unthinkable custom. God. They bargained everything; everything in Rapture actually *did* have a price!

It was an ethic, a code so foreign and shocking, he couldn't deal with it properly. And just as shocking was the inhabitants' complete and diligent adherence to it. They took it seriously indeed; from cradle to grave they bargained their way through life. Bargaining was part survival, part sport, part social form, part ethos. It pervaded everything they did, shaped not just their economy, but their very lives, even to the most intimate functions.

And Whiskey Daniels was the ultimate product of this bizarre blend of frontier desperation and survivalist philosophy. He had learned to handle himself with women of his own class and station. But nothing in his life could have prepared him for anyone as extraordinary as Whitney Daniels, trader, distiller . . . and virgin.

A wave of dry heat fanned through him as the memory of the feel of her materialized beneath his skin, pressing, rousing. He closed his eyes, giving himself over to it, knowing it was useless to fight it. But a moderating chill followed when that dangerous glint in her eye reappeared in his mind. The clash of hot and cold made him shudder.

He was going to be sorry, she'd said. And suddenly he knew she was right. He could feel it in his bones, disaster approaching, relentless and inescapable. Twice before, his life had been wrecked by women who'd found and exploited his weakness. And his uncontrollable desire for Whitney Daniels made him fear it was about to happen again.

"Where the hell is he?" Townsend strode through his camp that evening, looking for Wallace to have him ferry a message to Laxault, at the Daniels farmstead.

"Don' rightly know, Majur," Benson offered nervously, glancing around him at the mostly empty tents.

The major pounced on that anxious gesture and scoured the premises visually. Something was wrong about the camp, he realized. "Then where's Kingery . . . or that Ned Wilson and his partner in idiocy, Albert Sipes?"

He began to stalk the paths, peering into tents, then stalked the perimeter of camp, finding a total of six men . . . out of thirty-six.

"Dammit—there's no patrol out," he roared down at Benson, who blinked frantically. "Where the hell are they?" He didn't actually expect Benson to know, so he turned on his heel and headed for Dedham's taproom, thinking they'd probably congregated in its warmth. But the tavern was empty as well, except for Uncle Harvey, who picked up his broom and braced it across his chest defensively at the sight of the major's blatant anger.

Frustration mounting, Garner roared back through his camp. And this time raw anger got the best of him. He snatched Benson up by the coat front and gave him a throttle that promised greater retribution if answers were not forthcoming. Answers came slowly. The muscular Dem Wallace was likely down at the widow Donner's cabin, splittin' wood. Ned and Albert were likely at Aunt Sarah Dunbar's, fixin' shed roofs and shuckin' corn from harvest. Kingery, he was likely at Uncle Radnor's, helpin' to repair the smith's bellows . . . and on it went. Every damned one of them was out fraternizing with the locals. No, not fraternizing—*working*. They were working for the locals. Threshing, chopping, repairing, husking, stacking.

Townsend stood in the middle of his deserted camp, quaking

with volcanic rage. *"How dare they?* Desert their duty and defy their commander to work—*work*—for these treasonous rabble?"

"F-food, M-Majur," Benson choked an explanation as Townsend towered over him threateningly. "They be workin' f-fer their s-suppers."

"Food?" Townsend whipped upright and stared at him. "Food? They're working for the food these locals refused to sell us?"

"They'da s-starved a long time past, Majur," Benson ventured to explain, "if'n Aunt Sarah hadn' ta seen they wuz fed proper. I be dwindlin' away meself . . ." He looked balefully down at his baggy coat and the breeches that were bundled into his belt. His paunch was gone, his fleshy face was loose and haggard-looking.

Townsend was speechless, staring at him with newly opened eyes. He hadn't seen it, his own aide, dwindling before his very eyes. His Townsend obsession with succeeding in his duty had usurped awareness of everything, even the growling of his own belly. He looked down at his own middle and was shocked at how loosely his coat front hung, at how loose his tight breeches had become Lord, what had happened to him?

He'd been so caught up in his pursuit of the elusive stills, he hadn't noticed his own men deserting, aiding the enemy. These crafty rubes had used food to get his men to do the work of the traitorous distillers that were off in Pittsburgh—*defying the very federal authority he'd been sent here to uphold!* The irony of it collected in his throat, a huge lump that was impossible to swallow. He burst into action, rousting his remaining men to accompany him. And he struck out to snatch his wayward men from the jaws of opportunism.

He collected them bodily from every dwelling and farmstead in and near the settlement, and they quailed before his very controlled fury, expecting the worst from their Iron Major once they were back at camp. But at dark, when he'd collected most of them, he left Lieutenant Brooks to implement discipline on a few chief offenders, sought the solitude of his room in the inn.

Mingled with his anger and frustration was an irksome sense

of failure to take things in hand, to secure proper provisions. These locals had realized from the first day where they were vulnerable, and had used it against them with diabolical effectiveness. From that very first day—he looked down at his chest—*they'd had him by the damned buttons!* And they knew it.

He stepped to the door and roared for his aide. When the fellow appeared, puffing and obviously dreading his commander's wrath, Townsend stripped his coat from his shoulders and held it out to him. "Cut the damned buttons off, and then find me something suitable to replace them."

Benson did as he was told, his eyes wide. When he had finished and brought the double handful of gold pieces to the major, he was held at bay with a dark look.

"Carry them to Dedham. Tell him they're to be used for the purchase of food for my men." The major spoke through clenched jaws, avoiding Benson's sober nod of understanding. But when Benson reached the door, the major called him back and fished through the glittery fastenings to extract one, then dismissed him on to his task.

Townsend stood in the quiet of his room, looking at the teeth marks in the button he held, feeling every bit as hollow as that squashed bauble.

In the two nights that followed, the chase in the hills became frenzied in the extreme, and Uncle Julius and Uncle Ballard came within a hairbreadth of being caught. The Iron Major's determination had apparently been strengthened by his improved diet. And his gesture of sacrifice, rendering up his fancy buttons to provide them food, had built something of a bond between him and his men, and they followed more willingly now. Then, when they uncovered a barrel of new whiskey that had been hastily buried in the abandonment of a still site, the major promised it to his men when the distillers were caught, and they began to search in dead earnest.

Whitney had sent word for the old uncles to dump the fermenting mash altogether and to bury the still, literally, in the ground. One of the Delbarton bucks was dispatched to help them and to see that they arrived safely at the Daniels farmstead to stay for a while. Their presence in the Daniels household was duly reported to the major, who sent his lieutenant to investigate. It was explained to the lieutenant that Whitney's two old uncles had come for a visit, pure and simple. The major snarled that nothing about Whiskey Daniels or her household was either "pure" or "simple," and declared they should be watched all the more carefully.

Whitney saw the noose tightening on her people and implemented her plan. She was going to see that the major was forced to withdraw from the valley in disgrace and haste. His much-vaunted Townsend pride was the key. A man of his exalted social standing would far rather suffer a minor military setback than spend his life yoked to a whiskey-drinking Jezebel. And that was the choice he would face when Uncle Ballard and Uncle Julius caught them together in his room, in his very bed. She'd plant herself in his bed while he was on patrol and have Robbie Dedham fetch the old uncles as soon as he returned. There would have been just enough time for the obvious to have occurred, except, of course, that it wouldn't have occurred, when the old uncles would break in on them, toting squirrel guns and demanding the major do the decent thing by her.

Whitney's grin always faded when she came to this part of her plan. He'd be outraged at the prospect of a shotgun wedding, and so would she. Then she'd propose an alternative—his withdrawal from the valley—and they wouldn't let him out of the room until he agreed and called his lieutenant to issue the orders. It was a simple plan actually, one that targeted the major's one flaw, his one weakness . . . his pride.

She'd finally gotten the old uncles to agree, though they hadn't liked the idea at first. Now the only difficult part would be the time between the major's arrival and their discovery. Her eyes fluttered closed and she quelled a stubborn quiver in her loins. She'd deal with that when the time came.

"Majur!" Benson ran to meet him as he came from stabling his mount the next afternoon. The all-night patrol had netted only days-old fire sites and old tracks that always managed to disappear into streams. So they'd spent the morning desperately combing cold trails they'd already searched, for signs of more recent activity. He was exhausted and bitter and desperately in need of some hot food and a bit of sleep. What he got was "Th-the colonel . . . he's come! Th' lew-ten-ant set me out to warn ye, Maj—"

Townsend saw the tie-line of horses at the side of the tavern at the same moment the tavern door swung open. Just inside the doorway stood the paunchy, flint-eyed shopkeeper, Colonel Oliver Gaspar, his commanding officer.

Ten

"Well, Major." Colonel Gaspar appraised Garner Townsend across a tavern table and a temple of pudgy fingers with dirt embedded under their ragged nails. "I must say, I am surprised by your lack of progress here. We were reliably informed that this valley was a hotbed of traitorous activity, yet you've made only one arrest, and nabbed not a single still." The fleshy folds around his dark eyes tightened and narrowed accusingly.

"And the supplies that were to be sent after us, Colonel?" Townsend parried regally. "They never arrived. Hungry men are more apt to search for food than for outlaws and traitors."

"Discipline in your ranks is your responsibility, Major . . . *results* are mine," Gaspar sneered, goaded by the Bostonian's air of condescension. "To that end, I offer a bit of news that may enable you to redeem your sad efforts here. The meet of distillers in Pittsburgh broke up two days ago and the treasonous wretches are fleeing to their burrows. They didn't have the backbone for a decent fight. Put down their guns when they saw our forces massed and realized President Washington would permit no such treason. But some have vowed to continue resisting the tax, and may be headed here. Let us hope you can manage to arrest them when they arrive."

"I cannot manufacture evidence, Colonel," Townsend said, gray with suppressed rage. "How am I to prove they are distillers if they have no stills and no liquor?"

"It is not up to you to prove it, Major. I will not go back to my superiors empty-handed and they will not go back to the nation's courts without the leaders of this fiendish plot against our nationhood. Your duty is simply to make arrests, Major. The courts will do the rest." He rose with a cold smile that revealed yellowed and decaying teeth.

"My aides and I shall leave first thing in the morning, Major, and depend on you to take the steps necessary to insure a commendation for us all. But for tonight, my aide and I shall require accommodations in this establishment."

Night fell over the Rapture settlement like an icy black cloak. No moon lit the dimness, and even the stars seemed to be hoarding their light in the inky sky. Whitney sat with the old uncles in the kitchen after Aunt Kate went to bed, and reviewed the night's plan one last time. Uncle Ballard yawned and nodded and Uncle Julius frowned and agreed and they toddled off to Black Daniels's bed, where they'd been sleeping these last two nights.

Whitney waited in the quiet darkness of her room until she was sure Aunt Kate was fast asleep. Then she dressed in her breeches and boots and slipped from the house, sticking to the shadows to avoid the six soldiers who now watched the house night and day. She kept near the main road, her heart drumming, her hands growing icy in her coat pockets. There was no time for second thoughts now, she chided herself. No time for squeamishness or wretched misgivings. And for heaven's sake, don't think about what he'll think when he finds you in his bed, she grumbled mentally. Just tell him it's nothing *personal*.

She slipped through the settlement, from cabin to cabin, silent as a shadow, and eased into the tavern through the kitchen door. The stairs creaked under her feet as she made her way up in the darkness. The major's door groaned slightly on its rough iron hinge, and she held her breath. But the quiet continued, uninterrupted, and she released her breath and closed the door behind her. As her eyes adjusted, the placement of the room's meager furnishings became clear, and she looked at the ghostly outline of the bed and swallowed hard.

Removing her coat and boots, she placed them neatly aside and paused. The breeches had to go as well, she knew. But halfway through unbuttoning her shirt, she stopped, feeling an unwelcome fluttering in her middle. She left the shirt half buttoned and crawled beneath the covers of his bed. Lying rigid and cold beneath the quilts, she tried to turn her mind away from his impending fury, tried to focus on the fact he soon would be gone from the valley.

Gone. It was a depressing thought, she realized with no small alarm. He'd pack up and leave, hating the very ground she walked on, and she'd never see his sculptured face, never watch his lean, muscular body move, never feel the heated press of his mouth and his body on hers again. And that silky hair, those lips . . . she turned her head to the side as if warding off those unwelcome remembrances, and her head filled with his lingering male scent that clung to the bedclothes. Her blood began to flow again and her body began to warm as his bed stood proxy for him, cradling her in its arms. She sighed and breathed deeply, holding this much of him inside her. She didn't want to think about what it would be like in Rapture after he left. She didn't want to think about how much had changed, within her and around her, in so short a time.

"Good Lord!" Kate Morrison bolted upright in the middle of her darkened bed, having to hold her pounding heart in her body with her hands. The entire house was shuddering, reverberating with a thunderous snarling sound that made the back of her neck prickle. She got her bearings and took a deep breath. Either the house was being attacked by packs of ravenous wolves, or it was the old uncles, snoring again. Merciful heaven, how could even they sleep through the monstrous racket they made?

Kate slipped from her bed, drew on her shoes and a woolen wrapper, and lit a candle to see her way down the stairs. She had to knock loudly, for some time, on the old uncles' door before the deafening volume was reduced by half. And shortly she was met at the door by a foggy-headed Uncle Julius.

"You're doing it again, Uncle Julius," Kate fairly shouted above Uncle Ballard's snoring. "I'm sorry, but I can't get a minute's rest. Can't you do something?"

Julius scowled and scratched his head, blinking at Kate. Years of living together had inured the old brothers to each other's nightly thunder. But he seemed to hear it now. He shuffled back to the bed they shared and rousted Ballard, trying to get him to turn on his side, to no avail. Finally, he climbed on the bed and bent next to Ballard's ear and shouted, "Wake up, y'old fool!"

Ballard came flapping up in the bed, disoriented in the extreme: "Wha-what? Is it time?"

"Hush up, Ballard." Julius hauled him up out of the bed by the arm. "Ye wuz snorin' so bad agin, ye woke Katie here. Come on, I'm takin' ye out to th' barn to sleep."

Kate didn't object. In fact, she helped them gather their blankets and gave them her new candle to light the way. She climbed the stairs and slid back into her warm bed, praying for a bit of rest.

At that moment, a mile and a half away, Robbie Dedham was on watch from the depths of the straw pile beside the stall where the major stabled his horse. His job in Whitney's plan was pivotal, and he'd earned his position of trust by his reliability and quickness. He watched restlessly past the witching hour, and on past the hours of two and three o'clock. At half-past three, he was roused by sights and sounds of the major stabling his horse, and held his breath until the major left. He flung off the straw and slipped to the stable door. The clearing was deserted and he crept out, running from cabin to cabin like a night-hunting fox, on his way to fetch the old uncles at the Daniels farmstead.

But when young Dedham reached the Daniels house and slipped through the shadows and the unlatched door, he found Black Daniels's bed empty. No Uncle Ballard, no Uncle Julius. He sneaked through the house, looking for them, finding nothing but darkness and quiet. Where could they be, he wondered, and what would he tell Whit when he didn't do what she'd asked? The ghostly quiet and unfamiliar shapes of the interior of the house began to work on his nerves and he exited quickly, forgetting to muffle the bang of the kitchen door.

As he slipped past the barn, his eyes widened on a dim, unearthly glow coming through the half-opened door and he was drawn closer, his heart thudding and his palms sweating. There

was a growling, snarling rumble coming from the opening . . .
growing louder with each step. The growl of a mountain lion
about to pounce, he thought, or the ravenous rumbling of Old
Scratch himself, doin' his mischief in the dead of night. He froze
as the hellish noise seemed to stop. Then it thundered out again,
twice as loud, and he strangled a cry of panic and began running,
like a scared rabbit, straight across the yard and down the path
toward home.

There was a rush around him, and Old Scratch grabbed and
clawed at him! He fought the Old Tempter's clutches like a devil
himself and jerked free, running as though his soul depended on
it. He heard the fiend's growls and breathing and his footsteps—
cloven hoof-beats!—behind him for a ways. Then miraculously,
as he prayed for deliverance, the devil gave him up to the good
and he fled on through the night alone.

"Who was it, Sarge?" Dem Wallace, jogged to a stop beside
his gravel-voiced sergeant. "Did ye get a good look at 'im?"

"I think it were that innkeeper's kid . . . pro'bly jes pilferin'
about," Laxault panted. He drew a deep breath and ordered, "Git
back to yer place, Wallace, an' stay warm."

Kate Morrison was awakened, for the second time that night,
by the sound of the kitchen door banging shut. And just as she
was drifting back to sleep, there was a muffled cry and she was
wide awake, sitting up in bed again. Her first thought was the
soldiers sneaking in, sneaking up. With a stifled gasp she flew
across the hall into Whitney's room, calling her.

But Whitney's bed was empty. Kate lit a candle and stood
looking down at the undisturbed bedclothes. The horror of it
dawned on her; Whitney's bed hadn't been slept in at all. She
searched the house. No Whitney. She donned her heavy wrapper
and shoes and trekked out to the barn. There were Julius and
Ballard, still snorting and roaring; no Whitney. She went back

to the kitchen and lit the oil lamp, her heart racing, her hands icy and shaking.

Whitney was gone. But she couldn't be at the still, Ballard and Julius were *here*. Where could she . . .

There was only one other place she could have gone secretly in the dark of a cold, moonless night. Kate sank weakly into a chair at the table, feeling suddenly bleak inside and helpless. Her sweet little Whitney had finally succumbed to her fascination with the Iron Major. She had gone to be with *him*.

The door hinge creaked loudly and Whitney stirred in the warmth of the major's bed. After a moment, her eyes flew wide and her heart gave a convulsive leap in her chest. Just inside the door stood the Iron Major, taut, searching out the source of the change he sensed in his room. She froze, watching his dark head as it made a visual sweep and turned to fix on her. His eyes were bright silver disks in the dimness, and pulled her from the lethargy of sleep. She rose onto one elbow, baring a creamy shoulder between sliding shirt and quilt. Hot and cold clashed violently inside her, just from witnessing the outline of his body.

She waited, holding her breath, for him to speak and give some indication of his reaction. It was a long moment before he broke the silence, and the deep, invasive rumble of his voice was far from comforting.

"What are you doing here?"

It echoed about in her body, vibrating inside her from toes to fingertips, and causing an abrupt tightening of the sensitive tips of her breasts. Every inch of her bare skin contracted into goose flesh beneath the quilts. Her instinctive bodily response to him was alarming. But not completely unexpected, she reminded herself sternly; she'd responded in the same shameful ways before and survived it. She had a mission to accomplish here. Talk—she thought—you have to make him talk—to buy time.

"I . . . was cold," she murmured half truthfully, finding her voice had a sleep-lulled quality. His eyes fled her briefly to discover her boots, sitting by his open leather kit, and on the breeches draped over the stool beside them.

"If you were cold, wench"—he had to swallow to finish his thought—"you might have left your clothes on."

The Iron Major had trudged up the steps to his room with every joint and sinew in his body in a state of agonizing protest. Everything about him had been cold and frustrated and hardening irreversibly, even his anger. Then he stepped through his door to find her lush warmth in his bed, and in one heartbeat the slow contraction of his entire being halted and began to reverse. He fastened on her light eyes, on the glow of her skin, and ached at the sight of them. A wave of fluid sensation washed over his tight skin and lapped at his loins, melting the killing frosts of a lifetime of impossible demands and coldly imposed duty.

"I didn't think you'd want dirt from my boots in your bed," she answered in a whisper that beckoned him forward to catch it all. She watched him lurch and stop and felt both the pull of longing in his look and the push of pride that had halted him. The battle he was waging for control of his responses was occurring inside her as well, icy contempt or passion's heat, the pain of righteous victory or the sweet pleasure of surrender.

He was so tall and straight and strong . . . and hungry, so very hungry. Whitney could feel him reaching for her, tugging at her senses, and beguiling her reason. Talk—for heaven's sake. Just keep him talking—

"I wanted to . . . talk with you." She tried to sound reasonable, as though those little fires weren't racing along her nerves to throw themselves into the growing flame in the middle of her, as though she weren't sitting half naked in his bed waiting for him to . . . A serious tactical error, she realized, shedding her breeches along with her boots! But she had to be sure it would be convincing.

"Are you sure that's what you wanted, wench?" he breathed, taking another step forward and finding his hands reaching determinedly for the makeshift bone buttons of his coat. "Talk?"

She nodded, her eyes glued to the graceful movements of his hands and widening as each protective fastening unleashed more of his body into the covert battle of wills being waged between them. Where were Uncle Julius and Uncle Ballard? It shouldn't take them this long to get here!

"I didn't want you to leave thinking . . . I don't want you to think . . . I don't . . . want . . ." Words deserted her totally as she watched his coat slide down his shirt and saw him toss it aside. "I . . . I've never seen you without your coat." Her uncensored thoughts escaped in a rush, making her blush furiously when she realized how girlish and naive they sounded. But a moment later she was lost visually in the expanse of fine linen across his wide chest and in the sinuous folds that skimmed his ribs and tucked into his narrow waist. He was so large, she shivered noticeably, and so . . .

So soft, he was thinking as his eyes probed the top of the quilt hungrily for the swell of her breasts . . . and so damned much trouble. He should chuck her out on her curvy little bottom, or sound some outraged alarm, or just run like hell. Every minute she sat there, the peril to his ambitions, his dignity, his aristocratic life increased. She was a hot piece of temptation, a green-eyed bit of earthly torment. And for him she could prove the road to a final failure of honor and a lifetime of disgrace. But he couldn't make himself move, much less run. Disaster was breathing down his neck, and he still couldn't seem to take his eyes from the lure of her skin, from the impudent tilt of her nose.

When he finally managed to move, it was to lean down and remove his tall boots.

"What is it you don't want me to think, Whiskey Daniels?" He straightened a minute later, his temperature rising a degree for each small step he took toward the bed. His senses were so roused, he could smell the faint, spicy fragrance of her from six feet away. His blood pooled in his loins, starving his brain so that he couldn't maintain a rational chain of thought, or resist the urge that impelled him toward her.

The knot that had formed in her throat drew tighter as she watched him approach on silent feet, stalking her. His coat and his boots were off. Oh . . . Her mouth was drying and her lips felt thick and very sensitive, and for some reason she was afraid to lick them. When his long leg smacked into the wooden bed-frame, she started and her heart thumped erratically.

"What don't you don't want me to think?" he asked with a

low, compelling hum in his voice that betrayed the fact that every cord in his body was vibrating.

"I . . . I don't know." She looked up at him, towering above her, and felt a panicky shiver. She was going molten and liquid inside, recalling what it felt like to be held in his arms, to have his body pressed tightly against her tingling breasts and his hands molding her. "No—I mean—I . . . I wouldn't want you to think I hold anything against you. It's . . . nothing personal, Major."

As Garner Townsend stood there in his darkened room, staring into her luminous eyes, the heat that had been charging its way up his spine finally reached his muddled brain and breeched the last bastion of his legendary control. Desire exploded to life in him, freed, exultant. His entire body ignited.

"Wrong, wench," he whispered hoarsely. "It *is* personal. About as personal as it can be." And there his thinking stopped and feeling took total control. To her dismay, he eased himself down onto the bed, facing her. And when his hands came up to cradle her face, she rippled with involuntary pleasure at the contact. He was making her forget things . . . *every*thing.

"I meant . . . I know it's been hard . . . between us . . ."

"Hard . . . I'd say that describes it perfectly," he murmured, "and it's about to get harder still." His lean body flexed in one long, sensual undulation that demonstrated his point stunningly.

"Oh, Major—" She was in a dry, crackling panic now.

"Garner," he corrected her, leaning closer to join their breaths. "Call me Garner." It was a silky, irresistible invitation that poured into her on the air she breathed.

"Garner." She tried the sound of it, and just as the final "r" tightened her sensitive lips, his tongue darted out to stroke them. Fire flashed through her cheeks and spread down over her throat. "Garner," she murmured again. And again she was rewarded by another tantalizing stroke of liquid velvet. "Garner . . ." she shamelessly begged for more. "Garner . . . Garner . . ." And each time the stroke of his tongue lingered a bit longer, explored a bit more. It was hypnotizing, an intimate game that seemed as natural as breathing and as earnest as it was pleasurable.

She waited, head tilted, face raised, for him to join their mouths more fully, and when he hesitated, she opened her eyes and blinked to focus them. His eyes were closed and she could feel the warm tendrils of his breath against her lips and cheek as he spoke.

"What is that scent . . . on your breath?"

"Teaberry," she whispered against his lips, feeling him taking in, savoring, the breath she released. It was so intimate, so adoring that it sent a slow spiral of warmth plunging through her.

"It's wonderful . . . intoxicating. Say it again."

"Teaberry."

He breathed her deep into the middle of him, filling his head, his lungs, and even his heart with her. "It's just like you. You're intoxicating too, Whiskey."

"Whitney," she corrected him, brushing the tip of his nose with hers.

"Whitney," he repeated obediently, giving her control of the game and enjoying a luscious reward for his generosity. Her tongue drew a sinuous stroke across his parted lips, and his hands tightened gently on her face. "Whitney," he said again, demanding just compensation for his tractability. And again and again: "Whitney . . . Whitney . . ."

The game ended as naturally as it had evolved, dissolving into the deepening pressure of lips on lips and the mutual seeking of tongues. A shudder of pleasure coursed through her. She shouldn't enjoy this so much, some ravaged bit of reason nagged at the edges of her consciousness. But for the life of her she couldn't seem to remember why. He'd kissed all caution, all prudence, all her legendary guile from her. And when he growled from deep in his throat and crushed her to him in a feverish embrace, she gave up thinking altogether. Her arms slipped around his lean ribs and her hands filled with the rippled muscles of his back.

The heat of his wild kiss seared through her, purging all resistance, all other sensation. When she floated back to conscious awareness, she was clasped against his hot chest, too weak to support her head, resting it on his collarbone. His hands moved to the long, carelessly woven plait of her hair, unbinding and loosening it. He spread her hair over her shoulders and she saw him lift a handful to his face, nuzzling it. Then he took her by the shoulders and set her back a few inches.

"I want you, Whitney Daniels," he murmured, ripping the quilts from her and determinedly reaching for the few fastened buttons of her shirt.

The frigid air and the searing intensity of his movements clashed, rattling some of the languor from her love-lulled senses. He wanted to take her like a man took a woman, she realized. The thought roused vague confusion in her. As her last button gave and he swept the fabric aside, uncovering her breasts, she grasped his wrists and held them. They were hard and powerful and trembling; his entire body was trembling. And a moment later she realized she was trembling too.

"You want me too, wench," he whispered against the grip of desire on his throat. He caught the silvery glow of her eyes with his and lifted it, unveiling the raging fires of need she'd built in him since their first encounter. His desire rushed over her cool skin like a hot wind that carried in it the scent of paradise.

"You want me"—her tongue flicked out to moisten her dry, swollen lips—"and I want you."

"A proper bargain if I ever heard one," he said quietly, so attuned to her and her responses that he could almost feel the tilting of the scales in her mind as she weighed the trade. And for some unfathomable reason, making a proper bargain of loving her mattered very much.

"A proper bargain." He set the words resonating in the very fiber of her being. "It's what you came for."

Something in her tried to deny it; there was more, something more. . . . But the flame of desire in his light eyes claimed her reason before she could fully recall it. Perhaps she didn't want to recall it. Perhaps he was right, she had come to seek his loving. The rightness of his touch, the tender command of his kiss, were so perfect that she shoved the uncertainties aside and accepted the bargain he offered.

The force of her hands on his wrists eased so that her fingers only rested on him. In the dim light she saw the flash of his white, even teeth in a lusty grin of triumph. As his hands moved to cup her breasts, they carried hers along, and soon her fingers splayed over the supple strength of his hands, caressing him even as he caressed her. She arched against those heavenly sensations, gasping, and heard an impatient growl from deep in his throat as his hands withdrew.

He fairly ripped his shirt from his shoulders and only half unbuttoned his breeches before shoving them down. Then he returned, sliding onto the bed beside her, reaching for her with eager hands. He captured her waist and slid his hands up her ribs to brush her tightened nipples.

"You have such beautiful breasts," he said against her tingling lips, then continued his descent into the sleek, wet recesses of her mouth. He pressed her down onto the straw-filled ticking with his body, luxuriating in the cool softness of her skin against his inflamed length. His hands traced the valleys and curves he'd possessed many times in his mind, claiming them, branding them with his touch.

A slowly winding spiral of pleasure was begun in the depths of her loins, coiling through her in relentless cycles that were similar but never quite the same. Heat rose beneath her skin to meet his hands wherever they roamed her, until she was deliciously warmed and wriggled with small raptures. Then his kisses left her face and covered her ear and throat and trailed a familiar path downward. But this time it didn't stop, and when his warm mouth reached one pebble-hard nipple, she held her breath. He took her nipple into his mouth and sucked it, sending wild vibrations of pleasure all the way to her woman's hollow, where they focused into one burning, pulsing point of desire.

She went taut and her muscles tightened instinctively around that shocking concentration of pleasure, creating yet another overwhelming wave of raw, sensual delight. What was he doing to her . . . what was happening to her body? His hand followed the path of those unthinkable joys to the curls at the base of her sleek belly, and his fingers invaded the silky moistness of her womanly cleft. She gasped and stiffened and her hand flew to hover over his uncertainly. But the slow, knowledgeable circling of his fingers around that burning pleasure-point charmed her anxieties and stirred a steamy sense of expectation in her. When his hand withdrew, her hips arched to follow it partway.

Beginning again with kisses, he took her deeper into that swirling, unending vortex of sensual experience. Her hands began to move over him, seeking and exploring the varied textures of him. Everything about him spoke a paradox: the silky rasp of his chest hair against her breasts, the soft hardness of his lips, the rugged refinement of his back and arms, the gentle power of his long, graceful body. She embraced him, urging him above her, reveling in his hard weight as his body engulfed hers.

She knew what happened next; she'd heard the bucks talk about it. But she had never realized what it truly involved for a woman, never imagined what it would feel like to be opened by a man, to take part of his body inside her. She felt his shaft hard and foreign against her belly as he lay atop her, and felt the dull throb of desire in her body's opening. The tantalizing rasp of his swollen staff against her clothes that morning in the woods came rushing back. How much better would it feel with nothing between them?

The passionate wriggle that wanton possibility produced in her brought his head up, and his teeth flashed dimly before he kissed her nose, her eyelids, her chin. She was issuing the oldest invitation known to man, and he was going to accept in the most emphatic way possible. He nudged her legs apart and felt her breath stop at the unaccustomed position. The tension underlying her eagerness finally translated properly in his steamy thoughts. She'd never done it before. That much filtered through the barriers of reason that passion had erected in his mind. He remembered that much, and wanted to remember no more. He would be her first. The knowledge washed through him in a possessive flood, inundating every part of his male psyche, rousing the primitive urge for ownership, for dominion.

"I don't want to hurt you, my hot little Whiskey." He began a litany of desire, spoken between kisses into her ear, along her neck, down the dewy valley between her magnificent breasts. "I'll make it as easy as I can. You must tell me what you're feeling . . . and if I hurt you." He fit himself gently against her moist inner flesh and thrust slowly back and forth, rubbing against the little pearl of flesh that held the key to the mysteries of her response. He felt her breathing return, felt the racing of her heart against his chest. Her legs trembled as she braced and rocked beneath him.

Over and over he stroked her, watching her passions rise, feeling her movements growing bolder as she clutched his back, her frantic hands devouring every bit of him they could reach. Never in his life had he exercised such restraint, nor imagined such pleasure could result from it. When her legs rose and slid around his, trapping them, pulling him closer, he knew the time had come. He moved slightly, sinking his arms beneath her as he began to sink his shaft into the tight, silky sheath of her flesh.

Slowly, he pressed forward, pausing, allowing her to accept him, kissing away her tension. She stretched to enfold him, felt him rising in her, filling her trembling body by tight, breathtaking increments. There was momentary discomfort that made her bite her lip, but no rending pain, no harsh maidenly sacrifice. And soon the tightness gave way to a sense of fulfillment that escaped as a soft, tattered moan.

"Tell me, Whitney," he demanded softly, withdrawing a hand from beneath her to stroke her warm face.

She nodded and her eyes fluttered open, glistening with wonder. "It's . . . you feel so . . . you fill me and it's so hot and tingling. And I just want—" She bit her lip and flushed violently.

"Want what, wench?" He felt the sudden heat of her blush against his lips as they rested on her cheek. "What?" He caught her chin and made her look at him as she whispered, "More."

Need exploded inside him, and he crushed her to him, thrusting fully inside her in a single heart-stopping motion.

"Ohhh—Whitney—"

He heard her groan and he soared at the seductive pleasure carried in the throaty sound. He began to move rhythmically, his powerful body flexing, caressing her, lifting her into a bright, steamy cloud of sensation that swirled around and within them, joining their separate experience. Each thrust carried her higher, faster along some unseen continuum of pleasure, along a vector that expanded magically as time slowed and reality was left behind. And as he ground sinuously against her tender flesh, she began to quake and contract, whimpering with delight. Her senses exploded; her very body seemed to dissolve into a fierce

white-hot blast of elemental heat. And in that boundless, exploding star of pleasure she felt his essence mingle with hers as he
buried his face in her hair and erupted, pouring his passion into
her soft, responsive frame.

Joined in sweet release, they floated a long time, shivering
with aftershocks of pleasure. When he would have slid his weight
to the bed beside her, she stayed him with a tight hug that reached
far deeper than his ribs. For that splendid, glowing moment, his
entire universe was contained in the circle of her arms, in the
sweet, steamy bit of paradise they had created together.

He finally lowered to the bed beside her and pulled her warm,
pliant body against him so that they were pressed pleasurably
together at several points. She lay quietly in the circle of his arms,
leaving both his hands free to roam her back, to caress her bottom, and explore her delights in more leisurely fashion. When
his fingers drifted into a ticklish crevice, she tightened and wriggled to escape. He rumbled amusement and sent his hands to
other regions that caused her to release a shuddering sigh. He
kissed her tangled hair and felt her relax against him.

"I wish I'd known it would be like this," she whispered against
his breastbone, moving his chest hair enough that it tickled. He
shivered.

"I'm glad you didn't." He didn't want to have to explain the
remark even to himself, and was very glad when she just nuzzled
the middle of his chest like a sleepy kitten and sank deeper into
satisfaction's lulling arms.

"Charlie said I'd like it. . . ."

"And did you?" His heart stopped briefly and began to beat
again when she answered.

"Yes . . . umm, yes."

Beneath the gentle pressure of her cheek against him, his chest
seemed to be melting, caving inward, exposing a strangely
shaped void that he hadn't realized was there until he came to
Rapture Valley. Until that very moment, Garner Townsend hadn't
known what to call the hollow feeling that made itself known in
the dark of recent nights, in the pit of his stomach. He had
mounted the stairs each night, dreading the solitude, the empti-

ness of his bed, not understanding it was pure loneliness that beset him.

But Whitney Daniels had been there tonight, in his dark, silent room in his cold, empty bed. She had filled his arms, invaded his polished, hollow self with her warm, inviting curves, her responsive mouth, and her delicious eagerness. And he knew this was exactly what he'd craved since the moment he'd first set eyes on her.

Sliding into a world of dreams, she felt him draw the quilts over them and felt his leg sliding up hers to lie possessively across her hip. And for some reason, that claiming motion pleased her. A dreamy, satisfied smile appeared at the corner of her love-swollen lips. It was a new kind of look, a potent blend of "Daniels" and "woman." It was her unique contribution to the Daniels repertoire of expressions of delight.

Eleven

Kate Morrison sat at her kitchen table in the gray light of dawn, staring into the past with eyes that were red and swollen from crying. Across the years she again heard Whitney's mother, Margaret, confiding her undying passion for the restless and adventurous young patriot soldier, Blackstone Daniels. Margaret was destined for better things, their ambitious father had said, refusing to allow their marriage. And spirited Margaret had taken up the reins of her life herself and married the love of her heart anyway. Nothing could have dissuaded her from slipping from the house to go to him at night, from eloping with him, or from moving west with him after the War of Independence. Through hardship and sacrifice, Margaret had loved Blackstone fiercely, and had gloried in the devotion he bestowed on her in the years they had together.

Now Whitney was following in her mother's footsteps, casting everything aside for the wanting of one man. Only this time the roles were reversed; it was Whitney who had little standing or wealth to speak of, and the man came straight from Boston's elite society. The handsome, hard-nosed major had nothing to gain from an alliance with a wild and impetuous frontier girl except a cynical bit of pleasure. Kate knew all too well the convenience of a gentleman's passion. And she ached to think of the pain her sweet, spirited Whitney would suffer when she learned the callous major had only used her to slake his animal urges.

"Oh, Whitney," she whispered, burying her face in her hands, "forgive me for not warning you."

* * *

In the waxing predawn light, Black Daniels crept closer to his home, watching the soldiers as they watched his house. His eyes narrowed furiously. The wretches had found him out, he snarled silently. If they'd harmed Kate and his Whitney in any way, he'd see they paid for it with their very lives. He rolled his broad shoulders under his deerskin coat and lifted his musket to creep toward the back of the house in silent shadows.

There was a dim light coming from the small glass window in the kitchen, and Black stroked his bristled chin as he evaluated it. Someone was up and about quite early. He tightened and launched himself from the grape arbor toward the kitchen door. He burst through the door like a typhoon and slammed it behind him, pushing a chair against it.

"Oh!" Kate startled and whirled, clasping her throat as her heart leapt into it. "B-B-Black!" She launched herself at him, clutching his arm and his coat front frantically. "Oh, Black, thank God you're home . . . and safe—oh, Black—"

"Kate—are you all right?" He took her by the shoulders, searching her rumpled hair and nightclothes and her tear-ravaged face. "Holy heaven, what's happened? What have those monsters done to you?"

"N-not me," Kate said, wiping her eyes in order to see through her tears. "I-it's Whitney . . . she . . ."

"Merciful Moses!" he swore, giving Kate a compelling shake. "What have they done to her?"

"She's gone, Black." Kate shook her head and tried to get a grip on herself. "She's gone to be with him. I had no idea. He's a gentleman, and rich and handsome . . . and they've fought like cats and dogs—"

"Who, Kate?" Black demanded, his entire being igniting. While he was off protesting and bargaining for their freedoms, the jackals had invaded his home to abuse his family. The cold and fatigue and hunger of the perilous trek from Pittsburgh—hiding in the hills by day, traveling at night—were suddenly forgotten. "Where have they taken her?"

The desperation in his voice made Kate realize she had to explain more to prevent compounding the disaster. She dragged him to the table and made him sit. "They haven't *taken* her anywhere, Black. She went on her own, of her own free will . . . at least I think so."

"Went where, Kate?" Black's dusky features, so like Whitney's, darkened in confusion. "Tell me!"

"She wasn't in her bed when I checked tonight, and I think she's gone to be with their commander, Major Townsend. He's staying at Harvey's inn, and his soldiers are camped beside. Black . . . Whitney's a full woman now, and the major is so handsome and so arrogant. And I've seen what passes between them. She's tried to protect your still and the valley folk, but she's no match for him, Black. He's a great, cynical beast of a man who'll use her own passions against her and gobble her up for a morsel. Oh, Black, if only you had been here!" Kate dissolved into tears.

Kate's anguished revelations filtered brokenly through his own sense of guilt at having left them. The soldiers . . . Whit had been overpowered by some fancy-ankled officer. The knowledge slammed into his gut like a fist.

"But Whit always held her own with a buck."

"She's never met a *gentleman* before. She has no idea how treacherous they are. And her damnable Daniels pride—she honestly thought she could best him. He's all she's thought about for two weeks, and it was painfully clear what he wanted from her." Kate's anguish turned outward. "It's part my fault, all my talk of elegant life and fine gentlemen, but you bear the blame as well, Blackstone Daniels. Raising her like a buck, letting her talk and bargain her way through everything in life."

Black thrust himself up, goaded savagely in the most vulnerable areas of his being, his pride as a father and his love for his precious daughter. His face bloated with fury, his fists trembled at his sides.

"If he's dishonored her," Black vowed tightly, "I'll kill the bloody bastard." He lunged for his musket and the door.

The early wisps of dawn slid through the cracks in the shutters, stealing around Garner Townsend's room like thieves bent on pilfering the dreams and pleasures of the naked lovers entwined on the sturdy rope-and-post bed. The pair slept soundly, unaware that the bargain they'd consummated in the quiet of the night was dissolving in the light around them. When the first sounds of the angry commotion reached through the doors, both stirred, still wrapped in their shared warmth.

The major opened his eyes and let the reality of Whiskey Daniels's naked body ensconced cozily against his bare frame sink into his senses. The sensations were marvelous—her soft, warm curves, the gentle pressure of her hip against his loins, the ripe swell of her dark-tipped breast against his palm . . .

Whitney was confused at first, wakening to the feel of a hard male body pressed against her bare skin. But a slight turn of her head brought her languid gaze to his beautiful gray-blue eyes, his boldly sculptured mouth, his patrician cheekbones.

Their gazes locked as the pounding reverberated around them, coming from the hallway. Each tightened, feeling a vague but growing sense of alarm at their location and at the intimate juxtaposition of their naked bodies. Then the harsh sound of arguing assaulted them, rattling exposed nerves.

Blackstone had run most of the way from his farmstead, with Kate's heated accusations burning inside him. Laxault and two of his men trailed doggedly behind, but were no match for his emotion-spurred speed. He charged into the tavern and up the still-dark steps to assault the first door he came across. Harvey sprang up in his bed, gasping, and Black snarled and backed out, headed for another door.

Three soldiers were thumping up the steps, roused by Black's charge through the taproom, where they'd been sleeping. Harvey threw himself into the thick of them, demanding they retreat even as Black stormed out of the second room.

"Curse it, Harvey—where are they?" Black whirled and lunged for a third door over Harvey's frantic objection. The planking slammed back, startling the room's two occupants, a portly man in the small rope-and-post bed and another fellow bedded on the floor. They jerked upright, bleary-eyed, to find Black standing, braced, inside the door with his musket trained on them. "Where the ragin' thunder is she?" he stormed. "What have you done with my little girl?"

The fat fellow sputtered outrage and the skinny one on the

floor tried to rise to his commander's defense. Black's gun lowered menacingly to the skinny one's nose and shortly both were denying anything, everything, and threatening that they'd have him shot for such a heinous violation of their governmental sanctity. Black growled and stalked out, headed for the fourth and final door.

The old uncles, Whitney's melted mental processes managed to deduce as she huddled under the quilts and stared helplessly at the door. They'd come too late! She'd already spent the night in the major's bed—in his arms!

She turned a panicky look on the major, who had just risen from the bed, catching sight of his bare buttocks and thighs as his breeches slid over them. Her eyes slammed shut, but not soon enough to prevent the sight of his bare chest, his powerful arms . . . and manly parts. Every muscle, every line of him had burned into her very body during the night just past. *Into her body.*

The door slammed back and she started, grabbing the quilts tightly around her as the door burst open. Garner instinctively jolted to spread himself between Whitney and the open door. In charged Blackstone Daniels, with blood in his eyes, wielding a gun.

Everything froze for a moment as mutual shock bore in on the three of them. Instead of the old uncles, there stood Whitney's own pa, gun in hand, quaking with anger.

There she was, Black craned his neck to see, and recoiled; his little Whitney, her hair atangle and obviously naked . . . in a man's bed . . . a federal jackal's bed!

Garner Townsend swallowed convulsively. There was no doubt of the identity of the wild man braced in the doorway, ready to blow him to kingdom come. The fellow bore a weathered, male version of the very face he had spent the night making love to; it had to be her father!

"Pa?" she choked.

"Dammit!" Blackstone Daniels cursed for the very first time in anybody's memory. "You black-hearted blow of the devil's own seed. You plunderin' spawn of perdition. Dishonorin' my own flesh and blood! No need to say prayers, cur," he spat out,

his eyes wild, his frame trembling, "whatever you've got to say to the Maker you can say in person!" And he raised the muzzle of his gun.

"No!" Whitney just managed to grab a quilt about her as she lunged from the bed to stand between them. "You can't, Pa! It'd be murder! It's not what you think, honest, please, just listen to me—"

But turmoil erupted at Blackstone's back, and he lurched to the side, planting himself firmly against a wall as three half-clad forms grappled past Uncle Harvey to shove into the room. And for a second time, everything seemed to still.

"Get him—arrest that man!" shirt-clad Colonel Gaspar shouted, pointing at Black. But when the unarmed soldiers jolted forward, they were stopped in their tracks by the bore of Black's musket as he ordered them to stay back. Gaspar swept a hot gaze over Whitney's alluringly exposed form, then rounded on his half-clad major. "Just what in the hell is going on here, Townsend?"

"He's gone and disgraced my daughter," Black growled before Townsend could speak. "And I'm here to kill 'im for it!"

"No, Pa—"

"The hell I have," Townsend protested, feeling a sickening wave of humiliation pouring over him. Caught . . . again . . . by a furious father and a nasty little weasel of a shopkeeper. "I returned after night patrol and found the little witch in my bed. Ask her . . . go on!"

He turned on her, his entire being in turmoil, his gentlemanly standards in complete shambles. Last night he'd loved her, held her, adored every delectable part of her. And his first impulse just now had been to protect her, to shield her from this invasion, with his very body if need be. But it had turned out to be her own father, and Colonel Gaspar was standing there demanding an explanation, and suddenly his chivalrous impulses horrified him. Protect *her?* He was the one in imminent danger of life and limb . . . caught in a debacle of lust.

Oh, God. It was happening *again.* Just as he feared it would. He'd felt it coming, watched it approach, felt its hot breath on his neck every time he encountered her. Disaster in female guise . . . in the person of quixotic, irresistible, and treacherous

Whiskey Daniels. And as he stood, like a great granite statue, staring at her vulnerable girlish form, he forced himself to recall their other encounters: the modest humiliations, the small spectacles she enjoyed making of him, and that last, all-too-calm threat. He'd be sorry, she had said, and she'd meant she would *make* him sorry.

He shuddered visibly, revolted by his own weakness, by the unthinkable desire for her that lodged even now in the middle of him. He knew this humiliation all too well.

"Tell them," he demanded, his voice hoarse with pain-spawned anger. "God, you probably planned this little exhibition, didn't you? Having your father break in on us, wielding a gun, *after the fact.*" As he spoke, the awful certainty of it drilled through him. It was perfectly in keeping with her crass, unthinkable ethic: everything has its price. And the price of escaping this disgrace was undoubtedly to be his withdrawal from the valley!

The sight of his disgust, his anger, after what had passed between them in the night, slapped every possibility of response from her faculties. All she could do was stand there, feeling crushed and defenseless, feeling the weight of her own plot on her bare shoulders. It was true. She'd come to his bed as a Delilah, to ensnare him, to get him to leave the valley. And in seeking his ruin, she'd somehow found her own.

"Liar!" Black jolted forward, outraged by the arrogant major's charges and stunned by the pain and disbelief in his daughter's face, in her very body. He'd never seen her look so small and pale and hurt. "You miserable bastard. Blaming my daughter for the perfidy of your own deceitful lusts. I'll kill you for stealin' her innocence!"

"She's no innocent," Garner snarled, feeling his stomach turn and his chest squeeze at the pain that seemed to be draining the spirit, the very life from her. "There's not a more scheming, deceitful Jezebel on the face of this earth."

Whitney stood, naked and wrapped in a quilt, still bearing the traces of his loving on her body, feeling their hot eyes on her. Caught in her own wretched plot, undone by her own hand. How could she tell her pa?

"Blackstone?" came a familiar voice. "Whitney—is she there? Is she all right?" Her aunt Kate struggled and wriggled through the soldiers who clogged the hall and doorway and stopped dead at the sight that greeted her. "Precious Lord."

Whitney saw her aunt's horror through a blurry haze, felt Garner Townsend's hatred like a suffocating hand on her throat, felt her pa's bewildered rage, and the others' lurid curiosity. She burst into tears, great, awful, gulping sobs of them. She ought to think, ought to talk, to parlay this humiliation into some advantage. That's what a real trader would do, she knew. And all she could do was *cry* like a weak-kneed woman.

Kate gasped and ran to cover Whitney's exposed form and shield her against prying eyes. "Oh, Whitney, what did he do to you?"

"That's bloody well obvious." Black raised his musket again and found himself staring down it at the short, squat man with the bullfrog face.

"Shoot him and I'll hang you for murder," he croaked.

"And just who in blazes are you to be giving orders?" Black demanded.

"I'm the major's superior, his commanding officer. And if a wrong has been done here, I'll deal with it." Then he turned on the major with wicked fire in his eyes.

Colonel Oliver Gaspar had watched the bizarre proceedings with vengeful fascination. His gaze narrowed ominously on the handsome pedigreed Bostonian. It was exactly the sort of thing to expect from a rake . . . the seduction of a poor farmer's daughter.

"It's clear you've disgraced both yourself and your post, sir." The little round colonel tore into Townsend like a human cannonball. "I've a notion to cashier you out and send you packing. I'll not allow such a blot on the record of my command!" He whipped a glance at Kate leading Whitney to a seat on the bed, and his resentment of what could be termed only the major's "carnal opportunism" was fanned to furious heights.

"C-Colonel—" Townsend's blood boiled up into his face. "Dammit—you can't take the word of a—against a Townsend!"

"Of a what?" Black stalked forward, trembling with fatherly fury. "You steal her innocence and then call her foul names—"

"Silence, all of you!" Gaspar grasped command at the center of the room, seizing the chance to wield a blow against his "betters." "Like most men of your ilk"—he turned on Townsend— "you believe your wealth and standing insulate you from the consequences of your licentious and immoral behavior." He jabbed a pudgy finger at Garner. "You've compromised both yourself and your unit. And it is only in their interest that I shall see the situation repaired. Now, either marry the girl, or I shall allow this man to shoot you. And though I personally favor the shooting, I suspect you may find marriage the lesser evil."

Every muscle in the room stilled in shock at the ultimatum. *Marriage,* it rumbled through the teary haze in Whitney's head, *the lesser evil.* She lifted her blotchy face from Kate's shoulder, her reddened eyes wide with horror.

"Marry—*no!* You can't make him marry—"

"He will indeed, girl," Gaspar growled. "And you must face the consequences of your action as well, submitting to the yoke of marriage."

"No." She jumped to her feet. "I won't! You can't make me . . . or him. It was just a bit of bedding." She wiped her wet face frantically. "Nothing of importance . . . I . . . I do it all the time."

"See there." Townsend first seized her unthinkable admission, then turned on her with the turmoil of his being in his stormy face. She'd had other lovers? The very idea of it poured through his middle like molten lead.

"A bargain, we just struck a bargain. He's probably already got a wife," she protested, the very idea making her sick to her stomach. She had slept with him, given him her whole self in loving, and didn't even know whether he was married or not.

"He's an unmarried man." Gaspar's dark eyes glowed nastily.

"Well, I won't marry the likes of her," Townsend declared. It was pure madness, the ache to possess her, the desperation to escape her. "The little trollop . . . she drinks like a man, lies through her teeth, and runs the countryside at night with a pack of men. You heard her, she does it all the time."

A choked sound came from the bed beside Whitney. She

turned and found Kate staring at a small dark stain on the ticking. Black's eyes found it too, and then the colonel's. And when Kate rose and backed a step, Garner Townsend saw it too.

"You'll marry the girl," Gaspar sneered with malice, "or you're finished, Townsend."

There were a few further attempts to dissuade the vinegary colonel, all futile. The little man's determined prejudice against the son of an aristocratic house bordered on the fanatical. And when it became clear he could and would force them to go through with the marriage, they tried to use the problem of arrangements to forestall it. There was no preacher in Rapture Valley, no one to tie the knot. The colonel smiled wickedly and sent for his aide-de-camp, a newly ordained preacher, and his own son-in-law.

It was an hour later that Whitney was summoned down the stairs to the tavern and her wedding. The nuptials were delayed that long only because of Kate's insistence that Whitney be permitted to "freshen up" and that she be allowed to send for a dress to wear at her vows. As she washed and dressed, she couldn't meet her aunt Kate's doleful looks. And as she descended the stairs, she couldn't bear to look at her pa or the neighbor folk who had crowded into the tavern to witness the spectacle of her being hastily wedded to the Iron Major.

Half the tavern was filled with locals, the other half with soldiers of varying hues and classes. Townsend stood by the blazing hearth, towering dark and smoldering with resentment. Kate had to nudge Whitney across the room to his side and had to stay beside her to keep her from bolting.

Whitney hardly saw the fellow that married them, except for his boots. She couldn't raise her eyes past the crude bone buttons on the major's splendid blue coat. The military preacher said the words and waited patiently for the major to take her hand and repeat them. Garner's voice was deep and his touch was hot on her fingers. "Love," "honor," and "protect," she heard him say with a strange tenor to his voice. And when she was asked to make similar promises, she had to fight a terrible squeezing in her throat to speak at all.

She raised her face to him, her eyes luminous with apology as she spoke those awful words that sealed their fate. To love him . . . to honor him . . . and to obey. They were good and decent words, meant for the binding of lives, for the hallowing of loving bargains. They were meant for decent women. She ached at the thought. Not for Delilahs.

Garner Townsend watched the misery in her face and, oddly, almost forgot his own. He kept recalling that she'd rather have been branded a harlot than speak these words with him. However clever or treacherous she was, he couldn't bring himself to believe she could have pretended the volume of pain in her face earlier, as she stood wrapped in a quilt, hearing him denounce her. And God help him, this very minute he wanted to pull her into his arms and comfort her. These vows were a punishment, and would undoubtedly ruin him forever in his family's eyes. But right now all he could think about was that small dark stain on the ticking of his bed and his perverse pleasure in the fact that Charlie Dunbar had nothing to do with it.

Lord, she was making a sickening sentimental slur of his thinking again. Let him get within arm's reach of her, and he couldn't reason, couldn't string a coherent sentence together. Good Lord—he was being yoked to her for life. He was doomed to spend the rest of his wretched life acting like the village idiot.

Suddenly it was over and he was advised to kiss his "bride." His gut contracted, his muscles coiled all over. She stood before him, her eyes wide and wary, looking like she would bolt at the slightest movement. No breath was taken or let in the silence that stretched around them.

Why the hell not, his baser self snarled; the damage has already been done. He tilted her chin up and held it while he placed a shocking, openmouthed assault of a kiss on her cherry-red lips. Then he pulled away and did an abrupt about-face to wade through the crowd for the door.

Confusion erupted all around Whitney as she stood, feeling the angry heat of his mouth still burning hers. Tight-lipped Black wouldn't look at her, and teary-eyed Aunt Kate hugged her and wept openly. The colonel placed a gentlemanly kiss on her hand, and Rapture's people crowded close to congratulate her on her clever marriage bargain. Uncle Harvey and Aunt Harriet and Aunt Sarah and the Delbartons acted as though she'd just made the deal of the century rather than been forced to wed an enemy to Rapture's way of life and to her own father's freedom. She was too stunned to respond on any level.

The colonel and his entourage of eight followed Townsend outside and called for their horses straightaway. Gaspar pulled on his gloves and cast a satisfied glare at the gentlemanly Bostonian whose life he had gleefully turned inside out.

"I am willing to forget this incident, Townsend." He smiled coldly. "It need never be reported above myself, now that matters have been set to rights. Providing . . ."

"Providing what?" Townsend spoke through clenched jaws, physically fighting the urge to throw the warty little toad onto the ground and pound him into oblivion.

"Providing you complete your task here. Bring in the liquor and the distillers, as is your sworn duty. One more week, Major, that's all you have. Then you'll pull out and report to me and the rest of the division at Pittsburgh." He turned to his aide for assistance in mounting and stared tauntingly down at Townsend's fury. "One week, Major."

Garner stood watching them ride off, quaking with unvented rage. The nauseating little wretch breezed in to inspect, forced him to marry Whiskey Daniels, and breezed back out with a command that he— He froze.

Merciful Lord. He'd just married one of the distillers Gaspar insisted he arrest! And the kingpin of the entire illegal operation in the valley was now his bloody father-in-law! His entire body seemed to combust spontaneously . . . he was on fire. And there was only one way to put the inferno out.

"Laxault!" he bellowed, striding through his muttering men, making straight for the center of camp. "Where the hell is that barrel of belch-fire stew we found?"

The Iron Major spent the rest of the day and most of his wedding night getting drunk as David's sow, for the first time in twelve years. His men drank with him, though none quite matched his intake. His functional capacity for the potent, water-mixed whiskey was nothing short of amazing considering his abrupt conversion from abstinence. The men of the Maryland Ninth watched with a growing reverence for their commander. He was a man's man, their Iron Major, worked the hardest, bedded the choicest wench, held the most liquor. . . .

It was late in the night and most of the men had crawled off to their tents when Laxault and the lieutenant sobered enough to give the major an assist to his bridal bed. They found his upstairs room in the inn reclaimed by Dedham's children, snoozing peaceably, and they scratched their heads in bewilderment.

The lieutenant, being the critical-thinking sort, ventured the opinion that the major must be expected to stay with his bride and her family from now on. Laxault agreed it seemed reasonable. The major, who had just slid past the pale of consciousness, could voice no objection, so they loaded him across his horse and walked him the mile and a half to the Daniels farmstead. They banged loudly on the door and roused the household from their beds, though not actually from sleep, since no one had managed that. They teetered inside, under Black's furious glare, muttering, "He be a trifle jug-bit." Then they dumped him on Kate's French settee and tottered out, their duty done.

Whitney stood on the stairs, staring at her "jug-bit" groom, and didn't know whether to laugh or to cry. The stern, superior, abstemious Iron Major, drunk to insensibility on his wedding night. Her wedding night. Her throat tightened and her eyes prickled and she fled back up the stairs to her room.

He was still there the next morning when a somewhat more controlled Whitney came downstairs to the aromas of bacon sizzling and coffee boiling. She stood in her skirt and shirt, staring down at his handsome features, now a bit gray from the combination of beard growth and overindulgence. She impulsively brushed a wisp of his dark hair back from his forehead and he stirred. There was confusion on his face as his bloodshot eyes opened and he saw her and his surroundings. But as he opened his mouth to speak, his shoulders twitched convulsively and his hand clamped over his mouth. He was on his feet in a flash, staggering toward the door. He managed to empty the contents of his abused stomach on the ground outside beside the stone steps.

Whitney watched him there, on all fours, suffering the humiliation and the agony of the drink's aftermath. She stood by while he finished, then silently helped him to his feet. Drawing his arm across her shoulders, she grabbed him around the middle, and led his tortured body up the stairs to her bed.

"You?" he rasped as he sank back onto the bed.

"Yes, me," she answered softly. "You're probably right, Major. A man who can't hold his liquor any better than that just shouldn't drink at all." She watched his reddened eyes squeeze shut as though the sight of her only added to his agony. But she screwed up her courage and made herself stay, telling herself it was her fault he got married and then got drunk and sick. She owed him this much.

Through the day, she was there to hold his head as he heaved, and to periodically wipe his burning face with a cold cloth. By late afternoon his system was purged and he finally lapsed into a healing sleep. She sat with him in the waning light of evening, reading in his drained, miserable face the bleakness of the marriage she'd been forced to make.

Caught in her own trap, she sighed despondently. How could so much have gone so wrong with such a simple plan? It was a fiendish bit of luck that Pa came home when he did and a pure conspiracy of fate that the major's commander happened to be there—with a nasty streak of righteousness in him that he insisted on inflicting on others. But the worst of it, by far, was her own wretched and incomprehensible behavior, starting with the way she'd allowed her brain to go to mush the minute the major peeled his coat from his broad shoulders.

Unbidden warmth welled in the center of her even as she recalled that stunning physical surrender. He was so big, it was like having a wall fall on her. Very softly. And who'd have guessed that the sensual motions of his hard body would be as gentle as they were powerful, that he'd be so tender and so careful in fulfilling a bargain with her?

A bargain. A deal between a man and a woman. It had always sounded so neat, so sensible . . . almost reassuring. And remote.

But there was nothing sensible or orderly or remote in what she'd experienced in Major Garner Townsend's bed. It was hot and unpredictable and shockingly personal, as intimate as breathing. It was as though they shared each other's very bodies for a time. The realization took her breath away.

That was exactly what they'd done, shared both bodies and feelings in the most powerful way possible. She'd looked into his handsome face and glimpsed a deep tenderness and a soul-deep hunger he kept caged inside his ironclad being. And she'd revealed the vulnerable, inexperienced girl that lay at the heart of her, in a way she'd never done with anybody in her life, not even her pa. She'd never be able to look at him now without thinking of that tender, sensual man inside him, and wanting to experience him again. And after the terrible humiliation of being caught bedding her and being forced to wed, he'd never be able to look at her without seeing the scheming, conniving Delilah who had come to his bed to hold his pride for ransom. He would come to hate her more and more, while she seemed doomed to want more and more of him.

At the root of that futile wanting was the drastic change that was occurring in her deepest self. Her body sprang to a life of its own whenever he was near. And her feelings ran strangely deeper and shallower, both in the unplumbed depths of her heart and just beneath her skin. And where was her Daniels gift of gab when she had needed it? Where was her uncanny instinct for burning a profit in any situation? And how was she going to deal her way out of marriage to the one man who knew how to make her forget her pa, her people, and everything she had ever learned about bargaining?

Broad-shouldered, gray-templed Black Daniels trudged up the steps that evening to peer, unnoticed, through his daughter's doorway. He watched her troubled manner and the tenderness of her touch with the arrogant easterner. Something in her movements, in the sweet pensiveness of her expression, spoke of his wife, Margaret, in a way he'd never seen before. Whit had always been the pure mortal image of him: brash and daring, and quick with her tongue and wit. She had his wide, heavily lashed eyes, his dazzling smile, his agile hands, and his nose with the Daniels dent in the tip. She had his swagger, his explosive charm, his gift of gab. It was a pure shock now for him to see her garbed as a young woman and to realize how very like her mother she was, down to the fierce loyalty of her heart and the stubbornness of her desires.

Kate was right about Whitney's womanly transformation, he realized with a gut-deep sense of loss. And she was probably right about Whit's weakness for the gentlemanly cur too, for he couldn't imagine any buck taking Whit's virtue by force without losin' a bit of blood. She was too dirty a fighter.

He quivered, stung by the implications of it. The handsome bastard had stolen his daughter and his partner and the second love of his life, all in one fell swoop. It was more than any man had a right to take. And he had shown just how little he valued that precious plunder when he stood there in Dedham's inn calling the pride of Black Daniels's heart a trollop. It made Black's blood boil and made his hazel-green eyes snap with flint-struck sparks.

Whatever a fellow took, he had to pay for, one way or another. Nothing was ever free in life. And as he stood there, watching his daughter's somber face, Black Daniels determined to make the fancy bastard pay, and pay well, for his foul bit of larceny.

Twelve

Whitney waited that night until her aunt Kate and her pa had gone to bed before she pulled a quilt from her trunk and crept down the stairs to spend the night curled on the settee. They found her there the next morning, an exile from her own bed. Black heated furiously at the sight of her strained features and crumpled form, and he charged halfway up the stairs to evict his sponge of a son-in-law from his house before Kate managed to drag him to a halt. Their harsh words woke Whitney, and when she demanded to know what was amiss, both Kate and Black glowered and mumbled and retreated to the kitchen and barn to finish morning chores. Whitney watched them go and bit her lip, raising her eyes to the ceiling and the bed above it.

Upstairs, Garner Townsend stirred, confused by the softness and warmth of the bed around him. His tongue seemed to be several feet thick and some fiend had imbedded glass splinters in his eyelids. When he raised his head to look around him, thunder exploded in his too-tight skull. He flopped back, grabbing his head between his hands, writhing. After a few minutes of intense breathing, he managed to sit up and swing his legs over the edge. And he found himself in Whiskey Daniels's bed, bootless, shirtless, and with a taste in his mouth like the bottom of an old fish barrel. His belly was sore, his throat was dry, and he felt like he'd been pounded all over. He had no earthly idea how he came to be there.

His gaze fell on the basin on the floor beside the bed, and on the chair beside it. A folded cloth draped the edge of the basin and he had a quick flash of memory—Whiskey bending over him, touching his hot face with her cool hands. Recall slammed through him like a hammer, and his scratchy eyes closed. Oh, Lord . . . he'd been stewed like a turnip. And sick. And *married!*

It was dinnertime when the Iron Major, gray-faced and granite-hard, ducked through the kitchen doorway to confront his bride and her hostile family. He'd spent the last half hour preparing, arguing with himself. It was untenable, unthinkable. The two of them, *married.*

Three faces turned to him as he straightened, but it was Whitney's form that claimed his burning eyes. She was seated at the table, wearing skirts, her copper-kissed ginger hair combed and plaited neatly into a rope that lay on her shoulder. Her eyes were very green, her lips were cherry red, and her satiny skin was blushing apple pink. He'd never seen her looking more appealing, or dreaded the sight of her more.

"About time you dragged yourself out." Black Daniels lurched from his seat at the table with his shoulders braced, his fists clenched. "Don't stop there, just keep on goin' "—he flung a finger at the door—*"out."*

"Blackstone, remember—" Kate hurried from the hearth to catch his sleeve.

"Drunk as a slug on your weddin' night, so sick and disgustin' you drove my daughter from her own rightful bed. This is *my* house"—Black jerked a thumb at his thick chest—"and she's *my* daughter. And you're not welcome in either."

"See here, old man—" Garner flinched privately at the charges, but his drink-pickled eyes were a fair counterfeit of bloodshot fury. "I don't know how I got to be in your daughter's bed, but I've a fair idea how she came to be in mine. Was it your idea or hers?"

"Out!" Blackstone roared. "And never show your randy hide around here again. You stay away from me and mine."

"Yours?" Garner growled, red rising up into his ears as he stalked closer, looming over Whitney's chair. He was being ordered out? Away from the woman who'd just violated his honor, his family name, and possibly his future to possess?

"Yes, mine. My house . . . my daughter." Black stalked to the other side of her chair, nearly nose to nose with the Iron Major, above her.

"Dammit . . ." Garner vibrated, his intentions whiplashing at this unexpected turn. Now that he'd served his purpose, now that his military ambition lay in shambles and his name and honor were blackened, they would just dismiss him and go on with their precious dealing and distilling as though nothing had happened. He turned on Whitney with billowing flames in his eyes. Her! How dare she belittle and ignore what happened between them. He'd taken her blessed virtue, for God's sake. And how dare this scruffy, backwoods lot disregard something as momentous as marriage to a Townsend!

"Just leave, and let the two of you get on with your treasonous little enterprise, is that it? Well, it was you who made my bed yours, wench, and by God you'll lie in it. I was forced to speak vows with you and like it or not, you owe me. You're coming with me."

Whitney pushed up from her chair, surprising them both back a step. "Y-you can't be serious—"

"I may be yoked to her, Daniels"—Garner turned on Black furiously—"but it doesn't change a thing for you. You're a distiller and I'm still duty bound to hunt you down. And I'll do it—see if I don't!"

He dragged Whitney out the door into the cold, sunny yard before she realized what he intended. Black jolted after them, with Kate hanging on to his arm, struggling to hold him back, begging him not to make things worse.

"Just what do you think you're doing?" Whitney shouted, casting a frantic look back over her shoulder at Kate and her father as she tried to dig her heels into the dusty yard.

"I said you're coming with me, wench." Garner turned and reeled her toward him, grappling for a firm hold on her other arm. "You're my *wife,* remember?"

"You don't want me. You let me go!" She pried his fingers

futilely and shoved at his hands, twisting and turning so that her legs tangled in her own treacherous skirts.

"Wrong, wench. I do want you . . . where I can see you every damned minute of the day for the rest of the time I'm stuck in this pest-hole valley. That way I'll be sure of what you're up to."

"No, you can't make me go!" She found herself clamped hard against him and scuffled wildly, panic rising, her heart thumping painfully in her chest. He was taking her by force—making her his hostage. She wrenched violently about in his arms, and in the frantic flurry of battle reverted to the defensive habit of a lifetime. She raised his hand near her mouth and sank her teeth in!

"Owww!" he howled, releasing her and contracting around his throbbing wound. *"Dammit."* She skittered back, glaring venomously at him, and when he raised his gaze from the savage teeth marks on his hand, he caught Black Daniels's wicked smile and vengeful sneer.

"I taught her that."

Garner quaked for a moment, then exploded, pounding his shoulder into her middle and upending her across him. The blood raging in his head nearly obscured the sight of Black Daniels being restrained by Whitney's Aunt Kate, who had wrapped herself bodily about his middle and wouldn't be dislodged.

"I'm taking her, Daniels!" Garner outshouted her screeches and dodged her thumps, clamping her legs tight against his chest to keep her from thrashing off his shoulder. "And there's not a damned thing you can do about it!"

People came out of their houses to watch as the Iron Major strode into Rapture with his bride of one day slung indecorously across his shoulder. His face was bloodred, he was panting and steaming, and the fire in his eyes was hot enough to light damp kindling.

Resistance had long since been pounded from Whitney on that furious trek, and as she glimpsed boots and skirts, and suffered upside-down grins and stares and the giggles and hoots of the local children, she clamped her hands over her face and wished she'd just die and get it over with. Such humiliation—she managed a groan—a Daniels in such straits.

He charged into the inn and up the stairs, kicking open the door of the room he'd used and dumping her on the bed. He stood over her, his fists planted on his hips as she reeled and struggled to rise. He was panting, hot, furious . . . bewildered and infuriated by his own possessive behavior. And a moment later he was assaulted by waves of sensual memory and spurred mercilessly by pride. Lord, he was in pure primal chaos!

She righted herself enough to realize where they were and that he'd forcibly claimed her as his hostage . . . or *property!* "You . . . can't do this . . ." she protested.

"Do what, wench?" he snarled, thrusting the provocative picture she presented aside as though it were poison. "Can't haul your precious bottom wherever I please? Can't despise you for what you've done to me? Can't blame you for the disaster you've made of my life? Oh, I can and will, wench. You belong to me now."

"B-belong to you? That's absurd." She tried desperately to think, to find a way to explain, to reason with him. The weight of his anger settled on her heart, forcing the desperate truth from it. "Look— I never meant— I wanted only to make you leave Rapture. I never wanted to marry you. I don't want to be married to anybody!"

"You don't, do you?" He released a bitter laugh that stung something in the middle of his chest as it escaped. He watched her rise and step closer, her eyes swirling with desperation as she gathered herself. He braced as she came closer. He could feel the warmth of her invading him again and was helpless to prevent it. Some part of him ached for it, wanted it still, even after everything that had happened.

"Marriage wasn't part of our . . . bargain," she muttered desperately, meeting his eyes, searching his tightly guarded expression. She knew she risked much by recalling, by conjuring the stunning intimacy they'd shared in the sheltering darkness of his bed. His beautiful eyes suddenly bore traces of pain that had been etched by passion's burning passage. How could he seem so fierce and yet so vulnerable with the same look?

The air charged between them as each relived the sweet, steamy moment when the conditions of their joining were agreed.

He had wanted her; she had wanted him. There had been no more than that, a splendid simplicity of desire freely given and returned. No promises, no conditions, no entailments. That same compelling desire was exerting its pull between them now, somehow stronger for having been so briefly and so memorably freed.

But simplicity of desire was a pure deception, Garner understood. In seizing that bit of paradise, he'd abandoned the rest of his world, his connections, his obligations, and brought chaos down upon himself in the process. Nothing was ever as simple and as wonderful as the joy he found in her arms. Everything, he was coming to see—including that earthly paradise—had its price. Perhaps Rapture's folk weren't so far from the mark after all.

"This time it appears you got a bit more than you bargained for, wench." He reverted to harshness to hide his own turmoil.

"But—marriage—it's a bargain of sorts too." Her resistance to him was melting again, making it difficult to think. "There has to be something we can do, some way to undo it."

"Not unless you can persuade the Almighty to change His mind, wench. We swore vows before Him, and I've been given to believe He takes such things rather seriously."

Those words, ground from his soul, were the final knell against her freedom; he was going to make her stay his wife. A shiver went up her spine. She could only begin to guess what being married to a man like the Iron Major entailed. But for starters, he seemed to think it gave him license to manhandle and humiliate her as he pleased.

She dropped her gaze, and her shoulders drooped as she turned away. The riot of feeling occurring inside her prevented her from seeing his exit, from hearing the latch jiggled and jammed from the outside. *More than she bargained for.* His words taunted her. She'd bargained for a bit of pleasure, a sweet bit of womanly joy. And she'd gotten *married.* She'd forgotten her pa, her people, her pride the minute he took her into his arms and worked his gentlemanly raptures on her susceptible body. She was probably getting just what she deserved.

She went to the window and threw open the shutters to admit the cold afternoon air and sun. Her eyes began to burn as they swept the symmetrical rows of blotchy canvas tents in the camp below. A movement at the edge of the camp caught her eye, and she recognized Charlie as he stood up, facing her, his concentration focused on the sight of her in the major's window. His features were indistinct, but something in his rigid stance, the intensity of his searching look spoke his anger. His image swam before Whitney's eyes as she watched his shoulders round and his gaze drop. He turned away and shuffled slowly to the far side of the tree. She blinked hard and squeezed the burning tears from her eyes.

. . . more than she bargained for.

The tavern was nearly filled with his men when Major Townsend descended the stairs. They'd been there when he had carried his bride up the stairs, and they had drunk a rowdy round to his connubial bliss. Now every one of them stopped dead, staring at him. He was a very different man from the fancy gent who'd ridden imperially at their head and insisted that everything be done with polish and precision. His elegant coat was held together with bits of bone, hair was unkempt and shaggy, there was a three-day shadow on his face. And there was a lean, hard look to him, a flint to his eye that spoke of hard times and even harder luck. Now, here was a man they could understand, a man they could follow.

"Just what in hell are the lot of you doing in here?" he growled, facing them.

"We wuz jus' havin' a tilt, Majur," Sergeant Laxault rasped, raising his tankard in evidence. "And we wuz waitin' . . . fer orders."

Garner's eyes narrowed on the tin cups they held in their hands. "Having a tilt of what?" He turned on Uncle Harvey, who stood behind the bar with a cherubic deviousness to his little smile. "Where in hell did you get that swill you're serving, Dedham?"

"Oh, I ain't charged 'em nothin' fer it, Majur." Uncle Harvey's grin broadened. "It be jus' the dregs o' that barrel ye cracked open at yer weddin'. There were quite a little bit o' it left."

"The hell there was—" Garner sneered. He had no lucid recollection of anything past a third cup of the swill, but he was sure that with all his men participating vigorously in his "bridal fête," there couldn't have been much left. The wily little inn-keeper had simply taken advantage of the situation to import some new brew . . . and they both knew it. And they both knew it was the major's behavior that gave him license to do it.

"Get rid of the rest of it, Dedham, or I'll smash the barrel myself." Then he turned on his men. "Put that rot and ruin down and get back to camp. We have a job to do."

They looked at each other, grins aborning, and did exactly what they were told.

Everywhere Garner Townsend went that afternoon, he was greeted with muffled grins and terse nods that bore a knowing, conspiratorial air. Uncle Radnor called him "son" in passing, Aunt Harriet Delaney mentioned that she had made pies that morning and offered him one to take to his bride, and everybody punctuated their answers to his questions with a wink. The pat-tern that had developed over the last two weeks was utterly re-versed; nobody stopped talking or withdrew when he approached, nobody hid what they were working on or what they were eating or drinking, and instead of avoiding Dedham's Tav-ern, everybody made it a point to bring in something to swap and the trading was brisk and spirited all day long.

It worked on him as he went about the settlement, the sly, knowing quality of their actions, their new casualness with re-spect to him. By dusk he was in a ripe mood, growing inversely more surly as their spirits rose. Lieutenant Brooks was more than happy to lead out the first patrol that evening, and at dusk he watched with a sour expression as they tramped off into the woods. He knew they'd find nothing. He turned back to the camp and strolled through it, steeling his nerve before going inside to face *her*. He soon found himself near the far edge of camp, feel-ing Charlie Dunbar's resentful stare like a physical prod.

He stopped, staring at the strapping, muscular buck who had hoped to make Whiskey Daniels his wife. Charlie had wanted what he himself had taken, her virtue, the legal rights to her sensual, unpredictable person. Something in the bleakness of Charlie's resentment struck a resonant chord inside him. Would he have felt the same way if Charlie Dunbar had been the one to bed then wed her? A long, suffocating moment later, he was calling Charlie's guards, instructing them to remove the shackles and set Charlie free.

Tension settled on the camp in the closing darkness, and as word of Charlie's release spread among the men, they raced to witness it. Charlie's gaze never wavered from the major as his bonds were loosened and removed. His muscular arms flexed as his fists tightened and his brown eyes heated so that they glowed like living coals of resentment. He knew why the major was setting him free, just as he knew the real reason the major had kept him in chains these last two weeks . . . and he hated it.

They faced each other briefly, and Garner jerked his head toward the clearing path. Charlie strode for his home without looking back. Garner watched until he was out of sight, ignoring the hushed talk around him, then headed for the tavern.

But he stopped short of going inside, leaning wearily against the wall, looking about the placid clearing. He dreaded facing *her,* especially since he had locked her in his room for the afternoon. Not an especially bright thing to do, he realized. She'd be venom-spitting furious by now and he was in no mood for one of their volatile confrontations.

He finally surrendered to the urge to think about her and about what had happened to him. He had wanted Whiskey Daniels with every straining sinew of his man's body. He had ached to possess those saucy lips, those sleek, muscular legs, that firm, rounded bottom. And he'd finally had them. Lord, how he'd had them. He'd never experienced such sensual delight with a woman— never gone to sleep in a woman's soft, silky arms before.

He tried to shake off a sudden and very unwelcome arousal. He'd been foully seduced, then generously pleasured straight into paradise. He'd been ruthlessly driven to drink, then tenderly nursed back to health. He'd been forced to marry a backwoods wench who strutted and bargained and *bit* him, and who brought him to full crowning tumescence every time she came within three feet of him. He'd wanted her; well, now he had her. What in bloody hell was he going to do with her . . . for the rest of his natural life?

The sound of his name roused him from such dread reflections. He looked up to find young Robbie Dedham staring at him with another of those worrisome grins he'd been seeing all day on the faces of the local folk.

"Where'd ye want yer supper tonight, Uncle Townsend? That Benson o'yers sent me to ask. Up in yer room or down in th' tavern wi' the rest of us?"

"*Uncle* Townsend?" He stiffened, looking at Robbie's guileless countenance. "Uncle *Townsend?*"

"Wull, I don' rightly know yer Christ-un name." Robbie read his shock with a puzzled frown.

Garner stared at him stupidly, unable to summon a single thought.

"Ain't Uncle Townsend all right?" Young Dedham took a wary step back. "Uncle Majur sounds kinda odd."

"Dammit." Garner merely breathed it. He was one of the "uncles" now, at least to young Dedham and Rapture's juvenile set. They'd accepted him into their midst, into their society as if . . . *as if he'd married into the bloody family!*

Good God. That accounted for the strange tenor of their interactions with him all afternoon, accepting and even discounting his presence, going on about their lives with an air of relief. They'd included him, accepted him into their midst, into their bizarre communal family. Those grins and winks and little offers of pie and small talk were all gestures of inclusion.

"In—in my room, thank you," he managed to say. It was a full minute after Robbie left before he could peel himself from the side of the tavern. His head was buzzing as he entered the tavern, but not so much that he couldn't see the Delbarton bucks at their usual table and Uncle Radnor and Uncle Ferrel by the fire, all drinking whiskey. He turned on Uncle Harvey, pointing furiously at their cups.

"I thought I told you to get rid of that swill."

"Well, I am"—Uncle Harvey grinned broadly—"jest as fast as they can drink it up. 'Twixt them an' yer boys, it'll be gone by mornin', son."

Garner's eyes closed and he shuddered visibly. *Son.* Not even his own father ever called him *son.* He turned and tromped up the stairs, his insides strangely liquid and draining toward his boots. What was happening to him?

Pausing in the dim upper hallway, he struggled to collect himself, and after a deep, restoring breath, he reached for the door latch and froze. It was open, freed! He trembled for one agonizing minute as the pressure built inside him, then lurched through the unlocked door, knowing she'd be gone.

Whitney darted up from her chair as he came hurtling through the door. He stopped, just inside, his booted legs spread, his chest heaving. Surprise registered on his face when he saw her, and after a moment he eased and made quite a business of straightening his coat front. His ears grew red and he lifted his square chin to an arrogant angle as he surveyed the room, then her.

I must look a mess was her very first thought. Eyes red, nose swollen. Crying was all she'd managed to do that afternoon. She'd been interrupted twice, once by a fellow who described himself as the major's "aide," Benson, and a second time by Robbie Dedham, who came to bring a new candle and extra blankets. The door latch had been jammed, Benson explained, scratching his head over how it came to be so. Then, just minutes ago, Robbie and Benson had both returned with a tray of food, a small pot of coffee, and word that the major had just released Charlie Dunbar. And Whitney's afternoon-long struggle to gain control of her feelings went for naught. She had put her face in her hands and sobbed again.

And now here he was, looking her over like a mare on the block. She moved woodenly, keeping him in sight as he closed the door and came forward. She stiffened and had to stay the urge to run a hand up over her hair.

"You let Charlie go," she declared softly, losing her battle to avoid his eyes. They were so blue and clear just now, in the candlelight.

"How did you hear—"

"Robbie and that fellow Benson told me."

That explained the mystery of the unlocked door, though not the mystery of her continuing presence in his room. He nodded and waved her to a seat beside the tray on the bed as he settled on the other side of it.

"N-no, thank you. I'm not hungry." She wrapped her arms around her waist in a gesture that divulged an unexpected bit of insecurity in her.

"You didn't have dinner," he admonished, feeling strangely responsible and parental, and very uncomfortable with such feelings. "I'll not be held responsible for your wasting away, wench. Sit." When she didn't obey, he declared with greater force, "You have to eat, wench."

"Whitney," she whispered, feeling strangely hollow. "My name is Whitney."

A giant hand closed around his throat, forbidding a single word. He nodded and waved to the bed across the tray from him, and after a moment she settled there. Neither moved nor spoke for a time as each confronted the problem of their unsought union. It was done. And where did they go from here?

"You took care of me while I was . . . ill," he declared, trying desperately not to look at her reddened eyes and miserable face.

" 'In sickness and in health,' I said." She couldn't look at him either. "And a Daniels never goes back on his word."

Garner's chest grew crowded and his face darkened. He'd never felt less like eating in his life, or more hungry.

It was a somber meal and, despite the miraculous improvement in Dedham's cuisine, it was utterly tasteless as well. Afterward, Whitney made to carry the tray downstairs and he prevented her, saying that was Benson's task. Then he surprised her by asking if she would like to go down to the tavern's warmth for a while. She nodded and he took her by the wrist and led her out the door. In the darkened hallway she raised her hand between them, staring at the lean fingers wrapped possessively around her wrist.

"I won't run from you, Major. A Daniels never runs from anything." She turned her face up to his with a searching look.

He nodded and released her, feeling oddly hollow inside.

In the tavern she managed to return the Delbartons' greetings and settled by Uncle Ferrel and Uncle Radnor by the hearth. She watched strapping Mike Delbarton emerge from a huddle of heads over their table of cards and rise to snare the major's attention.

"How 'bout sittin' a hand or two with us, Majur?" he invited genially.

Whitney's head snapped up in time to catch Garner's unnerved look. He stumbled verbally, reddened, and declined with a choked "Some other time, perhaps."

Mike's grin broadened as he sank back onto his stool, and there were muffled but still audible comments about a fellow's first week of wedded life taking a lot out of him. And they turned with sly grins to glance at Whitney, whose face now matched the wheezing red coals in the hearth beside her.

She waited long enough to be sure they wouldn't connect her departure with their lusty remarks, and headed for the stairs. Her heart began to thud when Garner rose to escort her, and by the time they reached the darkened top of the stairs, her blood was roaring in her ears.

Once inside his room, Garner lit the single candle again and stood awkwardly, testing the wary truce between them.

"I should have sent for your things." He turned to his leather kit and pulled a clean shirt from it, thrusting it into her hands. "Perhaps you'll find that useful. Sleep well . . . Whitney." He fled, carrying with him the look of relief on her face.

Benson startled her with a knock some minutes later. She was still standing there, clutching the soft shirt to her, looking at the door. The pleasant-faced fellow had brought a tin box of live coals and a pitcher of fresh water and insisted on warming the bed himself, saying it was his duty. Something about "gentlemun's gentlemun," then he bobbed a bit of a bow that left Whitney speechless, and withdrew.

Recovering, she undressed quickly and doused the candle. She slipped into Garner Townsend's shirt and into his warmed bed, half wishing it were into his arms instead. As she lay in the drowsy warmth, she thought about his subdued courtesy after supper, and of his "servant," which was surely what Benson was, and about the fact that he wouldn't let her carry their supper tray downstairs. She had thought it was because he didn't trust her, but now wondered if there might be another, more gentlemanly reason.

For the first time, she wondered what his other life, in Boston, was like. He was wealthy, undoubtedly. Real gold buttons and such. Probably had servants. And family? Did he have family? She knew all kinds of things about him, his routine of hygiene and his culinary habits, his stubborn eastern loyalty, and his upright and uncompromising character. She knew how to make him lose his temper and how to make him moan with pleasure. But the really important things about him, the workings of his inner self—his ambitions, his fears, his longings, his past—were very much a mystery to her. Then the most nagging unknowns of all surfaced in her mind. What did her marriage mean to the future of Rapture's people? And what was a very proper Boston gentleman like him going to do with a wife like her?

Half of her questions were answered the next morning when she learned Garner had led out another of his patrols. When he returned, he nodded, took a bite to eat, and went straight to his bed. Whitney didn't see him again until late afternoon. She spent a very long morning seeing well-meaning well-wishers in Dedham's Tavern. Every woman in Rapture brought her something to set up housekeeping with and a bit of marital advice, both of which properly mortified her. Housekeeping? Her?

Late morning, Aunt Kate appeared in the tavern with a small leather satchel filled with her clothes and a worried expression. They hugged, and Kate cried a bit, and Whitney reassured her. When Whitney asked about her pa, Kate was tellingly silent, except to reveal that Charlie Dunbar had come to see Black and that they'd celebrated his freedom with half a jug of Black's best whiskey. Pressed further, Kate expressed her fears about Black's state of mind, about his angry vow to continue his distilling operations "come hell or high water." Whitney's first instinct was to go to him, to talk him into laying low until the soldiers left. But Kate was adamant; the sight of her would only agitate him further. Whitney watched Kate's departure with a horrible sinking inside.

She retreated to his room midafternoon, seeking a bit of privacy and some space to think. But as she entered, she came face-to-face with him, bootless, shirtless, shaving. He had whirled and coiled by reflex at the sound of her entry. But at the sight of her he straightened, seeming to grow before her eyes. And for a spellbinding minute, all she could see was the muscular symmetry of his wide chest and the lacy pattern of black hair over that tight, mounded flesh. The air between them charged quickly, and both turned away with flushed faces and constricting throats.

Later that afternoon he found her carrying a bucket of water from the creek for Louise Dedham and admonished her to leave such work for Benson and the Dedhams. When he made to take the bucket from her, she stubbornly thrust it out of his reach and he found himself pressing full against her. His fingers closed over hers, and a spark of excitement flashed between them as he brushed against her breasts, her shoulders, her skirts. She relinquished the bucket but he didn't move. He stood looking down at her tantalizing lips, refusing to separate himself from her. It was only Louise Dedham's unwitting intrusion that broke them apart.

By the time he escorted her to their room that night, Whitney was alive with tension, vibrating with a sensory hunger she could not satisfy with a mere glimpse of his long, muscular legs. Garner was no better off. All evening he had observed each seductive bend of her waist and sway of her skirts in an agony of awareness, craving the delights they concealed. His entire consciousness had narrowed to one driving reality; she was his. His woman. His wife. The knowledge had worked on his newly freed passions all afternoon. It was done; they were legally bound, entitled. The raptures that turned him inside out were his.

"Aunt Kate brought me some things today." She turned to him in the candlelight and found his eyes glowing golden with the reflection of it. Her whole body tightened and she simply held out to him the shirt he'd lent her the night before. When he didn't move to take it from her, she felt her heart beating faster and lowered the garment. "Of course, I'll be obliged to wash it first."

He reached for it belatedly, but her fingers now refused to

surrender it. As he pulled determinedly, her arms came with it, then the rest of her. Closer . . . closer . . .

"I have other shirts, Whitney. Lots of other shirts." When she was close enough, he transferred his hands to her waist, mastering her stiff resistance with gentle caressing motions.

"F-four"—she let the shirt fall to the floor between them—"you have four shirts."

"Unh-unh." He shook his head gently as he pulled her eyes into his and continued that relentless conquering of the space between them. "Forty. At least forty."

"Forty shirts?" She hardly heard what she was saying for the thudding of her own heart. "But you can wear only one at a time."

"True." He tightened around her so that her breasts crushed softly against his chest. A trill raced along his nerves and plunged into his loins. "Perhaps I should have some help . . . wearing them." His mouth lowered to her raised, parted lips. "Help me, Whitney."

Thirteen

His desire-roughened voice rasped over her skin, setting her entire body aflame with the need to answer. Her arms came up to circle him, and she raised onto her toes to open to his kiss. He tantalized her lips, nibbling and licking them, then delving into the spicy sweetness of her mouth. She met his tongue with hunger, holding it, savoring it, sucking it in gentle imitation of a larger fulfillment yet to come.

Shocked heat struck a spark, and desire exploded inside him. He groaned and clasped her to him as though he could somehow take her inside him, imprison her there. His hands flew over her waist and back, her shoulders and her tawny hair, wanting to cover her all at once. The eager rise of her response sent him spiraling beyond the reach of reason—careening toward paradise again.

Their potent, molten kisses drew heat and energy from all over their bodies, leaving them trembling. With burning faces and glistening eyes they parted and sent clumsy fingers to buttons and lacings. He ripped his coat and shirt from his shoulders, then peeled her skirt and petticoat from her, pushing them down into a heap about her ankles. Her shirt came off next and he replaced it with his, draping it about her shoulders, then caressing her hard-tipped breasts through its soft linen.

"It feels so much better on you," he groaned softly, sliding into a mischievous grin that dazzled her. She'd never imagined the natural hauteur of his aristocratic features could melt into such a rougish and charming expression.

He lifted her into his arms and carried her to the bed. She was clad only in his shirt and her boots, and shortly, he was removing the boots, running his hands over her trim ankles and slender feet, then up her shapely, muscular calves. His touch polished her skin, made it glow as he explored her. Every bit of girlish shock, every vestige of maidenly reserve, was drowned in the liquid flow of sensation engulfing her.

"I've watched your legs, wench . . . ached to touch them," he rasped softly, raising one of her knees and covering it with nipping kisses. "So strong and sleek, no wonder you run like a Thoroughbred." His fingers drifted down the inside of her upraised thigh, and she quivered and raised her other leg to clamp them together, trapping his hand between them.

"Want to inspect my teeth too, Major?" she purred, fighting the urge to wriggle against his hand, to let it slide to the burning flesh between her thighs.

"No." He laughed raggedly, bending closer as he raised his other hand, which still bore fading red marks from her bite. "I've had ample proof your teeth are sound. I'm about to set hands to you again, wench." His voice dropped, vibrating her extremities as he lowered his head and poured his breath over her mouth.

"Are you going to bite me again?"

"Do you want me to?"

She raised her chin to bring their mouths together and took his succulent bottom lip between her teeth, raking it gently.

He erupted, sinking both arms beneath her and shuddering at the heat of her kisses. And at that moment he lost himself completely in the marvel of her bright, passionate being. She was pure element, like the vaporous lightning that rose in the cauldron of a Scots-Irish still, like the roaring flame that separated rare liquor from its base beginnings, like the cool, dark earth that patiently yielded the grain that was both source and substance for the brew. She was passion and wonder and beginning; in her body were all the secrets of creation, the mystery and meaning of life itself, hidden and awaiting him, beckoning.

"I thought I must have dreamed that first time, it was so good," he whispered against the base of her throat. "God—how I've wanted you, Whitney, remembered the feel of you." His mouth reached her nipple and fastened on it as his fingers kneaded the cool, silky mound around it.

She felt him slide between her thighs, covering her, invading her, blurring everything but the pleasure of his driving strength. She chilled and burned in the cool air, giving herself over to him, wanting whatever he would do to her. His lips traversed the valley between peaks, and lavished the same irresistible attention on her other nipple before continuing downward. The brazen fire of his mouth on her belly set her wriggling, and he braced and cupped her sweet buttocks in his hands and nuzzled the gingery curls at the base of her belly. A moan escaped her as she watched him, crouched over her like a great dark cat set to spring and devour her.

"Love me," she breathed, the longings of her heart, mind, and body all compressed into that soft whisper. "Fill me . . . again."

His boots landed somewhere across the room and his breeches followed them into oblivion. He sank into her arms and her kiss, engulfing her in a steamy vapor of sensation that seeped into her blood. And soon his hardened shaft began to condense that feeling into the liquid heat of her flesh. He rubbed and tantalized her sensitive body, whispering her name over and over.

She arched and gasped and ran her hands over his back, then shyly clasped his buttocks as he had hers. He groaned and his body flexed to invade the creamy heat of her with a series of deepening thrusts.

"Oh, Major—"

"Garner—" he corrected her, stirring swirls of sensation in her hardened nipples with his tongue. He rested deep inside her, touching all of her at once, everything there was. "Is this what you wanted?"

"Yes, oh, yes . . ." She sucked air through her teeth in a rapturous hiss. The boundaries of her body seemed to have melted, merging her response with his. She met the sinuous commands of his movement eagerly, arching her hips, seeking more of him. And with her deepening response, his smooth, rhythmic motion strengthened, caressing her inside and out, bringing them together harder, faster. Each stroke took them higher, on rising, heated currents that rushed toward paradise.

She burned for completion, for the release of her tortured senses. And suddenly his motions slowed, became powerful exaggerations of loving that flung her through that last unseen threshold like a wave crashing onto pleasure's vast shores. The fragile barrier of being burst around her and within her shattered her senses like precious crystal, seared her nerves into wide-open streams of perception.

The storm of her release broke around him, sweeping him into its center, plunging him into that same breaking tide of release and fulfillment. She heard his moans coming from her own lips, felt his convulsive shudders as though they began inside her. And they were joined irrevocably in an intimacy ordained to conquer and rule the stubborn heads and hearts of mankind.

"Garner—" She wet her tender lips and managed a deep, shuddering breath sometime later. They lay much as they had loved, legs entwined, arms encircling, sinking into the soft comfort of love's sleep.

"Ummmm?" His dark head nuzzled the dewy skin of her shoulder lazily. His long-lashed eyes were lidded with deep satisfaction.

"I'm sorry I bit you."

"I must be drunk with you, my hot little Whiskey. I didn't feel a thing."

"I mean . . . yesterday."

He rumbled indulgently and lay his head back, closing his eyes "Oh, I intend to make you pay for that . . . someday. . . ."

When she raised her head to look, he was grinning like a devil.

The pounding at the door shook the darkened room in the middle of the night like peals of summer thunder. Garner sprang upright, his heart pounding and his eyes dry with alarm. The placid darkness of his room stayed him a half-second, then he bounded from the bed, his senses jolted to full capacity and his mind scrambling to make sense of their jumbled messages.

"M-j-rr!"

Brooks's frantic call righted in Garner's brain, and he stopped,

running his hands back through his hair, then shaking his head
to clear it. The cold air made him suck in breath as he cast about
for his breeches.

"Coming!" he yelled, finding his voice sleep-rusted, and
growling to clear it. "What is it, Brooks? This had better be
important—" And in the instant it took him to find and pull on
his breeches, he realized it *was* important. Otherwise, stoic
Brooks wouldn't be assaulting his door in the middle of the night.

"It's happening—tonight—now!" Brooks lurched forward,
nearly bowling Garner over the minute the door opened. In the
lantern light, the lieutenant's face was beet red and damp, and
he panted wildly. "They're moving the whiskey out now—right
now! Kingery spotted them while we were on patrol—out by the
sandstone cliffs—in the south valley! There's barrels and barrels
of the stuff!"

Garner quivered a moment as the news sank in, then erupted
into action, snatching the lantern from Brooks's hand and gathering his boots and coat from the floor. "How many?"

"Half a dozen or more." He frowned and lowered his eyes to
add, "Charlie Dunbar's with them."

"Dammit. Rouse the rest of the men. Have them on their feet
and marching in three minutes—I'll be there in two!"

"Yes, sir!"

Brooks tore out of the door and down the stairs as Garner
whirled, searching for his shirt. He spotted it on the floor by the
bed and sprang for it, coming up with it straight into Whitney's
bewildered stare. He froze momentarily and felt himself coiling
inside.

"Wha-what's happened? What's wrong?" She clutched the
quilts against her bare breasts. She blinked, trying to make sense
of the banging and shouting, and of the strange look on his face.

"The whiskey—they're moving it out." As he said it, his jaws
began to harden and his grip tightened on the soft linen in his
hand. He rose slowly, watching a spark of recognition strike her
eyes, and the way she quickly veiled it with her lashes. "I have
to go—" He backed a step and shrugged into his shirt, neglecting
the pearl fastenings.

"The whiskey? You mean . . . tonight? They're . . ." Full realization dawned as she watched him pull on his boots. Her heart lurched and began to pound frantically. "And you're going after them now?" The full horror of it condensed in her mind and rained through her like hailstones, stripping the middle of her bare. She struggled to the edge of the bed, taking the quilt with her. "Garner, you can't—"

He froze, his coat half on. His face was a hard mask, but it wasn't enough to protect the vulnerable parts of him from the sight of her. There she stood, wrapped in that same damned quilt, tousled from his loving, eyes like luminous green sapphires, lips trembling. Everything in him shrank from the lush reality of her, recoiling, contracting around a long-festering wound in him that she had reopened once again. A second time . . . the thought raked him like steel claws. He'd taken her to his bed again and for the second time had risen from her loving into pure turmoil. And disaster hadn't even waited for daylight this time.

"Can't?" His gray eyes narrowed and he braced, feeling his belly tighten for the coming blow. "Can't what?"

"It's my pa," she choked, taking a step toward him and stopping.

"Undoubtedly," he managed to say through clenched jaws.

"But . . . we . . . after . . ." She clutched the quilt to her desperately, acutely aware of her nakedness. She dragged her eyes from his in shame and rising despair. He'd boldly declared his intention to bring Black Daniels to "federal" justice, tossing it at Black's feet like a gauntlet, knowing a man like her pa would have to take it up. And she had watched it. She'd known a confrontation was inevitable, and still she'd gone to his bed. What could she say? Were there any words in the world that could dissuade him from the duty he held above all else?

"Did you know?" he demanded with a tight desperation that changed abruptly into deep, humiliated anger as he answered himself. "God. Of course you knew. It was all a part of the plan, wasn't it?" The accusation flailed him as viciously as it did her. He quivered, suspended between pain and rage, scarcely able to believe the unthinkable pain he'd walked into with his eyes wide open. Again. It had happened again, only the pain was worse, much worse.

"No, Garner, I didn't— Please—"

"You kept me 'entertained,' while they moved out the liquor. And, God—" He ran a trembling hand back through his tousled hair. "I certainly was accommodating, wasn't I? I even released your friend Dunbar so he could help."

"I didn't know," she whispered, seeking his burning eyes and feeling their fire deep in her heart. She moved toward him like a moth to a flame. "Pa was just so angry about me. And he hates the tax so. Please—"

He watched her come, feeling the sway of her body, feeling the pull she exerted on the very center of his being. He watched her grasp his sleeve and felt that same hand closing around his aching heart.

"There has to be another way."

"Another little Jezebel bargain?" He wrenched away and started for the door. "Not on your life. I have a duty to perform, and God knows I've let you interfere with it long enough. I'm going to bring Black Daniels in if it kills me." The cold intensity of his look as he turned back was shattering. "Now, there's a thought to warm the cockles of your icy little heart—perhaps I'll die in the fight tonight and leave you a rich widow."

The door slammed and her eyes squeezed shut. She grappled with it, fighting the suffocating waves of pain crashing over her. Garner was going after her pa. The man to whom she had given herself now hunted the man who had given her life and love and being. She staggered to the bed and sank weakly on it, staring through blurred, unseeing eyes.

They were both strong men, tenacious, principled, and proud. Everything about them clashed; their backgrounds, occupations, politics, their sense of duty. Their ironclad convictions had finally drawn them into open battle, and they met on the vulnerable ground of Whitney's heart.

She collapsed on the bed, burying her face in the pillow to muffle her sobs. Her bare shoulders quaked as she surrendered to the overwhelming pain of a heart being torn in half. Her father had been her world, her guide, her friend, her teacher, and the first love of her girlish heart. And Garner Townsend had ridden into Rapture on his big horse, with his arrogant jaw set and his gold buttons gleaming, and had ridden straight into her heart as well. She had come to care for the arrogant, impervious Yankee in ways she hadn't imagined existed. He made her burn with both anger and pleasure and challenged her wit and her spirit. He led her into new feelings of desire and tenderness and made her react in new ways, made her want new things.

She slowly calmed, and as her swirling emotions settled, she wiped her face on the rough pillow and took a deep breath. The problem was, she wanted them both. Probably typical of a Delilah, she sighed miserably, not being satisfied with one man. She sniffed and staunched yet another wave of tears. Garner knew she'd schemed and planned his first disgrace and now was convinced she'd used and betrayed him again. How could he think that after what they'd shared, in this very bed? Lord, he must think her a base and heartless creature, conniving and beguiling and betraying— No Daniels would ever—

Her very breath stopped. No Daniels ever sat by and watched something he loved destroyed without putting up a fight. What was she doing lying here, crying buckets and feeling sorry for herself?

She scrambled to her feet and dragged her jumbled hair back out of her face. She had to get out there, had to see they didn't kill each other. She stumbled on the blanket and looked frantically down at her bare legs. Clothes—she had to have clothes!

A heavy mist shrouded the low south valley in brooding expectation. All sound was muffled by the moisture-laden air and the thick blanket of wet leaves that covered the ground. The wet trunks of bare trees stood like stark sentries along the banks of the creek, but they sounded no warning of the impending clash of federal and local forces. The peace of the forest stretched on, unconcerned with the affairs of men.

Garner deployed his men strategically along the creek, focusing them on the pale sandstone cliffs above that glowed eerily in the light of predawn. They'd arrived in time to see the last of the barrels being loaded onto the backs of mules and horses. He quickly scouted the area, decided on his strategy, and now watched from a rocky outcropping on the far side of the stream, an outcropping the rebels would soon have to pass beneath on their way out of the canyonlike basin.

He counted the men through his field glass. There were nine, and he recognized every one of them. Black Daniels and Charlie Dunbar were prominent among them, and there was that Delaney fellow and the one they called "Uncle Sam" Durant, both of whom had appeared in the valley about the time of Daniels's return from Pittsburgh. Mike Delbarton and his brother, Cully. Uncle Radnor, old Uncle Julius, and even older Uncle Ballard . . . *God.* He couldn't even say their names without putting "uncle" before them. And look at it—they must have rounded up every four-legged creature in the whole damned valley to carry the stuff!

His face burned in the darkness as his eyes sought Black Daniels's striking features that were so much like hers. And the cold, relentless prickle of betrayal ran across his shoulders once again. His belly tightened with the expectation of violence. Perhaps he shouldn't have given the order to fire only as a last resort. Unbidden, Whitney's luminous eyes rose in his mind, pleading still. And he wiped them from his thoughts.

The water was shallow enough for easy crossing a short distance upstream, and Garner watched Black Daniels lead two horses with two more tied behind, across it. His shoulders hunched as the others fell into line behind, filing across the creek, headed straight into his hands. The thudding of his heart was counterpoint to the muffled tread of hooves, both marking the labored passage of time. And on they came, kegs jostling and swaying at the animals' sides.

Garner waited until they'd all made it across and were directly below the ledge where he hid, making for the nearby trees. He leaned back to get Brooks's attention and found him already watching for the signal. His mouth was dry, his gut was twisting as he raised his hand and saw Brooks rise to a crouch, raising his hand in response. Garner looked at the men below, men whose faces he knew, and he gritted his teeth and gave the signal.

Shouts rang out, and dark-coated figures hurtled down the rocky slope and charged from the nearby trees, scattering the column of men and animals in confusion. Black's party had no chance to reach for their guns, and in the mayhem that followed they dodged and then clamored to swing with hastily grabbed branches and bare fists at the soldiers bearing down on them.

Garner was in the first wave down the slope, launching straight for Black Daniels himself. Black recognized him by the glowing braid on his shoulders and bashed free of another soldier to meet him, swinging and snarling. They locked fists and grappled and thrashed, pushing for advantage—each half blinded by the personal rage in his own eyes. Black broke free only to charge again, slamming into Garner's middle, sending him stumbling back into the horses and cracking his head on a wooden barrel. He scrambled, managing to keep his feet under him, shaking his head to clear it. A split-second later, he lunged at Black's wide chest and they crashed into the underbrush together, grappling and pounding, fists connecting.

Around them, knives flashed in the dim light, and the snarls and grunts and shouts grew frenzied as the fight intensified. Then one by one, the heaving knots of violence stilled as Rapture's distillers went down before the overwhelming federal force. The old uncles first, then Delaney and Cully Delbarton and Mike and Uncle Sam and Uncle Radnor. And soon Rapture's men were either insensible on the ground or being restrained by Garner's men—all, that is, except Black Daniels and Charlie Dunbar.

Garner's superior size and hardship-honed endurance finally placed him above Black Daniels's thrashing form with just the right angle and just the right force to land a stunning blow to his jaw. Garner felt him go slack, and dragged himself to his knees, panting, dimly aware of Brooks standing by, then offering him assistance up.

The light was growing, the day approaching. And as Garner Townsend rose to his feet in the growing silence, Rapture's distillers lay at his feet, just as he had vowed they would.

He surveyed the damage and found a few of his men sustaining slash wounds—nothing serious, he was relieved to learn. They held the younger uncles and the bucks in vise-tight grips, awaiting orders. The major came forward to take command, his vision clearing, his face set like ruddy granite. He pointed back to Black Daniels's moaning, rousing form.

"Get him on his feet and bind him good and tight." Then he turned to locate Charlie Dunbar and found four—*four!*—of his men having a devil of a time holding the powerful buck. "And him, get him in ropes as well, Laxault!"

"Yessir, Majur," the gravel-voiced sergeant said as he stalked forward.

"Cut those barrels free and take the axes to them." He stopped at the sight of a dull red gleam on the crusty sergeant's hand and arm. "How bad is it?"

"Not so bad I can't swing me an ax," Laxault drawled with a fierce grin. "Come on, you shank's-mare dragoons"—he waved his good arm—"let's get to it!"

"The hell you will—" Charlie Dunbar said, lunging violently against his captors, surprising them and gaining enough freedom to swing and bash his way clear. Bluecoats rushed him, but he was already in motion, barreling straight for the Iron Major. He smacked into Garner's chest, shoving him, backward into a tree trunk before Garner could counter his momentum, and it was a long, seething grapple before the soldiers managed to pull him from their commander.

"Damn you, Townsend!" Charlie said, thrashing and jerking convulsively, spitting and red-eyed with rage. "It's all we got! You got no right to it—you an' yer fancy-arsed fed'rals!" He jerked to a heaving halt, and his burning eyes met Garner's in undimmed challenge. "Ye already took more'n ye had a right to!" Every man in the clearing knew exactly what "more" Charlie meant. "Fight me like a man for her, dammit!"

Anger, pure and unalloyed, erupted in Garner's middle as he stalked forward, his shoulders braced and his fists clenching. "Let him go."

"B-but, Majur—" Lieutenant Brooks protested, only to be overridden by Laxault's glower. *These two had a score to settle,* that look said, and a moment later Charlie Dunbar was freed.

Charlie lost no time making good his threat. He lunged for

Garner's throat and met a stone wall of resistance that jarred every bone in his body. He strained to get his fingers near that corded neck, but the Iron Major proved his name and yielded not an inch.

They grappled and staggered, locked in mortal combat until the major's boot snagged Charlie's leg and a herculean shove sent him sprawling backward on the ground. "Get up, dammit," Garner snarled, crouching with fists raised and eyes white-hot with anger. Charlie rolled and sprang to his feet, lunging with fists aimed for Garner's fury-bronzed face.

That blow was deflected, as was Garner's counterpunch, but the next connected viciously with his belly and the next with his jaw. Bright rockets of pain exploded in Garner's skull, showering burning sparks through his neck and shoulders, and somehow the pain shocked him onto a higher level of intensity.

He came at Charlie like a wounded bear, roaring, thundering. Time and time again his fists connected—bone and sinew crunched, flesh smacking flesh. And when Dunbar's fists plowed into his own head and body, he scarcely felt them. Something primal claimed him as he fought for undisputed possession of his victory, and for possession of the mate he had already claimed.

Whitney burst through the trees that lined the stream, frantically following the din of fighting. Her legs felt like mush, her lungs burned, and her ankle screamed pain from a fall she'd taken half a mile back. She ran toward the cliffs and the cave where her pa stored their whiskey, and stumbled to a halt as she realized the noise was coming from across the creek at the edge of the tall trees. She staggered and sagged against a stone outcropping.

The noise stopped, and across the creek men staggered to their feet, some hauling others up. She held her breath as more and more upright bodies appeared, some jerking angrily against restraint. It was over, and it was clear the bluecoats had been the victors. Tears blurred her sight.

Then a burst of shouts reached her, and she wiped her eyes on her sleeves, staring hard into the misty gloom. Shock had galvanized the soldiers; they were huddling into a circle, shouting, shoving. *It wasn't over!* She jolted forward, scrambling down the creek bank and to the ford, thrashing through the water to the other side.

"No!" Whitney's voice was just recognizable above the shouts and chaos of the human ring that surrounded Charlie and the major. She wormed and pushed her way through to the front, wailing at the sight that greeted her. Garner and Charlie, bloodied and pain-maddened, grappling furiously.

"Stop!" she yelled, darting for the middle of them.

Even through the mingled roar of pain and blood in his head, Garner heard her, and caught the flash of movement toward them. The shock cost him a split-second he couldn't afford to spend. "Whit—"

Charlie's lacerated fist snapped Garner's head back viciously, and he reeled into a clutch of his men, who just kept him from hitting the ground. Laxault rushed to intercept her, tackling her from the side and bearing her out of the way.

"No—I have to stop them!" She wriggled furiously in the burly sergeant's grip, but he held her fast. Before her horrified eyes, Garner straightened and shook groggily, searching for her and finding her held safely at bay. And the look on her face, the fear . . . the anguish . . . He lowered his shoulders and charged Charlie again, this time with the strength of two men.

Her presence had done something to him, had upped the stakes in some unexplainable way. And the raw desperation and anger her betrayal generated in him was now shunted into the seething turmoil that fueled his strength. He came at Charlie in a blind, heedless rage. His fists came like lightning bolts, and Charlie, sensing the change in him, fought with the desperation of a man staring into the jaws of defeat. Another rain of blows, another grapple and twist and a hard left to the gut, and Charlie went down to stay.

Garner staggered aside, his face and lip cut, his eye dark and swelling, his gentlemanly coat spattered with blood . . . and a cheer went up from the Maryland Ninth. Lieutenant Brooks hurried forward, offering him a steadying arm and a handkerchief. Those men not directly restraining prisoners crowded around, congratulating him on a "damned fine fight." It took him a minute to get his legs beneath him again, and his first thought was her. He squinted through the pain in his head and located Whitney, stilled, with Laxault's arms about her waist. Her face was red, her eyes closed, as though she couldn't bear the sight of her precious people, her blessed "family," in defeat.

He should have felt some pleasure, some triumph in his hardwon victory. God knows he'd earned it, every bit of it. But one look at her cheated him of all elation, of all pride in the very personal nature of his victory.

Dammit—he growled—nothing was going to interfere with his triumph, especially not *her*. He wheeled and roared orders for Charlie to be bound, and for the barrels to be destroyed, all but four, which were to be taken back and used as evidence. His men sprang to the task of splitting the oak barrels with raw enthusiasm. And as each cask was breeched, and a stream of the pale yellow liquor burst forth, a thirsty soldier was there to sample it before a second bash sent it gushing onto the thirsty ground. Soon the wrecking of the barrels took on a heady atmosphere of abandon and release.

Laxault dragged Whitney out of the way, toward the trees. As she turned her burning eyes from the destruction of her pa's proud labor, she glimpsed her pa himself, being set on his feet, his arms bound behind him. She came to life in Laxault's grasp, surprising him, and was able to wrest free. She was halfway across the clearing when Garner saw, and jolted to intercept her.

Whitney saw him coming and scrambled to a halt. Her eyes ached at the sight of his wounds, and at the cold fury and contempt in his battered visage as he stopped several feet away. He watched her and waited. She bit her lip and turned toward her pa. He was standing, captive but still defiant, watching her too.

She was buffeted by powerful waves of conflicting feeling. Her desire to go to her pa was matched by her desire for Garner Townsend, the Iron Major who had just defeated her and her people. In one breath she realized why they were both staring at her, their eyes hot, their stances challenging. She stood, fifteen feet from either of them . . . *being forced to choose.*

She tried to swallow her heart back into her chest. She

wouldn't, *couldn't* choose. They had no right to make her. And she did what any Daniels would do, confronting such a rotten deal. She turned on her heel and walked away.

Soon she was running.

Black Daniels and Charlie Dunbar were ensconced, side by side, in chains under what had become known as "Dunbar's tree," as soon as they returned to the settlement. In a surprising move, the Iron Major assembled his other prisoners and, after a stern lecture on the dangers of resuming any distilling operation in the valley, released them to their homes and teary-eyed families. He declared that only Black Daniels and Charlie Dunbar, the obvious leaders of the operation, would be shipped off to Pittsburgh to be formally tried and punished. It took some of the sting from news of the destruction of a whole year's production of "liquid currency."

The major cleaned up, had Benson doctor his face, and set out on horseback for the Daniels farmstead. He hadn't seen Whitney since she disappeared into the woods just after dawn, but her small leather case of clothes was missing from his room and he had a fair idea what that meant. His face and mood were dark indeed as he scoured the side yard of the farmstead, then dismounted to barge straight into the kitchen. Whitney started up from the table where she sat with her aunt Kate, and dashed through the keeping room. His battle-charged reflexes were quicker, and he caught her midway through the parlor.

She strained under his hold and refused to meet his look. Her heart wrenched painfully in her chest. "Why did you have to come—what do you want?"

"You." The pain in his face and in his gut made him brutally blunt.

"Am I under arrest?"

"God knows, you deserve it."

In the long silence she still refused to look at him, and confusion began to invade his anger. She seemed so young and so hurt, and he was a damned fool for letting himself think such things. She was a deceiver. An unscrupulous Jezebel who used his passion for her to undermine his sworn duty and his pride and dignity as a man. She'd read his fatal weakness fluently and seduced and betrayed him, and he'd allowed it. *Twice*. He wouldn't make that mistake ever again.

"You're my wife. Do you honestly think I'd arrest my legal wife, no matter how richly she deserved it?"

"Then—" She swallowed hard and started over, lifting her thickly lashed eyes to his stern face. "What are you going to do with me?"

"I'm taking you back to Boston with me," he declared, only now realizing the full, terrible ramifications of their marriage. He was going to have to take her to his home, to face his influential family. He shuddered. Beyond that catastrophe, he didn't want to think.

"Why? Why can't you just leave me here? If you're rich, can't you hire a fancy lawyer or something and find some way out of it?"

"No."

That single, awful syllable spoke plainly his disgust at the inescapable fact of their legal entanglement.

"Townsends don't make vows easily, but when we do, we keep them to the letter. 'Till death do us part,' whether we like it or not. Townsend wives belong in Townsend homes . . . in Boston." The ring of "Townsend righteousness" closed on her like the door of a stone crypt, sealing her fate. That infamous "Townsend pride" meant that "Townsend property" had to be secured. That's what she was now . . . Townsend property. She sagged and dropped her gaze. Her father's punishment was a bit of prison, but hers was far worse—a lifetime of living with the Iron Major.

"Get your things," he ordered with muted gruffness.

He waited for her to pack, and she paused at the foot of the stairs when she came down, looking around the snug keeping room, touching things with her eyes as though storing a few last impressions. Then he took her arm and led her through the kitchen. Kate was there, looking ashen and distraught.

"When will you leave?" she asked through a haze of misery.

"Tomorrow, at sunup," he answered.

"I'll come to see Blackstone this evening . . . if it's permitted?"

When he nodded, she turned to Whitney, fighting back the tears. The two people who had become Kate's whole world were being taken from her. She hugged her niece tightly, then drew away and forced her chin high as they left. From the window she watched as the major lifted Whitney onto his horse and swung up behind her. And when they rounded the first turn on the path, Kate buried her head in her arms and sobbed.

Fourteen

The Iron Major led his men out of the valley the next morning, marching them in a slender column down the same road that had led them into Rapture. Behind him came the spoils of his victory: four barrels of potent Daniels whiskey, two leaders of the Daniels "whiskey ring," and one tantalizing but treacherous Daniels female who just happened to also be his wife. The entire campaign had been a disaster from start to finish. But when he left this wretched valley, he thought, even when he got back to his life in Boston, it still wouldn't be over for him. He was taking the source of all his problems with him—Whiskey Daniels.

He shuddered as she rose unexpectedly into his mind, hot and intoxicating, lush and physical and so damnably responsive. He rescued his mental processes only by drastic measures: turning them to what lay ahead, his family's censure at this final disgrace, and a lifetime of suffering a volatile, consuming need for a woman who would invariably use that need against him. "Major Samson" she had called him . . . and how gleefully she'd shorn his head.

The valley folk came out all along their route to bid them a bittersweet farewell. The soldiers halted briefly and Laxault nodded to suffering Aunt Sarah Dunbar, allowing her a final word and a final hug from her Charlie. Aunt Frieda Delbarton surprised everyone, especially her boys, by impetuously hugging tough Ralph Kingery. And curvy May Donner surprised no one by wrapping her arms around strapping, thick-bodied Dem Wallace and delivering him a blistering kiss that would surely keep him warm in the nights ahead. Then the crusty Laxault jerked his hat in Aunt Sarah's direction and barked the column into motion again.

Whitney's first night away from Rapture Valley, alone in a cold, cramped canvas tent, was long and excruciating. The next afternoon, when the column of soldiers paused briefly on the hills overlooking the junction of the Monongahela and the Allegheny rivers, she stared at the town of Pittsburgh, below, and felt desolate inside. The three times she'd been there with her pa and Aunt Kate, the place had been a marvel, an adventure: fancy houses, wooden walkways, and stores and taverns and smithies and soldiers . . . people everywhere. But this time, as they descended the rim of the valley, it would be toward sorrow and separation, and she was in no hurry.

She waited until the prisoners were tethered temporarily to trees and their guards were off having a smoke of tobacco, and she slipped to be with her pa for a few minutes. She stood, her throat tight with confusion and her eyes burning at the bleak sight of him in chains. He looked up to see her beside him, and saw again the little wisp of a girl who had always awakened at the first crack of lightning and come to his and Margaret's bed. He pushed to his feet and held out his arms to her as he had those long years ago.

"Oh, Pa—" She buried her face in his deerskin coat front and let the tears come.

He let her have a bit of a cry, then pushed her back to look at her and wipe her cheeks gruffly with the backs of his knuckles.

"Pa, he says I have to go with him, but I can't. I can't leave you here. They'll lock you away in a prison of some sort—"

"A year or two . . . three at most," he snorted derisively, then broke into a wicked Daniels grin. "Think of it as—they'll be housing and feeding me for a while—at federal expense. I always said they weren't too smart, those federal boys. I'll come out best on this trade, mark my words." That grin broadened until she was drawn into it, returning it through a glaze of tears. "Recall, I was held by *lobsterbacks* durin' the great War for Independence. Now, lobsterbacks, they know how to make a fellow wish he'd just cock up his toes and get it over with. But I survived them and I'll survive anything this paltry lot can put to me. There's a cost and a profit to be had in everything, Whit. The worst part will be not seein' you and Kate for a while. But before it's over, I'll have my say on the tax as well. And I'll come see you in Boston as soon as I'm able."

Boston. The very sound of the place made her ill.

"I . . . I can't go with him, Pa. I've never been out of these two counties, and I don't know the first thing about living in a city or being a wife. I have to go back to Rapture. That's where I belong. And when the federals are gone, I can dig up the still." His eyes narrowed and she could tell he didn't like what he was hearing. The stare deepened to a knowing frown, and she felt him tugging at the real reason for her unprecedented retreat from a challenge.

"He . . . hates me, Pa," she whispered hoarsely. "He can't stand to look at me. We aren't married, not really, not like you and Ma. And we won't ever be. It's best all around if I just slip off back to Rapture." The misery in her face spoke of a powerful craving for the fancy buck she'd been forced to wed. Black flinched. He'd never seen her so full of longings, or in such low spirits. It worried him far more than any federal torture or prison that might await.

"And crawl under a rock and give up the blessed ghost," Black growled, bringing her face up quickly. What would happen to her while he was in prison, or, he made himself think it, if he never made it out of prison? He had to do something.

"Judas Priest, gal, you're a Daniels. Danielses don't run and hide when things get tough. We Danielses are born traders—it's in our blood, our very bones. A Daniels looks for a smart bit of profit in every trade. And by Gloriful Gabriel, that's what you got here, Whit, a bloody *trade*. Can't you see that? Fancy-pants, there, has taken your pa, your liquor business, and your blessed virtue . . . and now he has to pay for it."

He pulled her down to a seat on an exposed tree root and grasped her cold hands tightly. The flame in his eyes, part trader passion, part mischief, captivated her once again, carried her along with him. "Nothin' comes free in this life, Whit Daniels, not even happiness. You have to do something in the first place, before things can work out right in the second place." He paused at the frown on her face and explained. "I'm saying a fellow has to see to his own wants and needs, because nobody else will. You're wedded to that iron-arsed buck, Whit, whether you like it or not. And it's up to you to see you get the full measure of the bargain." His crafty Daniels glow deepened.

"Now, the way I see it, considering what he took, he owes you a livin', he owes you a family, and he owes you a good bit o' manly service. And you can't be a true Daniels unless you get every single thing you have comin' to you. Go on to Boston with him." He waved her on with an authoritative hand. "Squeeze him up and get all you've got coming. Make him pay. And let me hear no more talk about slinking off back to Rapture with your tail betwixt your legs. That's not the Daniels way, Whit."

He watched the light coming back into her eyes, watched her shoulders squaring and her chin lifting. He leaned closer with a crafty twinkle in his eye. "And if he's half as important as he seems to think he is, likely you can find a way to spring your old pa from prison a bit early—or at least make things a far sight more comfortable for him."

She laughed through blurry eyes and blinked them clear, borrowing his indomitable spirit, his cagey pragmatism, drinking them into the empty core of her. It was true, every word of it. She *was* a Daniels through and through. A couple of beddings and a few tears couldn't possibly change all the training and experience of a lifetime. She could bargain better, drink harder, run faster, talk smoother than anybody in Westmoreland County . . . except her pa. She was born with trading in her blood and this *was* a deal of sorts, even if it wasn't quite the usual bargain. What had she been doing, forgetting every sage and sensible principle she'd ever learned? The persistent heaviness in her chest eased.

"I tell you, it'll relieve my mind considerably, knowing you're set in sauce while I m away. And just as soon as they let me out, I'll hightail it to Boston too. By then you'll probably be used to fine clothes and high living in a grand house. . . ." Black trailed off, then his voice deepened with determination, and his quixotic face sobered. "You make him give you what you want, Whit, he's already got what he wanted."

"Probably even more than he bargained for," she murmured softly, getting a gleam in her eye as she recalled Garner's very words to her. It was all coming back now, her Daniels sense of self, her trader's insight, her nimble reason, and her pragmatic view of the world.

"That's my girl." He squeezed her hands, a wicked glint in his eye. "Anybody who can swap the spurs off a rooster can sure find a way to get a fair profit out of a marriage to a rich, handsome . . . stud."

"Paa—" She colored hotly.

"That man's a keg of dry powder inside, Whit, and you strike sparks every time you get close to him."

"Paa!"

"Well, sometimes a trader has to use every edge he's got. And, darlin', you've got that man honed like a razor." He grinned at his daughter, then pulled her to him and hugged her fiercely. In that long, sobering embrace, a terrible ache rose up in the middle of Blackstone Daniels, and it took every bit of his guile to muster the hallmark Daniels grin when they finally parted. "Do me proud, Whit."

"I will, Pa." They rose together and she gave him another quick, determined hug before turning back to her horse with a new heart.

Black watched her walk away and felt her dragging his heart away with her. He prayed he would live to keep his promise to come to Boston. He'd seen firsthand what treatment "whiskey rebels" received at federal hands. Men had died of exposure in "jail pits" dug into the frozen earth while waiting to be questioned as mere witnesses. After weeks of marching and waiting, the federal jackals were desperate for someone to vent their anger on. They came here to fight and found no great armed force of rebels waiting, only pockets of farmers and distillers who wanted the country they'd fought for to listen to them. The soldiers were deprived and frustrated and fight-randy, just itching for a scapegoat.

Much as he hated the buck for taking his Whit from him, he had to credit Major Townsend for treating him fairly. But the other federals hadn't bedded his only daughter. They'd have no reason to show justice or mercy to a known distiller like himself who had refused to sign a recanting pledge. He'd probably find himself in one of those frozen pits soon. And if he didn't come out of it, he at least wanted to know that Whit would be all right.

A movement at the side of his vision made Black turn, and he watched the Iron Major approach slowly and stop. It took a moment to register that he wasn't staring at Black, but past him, to Whitney's retreating form. He'd obviously seen them together. Black watched the frustration, the smoky, reluctant need in the major's eyes and prayed he read it rightly. It was a man's need for a woman, one specific woman, a special woman. It would have to be enough. He turned to watch Whit threading through the soldiers.

"You'd better take care of her," he growled with telling thickness. When he looked up, the major met his gaze.

"I will."

A commendation, at least. That was Colonel Gaspar's crowing assessment of what Townsend could expect for his sterling work in cleaning out the festering sore of treason, Rapture Valley. Garner blinked and his mouth opened, worked briefly, then shut. A commendation for letting a bunch of backwoods rubes and clucks bargain and humiliate him into total military impotence? For letting his volatile carnal cravings take complete control of his honor, sense of duty, and mission? For being caught, *literally,* with his breeches down? For arresting his own father-in-law after a bout of unbridled passion with his Jezebel bride? The whole idea of being decorated for such a fiasco was appalling, and that fact alone was probably enough to insure it would come to pass. Fate seemed forever bent on handing him success with one hand and perversely wrenching it away from him with the other. It seemed a fitting irony that the reverse should occur now—rewards and laurels when they were the last thing on his mind.

As soon as a report was filed and the prisoners were secured, Major Townsend surprised Gaspar with a request that he be released from the duty of the march back to Maryland. He cited the presence of his bride, and the inconveniences such a march would inflict upon her. The colonel smiled an oily, obvious smile, relishing his knowledge of how the inconvenience of a backwoods bride was inflicted upon the major. After a weighty pause, he agreed.

Whitney learned of their imminent departure when Garner appeared back in camp to announce that long-overdue pay was delayed yet again, that rations were short, and that he was turning command of the unit back to Lieutenant Brooks. Whitney protested and pleaded and resorted to down-and-out bargaining: ". . . After Pa's trial . . ." Then: "A week . . . all right, four days!" And finally ". . . Two days and that's my final offer!"

"Tomorrow," he growled, glancing furiously at the interest on the faces of his men as they gathered to watch.

"I won't go until I'm ready."

"The hell you won't," he declared. "I'll take you, kicking and screaming if necessary." But as Garner started for her, intent on removing her bodily, Laxault's burly frame intervened like a moving wall. He glared stolidly into Garner's angry face, then turned to Whitney, giving Garner his back.

"You go on, Miz Townsend. We'll see to yer pa." A chorus of agreement from the rest of Rapture's erstwhile enemies sent tears rolling unexpectedly down Whitney's face.

The morning they left Pittsburgh, Whitney appeared for traveling, garbed in her breeches and boots, and Garner looked her up and down and went granite-jawed. He insisted she change into skirts, or he'd haul her bottom back up the stairs of the inn and dress her himself. She seethed openly, stomped back up the stairs, and vengefully pulled a skirt on over her breeches. It was an omen, she growled disgustedly. He was apparently going to try to make her act like a "lady-wife" now. Well, she wasn't a lady. She was a trader and a distiller and a Daniels . . . and he'd just have to get used to it. After all, it was his idea to drag her off to Boston with him in the first place.

When they got to the stable where their horses were kept, round-faced Benson was standing by the door, his rusting musket on his shoulder and a faithful-beagle look on his face. He explained that the lieutenant had given him his walking papers early, figuring he might not survive the march back to Mary-

land . . . and he "jus' wondert if'n the majur might be needin'
the services o' a gentlemun's gentlemun."

Garner's eyes closed and he shuddered. "What do I look like,
Brother Benevolent?" When he opened his eyes, Benson was
scratching his head, trying to recall if he'd ever heard of the fellow.

Garner growled. The longer he stayed in this wilderness, the
more pests he seemed to pick up. He jabbed a finger toward one
of the two packhorses and ordered, "Mount up!"

The journey was difficult at times, impossible at others. At
first Garner tried to secure nightly lodgings in barns belonging
to suspicious and resentful hill farmers, who took one look at
his once-glorious federal uniform and wanted nothing to do with
him or the cash money he offered. Whitney watched his reined
fury at their refusal with a perverse mixture of empathy and glee.
She would have bargained them lodgings, but Garner went livid,
hauled her away, and forbade it in the most emphatic terms. They
spent two exceedingly miserable nights in the icy, early Novem-
ber rains before Garner relented and allowed Benson to try bargaining them a bit of hay in a dry barn loft for the night.

Things were terrible indeed between Whitney and her husband, and the closer they came to Boston, the harder Garner
pushed the pace. Whitney assumed it was because he was eager
to see his "almighty Townsend" family. It was in fact, however,
avoidance of his unbearable desire for her delectable self that
drove him straight into the jaws of his kin. He had determined
that the only way to live with Whitney Daniels and her devastating effects on him was to avoid her as much as possible. And
avoiding her at night in crowded inns where they shared a room,
and ignoring her over campfires built for three were exercises in
pure bodily agony.

When they reached New York, he hired a coach to carry them
the rest of the way in a more civilized manner, and in greater
haste. They would stop only for meals and changes of horses.
But the jostling, rocking motions of the coach soon rocked the
exhausted Benson to sleep, and Garner found himself facing her
alone again, knee to knee, across a quiet coach. With each passing

hour, his mood darkened another shade and his body grew more rigid. His hands soon clamped his muscular thighs like tourniquets and his jaw was set like mortar. Every sigh, every blink of her feathery lashes, every unconscious lick of her luscious lips, sent volleys of heat shooting through him.

Whitney read her own dread into his black mood, and believed his tension was produced by the prospect of facing his family with the circumstances of his forced marriage. And it finally occurred to her to ask a few questions about these Townsends among whom she would be required to make her life.

"The household consists of my father, my cousin Madeline, my grandfather, and myself," he ground out, adding with a huff, ". . . and now, you."

She bridled at his disdainful inclusion of her. "No brothers or sisters?"

"One brother, dead in childhood. My uncle died some years back and his wife soon followed him, leaving the girl."

Whitney recalled the pain of losing her mother and felt an instant bond with little Madeline. "And do they do anything, your Townsends, besides 'being rich'?"

Garner tore his eyes from her and stared out the coach window into the cold sunshine. "We have a large family business . . . which centers on the manufacture and sale of . . . rum."

"Rum?" She sat straighter, her mind working. "You mean Townsends manufacture rum? But rum is hard spirits . . . that would mean you're—"

"Distillers," he ground out irritably. And from the corner of his eye he saw the way her jaw loosened and the way she blinked and blinked again as if trying to absorb the unthinkable thought.

It shocked her into complete silence. Garner Townsend was a distiller, from a family of distillers . . . just like her. The knowledge rumbled around in her head for a few minutes and finally released a full wave of warmth through her. In some crazy way, it fit. And it probably accounted for the consuming fascination he held for her. Some part of her had recognized the distiller in him and responded to it in the most basic way imaginable. She should have known he was a distiller from his kisses. They packed the wallop of a double jolt of whiskey . . . or possibly rum.

And his family were distillers too. A second wave of relief poured through her, and the awful tension that had been collecting in her middle dispersed. The knowledge suddenly made his house full of strangers seem less daunting and far more accessible. A family of Boston distillers didn't sound nearly as bad as a family of Boston aristocrats, even if they were one and the same.

Sergeant Laxault returned to his camp outside Pittsburgh with a grim report. "Wull, we seen 'er pa," he growled, settling his burly frame onto a log beside the lieutenant, in front of a smoky campfire. The men of Major Townsend's old unit collected quickly to hear what had happened to their prisoners. "An' it looks like they been thumpin' on 'im, all right."

"Looks like a piece o' raw meat," Dem Wallace added angrily. "We never shoulda turned him over to 'em." A wave of anger went through the men.

"We had no choice," Lieutenant Brooks interjected resentfully. "Colonel Gaspar ordered it. There's nothing we can do about it."

"Ye mean, jus' like there ain't nothin' we can do about *no pay?*" stringy Ralph Kingery demanded.

"An' *no rations?*" Dem Wallace added furiously. "We jus' have to sit here and starve an' freeze? The hell I will. I'm due rations!"

"We shoulda stayed in Rapture," came lanky Ned's whine. "At least there we had us decent food."

"Hell, we're all hungry," Laxault growled like distant thunder and stood to face them. After a moment a crafty glint appeared in the grizzled sergeant's eye. "We be sittin' here, nursemaidin' th' evi-dence aginst Miz Townsend's pa . . . and dyin' o' thirst an' hunger. We got us a oppor-toonity here, boys. There's plenty o' soljurs that did get paid who're jus' as thirsty as us. I say"—he waved them closer and lowered his voice to river-gravel level— "we sell 'em some o' old Black's brew. We git money fer food, an' git rid o' the evi-dence aginst old Black in the boodle."

"Oh, no," the lieutenant protested, scrambling to his feet. "Tampering with evidence . . . it's . . . not right."

"Neither is them beatin' old Black," Dem Wallace declared with a determined scowl.

The men rumbled agreement, their eyes narrowing, their anger rising at the thought of four bountiful barrels of marvelous Daniels whiskey being used in evidence against their maker. There was something purely unnatural about it, they decided. And with the innate craftiness of hungry men, they overwhelmed and persuaded Lieutenant Brooks to turn a blind eye while the barrels were "spirited off" by "scurrilous persons unknown." And in a final act of rebellion against an arrogant officialdom that had used and abused and abandoned them, they bribed a guard to carry Black Daniels and Charlie Dunbar a bottle of the illegal, untaxed "evidence" as well.

The streets of Boston were cold, dark, and silent as the coach rumbled over the cobblestones toward the fashionable Beacon Hill part of the city. An occasional street lamp cast weak beams through the windows, illuminating Whitney's sleeping form in dim golden flashes before Garner's troubled gaze. It was the middle of the night, and his studied frown expressed second thoughts about his decision to continue driving, even though it meant arriving home in the dead of night.

The coach rumbled down Beacon Street, past the grand Hancock mansion, and soon reined up before an imposing Georgian brick house set back from the street by a carriage turn that led straight to a raised front portico with sweeping sets of steps down each side. Garner emerged from the coach onto the portico and sent the driver around to the side entrance to rouse the staff.

Shortly there was a rattle and a thumping behind massive white doors, which duly swung open. Garner carried Whitney's limp form past a white-haired fellow in nightshirt and cap, who was wrapped in a hastily donned robe and holding a fully lit candelabra.

"Master Garner. Sir—" The butler's eyes widened with alarm on Garner's rumpled state and several days' growth of beard . . . and on the burden he carried.

"Do we have guests?"

"N-no, sir."

"Good. The blue room, across from mine, send someone up to build a fire," Garner ordered quietly. "And see the fellow asleep in the coach settled in the servants' hall for the night."

The butler started and hurried after him with the candles. Garner carried Whitney up the sweeping stairs and down the wide upper hallway to a carved door. The butler, Edgewater, lurched ahead to open it for him, and he strode into a grandly furnished bedchamber to deposit her on a large draped bed. The butler stood by, dumbstruck, as his young master proceeded to divest the young woman of what he saw as a rather hideous felt coat and a pair of very worn boots, then carefully dragged the expensive brocade counterpane and down quilt from beneath to tuck around her gently.

"Tomorrow morning"—Garner turned on the incredulous butler—"Mrs. Townsend is not to be disturbed before half past eleven. Then see she's brought a full morning tray and a tub of hot water for bathing. I shall require the same for myself at half past nine." He pulled one lighted taper from the butler's blazing candelabrum and lit the candles on the marble mantel. He turned and found Edgewater staring at Whitney's unconscious form.

"*Mrs*. Townsend, sir?" A pair of hoary, imperious brows lifted.

"*Mrs*. Townsend," Garner asserted with authority. The staid butler jerked a nod and hurried out to see to his instructions. Garner sighed raggedly. He'd just negotiated the first of several hurdles in this latest homecoming.

The next morning at half past seven, a tidily starched and black-coated Edgewater met a sleepy servant in the upper hallway and relieved him of the morning tray bound for the Master Byron Townsend's chambers. Ordinarily it was a lesser servant's duty to deliver the tray, draw the brocades, and awaken the master, but on this morning the fastidious butler was determined to do it himself. He let himself into the princely, polished chamber and deposited the tray on the laquered table near the carved marble hearth. He stirred the fire to life and laid on another log.

"Half past, sir." He leaned discreetly near the edge of the master's bed, then withdrew to tug back the heavy brocades and open the shutters.

Byron Townsend stirred and sat up, rubbing sleep from his face with long, supple hands that continued back through dark, uncropped hair that was silvering at the temples. His long legs swung over the side of the bed and he blinked, appraising Edgewater's presence in his room.

"Has the paper come?" he asked, shoving his bare feet into kidskin slippers.

"The paper hasn't, sir . . . but Master Garner has." Edgewater busied himself with tying back the drapes.

"Home? You mean after I retired last night?"

"He and his party arrived *quite* late, sir," Edgewater intoned casually, transferring his attention to the tray, where he poured a china cup full of steaming coffee.

"His *party?*" Byron reached for his robe but decided to take the cup of coffee Edgewater offered first, scrutinizing the butler's tight-lipped air. "He brought people home with him?"

"Hardly 'people,' sir. One military sort of person . . . not quite officer material, I shouldn't think. And of course, his bride. Will that be all, sir?" Edgewater dropped a cool little nod and turned to go.

"His *what?*" Byron's deep voice halted Edgewater in his tracks.

"His bride, sir." Edgewater turned back with a raised chin and an offhand sniff. "I believe he did call her 'Mrs. Townsend' as he disrobed her, sir."

"As he what? Disrob—" Byron choked it off, reddening, hardening before the frosty butler's gaze. "He's married? When did that happen . . . and who the hell is she? Who could he possibly have found to marry out on the beastly frontier in the midst of a raging rebellion? Good God—he went out there to put down this wretched whiskey insurrection, not to dally with the females and rut about . . . and get—" He halted and stiffened further, now resembling a ruddy stone monolith in both posture and color.

"Married?" His volume increased now with each word. "How dare he—without permission? A bride! *Dammit!* Where

the hell are they?" He tore past Edgewater, jostling him aside, and thrusting the sloshing cup into his hands. He strode down the broad hallway, his nightshirt flapping, and began pounding furiously on the heavy mahogany panels of Garner's door.

"Garner Adams Townsend—I demand you open this door. At once." He paused, puffing and red-faced, then stormed inside, scouring the room, then the bed for his son and the questionable female connection. In the dim gray light, Garner lurched up, reeling and disoriented and clearly alone in the bed.

"Just where the hell is she, this 'bride' of yours?"

"Across the hall, sir," Edgewater offered smugly from the doorway. "The blue room, sir."

Byron stared at Garner's broad, bare chest and began to quake with impotent fury. "Dammit! How dare you do this to your family?" He wheeled, and strode across the hall with blood pounding furiously in his head and filling his vision. And after three solid whacks on the door, he cursed again and used the handle, muttering, "It's forty percent my house—"

Halfway to the bed he halted, watching Whitney rise shakily from the covers. Hair, light hair, lots of it . . . he could make out that much as she pushed up, rubbing her eyes and seeming confused. He stalked closer, peering into the gloom beneath the canopy and bed hangings. Her light eyes stared back at him from a very striking face.

"Who the hell are you?" he demanded imperiously.

"Well, who are you?" Whitney drew her chin back, blinking at his nasty tone, and casting a bewildered gaze around her. *And where was she?* She looked around wonderingly. In some big room . . . in a big, fancy bed. She looked down quickly and found herself dressed in her own shirt and skirt, and a quick feel beneath the covers confirmed that her breeches were still in place. How did she come to be—

"Just what do you think you're doing, invading my wife's chamber like this?" Garner lurched into the room, bare-legged, bare-chested, still buttoning his breeches.

"Seeing for myself the results of your latest idiocy." Byron tore his gaze from Whitney to impale Garner on it. "Married. Out on the bloody frontier. Good God."

"Yes, married," Garner stalked closer, "duly and legally so."

"Well, it cannot have been honorably done—else you wouldn't have come slinking home in the dead of night," Byron charged, coming unnervingly close to the mark with his thrust.

"A mere convenience of travel." Garner's jutting chin was matched by a stubborn-looking older version. "I was eager to be finished with the journey."

"Who is she?" Byron jerked a nod toward Whitney as she slid to the floor and came around the bed into the brighter light. He collected the details of her simple homespun skirt and mannish shirt and felt positively vindicated in his suspicions. "More to the point—*what* is she?"

Garner caught the shock on Whitney's face and his voice grated like a rasp on steel as he turned back to his father. "Out!" He stalked forward angrily, forcing Byron back out into the hall, using every bit of leverage his greater height permitted. "We'll discuss this later . . . not here . . . not now."

Whitney followed to the door as they argued, watching Garner and the man who looked enough like him to be his . . . his pa! Garner bested him by two or three inches in height, but their shoulders were of equal width and, in profile, their noses had the same straight slope and sharp tip and the same arrogantly flared nostrils. They both had brown-black hair, light eyes, and a tight facial musculature stretched over a strong, square frame. And when Whitney's eyes dropped to the gaping front of the fellow's nightshirt, she was a little shocked by the sight of familiar, dark chest hair, laced with strands of white.

". . . wasn't time for a letter or other communication," Garner growled defensively.

"Then you should have waited—put off the damnable vows—controlled yourself for a change!"

"What in damnation is going on out here!" came a raspy voice from just down the hall. Suddenly an old man, garbed in a nightshirt and sitting on what appeared to be a chair on wheels, burst from a door down the hall and rolled forward into the middle of the fray. He was rail-thin with thick white hair and a lean, hawkish countenance inset with faded gray eyes. "What's all the bile-raisin' uproar this hour of the bloody morning? Can't a man get any peace in the last wretched years of his life?"

"Garner is home," Byron said, then turned on the old man with combined fury and pain—after the old fellow banged into his unprotected shin with the sharp corner of the wheeled contraption. "Dammit, will you watch that bloody thing? How many times have I told you—"

"I can see he's home, lackwit."

"Merciful heaven!" A strident, girlish soprano sailed above the noise as yet another door opened and another white-clad, red-faced figure came hurrying out into the hall. "How is a lady to sleep with all this horrible racket? How perfectly thoughtless of you to argue outside my door when you know I always sleep until eleven."

A blur of fine muslin and swirl of dark hair thrust into the heart of the confrontation, jostling Garner and his father apart and sending the wheeled old fellow back a bit. It was a young girl in a flounced white bed gown who planted herself in the midst of them with her hands on her waist and the gown slipping on her bare shoulder.

"Cousin Garner . . . I see you're home from your dreadful old wars," she observed. Her thickly lashed eyes narrowed disapprovingly on Garner's bare chest, then found Whitney and narrowed even farther.

"Go back to bed, Madeline," Garner's father ordered the girl, thrusting a hard finger toward the door she'd just exited. "This is none of your affair."

"Who's she?" Madeline tossed her dark head and crossed her arms over her chest, refusing to budge.

"Exactly," the old fellow in the wheeled contraption snarled, squinting and craning his neck to see past the girl to Whitney's embattled form in the doorway. "Who the hell is she? Did you catch him with some hot little piece—"

"A conniving little fortune hunter, no doubt." Garner's father sneered, turning on Whitney with a gleam in his eye. "It seems Garner married her out on the frontier and has now dragged her home . . . in the dead of night."

"Married?" and "Married *her?*" the old man and Madeline chorused their disbelief.

"She's my wife." Garner took an intimidating step toward his father, his eyes now pale with anger. "And my marriage is my concern. It has nothing to do with you."

"Good God, Garner, you've married some backwoods trollop, of course it has to do with us!" Byron Townsend turned a burning stare full on Whitney. "At the very least, it's a family humiliation . . . married out in the woods, in secret . . ."

"It was *not* in secret." Garner collected the shock on Whitney's face and began to quake with raw anger. "We were married by the son-in-law of my commanding officer, Colonel Gaspar . . . with her full family in attendance."

"Well, indecently quick, then," Madeline tossed out with an arch, feline glance up and down Whitney's shape.

"Indecent, indeed," Byron added, raking her with his light Townsend eyes, pronouncing the judgment on both her marriage and herself.

Indecent. Whitney took the thrust square in the belly. Three hostile and belittling stares turned on her, adding to the insult. These snarling, sneering aristocrats were undoubtedly the much lauded Townsends—Garner's family.

"Indecent?" she managed to counter, coming out of her huddled stance with a fiery glow that was the spirit of Whitney Daniels. She raked a scathing, pointed glare across the expanse of bare muslin and bare skin that filled the hall. "Well now, if we're talking about decency, I think it's only fair to call to your attention that I'm the only person present who's fully *decently*—clothed."

Byron jerked his chin back and looked down at his nightshirt in surprise. Madeline's mouth worked soundlessly as she tugged the neck of her nightdress together and reddened. And Ezra glared down at his own knobby, hairy knees and bare feet and let out a rather nasty wordless oath. There was an instantaneous flurry of muslin, feet, and wheels. And three doors slammed resoundingly.

Fifteen

Whitney watched as dusky color flooded down Garner's neck, through his shoulders and chest; his turmoil apparently matched hers. Their eyes locked and held for a moment before a movement nearby intruded.

"E-Edgewater." Garner turned his head. "Breakfast and baths now, please." Then he took Whitney by the wrist and ushered her back into her room, closing the door firmly on the butler's huff. The flashing autumn fire of her eyes, the angry blush of her cheeks, the tangled fall of her silky hair . . . he had a devil of a time tearing his fingers from her arm now that they were alone in the dimness of her room.

"Your family, I presume," she said, her chest heaving as she fought to control a tangle of pride and ire and one other feeling that lodged somewhere between protectiveness and indignation. She did manage to recognize that there wasn't quite so much of the vaunted Townsend pride in his confirmation.

"Yes." His mouth tightened as though he'd just tasted something very sour. "They're . . . quite surprised to find me home so soon . . . and—"

"And married," she finished, when it became apparent he wouldn't.

"Their reaction is not unexpected." He straightened defensively. "I shall make a suitable explanation to them later. Meanwhile"——he waved a proprietary hand about him at the stylishly furnished chamber—"this is your room. Breakfast and bathe and make yourself presentable. I'll send for you later, when I'm ready to introduce you properly to my family."

He stood a moment longer, looking as though he might say

something else, but stopped and turned on his bare heel and left. He was across the hall with two closed doors safely between them before he realized he had been on the verge of apologizing for his family's unforgivable behavior. Never in his life had he thought of Townsends as other than Townsends . . . and thus exempt from the mundane course of ordinary human interaction. And if they were curt, cutting, even profane to others, including each other, it had never seemed to matter in light of the weightier concerns that occupied them.

But now, for the first time, he had had an unnerving glimpse of his father, his grandfather, and his cousin from another perspective, through another's eyes. He'd had an odd feeling that was surprisingly like embarrassment at the arrogance they displayed toward someone they didn't even know . . . toward someone as exceptional as Whitney Daniels.

Across the hall Whitney stood where he had left her, staring darkly at the carved panels of the huge mahogany door, with its polished brass fittings. "Bathe" he had said. "Make yourself presentable." How dare he! She pulled her shirt up vengefully and the mingled aromas of sweat and horses and woodsmoke wafted up. She dropped the fabric with a curl to her nose and a flame in her cheeks. Still, he might have asked in a more gentlemanly manner. She recalled his snarling father and cousin and grandfather and realized he might have also been a good bit less gentlemanly.

She shuddered. The Iron Major apparently came from an Iron Family. It was only the prospect of facing them again that made her reconsider her rebellious urges and looked around the dimly lit room for evidence of a washstand and her small leather bag of clothes. She'd not allow them to look down their noses at her again. She took a deep breath and snatched up the Blue Willow pitcher from the washstand, wondering how a body got water in this big, fancy place.

No, not just fancy, she caught herself. "Exquisite" and "blue." Very blue . . . or maybe "royally" or "opulently" blue. That's what her aunt Kate would probably call such color, *opulent*. A sudden wave of longing for her home and for Kate and her pa swept over her, and she had to shake it off physically to make herself answer a knock at the door.

A middle-aged serving woman dressed in starched gray and white stood just outside, balancing a linen-draped tray with one hand and reaching for the door handle with the other. Whitney fell back before her determined entry, and when the woman had deposited the tray on the table near the fire, she eyed the pitcher in Whitney's arms and went to pull back the heavy brocade drapes at the window and part the shutters to admit the morning sun.

"How would I . . . where do I get water?"

"It's coming, ma'am." The woman slanted a look at her that said it couldn't arrive a minute too soon, bobbed, and withdrew.

Whitney watched her leave, then turned to stare at the large, high-ceilinged chamber, now bathed in morning light. The bed was huge and draped with glorious satin brocades, and a counterpane that was trimmed with gold cording. The furnishings were all polished mahogany, made in a spare, graceful style: a table and straight chairs, a highboy, a wardrobe, a marble-topped washstand, and a needleworked fire screen. A thick carpet containing a dozen shades of blue covered the polished maple floor before a hearth and mantel made of carved white marble.

This was Garner Townsend's *opulent* home. Whitney put the pitcher back on the washstand and went to investigate the delicious smells coming from the linen-draped tray. Silver pots . . . two of them. And painted china and silver cutlery like her aunt Kate's, only grander. She handled the cup gently, turning it over and over with reverent fingers before filling it with coffee. Then she sipped and sighed and buttered a biscuit. At least he didn't intend to starve her.

By the time she finished, the little woman was back, ordering two fellows in to build up the fire and settle a huge beaten-copper tub before it. She informed Whitney she'd been "assigned" to help with her bath, and Whitney informed her pointedly that she was neither simple nor infirm, and needed no help. After a steely-eyed confrontation, Whitney resorted to a bit of bargaining and struck a deal; the woman could help wash her hair, then would have to leave her alone so she could bathe herself.

Soon Whitney found herself with clean, rose-scented hair,

soaking up to her neck in a steamy tub of water before a toasty fire. A whole tub of hot water . . . and scented soap. She wriggled her toes above the water's edge, wishing Aunt Kate were there. How she would enjoy this; she used to talk about such things with a certain wistfulness in her voice. Whitney now knew why. A body could come to relish this "bathing" business.

Half an hour later, the serving woman, who finally identified herself as Mercy, returned and found Whitney already dried and dressed in her other shirt and skirt, deerskin breeches riding covertly beneath them. Mercy had brought a tortoiseshell brush and comb, and set about detangling her hair and pulling it up into ladylike braids looped on either side of her head in the current fashion. Whitney protested and fidgeted, but Mercy was adamant and finally had her way. And when Mercy presented her with a hand glass so she could admire her new coif, Whitney gasped and bit her lip to constrain her incredulity. Mercy proudly announced that the style was fresh from the Continent and "all the rave" among the ladies in Boston. Whitney nodded, redfaced, and Mercy withdrew, clearly miffed that her skills had gone unappreciated.

Whitney plopped onto the narrow bench at the foot of the bed, looking glass in hand, and shook her head in disbelief. It was bad enough she'd have to face his prickly family soon, but to do so looking like a flop-eared beagle. She'd never seen anything so absurd in her life. She propped the handle of the mirror between her knees and dismantled the hound's-ear braids, Mercy or no Mercy.

She brushed her hair and waited, then brushed her hair again. It was several hours later, and Whitney's hair was shining indeed before Edgewater came to fetch her to the morning room and the family. Tension had coiled like a top string inside Whitney as she smoothed her homespun skirt, resettled her belt, and followed the butler. He led her through the broad upper hallway and down the sweeping staircase, and through a spacious tiled entry hall. They passed polished mahogany doors, gleaming brass-and-crystal sconces, thick Turkish rugs, and paintings in gilded frames. Regal reds and lush sendal greens and winking brass formed an intimidating palette of elegance wherever she looked.

Down a paneled hallway, he indicated an open door with his hand, then withdrew, leaving her alone. Her heart was pounding and her hands were cold as she took the final steps toward the open door and heard their voices. It was a very un-Daniels bit of trepidation that caused her to pause. What she heard in that pause stopped her entirely.

". . . forty percent of this house is mine," Garner was proclaiming in a deep and angry voice, the kind of voice he often used with her. "And forty percent of Townsend Companies and forty percent of the shipping and mercantile interests. *Forty percent.* This is my home, and my wife will live here with me whether you countenance it or not."

"You'd inflict her on us?" came a female voice. The cousin, Whitney realized distractedly. "A nobody from nowhere. Good Lord, Cousin Garner, she's lived among savages!"

"She's not a savage, she's my wife," Garner snapped. "She is unused to . . . eastern life, but she'll adjust."

"She looks like a charwoman, a scullion," the cousin intoned irritably. "All that hair—and my maid dresses better. I won't be seen with her, I won't."

"She is dressed appropriately for the frontier," Garner countered grimly. "Her appearance may be remedied by a simple outlay of coin."

"Which, no doubt, is exactly what she married you for, an outlay of coin," Byron Townsend charged in a voice very like Garner's, but with a harder, icier edge. "Well, she'll get nothing in this house."

"*Have* to marry her, did you?" broke in a worn crackle of a voice that obviously belonged to Garner's grandfather. "Caught bedding the wench and forced to do right by her?"

There was a shocked silence from the room, during which Whitney's heart rose into her throat. It was a brutal, constricting summary of their union; caught bedding and forced to marry. Dishonor set to rights. How small and tawdry it sounded. There was no room in it for the honest exchange of pleasure of their bedding, or for the days and nights of rigid control and denial that preceded that sweet lapse of honor.

"I knew it!" Garner's father exploded. "*Another* damned disgrace! You haven't got the slightest speck of self-control around women . . . no decency, no damnable honor at all. Madeline, leave the room."

"I will not! I have ten percent—"

"Let the girl stay, Byron," the old man said, a trace of lurid glee in his voice. "She's old enough to hear about the consequences of unbridled lust."

"It was not unbridled lust." Garner flamed guiltily.

"You went out there to fight honorably at Washington's side, to put down a treasonous rebellion, and ended up wallowing and rutting about in the muck with a crude little trollop instead of doing your duty. What else could it be called . . . disgusting, degraded animal lust."

Those steely, relentless words drove into Whitney like a spear. She was a crude little trollop who "wallowed and rutted" in "muck." And she dressed worse than a servant. She glared down at her thick, homespun skirt as though she could see it ablaze. It was all the worse for the fact that she hated the way she was dressed too. On a vengeful impulse she pulled at the ties of her skirt and pushed it contemptuously down over her hips to grind it underfoot. She ran her hands over her simple deerskin breeches and her boots and felt her Daniels pride flaming. How dare they? She was a Daniels . . . and blessed proud of it!

She squared her shoulders, lifted her chin, and strode into the study to face the snarling, dangerous pride of Townsends—*a Daniels walking straight into the lion's den.*

All four were arguing; every one of them making heated declarations that nobody else was listening to. Garner caught sight of her, stopped just inside the doorway, her booted legs spread so that they stretched and tightened that memorable deerskin around her shapely hips and thighs. Her fists were planted at her waist, her thick hair tumbled and swirled around her like a wild river, and her green eyes snapped with sparks—like fires in a lush forest. She was bold and breathtaking as the frontier that had shaped her, and every bit as untamable. As Garner straightened, staring at her, Byron stopped mid-diatribe and turned as well.

There was a strangled noise from Garner's cousin, and all fell churchyard quiet. Whitney took one step farther in and spread her booted feet again, feeling four sets of burning eyes upon her. She lifted her chin and thrust her shoulders back a bit farther, blissfully unaware that she thrust taut nipples hard against her shirtfront in the process. Garner flinched with pure horror at the sight, but was strangely unable to drag his eyes from it.

"I understand introductions are in order." She lifted her chin a quarter of an inch more, to a hard-trading angle, and tossed a hot, expectant look at Garner. When he didn't speak, she decided to introduce herself. "I'm Whitney Daniels, of the *Westmoreland County Danielses*. And I'm here because I wedded the Iron Major, here, a fortnight ago, and he insisted I come."

"Well"—Byron straightened and sputtered at her audacity— "I'll be damned."

"Very likely"—Whitney was pleased to agree—"unless you learn to curb your profane tongue. The major, here, has a nasty habit of swearing . . . and it's plain to see how he came by it."

"Good God, Whitney—" Garner started for her, his face dark, his eyes silvering with ire. But she stepped quickly aside and he halted, unwilling to chase her about the room in front of his family. Dread was creeping up his spine at the familiar angle of her chin and the trader's glint in her eye.

"You must be his pa." She returned Byron's bald scrutiny tit for tat, letting her gaze drift pointedly down his elegant gray coat, his snowy-ruffled shirtfront, and his snugly-tailored breeches. Then she moved on to face the old gent in the wheeled chair, taking in white hair that matched his shirt ruffles, a sallow complexion, and canny gray eyes set in pockets of wrinkles. "And you're his grandpa."

"I'm Ezra Townsend, you upstart baggage," the old gent snarled, glaring through narrowed eyes. "Nobody calls me grandpa."

Whitney leaned forward slightly with a glint in her eye. "I can certainly see why. And you"—she turned to the diminutive young girl with the dark hair, flashing hazel eyes, and pretty but petulant mouth—"must be his poor, orphaned cousin . . . Madeline, I believe."

The girl took a step back with an outraged crinkle to her nose. "Good Lord, she's even dressed like a savage. Breeches . . . men's breeches!"

But every male eye in the room was already fixed on them, and on the curvy delights they enhanced more than hid.

"I am *not* a savage." Whitney whirled to face them with a determined glow to her face. "I was born in Allentown and raised in Westmoreland County. I'm a distiller, just like you. My pa and I make the best whiskey in all of western Pennsylvania." She saw them shifting astonished stares to Garner and declared half-truthfully, "And the major married me because of a bargain that was struck between us. An honest deal, pure and simple."

She met Garner's silvery gaze for a brief moment and realized the depth of the stubborn honor that lay behind it, an honor that would not let him break a bargain or a *vow,* even though the keeping of it would expose him to his family's outrage. And in that long, heated moment she felt a strange rush of warmth for him inside her.

"See here, wench." Byron Townsend stalked toward her, his face dusky and his eyes silvering the way Garner's often did, only without Garner's tantalizing heat. "You'll not get a thing out of my son, or out of my family. Not one penny, do you hear? Do you think we don't know you trapped him into this marriage? You're not the first to try it, you little Jezebel—" He grabbed her by the wrist, clamping down punishingly.

"Delilah," she rasped ominously, trying to free her hand, "*not* Jezebel."

Garner watched in raw horror as Whitney's eyes blazed and she wrestled her wrist higher, bringing Byron's hand up—Dear God—Garner realized she was going to bite him! Blood roared in his ears as he lunged for her, watching her lips part—

He plowed into Whitney from the side, jostling her free and managing to wrap both arms securely around her waist from behind. Shock prevented her from struggling until they were a safe distance away, then she began to wriggle and struggle.

"Stop it, Whitney." He bent a harsh command near her ear,

tightening his arms furiously about her ribs. "Stop it, or I swear I'll—"

"Let me go. What's gotten into you?" she fumed, trying to pry his banded arms from around her waist.

"Behave like a lady, dammit," he growled into the torrent of her hair.

But it was already too late. His family's astonishment bore in on them. Good Lord, this was exactly the kind of spectacle he'd feared, dreaded in the marrow of his bones. All possibility of passing her off as untutored but otherwise acceptable had just been obliterated. Now his imperious family had witnessed Whitney Daniels in full, harrowing glory and knew the excruciatingly embarrassing state of his marriage. "Stop it." He gave her a shake. "Hold still!"

To everyone's surprise, especially Garner's, she did quiet, to slow, sinuous wriggles that drew Byron's and Ezra's hot eyes. Her face was crimson, her eyes flashed pure defiance as she writhed against Garner's body and his volatile loins.

"This is my wife, Whitney Daniels Townsend." He held her quieting form against him, his whole body focusing on her pressed against his highly reactive male parts. *Oh, God, not that—not now!* His voice dropped to a deep, menacing growl. "She's my wife, and this is forty percent my house. She'll live here . . . with or without your blessing. And if you find you can't accept that, then be assured: I'll take my forty percent of the Townsend Companies and use it to give you one hell of a beating. Do I make myself perfectly clear?"

Whitney wasn't sure if she imagined nods or not. But she had no chance to confirm or disprove her perceptions. Garner suddenly spun her around to seize her wrists.

"We'll return . . . after she has dressed for dinner." His face was a fierce mask, his eyes hurling silver lightning bolts as he demanded, "You will show her proper consideration, as she will give to you."

With that potent warning to both sides, he dragged Whitney from the room and through the main hall. When they reached the grand stairs, he overcame her deepening resistance by hauling her up onto his shoulder and carrying her to her room. By the time he dumped her onto her bed, her brain was blood-gorged and only partly functional. But outrage at his bullying remained, and she struggled to sit up, squeezing her eyes shut to clear her vision. When she opened them again, his thighs were braced hard against the edge of the bed and his arms were crossed resolutely over his lace-covered chest.

"You were going to bite him," he charged, his nostrils flaring, a vein in his temple pulsing visibly. "And by damn, that will stop here and now. This is Boston, dammit, not the bloody backwoods, and I'll not have you conducting yourself like a raging Hun!"

"Bite him?" She went positively scarlet. "Bite your father? What kind of savage do you take me for?"

Her question lay burning on the air between them, forcing each to confront harshly the mountain of obstacles that lay between them. He really did think she was an uncouth, ignorant wretch: the realization staggered her. And in the same moment he understood; his base expectations of her were no less objectionable than his family's.

"It was"—he twitched defensively and rubbed the hand she'd once bitten—"a reasonable expectation in light of my own experience."

"You're . . ." she had to swallow hard to force her voice past the huge lump in her throat, "the only person I've bitten in years."

In the crowded silence the sight of him braced and towering above her invaded her crumbling defenses. His wide shoulders were encased in fine black broadcloth, a creamy white brocade waistcoat hugged his ribs, and his chest was filled with a frosty waterfall of ruffles. She moaned silently, *he really is a fancy gentleman*. Her gaze worked its way up the lacy expanse to his bronze face and the heated glimmer of his light eyes. He suddenly seemed like a stranger. An elegant, demanding stranger.

"No biting," she managed to say. But it felt too much like surrender, and she had to add, "If you'll stop cursing. I hate it when you curse. It's foul and profane and a gentleman who finished five years at a Royal Military College in England ought to be able to think of something to say besides 'dammit.' "

"How do you know where I was educated?" he ground out. Around her he was lucky to be able to speak at all!

"I know a lot about you, Major."

He stiffened with raw alarm, trying desperately to rip his eyes from the taut wrinkles of deerskin that skimmed her belly. His blood was draining, pooling precipitously in his excitable loins. Bargaining again, he realized, but his proper indignation was drowning in the phantom feel of her bottom pressed against him, as it had been minutes before, wriggling against his manly parts.

"I'm not here to bargain." He took a giant step back.

"Just what are you here to do, Garner Townsend?"

She hadn't meant it to sound so seductive, hadn't meant to meet his eyes. And she didn't mean to flick her tongue over her top lip as she stared at the bold sweep of his velvety bottom lip.

Flames shot up the walls of his body and he trembled to contain them. His breath came hard as he visually traced the flare of her hips and sought the outline of the hard little buttons of her nipples through her shirt. He was hardening, aching . . . and forgetting what he'd come to do!

"Da—*blessit!*" he growled, making balled fists of his hands and squeezing them savagely. "I want those breeches. I don't want to ever see you in them again."

"What?" She leaned back on weakened arms, scarcely able to hear through the clash of impulses in her head. "My breeches?"

"And I want them now." He backed another step and jammed his fists onto his waist, spreading his shoulders formidably. "This minute," he demanded in a deep sensual rasp. "Take them off and put decent skirts on. In Boston, ladies dress for dinner. And by d—thunder, you will too."

"But—"

When she hesitated, he lunged at her, grabbed one of her legs, and pulled her boot off. She sputtered and protested, finding alarmingly little resistance in her desire-filled frame. When he reached for her other boot, she let him drag it from her.

"Well?" He halted, braced above her, his face glowing, his eyes hot with alloyed anger and need. Her parted swollen lips made no protest, but her green eyes lit with a glint of fire. If he wanted her breeches, that look said he'd have to take them from her himself. Against every bit of common sense he owned, he accepted her ultimatum and set his fingers to the horn buttons of her breeches. His knuckles brushed the smooth deerskin, stretched across her sleek belly, and excitement vibrated up his arms.

He clamped his jaw until it ached, and when the last button gave, his hands hovered hotly before seizing the top of her breeches and peeling them down her curvy hips. At first there was the shirt, then pale, soft skin, sleek rounded curves, and a patch of gingery curls in a neat little V. He froze, staring at the warm curls, sensing the sleek, tender flesh inside . . . feeling its liquid heat pulling him.

He straightened, quaking, unable to breathe for the desire squeezing his throat. She was looking at him with a dark, sweet invitation in her eyes and a promise of pleasure in lips swollen like cherries. He was trembling, ravenous. Once, twice, he'd loved her, burying himself inside her and losing some part of himself to her in the process. And twice he'd risen from her intoxicating loving into pure torment.

He reached for her, and felt a lightning bolt arc through his hands as he touched her satiny belly. He slid his fingers to the sides of her hips and down her firm, tensed thighs until he came to the crumpled deerskin about her knees. A third time . . . he could lose himself forever. The third time he wouldn't be able to stop, to resist this madness for her that made him so vulnerable. She'd find some way to use it against him, to betray him when it became convenient . . . or necessary. Then it flashed into his mind: Delilah, she had said to his father, not Jezebel. She was *Delilah* . . . to his *Samson*.

Whitney held her breath, watching desire flame through him with a life of its own. His fingers were like trickles of silver along her heated skin, and a familiar ache was swirling through the core of her. She wanted to surge against those hands, to feel his weight pressing her down into the soft bed, to feel the strong, rhythmic thrusts of his body inside hers, filling her. She wanted her woman's bargain with him . . . she wanted to love him and she wanted him to love her. She held her breath, knowing he wanted her, praying he would open his arms.

Then his hands closed on her breeches and he ripped them

down her legs and over her feet. She gasped, squeezing her eyes shut, feeling as though he'd torn her very skin away. Shame and hurt rocked her, and she bolted from the bed, her shirt and belt still in place, both shielding and revealing her bottom half. She pulled her shirt down angrily and faced him. He couldn't have made his rejection of her, his contempt for her, more plain. She forced her chin up to a stubborn angle and dared her eyes to fill with tears.

"You have what you wanted, Major. What are you going to do with them? I doubt they'll fit you." Her eyes dropped derisively to his breeches and filled with confusion at the evidence of his desire.

He stood there with her breeches wadded into one hand, his chest heaving, his face seared with private pain. "I'm going to burn them. And you're going to wear skirts and act like a marginally civilized human being. I'll be back shortly to escort you to dinner, and you'd better be in skirts." He stalked toward the door but turned back, his turmoil visible in every aspect of his frame. "And do something with that hair of yours."

Whitney watched as he slammed the door behind him. A moment later her legs melted beneath her and she scarcely made it to the bench at the end of the bed. She gulped air and gasped, feeling an ominous pricking in her eyes. Her hands curled into fists around wads of shirttail, and she refused to give way to tears.

What was she doing here? He didn't really want her, he'd just made *that* perfectly clear. Despite what happened to his body whenever they were close, he apparently hated her too much to actually touch her again. And his Iron Family certainly didn't want her there. They were convinced she'd wedded—ensnared him—for his money and his social standing. And she didn't *want* to be here. She'd come with him only because she was supposed to "collect" on her marriage bargain. A living, a family, a good bit of manly ser—

"Oh, Pa," she whispered through a choking in her throat. "How can I possibly make a proper bargain out of a marriage nobody wants?" Then the terrible truth of it struck her and she sagged, adding, "Nobody but me."

* * *

Sometime later Garner led a very subdued Whitney, garbed in her simple green wool dress, down the stairs and through the gleaming center hall. Their footfalls echoed on the hard walls and polished floors, auguring their coming encounter with the Iron Family. She glanced at the wrist Garner held in a viselike grip and lifted her chin another notch. She was a Daniels, she told herself, and Danielses were canny enough to bluff their way through anything, including dinner at a fancy table.

Byron, Ezra, and Cousin Madeline waited for them at the far end of a cavernous dining hall, and she felt Garner's hand tighten over her wrist. His restraining touch reached her embattled heart. He didn't trust her to behave in a civilized fashion. He didn't want her, *didn't trust her.* She raised her chin another notch to combat the sinking in her chest.

No taint of their earlier meeting was evident; politeness bordered on excess as Byron directed the seating. Whitney dragged her eyes from their stylish clothes to covertly inspect the fastidiously laid table nearby. The sight of snowy linen, tall crystal goblets, and myriad pieces of gleaming silver cutlery by each plate caused a squeezing sensation in her stomach. After some confusion, she found herself seated across from Garner and beside Cousin Madeline, who slanted mistrustful looks at her and leaned pointedly in the other direction. When servants in dignified blue livery began to serve, hovering over them to add and remove dishes, Whitney had to call upon every bit of acuity she possessed.

Food came in rounds: cold relishes and soups, puddings . . . by the time the steamed fish arrived, the dinner began to take on a surprisingly predictable flow: serve, chop, eat, sip, lean back, and let them remove. Though foreign to her experience, she realized that elements of such grand feeding were oddly familiar. She was surprisingly at ease with the heavy cutlery and her own insights into what was happening. She began to hear Aunt Kate's voice in her head, recounting details of elegant ways and fancy parties in her former life in Allentown. Whitney felt their unstinting eyes upon her, scrutinizing her dress, her simple hairstyle, and especially her manners. And she felt all the more empty inside for the debt she owed Aunt Kate, a debt she might never have the chance to repay.

"Well," Byron said, pushing back, fingering his tall wine goblet and leveling a stare at his son, "let us hear about your successes on the frontier. You must give us an accounting of your . . . adventures." He added a twist of a smile toward Whitney: too little and too late to be construed as genuine warmth.

"Oh, yes, do," Madeline crooned coquettishly. "Did you earn many ribbons and medals?"

"Never mind that, how many of 'em did you kill?" Ezra cut straight to the gritty score of military confrontation—the tally of bodies. He leaned forward on his wheeled chair and flicked a watchful glance between Garner and his bride.

Whitney felt their scrutiny and laid down her knife to withdraw her hands onto her linen-covered lap. Food stuck in her throat and she swallowed desperately as the quiet prickled up and down her neck. Garner was watching her; she could feel it, but refused to meet his gaze.

"There were no major military engagements on the entire campaign." He spoke in a carefully moderated tone. "The occasional skirmish, no more."

"No major battles? I've been scouring the papers for word—and not a single mention of you. So that's why. The gutless traitors saw you coming and ran for it," Byron sneered. "The damnable cowards. Only to be expected of the filth-spawned rabble who inhabit our frontiers, I suppose. Well, what did you do about it?"

"Washington departed after a mere few days, leaving the divisions to secure the area. I was part of that securing function."

"What the hell does that mean: 'securing'?" Ezra demanded, leaning forward and scowling such that his shaggy white brows met over his nose. "What in hell is 'securing'?"

"We were assigned territories to subdue and . . . clear of treasonous activity." Garner watched Whitney's paling face and chose his words with aching neutrality. "We were to search out and destroy illegal liquor and distilleries, and to arrest the distillers and their leaders."

"The treasonous scum," Byron said, pouncing on his revelations with pointed righteousness. "Half the lice-infested wretches probably need arresting on some account or other anyway. Most of those frontier scrubs are fugitives from proper society. Who in their right senses would choose a life of such squalor and animal deprivation unless some greater peril forced them to it? How many did you arrest?"

"I was assigned to clear a particularly difficult valley." Garner watched the heat rising in Whitney's lowered face, could feel the stiffening of her shoulders and a corresponding tightening inside himself. "We uncovered a large cache of contraband whiskey and arrested those responsible." Across from him, Whitney was hearing all he didn't say . . . her participation in the illegal trade, her father's arrest. He was carefully omitting her "shameful" connections, and the hot feel of his gaze on her drove the lesson home.

"And what of a commendation? Did you get one or not?" Byron prodded, unsatisfied with his son's sketchy report.

"It's likely." Garner saw the shudder that went through Whitney as he said it. "There was quite a bit of contraband . . . and resistance."

"Well, at least something useful will come out of this . . . episode," Byron sneered. "The damnable traitors should be hanged, every last one, as an example and a warning. I know the senti ments in Philadelphia are the same: a spate of hard-handed justice should be meted out on the lot of them."

Whitney's face came up, straight into Garner's dark gray stare.

"These low, animal sorts congregate on the frontier, thinking to escape lawful authority," Byron expounded furiously. "And they subsist in such deprived, degraded states for so long, they become like animals themselves, groveling in their own filth. Every standard of morality and decency abandoned. They tried to reduce the entire country to their pathetic anarchy and, by God, they failed."

Whitney's fingers were tight white knots in her lap, her body was rigid, her face crimson. Hanging, he had said. The western distillers deserved hanging. And the beleaguered folk who populated the frontier were vermin-infested criminals who wallowed in their own filth and had no pride, no loyalty, no dignity. Her pa was a "traitor" and her loving, extended family were low, crude animals . . . Uncle Harvey, Aunt Sarah . . . Aunt Kate. She couldn't breathe, couldn't blink, not even to avoid the darkness and anger she saw in Garner's features.

She trembled, trying to contain the tempest raging within her. She was an animal too. That's what Byron meant, probably why he had said it. He wouldn't defy Garner's ultimatum to degrade her directly, but he'd find other ways . . . meaner ways. And from the darkness in Garner's face, he probably believed it too. That's why he wouldn't touch her again. Blessed Gabriel—how it hurt. It was a small mercy when her tears defied her to fill her eyes and blur the sight of him.

Garner watched her struggle with his father's callous pronouncements. Her eyes were dark with pain, her body was rigid with the impact of those vile words. The almighty Byron Townsend had just reduced everything his Whitney was and loved to insignificant rubble. He read the desolation of her heart in the defiant tremble of her chin and, strangely, he felt it too, as though some part of her lodged within him.

Her whitened hands gripped the table edge as she pushed her chair back. Pride and misery warred in her heart-shaped face as she turned a blurred gaze on them, then strode out. Garner found himself on his feet, watching each painful step, and he turned on his family.

There they sat, the lauded and superior Townsends, with their smug ignorance and insufferable eastern prejudices in full array. Perhaps they actually believed it, the foul, poisonous doctrine of frontier inferiority Byron spouted like a self-righteous canticle. It was a mythology, he realized, created by his peers in business, his class, to insulate themselves from the human crises that prevailed on the country's harsh frontiers. And whether from true malice or mere arrogance, Byron had just wielded those judgments like a bludgeon against Whitney.

She had sat there, valiantly coping with the intimidation of a purposefully overset table and enduring their blatant contempt . . . forbidden to retaliate. He turned on Byron with blood in his eyes, his entire body quaking with towering rage.

"You insufferable bastard." His voice was raw with the long-fermented fury of a thousand sneers and slights. He was no longer in a mood to play the contrite son. "If you ever do anything like that to her again, I swear, I'll thrash you within an inch of your life." He slashed a fist across the table, sending several of the precious crystal goblets shattering on the floor. And he stalked out.

Ezra watched his grandson's passionate explosion and violent exit through narrowed, perceptive eyes. And as Byron cursed and Madeline gasped outrage, old Ezra finished his watered wine and smiled a crooked smile.

Sixteen

Whitney stood in her dusky room, staring out the long window. She felt utterly empty inside, as though everything vital to her being had somehow been ripped out. Only jangled bits of feeling and ragged hurt remained, crowding painfully into her heart and mind. Frightening images of her pa, dead, were mingled in her mind with visions of Garner's dark anger and his family's open contempt for her and her background.

She didn't hear the door open and close, didn't realize Garner stood in the shadows near the door, watching her. She sagged against the window frame and her square shoulders softened. How could she live here another day, bearing Garner's anger and coldness?

He stood watching her misery and felt the core of his anger drain through him, leaving a void inside him that he knew was tied to the pain she was feeling. His proud, quixotic little Whitney drank whiskey like a man, ran like a deer, bargained like a Baghdad merchant, and fought as dirty as a pillaging Hun. And yet she was proving vulnerable in the most unexpected ways. To words . . . as well as kisses. He swayed when the realization dawned: *his* kisses, his touch. She had wakened to womanhood in his arms and had responded fully, eagerly, to him each time he loved her. She had embraced her own stunning passions and his unbending self in the same tender moment, and in so doing had warmed the chilled core of his being.

Plunged into the steamy turmoil of a man's strongest needs and feelings, Garner felt physical waves of possession and protectiveness surging through him. He wanted her, wanted to discover and to claim the tantalizingly vulnerable parts of her, wanted to hold them safe. And in the grip of this compelling urge to comfort and protect her, he forgot all about protecting himself.

"Whitney—" He was mere feet away when he spoke, and she turned about with a horrified look. She wiped her wet cheeks with her palms and stiffened, raising her chin as she tossed a panicky glance about the room.

"I know I didn't wait to be . . . dismissed, or whatever it is you do. But I couldn't . . ." She fought a tightening in her throat to swallow, and died a little more at the emotion swirling in his finely chiseled features. His turbulent silence stirred her worst fears, and she backed a step, smacking into the window frame and open shutter as she sought escape.

"I didn't mean to make you angry. I'd never seen so many things to eat with. I know I probably did things wrong. But I didn't say anything about my pa . . . and I won't. I promise." Her jaw clamped shut and her throat closed, and the humiliation of breaking down in front of him was too much for her proud heart to bear. She struggled briefly to hold back tears, and when she lost the battle, she bolted.

"Whitney—" he growled softly, catching her, but unable to drag her closer without hurting her. "What my father said—"

"Is it true?" she blurted out, bracing and trembling as she searched the growing heat in his eyes. "Do they want to hang the distillers? Would they really kill my pa?"

Garner could scarcely answer as the volume of pain in her voice thundered through him. "No, Whitney, they don't hang distillers."

She sagged and he reeled her a bit closer before she halted him again. The bruising of her heart was visible in her beautiful eyes. And as a fresh volley of tears rolled down her face, all he could think about was holding her, sheltering her in his arms, kissing her tears away.

"My family . . . in Rapture . . ." She tugged her wrists closer, finding to her dismay that his hands came with them and his hard body was not far behind. "They're not animals . . . they're good people. They'd give a body the shirts off their backs . . ."

"Or the pies out of their ovens," he supplied, pulling her closer.

"And my pa's not a traitor. He fought in the War for Independence and took two British balls. He was with General George at Valley Forge. And Charlie's pa fought under General Green, and Uncle Ballard and Uncle Julius drove Henry Knox's ox team when he dragged his cannon across the mountains. They didn't try to bring the country down," she choked. "They just wanted—"

"—the freedoms they fought for," he finished for her, slipping a hand around her waist to bring her against him. He forced her tear-streaked face up to his and felt the shudder of her indrawn breath as she squeezed her eyes shut against the futile hope that he might believe her.

"And hardly anybody ever gets lice," she choked out on a sob.

"Just fleas." He nodded even though she couldn't see. He pulled her head to his chest and cradled it above his heart.

Warmth flowed from his hard body into her embattled core. His embrace, his soft words, the strange, comforting quality in his gaze both frightened and heartened her. He was holding her so gently. Or was it just the terrible loneliness in the middle of her, distorting her senses?

Her arms rose and halted midway, hovering near his waist in breathless uncertainty. Could he touch her like this if he really hated her? Then his fingers slid up her shoulder to her hair and cheek. She wrapped her arms around him desperately, burying her face in his shirt ruffles, embracing him and all he meant to her . . . for better or for worse.

"I'm sorry he hurt you, Whiskey." He clasped her fiercely against him and bent his head to whisper into her hair. "It won't happen again, I swear." The tremor of his body against hers, the hush in his voice, brought her face up to his.

He brushed her tears away on the backs of his knuckles and took her face in his hand, searching her with a hauntingly tender smile. Then he lowered his head to comfort her cherry lips and she melted against him, drinking him into her, filling her empty heart with his desire, accepting his comfort, borrowing his strength.

She opened to his mouth like a wild rose, silken and fragile, yielding her succulent nectar to his hungers. His tongue spiraled hers, beckoning, stirring a divine and primitive need for completion in her. She molded helplessly to his powerful frame, wanting him, reborn in his wanting her.

"Love me, Garner Townsend," she murmured, dazed, when he released her mouth to nibble the edges of her tingling lips and her chin and the line of her jaw.

"I will," he rasped, crushing her soft frame against his body. A groan erupted from his depths as the lightning between them set fire to his blood.

He scooped her up and carried her to the bed, ripping back the bedclothes to deposit her in the midst of them. He watched the desire flickering through her as he tore his coat and waistcoat from his shoulders. She lay there, her eyes glowing embers, her half-revealed breasts love-flushed . . . a wanton, irresistible angel.

When his boots and shirt came off, she sat up weakly, mesmerized by the symmetry and muscularity of his wide shoulders. She arched seductively, anticipating the feel of him against her bare body and within her burning heat. Clumsy fingers slid to the lacings of her woolen bodice, but he sank one knee into the bed and brushed her hands away.

"No—" he ordered hoarsely, "let me.

Time and again his hands strayed from their task to stroke her breasts, to savor the curve of her waist, to find the shape of her hip and thighs through her skirts. Then, with a primal male growl, he dragged her laces from their holes and tugged open her bodice. The sight of her, tangled in her clothes, half opened to him like some forbidden blossom, sent flame roaring into his loins.

"When," he half-groaned, rubbing trembling hands up the boning of her corset, "did you start wearing one of these?"

"I have to wear one . . . with this dress," she whispered, wondering at the strange, lidded look invading his handsome features. A new, focused intensity in his face took her breath as he dragged her dress from her with stunning precision. Her petticoat came next, and by the time he pulled her stockings from her, she gasped at the greed with which he undressed her. When he halted, staring hungrily at the deliciously trapped mounds of her breasts, she sent her fingers to the lacings of her corset.

"No—" he commanded, stilling her hands with his, "leave it."

"B-but won't it be . . . in the way?" she whispered, awed by this new glimpse of him as demanding, sensual.

"No, my hot Whiskey, it won't." He flipped the buttons of his breeches and shed them without taking his eyes from the satiny mounds she wanted to bare to him. He spread his desire-hardened body on the bed beside her and lowered his head to the voluptuous twin prisoners of fashion.

A small movement, a flick of his finger, and the dark, hardened nipple of one breast was freed to ride above its confinement. And while his mouth tantalized the proud, burning pebble, his finger released the other nipple to equally breathtaking stimulation between his thumb and finger. He twirled and nibbled and sucked the hardened peaks, making her gasp and wriggle. Through the steam in her head she realized her corset had become an extension of his hands, tightly embracing, molding her tender flesh, evoking her response.

And somewhere in that charged, erotic constraint, in the dueling of tongues and the hot press of bodies, he slid between her bare, silky thighs and began to stroke the creamy skin of her flesh in decreasing circles. With each knowledgeable swirl of his fingers she shuddered, responding to his sensual command. And each round proved the turn of a spiral that broadened, leading to the conclusion she craved. With wanton urgency she clasped his shoulders and sought his body with hers.

"Please—" She flicked her tongue over her dry, burning lips, then sucked breath through her teeth in a soft, delectable rush. "Garner, please—"

"Oh, Whiskey, love," he moaned, rubbing his sandy cheek against her nipple, then seeking her lips, "let it come."

Obeying his command, she gave herself over to the power of her own fiery responses and gasped, arching into his hand, aching for release. Once, twice . . . more . . . his strong fingers were guided by her desires. A wild, searing rush burst from the center of her, flinging outward, invading and claiming all of her. She clung to him, feeling the primal clash of pure elements within her, carrying her to the edge of existence, where all motion damped and muted into pure dazzling energy.

He called her back to him with tender kisses on her shoulders. And when she opened her eyes to him, they were filled with glowing coals not yet banked. Her voluptuous body rippled sinuously against him, opened, still seeking. Shifting slightly, she urged his weight onto her fully, and wrapped his buttocks with her sleek, muscular legs. She rubbed her liquid heat against his engorged shaft in seductive, thrusting rounds meant to conjure a like motion in him.

Garner sank his arms beneath her and joined their bodies. Fiery pleasure blew through him in consuming waves as he fought to contain his response. He moved with powerful rhythmic thrusts that rasped slowly against her burning flesh, carrying her with him. She arched against him, shuddering again and again, crashing through unseen barriers, one after another, as she soared higher and higher. And this time she called out his name and he came with her into the blindingly bright realms of pleasure.

In a starry night sky they floated, replete, drifting slowly back. Sometime later their fingers and legs entwined as they lay on their sides, facing. The steamy, charged haze between them lingered, exerting a powerful spell on their sated senses.

"You were right," she murmured, running her gaze over his sculptured face and his tousled hair.

"Um?" He opened his eyes, now smoky with satisfaction.

"My corset. It didn't get in the way."

"No, it didn't." His white teeth flashed a devilish grin in the dimness, and her heart quivered. "I'm rather fond of corsets, actually."

She was a little shocked to read the wicked glint in his eye so plainly. He meant he found corsets . . . stimulating. They brought his blood up . . . and other relevant parts of him as well. It was something of a revelation to her. He liked to look at half-dressed women.

"Well, I suppose that's reasonable," she announced a moment later, realizing that she had developed a powerful fascination in recent weeks for tall, glossy boots . . . and for snug breeches that hugged a man's tight buttocks and muscular thighs . . . and for the occasional glimpse of dark chest hair. "Anything else you're particularly 'fond' of?"

His grin went from devilish to positively dangerous. "Stockings. Sheer silk stockings . . . and . . ." He swallowed, staring into her sooty-lashed eyes.

"And?" she prompted, licking her itchy, sensitive lips.

"And . . ." He was about to say 'tight deerskin breeches," but thought better of it. "Bare skin. Especially yours."

"Oh, I was hoping you would say that." Her smile was both impish and desirous as she released his hands and pushed up to sit on her knees in front of him. Her fingers flew over her laces, ripping them out with seductive flair. And soon she peeled the bony restraint away, tossing it into the oblivion at the edge of their bed. "I really like bare skin better."

He laughed, his eyes riveted on her breasts as she spread herself over him, rolling him onto his back. Her knee inserted itself between his and she braced on her elbows above him. "Have you . . . seen a lot of corsets?"

He could read the drift of her thoughts quite clearly. "A few."

It didn't satisfy her. "Were you ever fond of one corset in particular?"

"No." That truth surprised him as it escaped. He'd never been exactly "fond" of a woman . . . before now. And it surprised him that he'd never even thought about women in such terms before. *Fond*. It was mildly disturbing. "I had more important things to think about."

"Such as?" She savored this closeness, this unprecedented sharing, relieved that there didn't seem to be another "corset" hiding in his heart.

"The Townsend Companies. My family has the distillery, a shipping concern, a bank, and a mercantile business as well as shares in other ventures. It's a diversified group, and managing them is a heavy responsibility, one I've been groomed for, worked for all my life. And I'm due to assume the helm soon. . . ." His pause was laden with hidden meaning. "It's a Townsend tradition, the son taking over. . . ."

"And your father, what will he do then?" she asked, watching the changeable lights in his eyes.

"Enter politics, hold office, most likely. That's what Ezra did until he became ill. That's tradition as well, politics in later years."

"It all sounds so . . . tidy," she observed, searching his expression. What she meant was "dull."

"Well, it's not. Things don't happen tidily. Control is actually voted by family shares, and the head of Townsend Companies has to earn both the family's confidence and his place at the helm . . . study hard, win a few military laurels, demonstrate sterling business judgment and impeccable character, and marry—" He halted and his ears reddened.

"Marry . . . properly," Whitney finished for him, beginning to see just how drastically their marriage might have affected his prospects. Just now his family's estimate of his character and his judgment seemed dismal indeed, primarily because of his "disgraceful" marriage to her. It produced a twinge of alarm in her chest and a very solemn look.

"You really want to control Townsend Companies?"

"I've wanted it, prepared for it all my life." He watched her deal with his revelations and felt the same uneasiness rising within him. No—he battled the unwelcome intrusion of larger problems—not now. Not yet. Just a little more time . . .

He ran a distracting finger down the length of her nose to her cherry lips. Her gaze warmed slightly, and she rubbed her chin gently on his chest, creating tickling sensations that vibrated through him all the way to his toes. His eyes closed as he concentrated on that sublime feeling, and a moment later they reopened.

She gasped as his arms flew around her and pulled her closer beside him. He rose over her in a single lithe and powerful movement, pinning her easily on her back.

"I have forty percent of Townsend Companies and I need sixty to control," he growled. "But right now I want a hundred percent . . . of Whitney Daniels."

Much later, in the chilled darkness of predawn, Garner picked up his beleaguered clothing, donned what he could, and padded

quietly across the hall to his own room. It was warmer than he
expected, and he realized a fire had been laid in the hearth even
though it was probably clear to all where he was spending the
night. Benson, he sighed. Only Benson would be so oblivious.
He pulled a heavy wing chair near the banked fire and sank into
it, propping his bare feet near the still-warm brands and bracing
for the disaster that always descended after he bedded Whitney
Daniels.

But the quiet continued uninterrupted. His body was at peace,
his passions truly slaked for the first time in his life. And with
passion's pathways purged, his thoughts were astonishingly coherent, focused. He'd made rapturous love to Whitney again and
again, too hungry for her, too intoxicated with her to stop. But
unlike the sickened aftermath of whiskey, the aftermath of *Whitney* was clear and calm, as was his view of the turmoil he'd
endured since the day he'd laid eyes on her.

He'd gone about in a perpetual agony of half-arousal, his body
reeling out of control, bursting into spontaneous flame whenever,
wherever she appeared. In front of his men or her whole village,
in a freezing wet forest or against a splintery barn wall—it didn't
make a bit of difference to his appallingly independent parts.
Wherever she appeared, his loins recognized her command . . .
and saluted.

He groaned, dropping his head back against the chair. It even
happened last evening, in front of his family. Lord, that was the
absolute limit, roused like a buck in rut from the mere sight of
two little bumps on her shirt and a few strategically placed wrinkles of deerskin. And all the while trying to explain and gloss
over the disasters already wrought by his volcanic and bewildering urges for her!

It was just in his nature, he had always understood, to be vulnerable to women in that way. Easily roused; easily had. And
after that first debacle at age sixteen, Chloe—he shuddered, he'd
spent years constructing impenetrable defenses against refined
womanhood. He taught himself to see absurdities in the elegant
affectations of the women of his class, concentrating on squelch-
ing and flattening his responses to the sumptuous gowns and
dresses worn by refined femininity. He had ruthlessly cultivated

immunity to the seduction of swishing skirts and fluttering fans and to the women who wielded them.

But Whitney Daniels was the perfect antithesis of everything he'd taught himself to beware. Straightforward, unaffected, seemingly unconscious of her sensual impact, she had startling preferences for breeches and bluntness, and equally startling indifference to his position and his money. She had absolutely nothing in common with the females of his class . . . except her penchant for betraying him in order to get what she wanted.

His vulnerability toward her was growing worse by the day, by the hour. Wanting her body to the point of distraction was bad enough, but every encounter with her roused increasingly more than simply lust. His face tightened as he recalled how hotly he'd defended her and how eagerly he'd comforted her. She'd seemed so hurt, so sweet . . . she had stimulated his feelings in a way that made "fond" seem pale indeed. And he didn't even want to think of the disastrous ramifications of that.

He was losing ground to her in almost every way possible, and it had to stop. He had to disentangle from her somehow, before she ruined both him and his chances for control of Townsend Companies. He had to keep her at a distance, and stay on guard against the wanting she conjured in him with a sway, a tilt of her head, or an unconscious lick of her lips. *Oh, God. How?* What could he do . . . where could he . . . ? *Think, man!* He had to find out what was happening at the offices. Undoubtedly a backlog of work was waiting for him. Perhaps he could stay . . .

Wait. A stroke of pure inspiration came to him. If uniqueness was her compelling sensual appeal, then perhaps there might be hope after all. Perhaps he could somehow camouflage her terrifyingly potent curves and kill two birds with one stone. She would be made acceptable to his family, and her unique sensual hold on him would be greatly diminished . . . well, at least to tolerable, resistible levels.

Lord, yes! That was exactly what he had to do. Make her look like the kind of spoiled, treacherous "lady" he could ignore. Clothes, fancy clothes . . . lots of them. That was the place to start.

* * *

The bed was empty when Whitney awakened the next morning. She turned over, wriggling with naked luxuriance in the soft sheets, and waiting for the achy echoes of pleasure in her body to damp before she slid from the bed. She donned her shirt, stirred the embers to life in the hearth, and threw back the drapes to admit the morning. The sun was surprisingly high. Her gaze swept the floor around the bed for some trace of Garner's clothes and found none. He was an early riser, she recalled with a trace of a smile.

As she collected her clothes and drew them on, she couldn't help recalling how they had been removed. He'd followed her defiant exit from the dining room, and instead of the furious lecture she expected, he had listened to her and taken her into his arms. She had been so lost, felt so empty, and he had reached past his family's outrage and past his own anger and prejudices to give her the comfort of his desire. Traces of his "comfort" still lingered in her body . . . and her heart. It was a tantalizing bit of the "more" she always seemed to want from him. Maybe there was hope for her bargain after all.

Mercy arrived with a breakfast tray, hot water, and a dark look at the open drapes and the crackling fire Whitney had built. Whitney watched her tidying the bed and changing the toweling on the washstand. It made her uncomfortable, having somebody else do personal things she was used to doing. As her memory enlarged to include more of the events preceding and precipitating Garner's stunning comfort, her face darkened too. The Iron Family thought she'd trapped Garner into marriage for his money and a life of eastern luxury.

"I'll be building up the fire of a morn and drawin' them drapes in future, ma'am." Mercy finally faced her with a tight, wary expression. "It be my duty. I'd have done it earlier, but I looked in an' you was sleepin'. And the young master, he said to let you sleep."

"Well then, what will you take for your service, Mercy?" Whitney stood and struck a trading pose, leaning back on one leg with her head slightly tilted.

"Why . . . n-nothing, ma'am." Mercy frowned so that the

crow's-feet above her wary brown eyes deepened. "It's my duty, ma'am."

"Not with me it's not," Whitney informed her. "Now . . . I'd be willing to help you with your chores every day for a bit of water and the wood I use at night."

"Ma'am." Mercy's eyes widened slowly as she realized Whitney was earnest in her shocking proposal. "I could never allow it, ma'am. It be purely unthinkable."

Whitney read her shock, and decided with her trader's logic that she'd insulted the woman by offering too little. Her face flamed as she realized that she was essentially a pauper in this great house, with virtually nothing of her own to trade. But then, she vowed, that had never stopped a Daniels from doing a bit of bargaining before.

"Well . . . you can draw the drapes and stir the fire, but I'll fetch my wood and water myself, then. If you'll just show me or tell me where the woodpile is, I'm handy with an ax."

"Ohhh, ma'am." Mercy splayed a work-reddened hand over her ample bosom and staggered back, shaking her head. "No, ma'am. Not me." And she exited in a flurry of proper gray skirts.

Whitney stood, crimson-faced at having done so poor a job of dealing, and even more determined to take nothing while in this house except what she earned in an honest bargain. No one was going to call her a greedy, conniving fortune hunter again. She'd take nothing but what was necessary for the "living" that was owed her; just food and shelter. She already had enough clothing for decency, and warmth.

She washed, nibbled some breakfast, and picked up the tray to carry it back to the kitchen herself. At the top of the stairs in the center hallway, she paused, realizing she had no earthly idea where the kitchen was. Footfalls from behind startled her, and she turned to find Benson hurrying down the hall toward her. His arms were filled with hearth brushes and a bucket, and his worn, oversized clothes and his ruddy face were smudged with ashes and soot. His whole countenance brightened as she returned his tentative smile, and he stopped a safe distance away.

"Ma'am!" He beamed at the sight of her love-polished cheeks and sparkling eyes. "Ye fairin' well, ma'am?"

"Well enough, Benson. And you? How do you like 'gentlemun's gentlemuning'?"

"Oh . . ." He flushed and looked down. "Wull, the majur, it seems he already had help thataway, so they give me the hearths to tend. It be all right, if'n old Edgywater don't come about too much." Whitney nodded in perfect sympathy. "Oh"—He hastily set his things aside to reach for the tray—"I'll take that for ye, ma'am."

"No," she said, pulling it back, "I'm taking it back myself, Benson. Just tell me the way to the kitchen."

"Oh, but, ma'am . . ." For every tug Benson made on the tray, she tugged it back.

"What in heaven's name is going on?" Madeline's voice wafted up the stairs, followed closely by Madeline herself. Whitney turned to face her and had to chew a smile from her lips. Cousin Madeline was wearing loopy hound's-ear braids on each side of her head.

"What do you think you're doing?" She turned on Benson the instant she landed on the top step.

"I were jus' offerin' to take the tray back—"

"I'm perfectly capable of doing it myself—" Whitney began.

"Don't be absurd." Madeline turned her pert young nose up at Whitney. "You can't go about *carrying* things. That's servants' work." She took hold of the tray herself, shoving it into Benson's charge with obvious distaste. "Take it off to the kitchen and then get back to your hearths. Henceforth, you're not to concern yourself with aught but grates and ashes." As Benson reddened and hurried off, Madeline turned to Whitney with a cool, assessing stare that aged her young face.

"Cousin Garner has left instructions that I'm to take you to a dressmaker this afternoon." She eyed Whitney's shirt and brown homespun skirt with obvious distaste. "Undoubtedly to make you more *presentable*. Make yourself ready midday."

Whitney recalled her recent resolve and realized this was a perfect opportunity to demonstrate her utter lack of interest in Townsend luxuries. Her lips tightened in a little smile as she leaned toward Madeline with a determined glint in her eye.

"I won't go," she declared flatly. "I already have all the clothes I need."

Madeline drew her chin back, surprised. Her fine nostrils flared briefly and her hazel eyes narrowed as she evaluated Whitney, searching for the scheme behind her unexpected refusal and finding none. "Suit yourself."

A small warm spot of satisfaction bloomed in Whitney's middle as she watched bossy little Madeline lift her skirts and sail down the hall toward her room. Then she descended the stairs with a spring in her step, recalling Benson's route of escape and intent on finding the kitchen herself.

In the hallway above, Madeline paused at her door to flick a smug little glance back at the empty top of the stairs. "Well, Cousin Garner," she purred, "you can't say I didn't try."

Whitney located the kitchen at the rear of the huge house, and the staff stopped dead at their tasks to stare at her. She inquired politely as to the whereabouts of the spring or well and the wood pile. After a bit of fuss and consternation by the head footman, she was shown a monumental pile of split logs at the back of the service yard. When she made to load her arms with some of it, she found herself staring into the head footman's outraged face, and then locked in a steely-eyed tug-of-war over the log in her hands. She tried bargaining him, offering to take some to the other upstairs rooms as well if he'd just let her have it.

Minutes later she strode back into the kitchen, her arms empty and her cheeks aflame. The wretched fellow acted as though the blessed woodpile belonged to him exclusively! She requested a bucket and directions to the well. No bucket, no well. She was close to losing her temper, when she noticed bread makings on the heavy maple table and decided to try bartering a bit of culinary skill for the wood and water she wanted. The gray-garbed cook just stared at her in horror, and there was a shocked murmur among the maids, the scullery boys, and the footmen who had collected as word of the young master's wife's presence in the kitchen had spread.

The rotund, rosy-faced cook spread herself between Whitney and the table, sputtering. Whitney was not so perplexed or so easily put off this time. Cooks of all stations were known to be jealous of their venue and their methods. Why, Aunt Sarah would hardly let anyone else even tend the fire when she made some of her special pies.

"Well then," she said, a gleam in her eye as she raised her chin, "ever heard of a Queensberry fruit braid?"

She saw the cook start, and realized yet another of Aunt Kate's snippets of grand eastern life was about to bear fruit . . . fruit *braid,* to be precise. She saw the cook wince and threw in her perennial trump, that irresistible Daniels grin. And shortly she was up to her elbows in flour and butter and fresh peeled apples and cherry conserve.

Edgewater stalked through the house, finding virtually no one at their proper duties, and when he saw the clutch of servants jammed into the kitchen doorway, he charged into the kitchen in high dudgeon. The sight of Whitney bending over the worktable, her sleeves rolled and her chin smudged with flour, was enough to cause a veritable explosion of indignation.

Whitney wouldn't have minded for herself actually. But he vented his anger on the cook and the others who were only watching. She wiped her hands and brushed flour from her skirts and retreated to what Edgewater called the "family" part of the house.

Now truly at loose ends, Whitney rambled darkly about the main floor, her hands clasped securely behind her back to prevent bumping or disturbing any of the "exquisite" things she encountered. There were two great parlors on either side of the center hall, filled with silk-covered furnishings and great, somber-hued portraits of old men who looked like they'd all bitten into the same sour persimmon. Probably Townsend forebears, Whitney deduced darkly. Why else would they keep such gloomy-looking faces hanging around? She studied the portraits and shook her head. There wasn't one she would have trusted in a horse trade; flinty, acquisitive eyes; pointy, interfering noses; and arrogant and unyielding chins. Garner Townsend was apparently from a whole line of Iron Forebears, she decided. And the question rose inescapably inside her: how did Garner escape being cast of solid iron too?

She quickly exited their collective disdain and drifted down a side corridor, peering into rooms and wondering where Garner was. Spying a half-open doorway, she crept closer and peered into a musty, shuttered room lined with what appeared to be shelves stuffed messily with books and papers. Its contrast to the bright, pristine state of the rest of the house was striking, and she ventured inside to investigate. Her nose curled at the air of stale tobacco and moldy dust, and she made her way to the window to throw back the shutters. A snuffling inhalation and a startled grunt came from near the fireplace, and she wheeled.

"You!" came a sleep-rusted voice.

Whitney found herself facing old Ezra Townsend, who was seated on his wheeled chair in front of the fire, shading his eyes from the intruding sun as he glared furiously at her.

"What the hell are *you* doing in here?" he snarled.

"I didn't realize the room was . . . occupied." She stiffened, her defenses well primed from the morning's several disastrous encounters. "I just saw the books and . . ."

"Humph," he snorted derisively, his gray eyes narrowing on her shapely form and the light of pride in her striking eyes. "What would an unlettered chit like you do with a book? Plundering, more likely. The whelp ought to keep you on a shorter rein."

"I *can* read, thank you." She crossed her arms firmly beneath her bosom for emphasis. "And a Daniels would never plunder. We take only what we've earned in a good, honest trade."

"That remains to be seen." Ezra wheeled a bit closer, looking her over with a proprietary air. She was a damnably fine piece of work, old Ezra decided, at least on the outside. "How did you do it?" he demanded. And when she canted her head to eye him mistrustfully, he clarified. "How did you trap him into marrying you? He's a fool sometimes, but he's no idiot."

Whitney's cheeks flamed as she met the old man's gray gaze straight on. "No, he's not. Nor is he an arrogant, profane tyrant . . . nor a wasp-tongued chit . . . nor a dried-up old prune!" She savored the sudden bit of color that leapt into the old man's sallow face. "He's a hard man sometimes, but he's not like the rest of you *Iron Townsends* at all. And thank God for it." She squared her shoulders as Ezra's mouth worked soundlessly, and then strode out.

"A-and stay out!" Ezra hurled at her back as she quit the

threshold. He grumbled, wheeling himself to the window to slam the shutter, which rebounded on him with a sharp bang. He slammed it a second time and again it refused to stay closed. Snarling a wordless oath, he turned his wheeled chair toward the open door to stare at it. And as he sat in the warm stream of sunlight, his temper drained, replaced by an intriguing bit of insight. So the hot little piece defended the whelp, did she?

Seventeen

Whitney charged upstairs to the meager sanctuary of her room, roiling inside. She plopped down on the bench at the foot of her bed and stared past her scuffed boot toes into the blue rug. She'd encountered his prickly family, his stuffy old butler, and his cowed and irritable servants, and offended nearly every soul in the household on some level or other . . . and it wasn't even noon.

She huffed irritably. It was an unholy affront to her trader's pride that they wouldn't let her bargain decently to meet her needs, or even let her do things for herself. On the one hand, they accused her of fortune hunting, and on the other, they refused her the dignity of earning her keep. But a Daniels was nothing if not pragmatic, and she was too astute a trader not to recognize a lost cause when she saw one. To continue to bargain and insist on doing the most basic tasks herself would only reinforce their already jaundiced view of her and expose both her and Garner to further derision. And while she didn't give a flea's ear what his wretched family thought of her, she was coming to care a great deal about Garner's place in their esteem and how they treated him. Their approval was crucial to the control of Townsend Companies that he seemed to want so badly.

His family, she thought with a shudder. Her pa had said Garner owed her a family. But this wasn't a family, it was a nest of vipers! They were cold-blooded and competitive and critical of each other in the extreme. They marked out their territories in "percentages," and defended them with all the charm and civility of snapping turtles. Whitney's frown deepened. They would never be *her* family, not in a million years! Imagine growing up in such a treacherous climate. How Garner had survived was beyond—

A warm wave of understanding washed over her. *He'd grown an iron shell, that's how he'd survived . . . a stern, righteous, unbending iron shell.* Garner's face suddenly rose in her mind as it had been last night, dark-eyed and smiling one of those rare, dazzling smiles, and she melted physically. Inside his iron defenses was a deliciously tender and sensual man, a man who had comforted her with his loving despite his family's obvious contempt for her and in spite of his own misgivings about her background and behavior. She had begun to think she'd only dreamed such caring, conjured it out of her own longings and need, but it was there all right.

Her sea-green eyes darkened like a wind-whipped ocean as she recalled the dusky heat of his face, the inflamed velvet of his lips, the caring that was evident in every movement, every nuance of his loving. She relived the way his powerful body trembled against hers, and the way it stopped trembling. Her troubled scowl of minutes before was gradually replaced by a glow that was sultry and feline and utterly new to her—a potent blend of Daniels and Delilah.

Garner Townsend owed her. Her pa was certainly right about that. But she didn't want Garner's money, and she certainly didn't want his family. That left the third part of the bargain . . . his "manly service." Chills rippled from her toes to her fingertips and the tips of her breasts at the shocking physical memory of his touch on her bare skin. Her lips tingled and she felt herself going warm and liquid inside.

If what her special trader's sense told her was true, she'd probably get more than she bargained for. That wickedly enchanting Daniels grin spread slowly over her face. *Maybe a lot more.*

That evening Madeline met her in the center hall with the announcement that Garner wouldn't be home for dinner—something about business—and that she'd taken the liberty of ordering a dinner tray sent to Whitney's room. Whitney read the intended snub in Madeline's spiteful little smile and squelched her first impulse to accept the temporary reprieve from his family. She strode past the girl and into the dining room to wait with ladylike patience while dinner was delayed and another place was set at the table. And under three pairs of hostile eyes, she managed cutlery and napkin with an aplomb that would have warmed Aunt Kate's heart. Her only gaffe of the evening was a request for a bit of whiskey in place of the wine she wouldn't be drinking—a request that was immediately and emphatically denied.

The next three days offered Whitney no chance to work at securing her bargain with Garner. He rose well before dawn, went to the company offices straightaway, and returned home late at night, precluding all possible interaction between them. He was avoiding her, she realized with a pronounced sinking in her chest. How was she supposed to make good her bargain if she was never even able to lay eyes on him?

Alone and adrift, she wandered about the house, studying things and trying to occupy her restless energies. But even Townsend House was only so large, and after nearly three days of solitary exploring and trying to avoid his prickly family, she gave up and made her way downstairs, determined not to shrink from them anymore.

She pushed open one of the sliding doors to the parlor and stepped inside, unaware it was occupied. She suddenly found herself eye to eye with Madeline, who was ensconced on the silk brocade settee near the fire, beside a very dignified-looking woman with graying hair. Talk ceased as the woman followed Madeline's narrow-eyed glare to discover Whitney standing near the door.

"I'm sorry." Whitney frowned uncertainly. "I didn't know if . . ."

"Well, since you're here—" Madeline put her teacup down on the butler's tray sitting by her knees and turned a vengeful look on Whitney. "You may as well clear it away." She waved a taunting hand. "Carry the tray back to the kitchen."

Whitney stood a moment, stung unexpectedly by the taunt and the gesture Madeline used regularly with servants. Since she insisted on going about dressed like a servant and acting like one, Madeline's look said clearly, then Madeline would be pleased to treat her like one. The fashionable woman gave her an unseeing glance and turned back to their interrupted conversation. Whitney bristled. She hadn't lived in a fancy house long, but she knew the insult that was intended.

"And Garner's wife . . ." the dignified guest inquired. "When will we get to meet her, my dear?"

"Oh, I doubt for some time," Madeline purred. "She was raised on the frontier, you know. Not used to our 'advantages.' Do you know . . . she won't drink wine. Only *whiskey*."

"Oh, dear. *Poor Garner*."

Whitney turned on her heel and shoved the door back angrily, striding out into the center hall, nearly colliding with Edgewater.

"Your *coat*, ma'am?" He stiffened at her request.

"It's not in my room and Mercy said you'd know about it. It's made of gray felt." She gestured irritably down her front. "With polished horn buttons—"

"It is indelibly etched in memory, Madame." He sniffed, with a jaded glance at her clothing. "I was under the impression that Madame would not be leaving the house until her new apparel arrived."

"Well, there won't be any 'new apparel,' thank you." She flamed and couldn't help glancing down at her simple homespun garments. She dressed *worse* than the servants, Madeline had said. She drew herself up straighter. "And you had better find my coat."

"I'm afraid that's impossible Madame. It's been . . . burned."

"B-burned?" Whitney was speechless. They took what little she could call her own and *burned* it? She finally found her voice on the bottom of its register. "How *dare* you?"

Trembling with hurt and ire, she pivoted, striding straight for the kitchen and the servants' hall. She had to get out of there for a while.

"I need a coat, any coat." She took a stand in the midst of the kitchen with her hands on her hips and her chin raised to a defiant angle. "And I'm willing to deal for it." The kitchen staff and other servants stopped dead in the shocked silence. Time was kept by the angry pulse of Whitney's blood.

"Here, ma'am." Over Edgewater's sputters and the cook's clucks and the shocked murmurs of scullions and footmen, Benson stepped forward, unbuttoning his own worn uniform coat. "I'd be proud to give ye mine."

Whitney's throat was too tight and her eyes were suddenly too full to bargain him properly. She simply accepted it and made to put it on.

"No." Mercy stepped forward, then hurried to the pegs near the kitchen door for her heavy brown cloak. She brought it to Whitney with a solemn "A woman's cloak's more fittin'."

Whitney nodded mute gratitude as she spun the cloak about her shoulders and strode out the kitchen door. In her wake, a confusion broke loose and the imperious Edgewater lost his temper and had to pound the table with his fist to restore order and send everyone back to their duties.

Late that afternoon Garner arrived home with an aching head full of numbers and a healthy dread of running into his unpredictable wife before he reached the sanctuary of his room. His efforts to avoid her had netted him too much work and too little sleep in the last three days. He was in no condition to combat his volatile urges toward her or to surrender to them. He quickly handed off his hat and voluminous greatcoat to a very terse Edgewater, but was intercepted by his petite cousin before he reached the stairs. Madeline dragged him into the east parlor and launched immediately into a detailed list of complaints against the household's newest member.

". . . duty to make you aware that your wife has the entire household in an uproar. She persists in disrupting the servants' routines, invading the kitchen, arguing over servants' work. She haggles and bargains for food and necessities like a common fishwife. Good Lord—she insists on carrying things and chopping her own wood and drawing her own water—as if she still lived on the wretched frontier! It's a pure embarrassment to the staff to have to deal with her."

Garner stood, stunned, with images of Whitney in a defiant trader's mode burning in his mind. Bargaining for food and water? He shuddered visibly.

"And she refused to accompany me to a dressmaker so that

she could be made *presentable* . . . absolutely refused." Madeline's lashes fluttered, and one dainty hand splayed over her throat as if containing the shock. "She said she didn't want or need new clothes and she wouldn't go. *Wouldn't go!* And she's been demanding *whiskey* to drink. Whiskey—like some crude savage—" She swooned, pressing the back of her wrist to her forehead, at which point Garner came to his senses and ushered her to the settee near the fire.

"She refused the *clothes?*" he ground out from between tightened jaws. The throbbing in his head had just gotten orders of magnitude worse. Dammit! He should have known she'd do something like this . . . ruin his plan by refusing the clothes. Then she'd set the whole bloody house on its ear and demanded whiskey to drink!

It was his own fault; blame sank deep claws into his Townsend pride. He'd left her to her own devices, expecting that she'd somehow come to terms with— *No,* he sternly made himself face the fact, *he'd run from her.* The turmoil she bred inside him had overpowered his manly sense of duty yet again, and he'd fled her. But there was no retreat from something as potent and devastating as Whitney Daniels. He should have known. She was something in his life that had to be confronted, met head-on, whatever the outcome.

". . . just demanded one of the servant's cloaks and left." Madeline was on the brink of a few artful tears.

"Left?" The news galvanized him. He grabbed Madeline's shoulders. "What do you mean, left? Where did she go?"

"I have no idea. She just threw one of her little fits and left, hours ago. She's probably gone for good."

Garner was on his feet in a flash, running for the stairs. His heart was pounding wildly as he burst through her chamber door and paused, scouring the room for signs of her. He threw open the wardrobe and slowly released the breath he'd been holding. Her clothes, such as they were, were still there. She wouldn't have gone without them. Scarcely reassured, he stomped back downstairs bellowing for Edgewater to have his horse brought around, then roaring for Benson and a second mount. He was going to find her, and when he did . . .

* * *

Whitney's steps slowed in the closing darkness. Dread weighted her feet. She stared down the cobbled street at the looming outline of the great house and wished she could have stayed the night on the common instead. She felt more at home in the big old trees and the frozen, weedy fields of nearby Boston Common than she did in the cold elegance of Garner's house.

"Poor Garner," Madeline's lady guest had said, and those words had echoed in Whitney's heart all afternoon. It was no secret that his family considered both her and her marriage to Garner a major disgrace. But it surprised her to realize that so much of their outrage seemed to be based on what she wore . . . and drank. And it bewildered her that they seemed to judge upstanding, gentlemanly Garner by the shortcomings in *her* wardrobe and *her* taste in liquor. An oddly protective urge swelled in her. He deserved better.

She sighed heavily and paused to look above. There was the evening star winking in the sky, and the cool crescent moon grinning down at her. She felt a wave of pure longing for Aunt Kate's womanly wisdom and her pa's infectious confidence. And she wondered if they were watching the same moon, the same sky, thinking of her too. The empty feeling she'd been fighting all afternoon deepened.

Roused from her musings, she entered the carriage turn and hurried up the steps, past a footman holding two horses at the edge of the front portico. Just as she reached for the great brass door handle, the door jerked open and she was bowled back, engulfed in an angry storm of camel-colored wool and heated male force. She stumbled back. A pair of strong hands narrowly kept her from tumbling off the portico, then pulled her into the light from the open door and tightened fiercely upon her.

"You!"

Whitney looked up into Garner's anger-bronzed face, and her heart stopped. He was huge, overpowering in his caped greatcoat, and he was furious. He growled something else as his eyes raked her wind-mussed hair and dropped to her cloaked form, but the sense of his words was lost in their leonine tone. He dragged her back into the center hall under the shocked gazes of Cousin Madeline, Edgewater, and half the household staff, and kicked the door shut behind them. The sound jolted her ears back to functioning. "Just where the hell have you been?"

"I—j-just went for a walk. On the common." She tried to straighten in his grasp, her mind racing to discern the reason for his fury.

"Out alone, in a city you know nothing about? That is the most irresponsible—" He caught the avid stares turned on them and stiffened abruptly. Pulling her roughly into the west parlor, he released her long enough to draw the huge sliding doors against their audience.

She braced as he turned on her, eyes narrowed, gloved fists clenched. What had she done to rile him so? In two long strides he was looming over her again, thundering loud enough for the entire house to hear.

"Your behavior is appalling, inexcusable! Going out without escort—without even a word—you could have been set upon or spirited off. I won't have it, Whitney Daniels! You're not to go out alone again—ever!" His hands closed hard on her shoulders. The shake he intended to give her dampened to a mere quiver as the warmth of her flooded up his arms, releasing a wave of relief in him. Her cheeks were cold-polished and her eyes were deep tidal pools beneath long, feathery lashes; she was whole and safe and here. But the melting of his worry laid bare other issues that were not so easily disposed of.

"In three short days you've managed to turn this entire household upside down! And by heaven, that will stop as well, do you hear?"

"What?" She fought his grip, her Daniels pride rising to replace her pained confusion. "What are you talking about? I've done nothing to your suffocating old house, or your precious family!"

"You've interfered with the servants' rightful duties, demanding *whiskey* to drink, *bargaining* for food and necessities, insisting on chopping wood like some charwoman, and carrying your own water. It's embarrassing to the servants and a disgrace to me."

"Well, I didn't have anything to trade for their services," she answered hotly.

"They're already *paid* to perform such duties!"

"Not by me!" She flamed.

"No—by *me!*" He jerked a thumb at his heaving chest, and released her abruptly. "I pay them in cold, hard cash. That's the way we do things in Boston . . . we *acquire* things with *cash money,* not by bartering and bargaining. You'd just as well get used to it, wench. If you want something in Boston, you pay for it with legitimate, federal issue dollars!"

"Well, I don't have any money—" Her throat tightened humiliatingly.

"Well, *I* do . . . plenty of it . . . all you'll ever need."

"I won't take your money," she choked, backing a step. "I don't like money. Money is the root of all evil—it says so in the first book of Timothy." Her eyes were very large and luminous now, washed with confused hurt. "I don't want your money. I don't want anything from you." She ground to a halt, knowing she truly lied for the first time in her memory. There *was* something she wanted from him, something she wanted with all her heart.

He watched her struggling with her emotions exactly the way he was struggling with his. And it nearly undid him. Anger was the only way he could counter this relentless slide into the steamy cauldron of his desire for her.

"We're married"—his voice thickened in spite of himself—"and as my wife you're expected to reside in a certain level of comfort and luxury, whether you want it or not. It's . . . required. You're the only wife I get, and that means you're going to live in this suffocating old house and put up with servants doing things for you, and you're going to act like a lady and dress like one." He stiffened above her as if stung. "That's another thing—" He began to heat all over again. "You defied my order—refusing to go to a dressmaker after I left explicit instructions you were to have new clothes."

"I don't want any new clothes. I don't need them." Her throat tightened humiliatingly. "And I won't take them. I won't take anything I haven't earned by honest sweat or in a proper bargain."

"Don't be absurd, wench. You don't have to earn things; you're my wife."

Whitney felt a telltale scratching at the back of her eyes and had to swallow a lump in her throat to speak. Her voice was small and tight.

"But I'm not your wife. You don't talk to me, you won't look at me. You don't bed with me. I'm not your wife. I'm just somebody you made a mistake with once."

That quiet charge sank into the middle of him like a knife into butter. Every word expressed with brutal accuracy the dismal state of affairs between them, and yet it wasn't really the truth. For nothing in that bleak summary expressed the desire for her that pushed him to the brink of insanity every time she came near, or the heaving tumult of feeling she stirred in him every time he looked into those big, warm eyes of hers and realized how easy it would be to love her.

He inhaled sharply, as if gut-punched. Suddenly everything in his chest was squeezing, crowding his heart so that each beat sent a quiver of pain through his chest. That was it, he realized with a horrifying wave of understanding. He loved her.

It tore through him like a lightning bolt, laying open his nerves and sinews to expose the complex new feeling for the first time. He loved Whitney Daniels. A flood of bone-deep wanting engulfed him, and in its wake came a full roiling panic. Loving at its best was fraught with pain and uncertainty. But loving Whitney Daniels was being destined for disaster, earmarked for oblivion. There were no halfway measures with a woman like her. Loving her meant risking everything he wanted, everything he was. And she'd already betrayed him twice.

Whitney watched as powerful forces clashed within him, understanding that she was involved. He wanted her, she knew, even though he didn't want to want her. And he didn't trust her; his allegations tonight were proof. Yet he insisted she was his wife and insisted she act like one.

"Blessit." He grabbed her by the shoulders and dragged her closer, his features now fierce. But a muffled cough issued from across the room, near the hearth, and his dark head came up, eyes blazing.

Whitney started and followed his angry gaze to the sight of Ezra Townsend's smirk. The old man was leaning around the back of his wheeled chair, which was parked before the fire. He'd obviously been there the whole time, watching, hearing every word.

Beyond mere humiliation now, Garner glowered furiously at his grandfather and pulled crimson-faced Whitney to the door. Under a horde of curious eyes, he dragged her up the stairs to her room.

"You owe me," he declared, looming huge and deadly potent above her, while deathly afraid of touching her. "You owe me a wife, a *fitting* wife. I'm sending for a dressmaker first thing tomorrow morning. You're getting new clothes whether you like it or not."

He turned on his heel and strode out, locking the door behind him. Halfway down the upper hall, he was stopped by the sight of Ezra and his chair being trundled up the stairs separately by their brawniest servants. When Ezra was seated again, he waved the servants off and sat staring at Garner with a knowing smirk. Garner lifted his chin and made a show of removing his gloves and shrugging his coat from his shoulders as he headed for the steps. Ezra's voice halted him.

"What a horse's arse you are sometimes, boy."

Garner turned, his back rail-straight and his face stiff with chagrin.

"You have what most men only dream of." Ezra laughed a rusty, ironic sort of laugh at his grandson's predicament. "A hot little piece for a wife . . . who doesn't know how to spend money."

Half of that night, Whitney paced her room, torn between stubborn hope and nagging despair. Something momentous had happened between them that evening, she could feel it. But for the life of her, she couldn't say whether it was momentously good or momentously bad. She *owed* him a wife, he said. Could it be that he really wanted their marriage bargain too? Or was it just his stubborn pride demanding a suitable wifely ornament for his Townsend ambitions?

There was a cost and a profit in everything, her pa always said. And it was painfully clear she'd cost him his "proper marriage," his family's approval, and now perhaps his reputation as well. "Poor Garner" echoed in her hollow middle. Maybe she *did* owe him a wife who wore feminine clothes and drank proper wine.

She sighed. All she knew for sure was that she was coming to want a lot more than just a bit of "manly service" from Garner Adams Townsend. She wanted *all* of him. Everything there was. And if that was lustful and greedy, so be it. She was a Delilah, after all, and probably entitled to a few desires of her own. In point of fact, she reasoned with a desperate bit of insight, that was probably what made the difference in women to begin with: Delilahs had desires and "decent" women didn't. And Delilahs not only had desires, they invariably did something about them. Like . . . going to the Iron Major's bed. Or like luring the "Iron Husband" into hers.

Her heart-shaped face began to glow with a dangerous blend of Daniels and Delilah. If she was ever going to have him, really have him, she was going to have to use his own wants against him, in the long-standing Delilah tradition. And just what *did* the Iron Husband want? Her beguiling smile and the gleam in her eye both deepened as she thought of their latest confrontation. *Her.* He apparently still wanted *her.* And he wanted her dressed like a lady.

There was confusion midmorning in the upstairs hallway of Townsend House. One of Boston's finest dressmakers had been wakened with a summons before dawn, and had hurried to Townsend House with the promise of a lavish fee burning in her ears. Now, however, the dignified little woman was huddled with her two wide-eyed seamstresses and Mercy outside Whitney's door, speaking in shocked whispers and watching the top of the stairs. They didn't have long to wait.

Garner came charging up the main stairs, his face set like flint, his eyes glowing hot. And in his wake trotted a superbly outraged

Madeline. He strode right through the clutch of women, sending them skittering aside in exaggerated horror, and burst through Whitney's door, When it slammed behind him, it released a nervous volley of exclamations. Little Madeline caught the dressmaker's shocked gaze and held it.

"If so much as a breath of this gets out, you're finished in Boston."

Inside the well-warmed room, Garner advanced on Whitney, his eyes blazing at the sight of her, clad only in a gauzy, thin-strapped chemise and strategically backlit by the bright fire.

"What in hell is this all about?" He stopped a defensive distance away, spreading his long legs, settling hard fists on his hips. "I've told you—you'll have new clothes whether you want them or not." His eyes locked on her glowing face to keep from straying toward more dangerous territory, and he began to tighten with unholy expectation. There wasn't any "safe" territory with Whitney Daniels.

"I won't wear a corset, that's all."

"Don't be absurd. All ladies wear them. Even *you've* worn one before." He realized her chin was set at a dangerous angle, and it jolted all his defenses to full alarm.

"Well, I won't put one on now. I've never liked them, and I refuse to put one on." She crossed her arms under her breasts, pulling the treacherous spider's web of a fabric tight over her taut nipples, and trapping his gaze in it. She could almost see the heat rising in him as his face and ears reddened another shade.

"The hell you won't," he growled, striding forward, then stopping dead in his tracks. *Corsets.* He felt the pull of her sultry green eyes and realized instantly what this was about. In a vulnerable moment he'd revealed his special weakness for corsets, and the little witch was blatantly using it against him. A *Delilah*—he recalled her own epithet—she would always use his impulses against him.

He whirled one way, then the other, searching the chaos of fabric bolts and wooden boxes and half-sewn garments draped everywhere. There they were . . . the corsets. Three of them, lace-trimmed and frilly, lay on the bench beside Whitney's bare, silky knees. Fingers of fire ran up the contracting muscles of his belly at the sight. This was no time to panic, he told himself desperately. This was a test of wills, of manly mettle, husbandly authority. And, by damn, he'd not be found wanting.

He stalked over to them, trying to look formidable, and snatched the closest one up, holding it out to her. "Put it on, Whitney. I swear—you won't leave this room until you have." She raised her chin another notch and her eyes darkened another shade.

"If you want it on me, you'll have to put it on me yourself."

There it was. The ultimate defiance. It was do or die. And a Townsend always did.

"Don't think I can't, wench," he warned, "or that I won't." Her only response was a defiant little smile that dared him to try. He growled and lunged at her, sweeping her off her feet and plopping her bottom down on the bench, atop the other corsets. He grabbed both her legs in a viselike grip and began to shove the half-laced garment over her trim feet and up her shapely legs.

It took a moment for him to realize that she wasn't resisting, that her legs were captive in his arms and her body wasn't even hinting at resistance. He eased and stiffened in the same moment. And when he glanced over his shoulder at her, his mouth dried with dread. She was leaning back on her arms, her eyes now emerald-dark, her lips parted, her skin glowing from the dual heat of the nearby fire and the fire within her. Her hip was pressed against the side of his ribs. Suddenly he was hot all over and trembling.

He fastened his eyes on the corset and pulled it up to her thighs, realizing he was raising her chemise with it. He was groaning inside. In a desperate move he stood and lifted her onto her feet. Now she would bolt or kick or shove it down, fight him. But she just stood quietly, her arms at her sides as he set lean, muscular hands to the corset and pulled it up her thighs and over her curvy bottom. He fought to keep her chemise down and to ignore the way the corset molded her soft, sleek buttocks as it glided over them. But the warmth of her body and the faint rosy scent of her skin were radiating through him, charming his senses, constricting his thoughts.

And shortly it slid into place around her narrow waist and nudged her full, hard-tipped breasts. He jerked his hands away, panicking at the impulses battering his legendary Townsend restraint. But he felt the challenging heat of her look and took a hard breath, pulling the rim of the corset up and over those seductive mounds. His knuckles brushed that excruciating softness, and something exploded in his loins, completing a massive arousal. He flinched and flamed. *Ignore it.*

He turned her gruffly by the shoulders to draw her laces from behind, and still she made no move to resist. With his hands shaking and his loins throbbing, he could scarcely coordinate the lacing and pulling. His eyes trailed the nape of her neck, her half-bare shoulders, and slid to her tightening waist and the sweet swell of her lush, inviting bottom. He was seized by an overpowering urge to pull that soft bottom against his hard front . . . to send his hands around that small waist . . . to set those succulent breasts free. . . .

He froze, his body rigid as the thought flashed through him: in this contest of wills, she was letting his impulses do her fighting for her. She'd roused him to pounding, agonized tumescence without so much as a touch, a kiss, or the slightest indication of desire on her part. She knew his weakness for her, and she used it against her. She was unraveling his self-possession like an ill-knit sock. And when it unraveled completely, what then? Would he lie in pieces at her feet?

She felt him still, felt the heat of his body invading her from behind, and her throat tightened. She turned slowly to face him, trying to read in his mood whether he would welcome her embrace.

But as they came face-to-face, he stumbled back a stiff-legged step . . . then another . . . and another. With each step the turmoil visible in his face and powerful frame increased. He didn't stop until he reached the door.

"Now"—his voice was choked—"let them dress you like a lady, dammit."

When the door slammed behind him, Whitney stood for a

minute, her chin trembling, her entire body flushing crimson with shamed heat. Lord, what did it take to make him set hands to her again? But a moment later she lifted her chin and raging fires of determination billowed in her eyes. Delilah apparently wasn't enough. It would take a bit of Daniels as well.

As it happened, they did dress her, and undress her, and redress her, over and over. And after the initial contretemps over the corset, and Garner's husbandly edict, Whitney proved the very model of cooperation. Madeline's cooperation was rather more conditional, she agreed to help choose suitable clothes only because Garner pulled her aside and threatened to introduce Whitney to her society *buff naked* if she didn't. Whitney dutifully stood and posed and turned and tried half-stitched garments. And when they spread swatches of luxurious fabric and bolts of lace and ribbons and trims before her, she found herself strangely moved to stroke them and hold them up to the afternoon light.

Apparently there had been a few changes in fashion since Aunt Kate retired to the frontier. Corsets were briefer, infinitely more bearable; dresses had higher waistlines, and petticoats were less voluminous and restrictive. Fewer things were starched; softer, more drapable fabrics were the order of the day. Stockings were silken and translucently sheer, making Whitney pause, adjusting a garter, to recall Garner's confessed weakness for them too. She'd thought it strange at the time that he could be amorously roused by something as commonplace as stockings. But then, she'd never seen stockings like these.

With each garment planned, each style and cloth agreed, she found her interest in womanly wear growing. And since no exchange of coin was involved, she relaxed enough to indulge her new fascination a bit. There were clothes for riding and for home and for visiting, for morning and daytime and evening wear. And though Madeline insisted there was absolutely no need for ball gowns, the little dressmaker clucked and insisted that Mister Townsend had specifically mentioned them . . . "something about the Hancock Ball . . ." Madeline's groan could have been heard all the way to Westmoreland County.

When the dressmaker left late that evening, Whitney had three new dresses and the promise of twenty more. And she had a headache, a burning nose, and itchy eyes from the lint and the strong smell of the fabric dyes. She took a bite of food from a tray that was thoughtfully brought up by Mercy, and climbed into the middle of her big, soft bed with a tired but pleased expression. She needed a sound night's rest. It was going to be the last un-interrupted sleep she had for a long while . . . if she had anything to do with it.

Eighteen

Garner arrived home from the company offices the next evening with a tightening coil of premonition in his gut. For the past day and a half he'd been walking around in a wretched half-roused state, unable to think, scarcely able to string a coherent sentence together. All creation seemed engaged in a conspiracy to fill his senses with Whitney in her absence. A breath of spice outside a bakery became the scent of her lips. An aura of light around a candle flame became the tarnished halo of her hair, the swish of a clerk's broom became the sway of her hips, and a rounded breakfast bun became . . . *damn*—the merest hint of her and his blood was racing through his veins, plunging toward his loins again. What utter misery, being trapped inside a body someone else seemed to control.

He shed his greatcoat into Edgewater's efficient hands, pulled his waistcoat down firmly, and tried to look more controlled than he felt. He joined Byron and Ezra in the west parlor before supper, and Madeline soon arrived with a cryptic reference to the absence of his "free-spending" wife. He was relieved to hear that Whitney had finally cooperated with his plan to clothe her in sumptuous, ladylike fashion, but couldn't help wondering if it might be too little too late. When Mercy appeared in the parlor doorway looking rather ashen, Garner knew his day-long sense of dread had been well founded. He bent to collect the message, then shot up straight, his face erupting red, his fingers clenching at his sides.

"Dammit," he growled, heading for the stairs in the center hall. His long legs covered the tiles quickly and mounted the steps by twos and threes.

Mercy was left to face the other Iron Townsends with a message from Whitney. "Mistress Townsend . . . she says yer not to wait supper on them."

Whitney stood by the blazing hearth in her room, clothed in an embroidered green silk wrapper and staring at the door. There were bees buzzing in her stomach and a faint hum of expectation in her blood. When the door burst open, she started and felt a shiver up her spine. He stalked inside, surveying both the room and her with irritation. When the door slammed behind him, it rattled the wall *and* Whitney's nerves. His long, muscular legs, his wide, black-clad shoulders, his big, supple hands set in gentlemanly ruffles—she'd never seen him look so big . . . so male . . . so determined.

"Get dressed," he growled, his deep tones vibrating her nerves.

"I won't," she said, steeling her nerve and lifting her head a few telling degrees. She could see the depth of resistance in his eyes.

"I don't know what your game is, wench, but I'm not having any of it. Dress yourself properly and come down to supper or—" He stopped, realizing he didn't have an ultimatum that made any sense at all. Or what? He'd dress her again himself? A slash of heat ran through him from head to foot. Not if his life depended on it!

"Get dressed or I swear I'll call the servants to do it for you," he finally snarled, though with a telling waver in his hostile tone.

"Then . . . I suppose"—she undid the ties of her wrapper and shrugged it from her naked shoulders, letting it glide down her bare body and drop into a shimmering pool around her feet—"you'll have to call them."

It took every bit of combined Delilah and Daniels audacity she possessed to stand there naked before him, daring him to call the servants to stuff her into her clothes. She saw him stiffen, watched as he fought to control his eyes . . . and lost. And there it was. Her jubilant trader's sense told her that light of yearning, that acquisitive glint in his eye was the first key to securing her wifely bargain with him.

He swallowed hard, feeling his insides turn to liquid heat, feeling his blood drain from his brain to collect in his already primed male parts. The sinuous curve of her stance, the impudent thrust of her nipples, the enticing fullness of her hips, the sleek taper of her long legs. How could his blood be roaring in his head this way, when it was all surging into his swelling parts?

"Or"—her voice grew noticeably huskier—"you can *bargain* me into them."

"Bargain?" he managed to ask, his temperature rising precipitously. "Good Lord—*bargain* you?" He shook his head to reclaim his senses and dragged his gaze up her body to meet hers. Her green eyes were lit with passion fires that held him rapt, unable to tear himself away.

"I almost forgot. Everything has a price with you, doesn't it? What is it this time, wench? What do you want?" A wicked little smile stole over her generous lips as she read the second sigh: demanding the asking price of her cooperation.

"I want your shoes . . . and stockings. I'll put mine on. If you take yours off."

"Wh-what?" He snorted his indignation. "Don't be absurd, wench. If you think for one minute . . . what makes you think . . ." He searched desperately for a bit of disdain in his churning being. "What in hell makes you think I'd take my clothes off to bargain you into yours?"

But even as he said it, the erotic ramifications of it slammed through him with the force of a stone hammer. The excruciatingly slow peel of his clothes . . . the tantalizingly slow donning of hers.

Her heart quivered at the third sign: belying interest in the desired object. She watched his eyes unfocus briefly, and it was all she could do to keep a calm mien. They still had "offer and counteroffer" to go. And a deal was never done until it was done. But the only weakness in her plan was the possibility that he might just turn and leave again before she got him out of his clothes. And he didn't show the slightest inclination toward that.

In truth, the possibility of leaving never crossed his mind. From the minute he stepped into the room, he knew he was being brazenly seduced, and his entire body had begun to vibrate in response to her irresistible sensual challenge. Now those tremors of anticipation had climbed his spine and rattled his brain. He couldn't think properly, couldn't make out what she really wanted from him. Not money. Not clothes. Not status. Inside him, the noise and confusion of his titanic struggle for control increased. Even if he managed to clinch this bargain . . . what would he lose in the process?

"Your shoes and stockings, Garner. For mine," she prompted, lifting one sheer, silky stocking from the bench beside her that was draped with an entire set of ladies' intimate garments. She rounded the bench, swaying, and sat down, raising one knee, pointing her toes . . . poised to slip a sleek limb into that snug, silken sheath.

His eyes burned as they fixed on the seductive arch of her leg, the erotic rounding of her buttocks pressed down on the bench amid velvets and laces. The fire in his loins crowned instantly. Anything . . . anything . . . just put it on, he groaned inside. Shoes—they were only shoes—he had other shoes! *Dammit—* part of him—yelled—*give her your shoes!*

He nudged his gold-buckled shoes off with a growl, then held his breath as she slid her toes inside a stocking and began to pull it up. His desires rose with it, inch by tantalizing inch, filling his throat. When she paused and her eyes flickered down him to his stockings, he leaned down and flipped open the knee buttons of his breeches and tore his stockings loose. Some part of his sanity slid with them as he pushed them down his calves and over his feet.

He straightened, knowing now that he was stripping more than just his clothes, he was shedding his resistance to her . . . baring himself. And for the life of him, he couldn't stop it. The other mesmerizing stocking inched its way up her leg and was tucked beneath a tied lacy garter. He held his breath as she reached for a pair of velvet shoes with dainty little spool heels and slid her feet into them. She rose to her feet, clad only in shimmery stockings and pink rosette garters and ladylike shoes.

"Now your coat. Take off your coat."

"What for?" he choked, his body aching, trembling, near the flash point of total explosion.

"For my chemise." She picked it up and held it against her breasts, watching his eyes fasten on the garment, watching him swallow with difficulty. An instant later he was removing his silk-lined coat with jerky, tortured movements. She smiled with covert sympathy and pulled the thin chemise over her head, letting it fall slowly over her hard-tipped breasts and down her hips into place.

He managed a rattled breath of relief that she was at least partly hidden—then he froze. The chemise left her legs visible below her knees and her rounded breasts and the curve of her waist were clearly outlined beneath the clingy fabric. *How could she possibly seem more naked with clothes on?* The throbbing in his loins had only increased.

"Your waistcoat and shirt for my corset," she demanded huskily, losing her own gaze and determination momentarily in the snug fit of his garments around his lean waist. Her knees were going weak. It was more than any "bargain" now, however important. Desire was swirling through her core, preparing her body for his touch. And a surge of sensual joy pulsed through her at the way his hands shook as they reached for his buttons.

Her corset slid up her legs, over her curvy hips . . . briefly raising her chemise, exposing the moist, gingery curls at the base of her belly. Her legs parted and braced in a pure sexual provocation of a stance as she settled the corset around her waist and tucked her breasts inside. She drew what laces she could and then walked toward him . . . a sensual prowl that immobilized him completely, stopping his breath, his blood, even his thoughts.

She presented him her back and lifted her fragrant fall of hair out of the way so he could tighten and tie her lacings. Operating outside his conscious will, his hands actually managed to do it, to tighten the cinch around her small waist, emphasizing its delicious contrast to her rounded buttocks . . . and deepening his torment. Corsets—God, how he loved corsets. And silk stockings, and skimpy little chemises . . . things ladies wore beneath the dresses he'd taught himself to loathe. And on Whitney's tantalizing body, such refinements were doubly potent.

She turned where she was, facing his hot bare chest, and gave his unbuttoned shirt a tug that sent it sliding down his shoulders into oblivion. He was braced, barelegged, and bare-chested, mere inches away.

"Breeches," she whispered up his throat as she lifted her face. "I want your breeches, Garner Townsend."

Quaking, teetering on the very brink of eruption, he let himself be drawn into her eyes, into the passionate tidal pools that held the promise of things he didn't even know how to want. All he knew was he wanted her with every aching sinew, every embattled impulse, every tortured part of his being. And whatever price she asked, he was going to pay. Trembling hands tore at the buttons of his breeches.

"Your breeches for my petticoat," she breathed, "fair is fair." She backed to the bench, reached for her soft petticoat, and stepped into it. And she saw him come for her . . . his breeches sliding down his tight buttocks, down his powerful thighs, baring his swollen shaft. A sharp trill of exultant desire ran through her at the sight of his passion. In the thrall of his focused male desire, she managed her final gambit.

"It seems you're one garment short. I—I still have my dress . . ."

"What is it you want from me?" he half growled, half groaned, seizing her bare arms. "What is your price, Whitney Daniels?"

In the heaving silence, eyes met and hearts stopped. Passion sizzled and crackled between them, scintillating, white-hot. The Iron Major was suddenly molten, caught in passion's roaring forge, waiting the shaping strokes of loving hands to give his being final form, to shape his destiny, to fashion his soul for a life of loving, or a lifetime of regrets.

"I want your loving, Garner Townsend." She poured all the passion of her bright being, all the warmth of her growing love for him into one breathless whisper. "Come to my bed . . . and love me. And I'll gladly wear your fancy clothes."

Garner stood, quaking at the very gates of paradise, unable to believe his ears. Love her? *That* was what she wanted? Lord, yes—he'd love her—he already loved her—would always love her—

"Yes." His banded arms crushed her against his hardened body and his dark head swooped to possess her mouth. "Oh, yes." He plunged into her spicy sweetness, demanding, devouring her eager response. She surged against him, engulfed by his desire and buoyed by her own. His long, lean body, his heated male scent, his velvety tongue, the hard press of his male desire against her belly, started a free-spinning wheel of pleasure in the center of her.

Her hands flew over his back, finding its mounds and ridges, unleashing its latent power. He groaned and sent his hands to cover her deliciously imprisoned softness, At the limits of her corset, he reveled in the contrast of boned binding and soft, delectable flesh. And he shuddered hotly at the realization that at the center of all that pristine muslin and proper restraint was a succulent coral blossom of womanly heat, waiting.

He fumbled blindly for the ties of her petticoats, refusing to take his mouth from hers for even a moment. A throaty, seductive laugh rumbled in her throat as she realized what he wanted and helped him find them. She slid her mouth from his long enough to whisper, "You don't want me to leave them on?"

"Petticoats . . ." he rasped between voracious nibbles of her lips, "aren't my favorites."

They were shed instantly, and when she felt him working the corset lacings at the small of her back, she sent her hands to still them. His eyes were black with need when they opened above her.

"Tonight I want your bare skin," he said with a crooked, desirous grin. "I want to love all of you, and only you. Just Whitney."

In seconds he had peeled her underclothes from her, all but her stockings. And he carried her to her bed and covered her intimately with his hands and eyes. His long, supple fingers teased her to quivering peaks of arousal. And wherever they led, his pleasurable mouth followed, blazing wet little trails across her breasts, her belly, and down her hipbones. He caressed the swell of her breasts and invaded the honeyed heat at the base of her belly.

She writhed and whimpered, gasped and wriggled under his touch, impatient for greater pleasures and yet unwilling to relinquish the smallest rapture. And with each stroke, the fires of need built higher in her, making her crave the completion that only his body could give her. "Love me, Garner," she moaned, arching into his hands, seeking him with her burning body even as she called to him with her woman's heart. "Love me . . . always."

Roaring heat engulfed them both as he slid between her smooth, muscular thighs. She wrapped her legs around him, urging him higher, meeting his forceful movements, reveling in the lean power of his beautiful body as it completed her own. His arms slid under her shoulders and his hands sank into her hair as he arched against her. A wild, powerful rhythm claimed them: giving and receiving, surrendering and conquering in the sublime, unending cycles of love. Wave after wave of need brought them together, ever closer to the bright, dimensionless planes of pleasure that could be reached only in a true joining.

Higher, hotter, closer . . . till gradually existence and movement slowed, time dissolved into pinpoints of pure, inexpressible feeling. Launching free of human bounds, she shattered unseen limits and soared through fathomless regions of joyous pleasure. And unerringly through the vast, uncharted reaches, he found her, and they were joined in spirit as they were in flesh.

A long while later she felt him nuzzle her ear and place a soft kiss on her temple as he slid to the bed beside her. She drew a breath, but when he pulled her warm, pliant body against his, she released a sigh instead of a protest. She opened her eyes and saw that he was watching her, a wry softness to his expression and an adoring warmth in his gaze. His dark hair was damp and tousled and his face and shoulders wore a sheen of spent heat. She'd never seen him so relaxed and unguarded.

A sweet ache settled in her chest. She trailed a finger down his square chin and down his breastbone, twirling it in the dark, lacy hair of his chest. He shivered.

"You realize, of course, that I'm going to have to wear corsets all the time now underneath those lady dresses."

"I—" he began, then cleared his throat. "I suspect so. And how perfectly wicked of you to remind me of it. You realize, shameless hoyden, that I'm not going to be able to look at you without recalling what you're wearing underneath. And if you're going to do that to me"—he glanced down at the way her palm was making circles over one of his hard, flat nipples—"you'd better be prepared to take the consequences. I'll not be held responsible for my urges if you continue to encourage them like that."

Her hand stilled and her eyes danced with mischievous lights. "Are you saying I might get more than I bargained for?"

"I'm saying exactly that, my hot Whiskey."

"More of your loving, your smiles, your time—which?" Her fingers swept his chest and up his throat to feather over his lips. A womanly glow lit her enchanting heart of a face. "I want them all, Garner. I want you in my bed every night, the way you are right now. And I'm serving notice, I intend to have you. If you go on ignoring me and avoiding me and resisting your urges to bed me, you'll have a fight on your hands." Her voice dropped to a silky, irresistible whisper. "And I can be a very dirty fighter."

And as if to prove it, she unleashed that devastating Daniels grin, aiming it straight at the vulnerable center of him. There was nothing in the Iron Townsend repertoire that could even come close to the soul-bending power of that bit of persuasion. It was like looking full into the sun, dazzling and disorienting in the extreme. His chest crowded with something bewilderingly close to raw delight. She apparently cared enough about him to fight dirty for him.

"I want to be a wife to you, Garner Townsend. A real wife." She raised onto one elbow and her jaw set in a demurely stubborn manner. "And if that means wearing fancy dresses and corsets and eating every bite with a different fork, I'll do it. And if it means learning to drink wine instead of whiskey, I'll do that too. And if it means living here with your Iron Family—"

She stopped and her eyes widened. What was she saying? Wear corsets? Give up whiskey? But even as her determination shocked her, she owned it. This was the tender paradox of Garner Townsend, the man inside the man; the one she had ached for, bargained for, and despaired of ever having. He was lying against her, warm and naked, staring at her with a soft-eyed wonder that was almost painful to behold. And she knew at that moment that whatever price he asked would be worth paying for Garner Townsend's loving.

He watched her glowing determination with a poignant fullness in his chest. "Would you really do that, my sweet Whiskey? Would you really wear corsets and put up with my family and learn to spend money properly?"

"I would if the trade was right."

"A bargain to end all bargains?" He laughed, caressing her with a bold, claiming stroke from thigh to breasts. Her eyes darkened with an ageless aura of mystery. "What was it you wanted . . . my time, my smiles . . . and loving?"

"More," she admitted recklessly. "Because I'm yours, Garner Townsend. *My* time, *my* smiles, *my* loving are all yours." And with a flash of inspiration she added, "A hundred percent yours. Isn't that what you once said you wanted, a hundred percent?"

No words on earth could have shot as straight to his core. *A hundred percent* . . . totally and completely his, only his. The thought set his heart contracting with a crushing wave of possession. He shot up onto one elbow and rolled her onto her back, sliding one leg possessively across her hip. His handsome features bronzed from the joy and heat erupting inside him.

"Do you know, all my life I've had forty percent of things." His voice was deep and ragged as he caressed her cheek and stared down into the warmth of her smile. "I can't remember ever having something that belonged completely to me, just me. Forty percent of the companies, of this house, my clothes, and even my pony when I was a child. Everything was always more *Townsends'* than *Garner's*. Until now. Now you're mine, wench. My woman." His eyes darkened with renewed hunger. "My wife."

Her mouth opened under his even as her body and her stubborn heart opened to him irrevocably. And when he joined their heated bodies again, she knew she'd just clenched the kind of deal every trader dreamed of . . . a true *paradise bargain*.

The next morning a discreet knock at the door awakened them, nestled side by side in Whitney's blue bed. Garner raised himself onto his elbows and called permission to enter. It was Benson, with a huge armful of firewood and a perfectly oblivious smile. Garner made sure the comforters were tucked securely about Whitney's bare shoulders, then waved Benson on to build up the fire. As Benson left, Garner laid orders for breakfast and hot baths for the two of them.

"Wake up, wife," he whispered into her ear, watching her stir. She was perfectly desirable, tousled and kittenish in the jumble of sheets and comforters. He slid down into the body-warmed bedclothes and curled on his side around her, pulling her legs up and over his hip. Watching her waken, he felt a strange sense of calm that he was coming to realize was the fruit of the night's intense loving. It was past dawn and he half expected to find himself in pieces. But his thoughts were lucid, his body at peace. It was remarkably like the other time . . . that first night at Townsend House, when he had comforted her.

It was ironic that she who wreaked such havoc inside his body should also be the one to restore him so completely. She deliberately roused his volatile passions, then just as deliberately satisfied them. And last night she'd roused his emotions, his pride, his complicated manly impulses for possession, and she'd satisfied them too. And in her wake, once again, his world became focused, comprehensible. It was a true revelation to him, this clarity of mind, this centered calm in the midst of him. And he turned this new sight upon himself, his life, and his family.

In the cold, circumscribed Townsend world of money and power, there was no room for anything as unpredictable as human desire. It had been condemned and exorcised from their collective being, and banished to realms of lesser mortals. Those who succumbed to its lure were deemed flawed in some basic way, vulnerable. And to be vulnerable in any way was anathema to the Iron Townsends. He smiled wryly at the appropriateness of Whitney's term for them. He'd spent twelve long, joyless years trying to recoup his standing with them, trying to prove he was an Iron Townsend too. In the process, he had ruthlessly denied his most basic needs as a man: the experiences of intimacy and emotion, desire for a woman, and his own need for autonomy and independence.

And with a wriggle and a kiss and the bite of a button, Whitney Daniels had barged right into the empty, aching core of him. And once there, she announced her intentions to stay and audaciously demanded that he love her. And she'd gotten everything she wanted. He loved her tantalizing body, her stunning eagerness for physical loving, but he loved the stubborn, intriguing paradoxes of her inner being even more. He loved the brash, reckless vitality of her that thumbed its nose at his family's god-awful propriety the way he never could. And he loved the tender, vulnerable young girl who had succumbed to her bewildering desire for him in spite of her loyalty to her father and her extended family.

Whitney watched him looking at her and wished she could have access to his thoughts. She prayed he wasn't getting cold feet about the bargain they'd consummated the steamy night just past. She raised her head to kiss his cheek and murmur "Good morning," and soon found herself wrapped in a warm embrace, being devoured in a very leisurely and very reassuring fashion.

When the Townsends eventually did descend the stairs, the entire house stopped to stare. The scandals over Mrs. Townsend's new clothes had provided juicy fare for household gossip. All were now shocked to see Whitney wearing a fashionable high-waisted velvet dress, forest green in color and trimmed with Alençon laces and velvet ribbons. Her thick mane was curled into ringlets and raised to a ladylike fall down her back. Around her throat was a creamy satin ribbon and over her shoulders was a lace-rimmed kerchief caught together at the front of her bodice by a carved ivory cameo. Her movements were surprisingly graceful in her heeled shoes, and she seemed quite at ease with her new style of raiment. None could deny she was the very image of a proper Townsend wife.

They exchanged glazed and potent looks across the dinner table that afternoon, scarcely touching their own food and positively ruining everyone else's appetites. Whitney's stunning transformation and Garner's ardent attention to her set Byron's teeth on edge and sent him straight for his coat and his business

offices. Madeline watched with a stiff expression then escaped
to her room in a royal huff. Ezra eyed them sharply and wheeled
toward his study with a particularly knowing sort of smile. That
left the two of them alone, and they whiled away the rest of the
afternoon with a belated tour of Townsend House and a walk on
wintry Boston Common. Their eyes and hands met often and
each wondering smile explored the new boundaries of their relationship.

But by evening, when they gathered in the parlor, the collective
Townsend pique had taken on proportions that made chilly in-
roads into the warmth that had developed between them. Garner
felt the weight of duty and family disapproval on his shoulders,
and reluctantly began to speak again of the offices and prevailing
commodity prices and shipping routes.

Whitney felt his withdrawal into that impenetrable Townsend
sphere, and her heart sank. She'd made good the third part of her
bargain, thinking it would be all she could possibly want. But
her coveted wifehood was scarcely a day old and, like a true
Delilah, she was coming to desire even more. It struck her that
when her pa spoke about a "living," he might have meant more
than just the "providing" part; he might have meant actually
living together, participating in each other's lives, sharing things.
She caught the covert smile Garner sent her and the intimate
promise in his eyes, and was reassured that he meant to share
her bed in a short while. But a strangely shaped little hollow
inside her wondered if they'd ever share more.

Garner went dutifully off to the Townsend offices the next
morning, leaving Whitney to her own devices for the day. She
wandered about the house, trying not to upset the servants by
being too helpful or too independent, and was generally successful. But midafternoon she managed to offend Madeline deeply
by asking what she did all day, every day. Madeline leveled a
scathing glare at her, collected a piece of ladyish needlework into
her sewing basket, and exited in a snit.

Minutes later she found herself standing in the hallway that
led to Ezra's study, and wondering how she'd gotten there. When

she turned to go, she came face-to-face with Ezra himself, humped over on his wheeled chair, creaking down the hallway toward her. He looked up just in time to keep from running into her, and stopped with an uncharacteristic fluster, struggling to turn the chair about to avoid her.

But the rough wooden wheels of the chair snagged on the hallway runner and he bobbed and shifted irritably trying to free them. Something thunked onto the floor from his blanket-covered lap and rolled toward Whitney's feet. A bottle . . . a brown, thin-necked bottle with some sort of liquid in it. She picked it up and stared at it, then at Ezra, who bristled, reddened, and pulled his neck in defensively.

"Out of the way, woman," he growled, deciding on a frontal strategy and struggling to reroute his half-turned chair back to its original course.

"You dropped this."

But his bushy white brows knit into a solid line and he batted both her and the bottle aside, making furiously for the door of his study. As he passed, she heard the unmistakable clink of still more glass bottles coming from beneath the blanket spread across his knees. Just as he reached the door, a second bottle thudded onto the hardwood floor, skidding and spinning to a stop by the door frame.

Ezra's sallow face flushed, but he forged straight ahead, leaving Whitney to collect the second bottle and trail after him. She caught him in the study, and planted herself in front of him as he wheeled obstinately toward the littered mahogany desk. On impulse, she grabbed a dangling corner of the blanket and gave it a tug.

"Wh-whaaa—?" he sputtered, and clutched futilely. Four more bottles were tucked about his lap and between his knees on the chair. He huddled, glaring at her. Caught. Red-handed.

Her green eyes danced over the incongruous sight, then settled on the two bottles she held in her arms. The blend of pride and petulance in his withered face tugged at something inside her, reminding her of Uncle Julius's and Uncle Ballard's mulish spells. She worked the cork of one bottle free and took a sniff. A sweet brown vapor filled her head and seeped into her blood.

Rum. She closed her eyes briefly, analyzing it, absorbing it. Then she leveled a searching look at Garner's grandpa, caught sneaking spirits into his study. He stared back with a wary gruffness, as if waiting for her to say something. When she didn't, his bushy white brows lowered farther.

"You goin' to tell them?" he demanded.

She straightened with a keen, thoughtful look at him as she realized who "them" was. "It seems to me a man's entitled to a tilt or two in his own house."

"It's only *ten percent* mine." He peered at her from the corner of his eye. "They won't let me have any. Ever since I was struck, all I get is a glass of wine at supper." His sharp nose made a rather interesting curl. "Even that's damnable watered down. Pure souse."

Their eyes met as each studied and evaluated the other. He crossed his arms over his thin chest and his mouth pursed stubbornly. She matched him, crossing her arms around the two brown bottles with a deepening frown of speculation.

"They won't let me have any spirits either," she mused. "I'm supposed to learn to drink wine." She made a face and shuddered at the idea, and the corner of his mouth twitched.

Silence fell again as they regarded each other. Her eyes narrowed; his crinkled at the corners. She chewed her bottom lip. He puckered his mouth a bit more. A stubborn Townsend scowl tightened his face even as a Daniels glow lit hers. They watched each other's eyes widen, began to read each other's thoughts. Was it possible . . .

"Get the glasses!"

"Right." She came to life, dumping the bottles on the desk and following the finger Ezra flipped toward a dusty, lacquered cabinet in the corner. She hurried back with two thick glass tumblers and, at Ezra's order, left them on the desk to pull over one of the leather-covered wing chairs. Soon they were nearly knee to knee beside a row of brown bottles along the edge of the desk.

Ezra poured while Whitney watched, and when her gaze narrowed on the unequal portions, he brought the level in the glasses even. Their glasses rose in a conspiratorial salute and down went the rum.

"Ahhh." Ezra leaned back, savoring the clean bite of the pungent brew, and watched Whitney's clear eyes roll as she examined the taste of it. She melted physically and her eyes sparkled as she took another assessing sip.

"It's good." She nodded and inhaled again over the liquor. "Not quite Daniels whiskey, but it's still mighty fine spirits." And she held out her glass for another shot.

Ezra poured them both another and leaned forward in his chair with righteous indignation. "They won't even let me drink my own rum. Won't let me do anything I want anymore. It's always 'your health' this and 'don't be absurd, Ezra' that. My old father made me quit the distillery when I hit fifty, so's to make room for Byron. Made me run for office . . ." His face soured and Whitney chewed back a surprised laugh as it took on the same persimmon look of the other Iron Forebears. "God a'mighty, I hate politics. Always did. People on your neck day and night, do this, vote that, and you have to look interested in every damned-fool idea that comes along. Everybody either has his hand out or in your pocket. Byron's the real politician—" He paused, realizing she was listening, and pulled his chin in suspiciously. It had been a long time since anybody listened to him.

"All I wanted to do was run the distillery. That's all. I was good at it too, made the best damned Boston rum."

"You did?" Warmth blossomed in her winsome features. "I miss it too, the distilling. Scenting the grain, tasting the water, the yeasty, sweet-sour smell of the beer before it's cooked, the crackle and the smoke of Uncle Ballard's hickory fire under the still on a frosty autumn night . . ." Her tone and face became wistful.

"Y-you actually distilled whiskey yourself?"

"Of course." She came back to the present. "My pa and I distilled the best whiskey in all of western Pennsylvania. Pa says it's in a body's blood or it's not. I've got the senses for it, true enough."

A dazzling smile spread over her smooth, delicate features, rattling Ezra's rusty faculties, sweeping him up in its net of charm. It was a minute before he could reclaim his eyes and the power of speech.

"That's how you did it, isn't it?" He swallowed another gulp of rum and squinted against her unnerving impact. Beautiful and spirited and sensual only began a description of her, his grandson's unusual wife. She was a consummate "trader," a woman who disdained money and all its power and trappings, and now a rum-drinking distiller with a hundred-proof smile.

"Did what?" She laughed, rich and potently.

"That look . . . that's how you hooked him. Had to be something special. He's hardly gone near a woman since that hot little English piece some years ago."

"Little English piece?" Despite the buzz of the rum in her head, the tidbit brought her alert instantly. Nuances of things Garner and his family had said came rushing back to her. The way Byron had greeted news of their marriage: something about other "idiocies" and disgraces and about her not being the first to try fortune hunting with Garner. With a man as handsome and virile as him . . .

"He had problems with a woman before?"

"Women. Two of 'em, at least. Got the damnedest way of collectin' women and trouble, that boy has. The first when he was sixteen—got caught in the stable with a gal fixin' to make sure she was going to be Mrs. Townsend. Byron was giving his cronies a glance at his new stallion—the gal's father among 'em—and they came across the whelp all tankered up an' playin' stallion himself." Ezra chuckled wickedly, his faded eyes coming alive with the recollection.

"There was quite a stir because she was older than him, and turned out to be right worn at the heels . . . a damned public ledger, if you take my meanin'. Well, he was packed off to England in disgrace. Did a fine job of all that military trainin' at the Royal Military College. But then, after he finished, his best friend's betrothed took a hard-climbin' fancy to him—plopped a buttered bun right in his bed. There was a duel, of course, and he wounded the youngblood. Came home with his tail between his legs and he's not taken a drink nor hardly looked at a female since.

"I told Byron, 'Leave the boy alone—he's just got to get the urge out of his system.' But Byron, he's just like his mother was,

no damned urges at all. Didn't understand a bit of it. It wasn't
the whelp's fault he was born handsome and rich . . . and randier
than most." Ezra laughed at Whitney's wide-eyed flush of color.
He couldn't know he'd just solved part of the mystery of Garner
Townsend and of his desperate resistance to her.

Apparently she wasn't the first Delilah he'd encountered.
Twice before he'd been disgraced in his almighty family's estimate, by his "urges" toward women and his entanglements with
them. He'd been sent all the way to England to escape a disgrace,
and ended by getting involved in an even worse one . . . wound-
ing his best friend over a Delilah.

Now she'd involved him in yet a third disgrace, one far more
devastating for its impact on his life. She'd done the same thing
to him the others had: used his own desires to suit her own pur-
poses. And in fulfilling her desires, she had dragged him into
embarrassment after embarrassment, into humiliating breaches
of his personal code and degrading confrontations with his commander and his family. It was a miracle he could even bear to
look at her, much less smile at her so warmly and touch her so
gently and love her so compl—

Love her? She froze, glass in hand, sitting on the edge of the
chair. Was that what lay in the depths of his well-guarded heart?
Love? Was that what roused his powerful desire for her and urged
him to comfort and defend her and to lay such tenacious claim
to her future? She felt a sudden flush of warmth for him rising
in her middle, crowding into her chest. His concern for her welfare and for her acceptance in his world suddenly took on a whole
wealth of meaning. He'd declared that she owed him a wife . . .
then he'd comforted and pleasured and provided for her as though
she were the cherished choice of his heart. The thought multiplied
that warmth a thousandfold, sending it surging through her in
joyful waves.

He was absolutely right, she *did* owe him a wife. A devoted
wife. A wife he could be proud of. A loving wife. And she did
love him . . . with every particle of her being. And he was going
to love her too someday . . . see if he didn't!

"I said"—Ezra was leaning forward in his chair, holding the

dwindling bottle poised over her glass—"are you ready for another?"

Whitney came back to reality, blinking at him, then at the
empty glass tumbler she clutched. "Oh . . . well . . ." She licked
her lip ruefully, then covered the top of the glass. "I don't think
so. You see, I have to learn to drink wine. I mean, I want to learn
it. And I may as well start now."

Ezra's face puckered as he read the determined glow in her
face with uncanny ease. "Givin' it up for him, are you?"

She flushed, but his assertion struck a spark in her that soon
illuminated her whole countenance. It wasn't quite "giving it
up," she thought. It was more like a trade, relinquishing a bit of
spirits to gain another little bit of Garner's heart.

"Damnation," Ezra swore, plunking the bottle back on the
desk beside him and looking testy. "I just find me somebody to
drink with—" He crossed his thin arms over his chest, humped
back in his chair, and glared at her. But as she sent him a wistful
smile, he jolted to life again before her eyes. "Well, then, I'll
teach you to drink wine. I know all about wines."

And before she could react, he was fumbling jerkily to turn
his chair toward the door. "Don't just sit there, woman—give
me a push!"

She jumped to her feet and, as they reached the door,
Ezra began shouting for Edgewater in the remnants of a
once-impressive baritone. The butler met them in a rush, in the
hallway outside the study door. Ezra drew himself up imperially
in his chair and summoned his best Townsend sneer of command.

"Wine . . . in the dining room. Bring me a bottle of that snippy
little Chablis we had for supper two nights ago and a bottle of
our best claret . . . and a smooth sherry . . . and some of that
most excellent Madeira and a good, sturdy Moselle and a hearty,
bedrock Burgundy—"

"But, surely, sir—" Edgewater looked from Ezra to Whitney
with one of his habitual sniffs, and quickly sniffed again, and
leaned closer and sniffed yet again. His long, sober nose curled,
and he stiffened at the aura of rum about them. "I should think
you'd already had your fill."

"And bread, dammit. And goblets, plenty of them." Ezra's

wrinkled face darkened, taking on the semblance of a prune at his chief houseman's hesitation. "It's still ten percent my house and ten percent my cellar. And if you don't bring me the wine I want—by damn, you'll be out on one hundred percent of your arse."

Whitney had to stifle a giggle at the way Edgewater blanched and jerked his arms. He heeled and made straight for the kitchens and the wine cellar, his black coattails flapping so that he resembled a wounded crow. Ezra drew a deep-satisfied breath and motioned Whitney to wheel on. "The dining room, woman."

Nineteen

That's where Garner found them when he returned from the offices that evening, in the dining room, surrounded by bread crumbs and more than a dozen open bottles and drawn decanters of the Townsend cellar's best wines. Ezra was slumped against the back of his chair, snuffed like a wick and snoring loudly. Whitney was awake for the most part, with her cheek propped in her palm, repeating names and vintages and characteristics of vintages, in the manner of a schoolboy memorizing Latin.

Under Edgewater's and Madeline's indignant looks, Garner strode in to collect his wayward wife. The sight of him kicked up a spark of recognition in her wine-weighted eyes, and she managed a small, lopsided smile as he demanded to know what in the devil she thought she was doing.

"Ohhh . . . yourrr gran'pa wuz teeeching me wines . . ." She fell nosefirst against his braced stomach and spoke into his loins. ". . . ssso you'lll be proud uv me."

He stood there, her sweet frame melting into him, his outrage cheated by her candor. Hell. She'd apparently gotten to crusty, embittered old Ezra the way she'd gotten to him. He took her heart-shaped face in his hand and tilted it up, feeling the pull in the center of his chest that he associated only with her. Drunk as a skunk, and she still exuded that open, guileless quality that made all her perfidies seem hopelessly like virtues.

After his first irate flush of embarrassment, he realized that the "disgrace" of it didn't seem to matter to him. What did matter was that he *wanted* to believe she'd gotten drunk while keeping her promise to learn to drink wine so she could be a "proper" wife to him. He wanted to believe she cared about more than her unholy Daniels pride in a bargain and the pleasure he could give her. He wanted to believe she was coming to care about him . . . to *love* him . . . if even a little.

He collected her into his arms and she snuggled drowzily against him as he carried her through the pall of Madeline's resentment and Edgewater's disdain. They trailed him into the center hall, exchanging disapproving looks as he carried her up to her room.

The next morning Garner leaned near her ashen face with a vengeful grin. "You're probably right. A woman who can't hold her wine any better than that probably oughtn't to drink it." She opened her mouth to respond, but clamped her hand over it and lurched over the side of the bed toward the basin he held.

When she'd regained her breath and her reason, she stared up at him from the tangle of her hair and bedclothes. "I'm sorry. Your grandpa offered to teach me about wines and—Lord—they do sneak up on a body."

"I can see," he said, sitting on the edge of her bed and stroking her pale face in gentle remonstrance, "that it's dangerous to leave you alone for very long. What am I going to do with you, Whitney Daniels?"

"Whitney Daniels *Townsend?*" she managed to ask. "I am Mrs. Townsend now."

Garner laughed. "You certainly are."

With Garner's and Mercy's careful nursing, Whitney was back in form in two days, vowing to imbibe neither wine nor rum except under great duress. Garner watched her mischievous exchanges with Ezra over the supper table of an evening with a certain anxiety. But she proved a woman of her word, drinking only coffee with her meals, as he did himself, and he began to relax, shaking his head at the rusty laughs and quips she elicited from his grandfather. They honestly seemed to like each other. The idea of it genuinely surprised him. Imagine the old boy actually *liking* somebody.

He tried to think of ways to keep Whitney busy, out of Byron's ever-present contempt and out of Ezra's eccentric influence. What did lady-wives do all day, every day?

"A-absolutely not!" Madeline had sputtered, outraged by Garner's suggestion that she include Whitney in the occasional social invitations she received. "She's uncouth and unpredictable, and I'll not be embarrassed by her crude conduct before my acquaintances."

Garner glowered, thinking about it. Unpredictable, certainly. But Whitney's manners, even that first night at Townsend House, were anything but uncouth. In fact, they were astonishingly good, considering her limited experience with elegant customs and polite society.

It didn't take a sage to understand the pique that lay behind Madeline's refusal. She was used to being the only female in a house full of men. And though Townsend men never coddled anybody, not even little orphaned granddaughters and nieces, she had been given her way in many things, including the pensioning of her old governess last year. Since then she'd had precious little direction for a young girl of sixteen. It surprised him that her lack of supervision hadn't even occurred to him before now. "My acquaintances," she had said. Garner frowned. Did she have any friends?

Madeline's refusal left Garner with few possibilities for Whitney. Household duties, ladylike amusements of music, drawing, and needlework, and the consummate feminine pastime of shopping—none of them seemed the least bit promising. In desperation he stole occasional hours from the office to squire Whitney about the city himself.

He finally acceded to Whitney's persistent request to be shown the Townsend distillery. He collected her one bright, cold afternoon in the plush Townsend carriage and escorted her to the south end of the manufacturing district.

It had been some time since he'd visited the large three-story brick building where Townsend rum was brewed and distilled. When the family's business enlarged to include other concerns, the company offices had been moved to a more fashionable and financial district of town. There had been no need to oversee the distillery on a regular basis, so long as it continued to produce profitably. Thus he was a little surprised to see the neglected state of the brick building's wooden doors and shutters and the rags stuffed into holes in the dirty glass windows.

The exterior proved a harbinger of the dirt and disrepair inside the distillery itself. Moldy straw littered the worn brick floors, and half-rotted crates and old barrels were stacked helter-skelter against the walls. The atmosphere was thick and soured, as were the workers they encountered in the dimly lit sections of the fermenting room and stacking house.

Garner found the master distiller and was soon involved in a heated discussion regarding the state of the place. That left Whitney free to investigate further on her own. The scruffy, ill-clad workers followed her into the sweltering heat of the great still itself, then into the finishing room, where she respectfully asked to taste the newest batch. They scrutinized Whitney's elegant velvet skirts and fitted shortcoat and ermine muff, and denied her request in rather salty and confrontational terms.

But she was not set back in the least by their gruff manner. She turned a rather fierce smile on them. "Oh, I'll have a taste . . . if I have to draw it myself." After a steely-eyed stare, she was handed a battered tin cup with a sampling of a just-tamped barrel. Under their glowers she tasted it and tried not to let her opinion show on her face.

"Wull . . . ?" came a sullen query. Before she could answer, Garner strode into the finishing room looking for her. He wasn't particularly pleased to find her in such rough male company, or with a cup filled with rum in her hand.

"I was just tasting," she explained, holding her ground as she held the cup to him. "And I think you'd better taste as well. This isn't anything like the Townsend rum your grandpa gave me the other day."

Against his better judgment, Garner did taste. And the sour, watery brew turned his jaw to granite. He hastily ushered Whitney outside and into the waiting carriage, and they were halfway home before he would respond to the gentle pressure of her hand on his arm.

"You were disappointed," she said, summarizing both their reactions. Apparently Townsend "distilling" was afflicted by the same profit-blind disinterest that affected the Townsend family itself.

"Blessit." He pounded his thigh with a gloved fist. "Townsend rum has been the foundation of our family fortunes since the beginning. And to see it sink to such a foul state. That swill's a disgrace to the name."

Whitney watched the muscles work in his jaw and felt some of his turmoil in her own middle. A distiller's product was a distiller's pride. "So, do something about it."

"Like what?" he snapped, realizing how harsh it sounded and scowling at himself. "Turn it over to you?"

"Me?" Her eyes danced at the way he read her thoughts. "Why, that's a splendid idea. Except . . . I don't know anything about rum. But your grandpa does, and he hates just sitting around all the time. He could teach me, or *us,* and we could . . ."

Garner's dark glare brought her to a halt. "He's a sickly, difficult old man, Whitney."

"You think so?" Her eyes sparkled at the way he didn't reject her involvement out of hand.

"He's an invalid in a wheeled chair—"

"That he uses like a battering ram. Have you ever tried *pushing* that chair of his around?"

He turned to her fully, searching the clear jewels of her eyes and the peachy moistness of her cheeks. "What are you saying?"

"Only that I think he's much stronger than anybody credits." The warmth of her smile had resolve melting in the middle of him again. "He is an Iron Townsend, after all."

"I'll think about it."

Garner did think about it. All afternoon, as he showed her the city, he thought of little else. And it slowly came to him that a rather unique opportunity had just presented itself. Whitney wanted something, even if it was a chance to pursue her old trade in unthinkable partnership with his irascible grandfather. For the first time he was in a position to do a bit of bargaining himself.

He ordered the driver to take them to the large, bustling open-air market. His eyes narrowed craftily as he observed her excitement when they disembarked into the frosty sunshine. The trader's gleam crept into her eyes, and he could feel the urgency mounting in her as she listened to the haggling and bargaining all around her.

"Ezra and the distillery. I'd warm to the idea much faster"—he stood close to her and murmured in her ear—"if you were to put your energies into learning to spend money like a proper wife." He fished in his waistcoat pocket and produced two bright coins, holding them up before her glistening eyes. "Here . . . try it. Anything you want." He waved at the myriad choices in the bustling stalls and carts. When she hesitated, he reached for her gloved hand and pressed them into her palm, closing her fingers over them. "Just ask the price, and if it's less than ten dollars, hand them the coins. But no bargaining."

Whitney swallowed. No bargaining. The coins seemed cold and foreign in her hand. As Garner led her through the paths, up and down the crowded aisles, the sounds of trading beset her from all sides, setting her heart thudding in her breast and drying her mouth. She paused several times, eyeing items that betrayed her growing interest in feminine apparel, but each time, her throat tightened, her muscles stiffened, and she had difficulty hearing over the swoosh of her blood in her ears.

Her turmoil mounted as she felt Garner's patience thinning. "I'm sorry, I can't." She thrust the coins back into his hand and fled toward the waiting carriage.

Townsends, however, were long known for their persistence in the face of overwhelming odds. And in that regard, Garner was the Ironest of Townsends. He waited two days and rather astutely mentioned that Christmas was fast approaching and suggested that she might wish to send something to her father and her aunt. The conflict in her heart was visible in her face at the mention of them. Her green eyes darkened and her mouth grew pensive, but she did agree to shop.

More and more frequently of late, she had sent her thoughts back to Rapture and her pa and Aunt Kate, wondering and beginning to worry. Kate had promised to visit Blackstone in Pittsburgh and to write Whitney about the outcome of his trial. Now, after almost six weeks, Whitney grew concerned at the silence.

Surely the trial was over by now. Had something awful happened to her pa, or to Aunt Kate?

On the appointed morning, she allowed Garner to take her to the mercantile district, but her heart was clearly not in it. She reluctantly selected a pipe and some tobacco for her pa, and a warm knitted wool vest and cap, but when it came time to pay for them, she refused to take her hands from her muff, or to meet Garner's eyes. He stood, watching her somber mood, sensing the turbulence beneath it, then paid for the items himself. He ushered her straight into the carriage, dropped the packages onto the opposite seat, and took her by the shoulders to make her look at him.

"What is it, Whitney?"

"It's nothing, I—I just don't like using money. It seems . . . too quick, too easy, to be right." She managed to look up at him through her long lashes, hoping he wouldn't be too upset, or press her further.

"There's more to it . . ." he surmised, reading confirmation in the deepening color of her face. "What is it?" But even as he said it, he witnessed her furtive glance at the packages and felt the realization forming inside him.

"My pa, Garner," she whispered, unable to lift her eyes from her lap for fear of what she might see in his face. "I haven't heard from Aunt Kate. She was supposed to write me when . . ." Her throat closed before she could finish her thought.

Garner stiffened slowly. Her father. He should have known. She was undoubtedly missing her family, and thinking about how they came to be separated . . . and who was responsible for it. Dread opened like a dark, sinking pool in the pit of his stomach as he sat feeling her withdrawal and fearing it more than he'd feared anything in his life. He had to know, had to see. He lifted her face on his gloved hand and held his breath.

Her eyes were dark in the shadowy carriage, but there was no accusation in her expressive features, no anger or denial. In the depths of her unguarded gaze was a tiny, stubborn little flame that he slowly realized still burned for him, belonged to him. And as he sank toward that flame, his lips parting and his reason reeling, the sadness-tinged warmth of her enfolded him. She welcomed his kiss and accepted the comfort of his touch. He pulled her against him and delved into her yielding sweetness, savoring both her response and his relief.

When he drew back there was a telling wetness on her lashes. He absorbed some of her heart's ache with his gloved fingers, so that his smile bore traces of her hurt. "I'll have our lawyers send a legal representative to see that he's being treated fairly. Will that ease your mind?"

"Yes." She felt her heart lightening. "Oh, yes."

Four days before Christmas, Garner entered the fashionable offices of the Townsend's senior legal representative, Henredon Parker, and in ticklishly vague terms assigned him the task of determining Blackstone Daniels's current legal status and of providing him legal assistance.

"I see." Parker knitted a graying brow over questioning eyes as he reached for paper and quill. "You wish me to send a representative of this firm to see about this Daniels fellow. And where"—he began writing down the particulars—"is the fellow being held?"

"In the town of Pittsburgh." Garner squirmed a bit and fidgeted with his wrist ruffles.

"Pittsburgh? On the frontier?" Parker's horror was soon cloaked beneath a solemn legal demeanor. "And what makes you think the fellow is being held there?" It was a question Garner had hoped to avoid.

"Because"—Garner swallowed hard—"that's where I took him after I arrested him." Parker's eyes widened in spite of himself.

"You *arrested* him?" Parker leaned forward onto his desk, intrigued.

"I was part of the military force that accompanied Washington into western Pennsylvania to put down the whiskey revolt," Garner divulged. "I need to discover what has happened to him."

"A whiskey rebel?" Parker sat back, thoroughly confused. "You arrested him and you wish to provide him legal assistance? Surely, Mr. Townsend, you can see that this is most irregular."

Garner summoned his most Townsend mien and announced,
"As it happens, the fellow is my father-in-law." And as if that
terse pronouncement should elucidate all, he rose and bid the
stunned Mr. Parker, "Good day."

Christmas came, lifting Whitney's spirits considerably. She
sent precious packages west, to her pa and Aunt Kate, along with
letters assuring them of her welfare and begging the same news
of them. Then she threw herself into a festive mood by decorating
the house with fragrant greens and shimmering scarlet ribbons.
The family mustered on Christmas Eve for their yearly attendance at church, and afterward assembled in the brightly lit west
parlor to receive a few guests, primarily business associates ex-
tending the obligatory holiday visit.

Whitney was the subject of intense scrutiny. She stayed close
to Garner's side and avoided the mulled wine punch that was
served. It was a profound relief to Byron and Madeline and Whitney, and something of a disappointment to Ezra, that she appeared so ladylike and did nothing outrageous or embarrassing.

With a sense of relief Garner watched Whitney's determination to adjust to her new world. She steadfastly refrained from
bargaining the servants, except in occasional circumstances that
caught her off guard. But it bothered him that she still refused
to use money when they went out to the shops. It was as though
some part of her still resisted her new life with him. It seemed
that two integral parts of her, her trader's pride and the deepest
regions of her heart, where it lodged, were both still beyond his
reach. Until he could penetrate that determined trader's instinct,
he was convinced, he couldn't gain access to the wealth of deeper
feeling that surrounded it. Determined to do something to bring
Whitney around to eastern ways of acquisition, he arranged to
leave the offices early one afternoon to escort her to the shops
again, a new plan in mind.

But as he waited in the center hall for her to make ready, Byron blew through the front doors, demanding to see Garner in his study immediately. Garner's gray-blue eyes paled a shade, and his jaw hardened as he read his father's combative mood. But he shrugged his greatcoat from his shoulders and strode back through the house behind Byron.

Whitney came downstairs to find the center hall empty; no Garner, no Edgewater. Garner's coat was tossed recklessly over the polished banister railing. The sound of voices from the west hallway drew her back through the house with a deepening frown. Madeline stood in the arched doorway at the rear of the center hall with her arms crossed and a similar frown on her face. Her glare heated as Whitney passed. Just outside the half-open door to Byron's study she found Ezra, sitting in the hallway, absorbed in the heated exchange going on inside.

Anxiety knotted the nerves in her stomach as she came to a halt a few feet from Ezra, reading the seriousness of the situation in his face.

"Nothing!" Byron's voice was clear and furious. "Nothing, ever, without getting tangled up in a scandal—some debacle or disgrace! You had a chance to redeem yourself and prove your mettle, to bring back a commendation, some badge of honor from that wretched whiskey rebellion. And where the hell is it?"

"The commendation must have been delayed." Controlled anger ran through Garner's deep voice like a rail of steel.

"Or *denied,*" Byron charged.

"That is not in my control, one way or the other—"

"This is typical of you, Garner." Byron pronounced his name as though it were something disagreeable. "You go out there to bring back laurels, and what do you bring back? Some wine-guzzling little tart—"

"Enough," Garner demanded, stalking forward. "I'll not hear another word defaming her. She's my wife, whether you like it or not. I wanted her, I married her, and she's going to live here with me. Accept it."

Whitney jolted toward the doorway, but was caught and restrained by Ezra's surprisingly strong grip.

"I *won't* accept it—having my house, my family turned upside down by a conniving little Jezebel." Byron's florid face was clearly visible through the doorway as he taunted. "You've moved her in—*inflicted* her on us. How long before her tawdry relations descend upon us as well? Cousins, uncles . . . or her whiskey-distilling father?"

Byron's charge slapped Whitney physically. At the mention of her father, her blood drained to her knees, leaving her heart thumping dryly in her chest.

"Damn you," Garner growled in a tone so calm it was chilling. "Leave her and her family out of this. Your real quarrel is with me, as it has always been. I may not be the son you wanted, but I'm the son you have. And there's not a damned thing either of us can do about it."

"Oh, yes, there is." Byron stalked closer, his eyes glittering. "I can see you never have control of Townsend Companies. I'll not turn control over to you and watch you fritter away what I've spent a lifetime building. You have no sense of dedication or duty and no appreciation of the responsibility entailed in managing such an important enterprise. Do you think I haven't noticed how you abandon your duty at the offices at the merest crook of her finger? You're gone half the time—"

Garner recoiled, resisting the urge to lash out physically. "I won't answer to you, to *anyone,* for my time, or on the conduct of my marr—"

"That's probably what you did out on the damned frontier too," Byron charged. "One sniff of her skirts and you abandoned your duty, and what little honor you had left!"

The charge struck Garner square in the chest. His face tightened and the dark centers of his eyes contracted. Byron read those subtle changes as the unwilling confirmation they were. "Good God, that's exactly what happened, isn't it? That's why you had to marry that upstart chit . . . and that's why there's no commendation. They don't commend officers for failures of duty and honor."

"Stop it!" Whitney wrenched free of Ezra's frantic hold and burst into the study, slamming the door back and startling both Byron and Garner. "How dare you?" She came to a stop halfway between them. "How dare you say such things to him?"

"Whitney, stay out of this—" Garner thundered, but she was too hurt, too angry to heed him.

"Duty and honor—you wouldn't recognize them if you tripped over them. There's not a man born with more loyalty to his country and to his duty than Garner Townsend, and you're forty kinds of a fool if you can't see that just because he's your son!" She swept a fiercely possessive look over Garner's bronze features and broad shoulders.

A pained, contradictory pride surged within her at the stubborn honor that lay at the core of Garner's being. It was that unyielding sense of duty and honor that had required him to arrest her father and crush her beloved whiskey trade. But it was the same uncompromising honor that demanded he fulfill the vows he'd spoken with her and made him protect and provide for her. It was that honor that demanded he replace her shattered world and perhaps someday the love of her heart. He was a man who had paid the price of duty, and he deserved better from those whose duty it was to love and support him—his family.

"You want to know what really happened in Rapture? You want to know just how disgraceful and dishonorable he really was? He did his military duty, destroyed the illegal whiskey, and arrested the valley's major distiller even after he'd spoken vows with me."

"Whitney—*no.*" Garner lunged around the table for her, but she darted back, her eyes still locked on Byron's burning face.

"It was *Daniels whiskey* he poured into the ground; whiskey I helped distill," she rasped, dragging the bottom of her register. "And it was *my father* he arrested. My pa was the one his duty, his honor demanded he arrest. And he did it. He did his duty for you and your bilious Townsend pride! And when his wretched commendation does come—"

"Dammit, Whitney!" Garner exploded at her, seizing her by the arms and pulling her toward the door as she scrambled to resist.

"No—stop—".

"Not another word, dammit—" Reduced to brute force by the uncontrollable emotions churning inside him, he ducked, ramming a shoulder into her middle and hoisting her up onto his shoulder. In three long strides he was barreling through the doorway, sending Ezra and Madeline back in shock. They stared, dumbstruck, as he carried her from sight and continued to stare at the end of the hallway as sounds of Whitney's protests drifted back to them.

A growl or a clearing of the throat—something—carried through their shock. And close on its heels came a storm of emotion nearly as intense as the one that had just passed by them.

"She's right, Byron," Ezra snarled, rolling himself partway into the room to face his son with the bitterness of years evident in his lined face. "You are a prize fool. But then, why shouldn't you be? You certainly learned from a master." After a long, acrid visual exchange, he fumbled to roll his chair backward into the hall and growled at his granddaughter: "Help me out of here, girl."

Byron turned rigidly aside as Ezra withdrew, stripped emotionally once again by his father's ever-present contempt. He battled back the chaos of anger and resentment that Ezra's scathing derision always unleashed in him. Ever since he was a young boy . . . no matter what he did or achieved or built . . . it was never . . .

He choked as pressure built in his chest and distended the veins in his neck and temples. His scorn of Garner's behavior was no worse than Ezra's disdainful treatment of him. In fact, the insight rattled every connection in his body, it was the very same.

Close on the heels of that painful realization came a recurrent blast of Whitney's fierce defense of Garner. How dare the chit presume to protect his own son from him? The shocking content of her claims was somehow overshadowed by the raw intensity of them. She defended Garner and his honor like a she-lion. A prickling sense of emptiness opened in Byron's middle. No one had ever defended Byron Townsend. Not his cool, elegant mother, nor his irascible, demanding father, Ezra. And certainly not the delicate, retiring girl he'd taken to wife to satisfy his family.

He felt suddenly very empty and very naked beneath his fashionable clothes. Hollow and vulnerable. For the first time in twenty years.

Garner's blood was roaring in all his senses by the time he reached the top of the stairs with Whitney's half-subdued form thrashing on his shoulder. Instinct led him to his own chamber. He strode to the bed and plopped her down on the edge of it, grabbing her shoulders as she swayed.

"What in heaven's name did you think you were doing?" He towered above her, wanting to give her the shaking she so richly deserved.

"I was telling the truth, the whole truth." As she shook off the dizziness, anger rose in its place. "It's about time somebody did. The things he said to you—he deserved to hear it!"

"You had no right to tell them—"

"I had every right." She shoved to her feet, pushing him back a pace. "He made vicious, little-minded charges about my marriage and my husband. Garner, how could you just stand there and let him say such things about you, knowing they were foul, blackhearted lies? He's supposed to be your father—this is supposed to be your family—"

"It *is* my family and I'll handle them my w—"

"Suffering Stephen. This isn't a family, it's a pack of jackals that have learned to bark percentages! Families are people who share their joys and good times and hold each other up in hard times. Real families want what's best for each other and believe in each other and help each other, no matter whose blood flows in whose veins. The folk in Rapture—Uncle Harvey and Aunt Sarah and even Robbie Dedham—they're my family as much as if we had the same blood. And they care more about you and are more of a family to you than your prickly, self-centered Townsends will ever be. Your father, Madeline—they don't care about you, they don't trust you or support you in what you do and want, and they sure don't love you—"

"And I suppose *you* do?" he thundered.

"Yes, I do!" she shouted, desperate to make some dent in that thick Townsend pride. "I *do* love you. I had every reason in the world to hate your guts, Garner Townsend, and I wound up loving you, wanting you with everything in me. It doesn't make any sense at all to me that they don't love you too!"

Garner fell backward, catching himself on one leg so that it seemed a jolting step. Every word went straight to the exposed core of him. He was suddenly battered by the impact of gale-force contrasts: his implacable, unforgiving family, and the openness and warmth of Rapture's people; the Townsend coldness and pride in excluding others, and the vital, generous inclusiveness of Rapture's eccentric family. They had accepted him even when he didn't consider himself acceptable. They'd drawn him into their lives when they had every right to mistrust and reject him.

But there was a contrast more shocking yet. His own family, whose very blood ran in his veins, scorned and derided him because of long-ago embarrassments that he had been too young and callow to avoid, incidents the rest of the world had forgotten years since. But his quixotic little Whitney, who had every reason to hate him, defended him, *loved* him. He'd accused and reviled her, arrested her father, destroyed her beloved family trade, and dragged her off to live in a "pack of jackals" that barked percentages at each other. *And she loved him.*

He reeled from the impact of it, backing a dazed step, then another, scarcely able to focus his eyes. *How could she?*

Whitney watched him recoil and felt a frightening gulf between them opening with every step he took. Her blood was pounding in her head, her chest was heaving. What had she said? She loved him . . . she'd told him she loved him . . . yelled it at him.

She tried to read the strange, shocked look on his face, and her vaunted acuity utterly failed her. She had recklessly made her last offer in the most important bargain of her life, and had no idea whether it would be accepted or rejected.

"Well . . ." The strange waver in her voice was caused by her heart beating in her throat. "I just mean, you're so diligent and upright and dutiful, everybody in Rapture thought so." She groaned inside as his eyes focused on hers and his scowl intensified. "And you're honest—you've always been honest with me. And honorable—you say you'll do something and you do it or

die. And you're strong and self-controlled even in the face of
monstrous provocation and . . . gentlemanly and temperate and
very moral— You wouldn't have bedded me at all if I hadn't crept
into your room like a Delilah."

"You think not?" He came to life, lunging at her, catching her
against his hardening body in a fierce grip. His face bronzed and
his eyes darkened. "Well, let me tell you how it really was in
Rapture, Whitney Daniels. From that very first afternoon, when
I found myself spread over your delectable little body, you're all
I thought about, your full breasts, your hard little nipples and the
softness of your lips, your long, sleek legs. For weeks I stalked
about Rapture in a state of blind, consuming rut, wanting to both
strangle you and throw you down and mount you on the spot.
You embarrassed or humiliated me every time I set eyes on you,
and all I could think about was what it would feel like to bury
my aching flesh inside you—to have you hold me in your arms
and feel your softness in mine."

His arms around her tightened, overcoming the last resistance
of her hands against his chest, and his head lowered above hers,
crowding everything else from her consciousness.

"You don't know how many times you came within a hairbreadth of finding yourself flat on your back, wench. On your
own bed, in the woods, against your damned barn wall, in the
middle of my own men's camp . . . your virtue lived a damned
perilous existence. It was just a damned good thing I didn't realize it existed until after you tried to bribe me with it."

He was holding her so tightly she could scarcely breathe.

"B-but I didn't try to . . . I wanted only a prop— "

"A proper bargain with me—I know that now. Dunbar clarified that little point for me. But, you see, I was all too willing
to believe the worst of you. Even while lusting after you with
every particle of my being. I was a pompous, arrogant, self-
righteous, *temperate, diligent, moral . . . sham!* I did abandon
my duty and honor. I knew you were involved in the whiskey
trade somehow, and I didn't do a thing about it. And I knew I
had no business touching you, kissing you, but I didn't do a
thing about that either. I wanted you more than I wanted com-
mendations or honor or my cursed family's approval. Dammit,

that's the kind of man I am . . . not some paragon of manly duty and moral rectitude! I married you because I was forced to, not out of any sense of honor. I arrested Black Daniels because I was forced to, not out of some elevated patriotic duty. And I brought you with me to Boston because I couldn't stand the thought of letting your desirable little body out of reach, not out of some noble notion of holy matrimony! That's the kind of man I really am—greedy, distractible, profane, lustful— Dammit, I'm lustful!" he growled, arching hard against her, making her feel the insult of his arousal.

"Now"—his eyes glittered with challenge—"do you still *love* me?"

Twenty

Whitney looked up into the turbulent depths of his soul, bared in his face, and recognized the importance of the intimate access he offered her. He risked opening to her the pain, the disappointment, and the raw, stubborn hope that lay in the depths of his being. The insight sent an ache slamming through her.

She bit her lip and nodded.

His eyes closed. And after a breathless moment his frame melted one desperate degree. "God . . . don't say that, Whitney, unless you really mean it. Say you want to be my wife, say you want my loving or even my money."

"I do want your loving"—she spoke through the tears in her eyes and voice—"and I do want to be your wife. But I also happen to love you, Garner Townsend. Greedy, distractible, lustful old you. Generous and tender and painfully honest you. Handsome, pleasureful, and capable you. I know exactly what kind of man you are." She slid her arms around his neck and rose onto her toes to hug him fiercely. "And I do love you."

One last instant of hesitation, one last heartbeat of doubt, and Garner's arms crushed her to him, surrendering to the storm of need roaring through his entire being. His mouth sought hers hungrily, tasting the saltiness of her lips, absorbing the joyful eagerness of her response. She loved him! He picked her up and whirled her around, delirious, giddy from the sudden release of pressure inside him . . . she *loved* him!

"My laces—" Moments later she managed to slide her passion-bruised lips aside enough to insist. But her mouth was soon captive again, being plundered with exquisite precision as his hands obliged.

"My buttons," he demanded in a voice like rough velvet, arching back to give her access while refusing to relinquish the delicious treasure of her mouth.

He pulled her from her dress, relishing the feel of her bound waist and the soft flesh mounded above and below it before stripping her corset from her too. His hands cupped her satiny buttocks and lifted her so that her body met his. Breast to breast, belly to belly, they pressed and kissed as her hands clasped and claimed him.

Again and again he arched, his body flexing, thrusting nearer, coming closer . . . closer . . . commanding, initiating her hot, liquid response. She wriggled against him, seeking the fullness, the deep, shuddering satisfaction that would come as he penetrated her. But he moved her back to the bed and continued his relentless stroking arousal. Bracing and rising above her, he watched hungrily the erotic undulations of her body and the way his veined shaft slid over her creamy flesh to part those moist, gingery curls again and again. She arched and mewed both pleasure and frustration, wanting completion and yet wishing the divine torture to continue.

"Say it again," he growled, braced above her, his eyes mesmerizing, black-centered rings of silver fire. There was no doubt of what he wanted. "Say it . . ."

"I love you," she rasped, finding his passion-bronzed face through her swirling senses. His fierce carnal grin took part of her breath, and the plunging weight of his body on hers took the rest. His kiss was sublimely savage and possessive as he wrapped himself around her, cradling her body beneath his.

"Again," he demanded, lowering the heat of his devouring kisses down her throat.

"I love you—" She was breathless with need, exultant in the power of his desire for her. "I love you, love you, love . . ." She arched as he tugged at her nipple and sent billows of pleasure spreading beneath her skin and swirling into her aching, empty flesh. Soul-deep desire welled within her. "Love me, Garner . . . please . . . love me."

His desire absorbed and focused hers. He knew what she wanted; he felt it as though it were his own unbearable craving.

She asked him to love her, and it was not just the joining of their bodies that she sought. She wanted exactly what he had wanted: the certainty of it rocked him. And only he could give it to her. He braced above her to stare into the seductive emerald lights of her eyes, collecting her senses in his.

"I do love you, my sweet Whiskey." He ran his hand over her cheek and threaded his fingers back through her hair, cupping her head. "You're . . . the very heart of me now."

Her breath stopped, setting her heart thudding in her chest as she searched the tension of his frame against hers. The tautness of his features told of passions held in check against a greater need, the need to love and to share that love. Joy exploded inside her, shattering all awareness but that one: he loved her!

"I'm your heart?" She shoved him back to search his face. "I embarrass you and interfere in your family and I can't spend your money properly . . . and you still love me?"

"I do."

"You were forced to marry me and bargained into bedding me. I've caused nothing but trouble in your life, your house, and your family . . . and you still love me?"

He nodded with a wry expression. "Is that so hard to believe? You just declared your love for a greedy, dishonorable, arrogant wretch who has lusted after you unceasingly from the first moment he set eyes on you. What makes you think I can't love a stubborn, impudent, conniving little wench who has taken advantage of my boundless lust for her at every turn?"

Her jaw drooped at his summary of their love, and he laughed, overcoming her shocked resistance to hold her tightly.

"I guess I am . . . stubborn sometimes." Her confession was muffled by his bare chest.

"Determined." His lips curled on one end.

"I don't mean to be impudent or disrespectful."

"Just truthful." His grin widened.

"And I don't mean to interfere . . ."

"Just to be helpful," he finished with a broad smile she couldn't see. And he felt her head bob against his shoulder.

Suddenly he knew. It was *love* that renamed all her flaws virtues and transformed her excesses into zeal in his mind. Fate, guided by the unfathomable wisdom of love, had cast Whitney's sweet flaws over the weaknesses in his own character, to strengthen and uphold him. And by some pure miracle she seemed to feel the same about him. He turned her face up to his, treasuring and sharing the wonder he read there.

"I need you, Whitney. God, how I need the warmth and the joy of you in my life. With you I feel alive, whole, for the first time. I do love you—"

His mouth descended on hers with a tenderness that drew her breath from her. When he raised his head, she lay utterly still, deep in wonder, listening to the quietest whispers in her deepest heart. After a moment his fingers on her cheek brought her hurtling back to him and she came alive beneath him.

"Show me—" she demanded with a fierce, passionate glow. "Show me how you love me." Her hands clutched at his back, and her legs wrapped him possessively, pulling him against her liquid heat. Caught in the updraft of her explosive sensual joy, he captured her mouth.

He joined their bodies with a driving thrust and absorbed her rapturous moan with his mouth, sharing it, completing it. They moved as one, thrusting, giving, holding nothing back as they mounted pleasure's tightening spiral. And with the hot brilliance of colliding stars, they shattered sensory bounds and bodily limits to reach that ultimate of joining. Then in lavish contentment they floated a long long time.

"Garner . . ." She rubbed her cheek against the hard pillow of his flexed biceps. "Will he really do it, do you think?"

"Will who do what?" he murmured, lifting lidded eyes to her.

"Your father. Can he keep you from becoming head of the businesses?"

There was a long silence in which Whitney could feel him wakening further, considering it. And she felt a decision in the determined relaxation of his lean, powerful body. "He can't do it alone. Legally he has to have Ezra's and Madeline's backing. Sixty percent."

As he said it, he marveled at how insignificant it all seemed just then. The ambition of a lifetime, uprooted, supplanted by the love of a lifetime. A curious twinge of warmth vibrated through him and he wrapped her in his arms. For the first time in his life, he wasn't seeing his future narrowing inescapably into a hard, linear, Townsend furrow. And he owed the emancipation of his outlook to the bewitching little Delilah in his arms.

Sixty percent. Whitney felt it resonate in the depth of her soul. He needed it. He deserved it. And since she was the one who had cost him the coveted control of Townsend Companies, she'd have to be the one to see it restored to him. With that fierce new resolve in her heart, she snuggled against him and drifted to sleep.

The hour was late and the sun had set when Garner blinked and rolled onto his stomach, squeezing his eyes tighter shut and refusing to heed Whitney's soft, insistent call to rise and dress for supper. He was adamant; he would allow no promise of food or recitation of obligation or prodding of propriety to roust him from his warm bed. Whitney stood in her chemise, watching his very stubborn repose, and a wifely glint appeared in her eye. She removed her chemise and peeled back the covers slowly, baring his insolent male frame.

It was all Garner could do to lie still when he felt her cool, satiny skin slide over him and realized from the concentration of her weight she was likely sitting—very warmly—astride his buttocks and lower back.

"Oh, God, Whitney! Are you biting me?" Every muscle in his body contracted violently. She'd found that special spot halfway down his back, halfway to his right side.

"Umm-hmm." She did it again. He jolted, then writhed, clutching handfuls of sheets. Her laugh, husky and voracious, prepared him for it the third time, and he managed to embrace its full erotic impact.

Suddenly he was wide awake, and he was on fire. He tried to turn over but she pushed his muscled shoulder down insistently and began a series of determined and delectable little bites up the center column of his back to his neck. His eyes closed as he surrendered to the pleasure raining through him.

"If—" he managed to say through clenched jaws, twitching and flexing with escalating arousal, "you're determined to do that . . . please do it in places that won't shock my valet too badly."

Again came that devastating Delilah laugh. "Perhaps you should make Benson your valet. He wouldn't notice a thing." Her little bites had muted to sensual nibbles by the time they reached his earlobe. She raked it with her teeth and purred.

"Benson. I'll . . . consider it," he rasped with deceptive surrender. A moment later he snapped around to snatch her wrists and pull her to the bed. A second silky move brought her beneath him, squealing mock outrage and wriggling to escape. "But first . . . I have a score to settle with you, wench. You've a habit of using your teeth on me, and I told you I'd make you pay for it someday." His voice was a primal growl as he spread her arms and pinned them to the bed. "Well, someday has just arrived."

"No—Garner!" She writhed, her eyes widening as he bared his teeth with lecherous menace. "No—really—ohhhhh—"

He raked his teeth over her bare shoulder, then tightened them deliciously on one succulent spot. She sucked breath and wriggled helplessly, her eyes widening even farther when she saw where his eyes drifted next.

"No, Garner—oh— OH!— ohh—oooooh . . ."

From her breasts to her sensitive inner elbows to the supple bend of her waist and the sleek plane of her belly, he gently consumed her, firing her passions and ignoring her pleas. He tantalized her hipbones and the backs of her knees, then roused her to frantic heights as he nibbled his way up her inner thighs. He made one last tidbit of the downy skin of her thigh just below the patch of gingery curls, then rose, sliding upward onto her softly undulating body. Desire squeezed her throat, permitting only a tattered moan, a plea.

"That's what you get for biting me," he growled hoarsely, and her darkened eyes fluttered open.

"You mean . . . every time?" she breathed.

"Every time."

"Anything . . . else?"

"Umm. This."

His eyes closed and her eyes closed. Neither breathed. A long, penetrating moment later, Whitney felt his lips against hers and spoke into them. "About Benson . . ."

"Ummm?"

"You're going to need him."

"Interfering ag—ohhh!—Whitney!"

The day after the great explosion, Whitney rapped on the door of Ezra's study and smiled when she heard Ezra's crusty permission to enter. She slipped inside and closed the door carefully behind her with a warning finger to her lips. *Edgewater . . . lurking outside,* the gesture said. And from the folds of her skirt she produced a bottle of Ezra's favorite, Townsend rum. He grinned.

"I do love this stuff," he mused later, savoring the last swallow in his glass and eyeing her and then the bottle. He huffed disgust as she corked it firmly. She was getting to be as bad as the rest of them.

"Then how would you like to . . . taste it—every day? Distill it again?" she proposed.

Ezra came up straight in his chair, his eyes razor-keen on her trader's glow. "You mean . . . me at the distillery?" His heart began to hammer like a schoolboy's, and his eyes narrowed as they searched her. "What's in it for you?"

Whitney straightened and canted her chin to a modest trading angle. "Your ten percent." She saw Ezra's surprise and added, "For Garner."

"The whelp," Ezra snorted, looking away disgustedly. "Should've known."

"Not your true ten percent . . . just your voting ten percent," she clarified with a keen eye on his reaction. "He's a very good manager, you know. His judgment shouldn't be judged by"—she swallowed and made herself say it—"his urges toward me."

"I don't know why the hell not." Ezra turned back to her with a crafty glint in his eye. "A good businessman has to have a few urges . . . and follow 'em now and then. My voting percentage for a chance at the distillery again . . ." He didn't have to think for very long. A slow grin spread over his face. "I think marrying you might have been the best business move the whelp's ever made."

January progressed with a plodding gray succession of watery snows and a plague of bone-chilling cold. When the sun finally appeared one late afternoon, it was a welcome relief, so welcome that Garner could think of nothing but enjoying it with Whitney. He left the offices early to take her for a much-needed walk on the frozen common. They had just returned home in the lowering daylight and ordered a tray of hot tea and cakes for warming, when there was a flurry in the center hallway. Edgewater exited the parlor to investigate.

A human figure bundled in a shapeless fleece-lined deerskin coat, a floppy felt hat, and heavy boots caked with drying mud stood on the pristine marble floor of the hall, restrained in the grip of the footman who had answered the knock at the door. Edgewater's thin mouth drew thinner still as he hurried to enforce the footman's reluctance to admit such a creature to Townsend House.

"Tell this insufferable thatchhead to unhand me at once," a bold feminine voice intoned as the figure wrested about in the hapless footman's hands. "This is intolerable. I am here to see my niece, Whitney Daniels. I know she was brought here against her will and I shan't leave until I've spoken with her."

"Good Lord, it's a female," Edgewater pronounced, scrutinizing the bizarre camouflage of her clothing from a safe distance.

"Indeed." The eyes narrowed fiercely. "I am Kathryn Morrison, Whitney's aunt." Her voice rose in pitch and volume, "And I demand to see her!"

"What in heaven's name is going on, Edgewater?" came Madeline's voice from halfway up the stairs. And at the same instant, one of the front doors swung open, admitting an icy blast of air and the irate, greatcoated figure of Byron Townsend, whose approach to the doorway had gone unheeded in the ripening confrontation.

"Dammit, Edgewater!" he snarled, ripping his fashionable high-crowned hat from his head. "The least you can do is see the bloody door attended—" When his eyes fell on Kate Morrison, he stopped dead. His pale gaze narrowed, raking her rough, unwieldy garments. "What in hell is that?"

"I'm—let me go!" Kate jerked free of the houseman's hold and turned to face the arrogant prig that had just verbally neutered her. "I am Kathryn Morrison—"

"It's a Kathryn Morrison, sir," Edgewater sniffed with the air of just having created the new classification just for her.

"And what the hell is a Kathryn Morrison?" Byron demanded of his butler, ignoring Kate. "And more important, what the hell is it doing on the clean tiles of my hallway floor?"

Kate sputtered, jerking her floppy felt hat off to reveal a crimson face punctuated with flashing eyes and surrounded by a rumpled mass of dark hair. In spite of herself, she looked down at her dirty boots and the tracks they'd made on the pristine marble of the floor.

"Apparently related to a Whitney Daniels, sir," Edgewater intoned, enjoying the denigrating bit of repartee. "And demanding to see one."

"Good God." Byron turned on Kate with an oft-practiced sneer. "I knew it. We're being positively swarmed by these unsavory frontier types."

Proud, refined Kate Morrison had been traveling for more than three excruciating weeks, through intolerable cold and muck and deprivation. She'd weathered with fortitude the insults and hazards and unholy propositions that confronted a woman traveling alone through frontier provinces. And then to be further insulted and assaulted when she finally reached her destination—her endurance and tolerance came to an abrupt end.

"You pompous, inhospitable wretch." She advanced on Byron with blazing eyes and noted with satisfaction that he backed a step. She glared at him and deliberately stomped mud from her boots onto the floor. "I've spent weeks getting here, going without sleep and proper nourishment, half frozen, imperiled on every hand," she raged, stalking closer. "And by merciful God, I'll see my niece with my own two eyes and learn what that foul beast of a man has done to her. And you daren't stand in my way, you arrogant, overbearing boor—" She planted her fists in the vicinity of her waist and bellowed from the depths of her capacity, *"Whitney!"*

"See here, woman!" Byron thundered, astounded by her sheer capacity for volume. "How dare you invade my home, raving, and insulting me—"

"D-do something, Edgewater." Madeline rushed down the steps in the midst of Byron's denunciation and gave the shocked butler a shove. *"Edgewater!"*

In the parlor, Whitney stood before the fire, enjoying its warmth and the warmth of one of Garner's ever-more-frequent smiles. Loud voices in the hall caused her to frown at the parlor door, and a moment later she went poker-straight before the fire, her eyes wide. "Garner, that sounds like—" An instant later she was in motion, Garner close on her heels.

Edgewater and Nolan, the footman, and Madeline were all pointing and yelling, demanding something be done and refusing to do it themselves. Just beyond them was Byron Townsend, still gloved and coated, his countenance beet-red and his jaw working furiously. And nearly nose to nose with him was . . . Aunt Kate!

Whitney blinked and looked again, disbelieving her eyes. "Aunt Kate?"

"Whitney?" Kate swung around, her fiery eyes flying to Whitney's womanly, velvet-clad form. She blinked as well. "Is it you?" She scanned the stylish dress, the sweetly sophisticated fall of curls down Whitney's back, the bloom of her beloved niece's face, and an eruption of emotions in her choked off all other words.

She took one mute step and hesitantly opened her arms. Whitney flew to her, engulfing her in a joyful hug that nearly bowled her over. Around and around they twirled, laughing and hugging, tears flowing, oblivious of the horrified stares leveled at their reunion. It was a long while before Kate managed to push her back to look at her and touch her face and hair.

"Let me look at you. Oh, Whitney, I've been half out of my mind with worry—"

"I'm fine, Aunt Kate, truly I am. How did you get here?" She looked over Kate's shoulder as if expecting someone else.

"I brought the wagon partway, then rode the horses when it broke down—"

"You came alone?" Garner approached with a solemn look on his face, aware he was intruding and yet unwilling to stop himself. "All the way from Rapture, alone?"

Kate hastily wiped her wet cheeks and returned his assessment defensively. "I did. If you'll recall, Major, I am alone now. I came to see if Whitney was all right."

Garner watched the slight trembling of her chin, and read the cost of her journey in the fine lines exhaustion had etched about her striking eyes. For some reason, the pained joy, the love that had shone in her face moments before, returned to engulf him. They had something in common, this woman and he; they both loved Whitney. The realization melted some of his reserve.

"Welcome, Mrs. Morrison."

Kate watched the subtle change in his face and the easing in his powerful frame. "Thank you, Major."

"Well, don't just stand there, Edgewater." Whitney turned a beaming smile on the outraged houseman. "Take her coat. Then fetch us some hot tea. She's positively frozen!"

After a tense moment in which Garner's gaze narrowed dangerously at him above Whitney's head, the butler stalked to assist Kate with her "wrap." The others stared with incredulity as a very womanly form was uncovered beneath the woolly barn of a coat. A sturdy, slightly outmoded wool dress with quilted bodice was revealed, fitted perfectly over a well-proportioned frame—small waist, slender arms, a very feminine aspect. Kate felt their shocked eyes on her, and her hands jittered over her clothing.

"I—I apologize for my unkempt state." She lifted her chin and spoke only to Whitney and Garner. "I went straight to a respectable inn, but as a woman traveling alone was denied lodging until I could produce an endorsement or reference." She drew herself up to address Garner. "I'm afraid I must impose upon you, sir, for such sponsorship, if you are willing."

Whitney put her arm around Kate's waist, her face glowing. "Of course he'll sponsor . . ." She looked up into Garner's handsome face, seeing the seriousness of his expression and only then realizing that he might not be as pleased to see her aunt as she was.

"There is no reason for it," Garner said with a calm and deliberate glance at his tight-eyed family. "We have plenty of room here. You must accept our hospitality, Mrs. Morrison."

"Oh." Kate flushed, trying not to show how much that "foul beast of a man" had surprised her. "Oh, but I couldn't. It would be far too much of an imposition—"

"Indeed." Bryon stalked into their line of sight, his gloved hands still clenched on the brim of his hat. "I'm sure your wife's frontier relations would be far more comfortable elsewhere. And there's the unfortunate matter of accommodations." He turned a scathing look on Garner. "I believe your forty percent of the bedchambers are already in use."

Garner twitched with the stifled urge to trounce his irascible father. "We have several unused guest chambers. However, she will probably find my own chambers more comfortable. You no doubt realize, I have not used them for some time now."

"This is intolerable—unthinkable." Byron reddened further. He stared heatedly at Kate, meeting the fiery lights in her striking eyes and fighting the way his gaze drifted determinedly down her shapely form. "You surely can't intend to lodge this creature under—"

Kate stared back with defiance, daring Byron Townsend to tangle with her again. And her eyes inescapably collected the details of a face strikingly like the handsome major's—older, graying at the temples, but with the same full, sensual mouth, the same aquiline nose and arrogantly sculptured bones.

"I accept," Kate announced without taking her eyes from Byron's flaming displeasure. "I'll be pleased to stay until I am settled."

Whitney gasped with delight and gave Kate a squeeze before she caught the second half of it. "Settled?"

"There's naught for me now in Rapture with both you and your father gone. I've decided to reestablish residence in a city, and it might as well be Boston as any other." She flicked an uncertain glance at Garner, who surprised her with a stiff smile.

"You're welcome to stay as long as you like, Mrs. Morrison."

"Dammit! In my own house—" Byron ripped his coat from his shoulders to pile it atop Edgewater. He stood with his booted feet spread and his hands on his waist, a posture Kate recognized from Garner's repertoire of impotent fury. Like father like son, she thought, returning his glare. He stalked off through the house to the sanctity of his study with a pronounced "Dammit!"

Garner and Whitney bundled Kate straight into the parlor. She was soon ensconced in a stuffed chair near the fire with a blanket wrapped about her knees. Her face was dewy and flushed like a young girl's from the unaccustomed heat both inside and outside her.

"And Pa?" Whitney knelt on the floor by her chair and took Kate's hands while Garner leaned his shoulder against the mantel nearby, stroking his chin thoughtfully. "I've been so worried. You promised to write."

"I did go to see him in Pittsburgh"—Kate squeezed Whitney's hands—"a week after you left. I managed to talk with him for a few minutes and give him some food and extra clothes. Then I heard two weeks later that they were marching the prisoners east, probably all the way to Philadelphia for trial."

"Philadelphia?" Garner frowned uncomfortably.

Kate nodded. "He's all right, Whitney, I'm sure. If anyone can get along in such circumstances, Blackstone can. His spirits were good when I saw him, and that's what it takes." She didn't want to worry Whitney with mention of the scars of a recent beating that had been healing on his face. "But he hadn't come to trial yet and there didn't seem to be a time set for it."

Whitney turned a wide-eyed look on Garner, and he assured her, "If he's being held in Philadelphia, we'll soon know it." She nodded with a wan smile, then forced a brighter expression as she turned back to Kate.

"And Rapture. How is everyone?"

"The same. Well, not exactly the same." Kate's delicate features were suddenly animated by the news she bore. "It seems some of your men found Rapture Valley quite to their liking, Major. After they were released from duty, several returned. The big Wallace fellow came back with his mustering-out pay to buy a few acres and hop over a broom with May Donner. They're waiting for the circuit preacher. In fact, there were two broom-hoppings. Frieda Delbarton and that Kingery fellow too. Her boys were outraged—they nearly strung him up! But Harvey Dedham intervened and made them put him down and listen to their mother." Kate smiled and shook her head. "It was a sight, the four of them hulking over him."

"And Aunt Sarah?" Whitney prompted. "Is she all right?"

Kate laughed. "She's pining for her Charlie, as you might expect. But she's being comforted in her trials by that sergeant fellow. Laxault, wasn't it? Well, he arrived not long before I left. He said he couldn't bear the thought of Sarah alone all winter without a man's protection, doing for all her young ones by herself." Kate laughed a low, musical sound. "I expect there'll be another knot to tie when the preacher comes this spring. And Harvey's adding two more sleeping rooms to his inn with the money from—" She bit her lip and darted a glance at Garner.

"With the 'wretched paper money' he got from me and my men," he finished for her with an exaggerated glare that was slowly transformed into wry acceptance. "The little hypocrite." He turned a challenging look on Whitney. "If he can overcome his reluctance to cash money . . . *anyone* can."

Whitney blushed, and Kate caught the intimate exchange of their eyes. Whitney's riposte was lost in Kate's absorption in the warmth flowing between her and her husband.

Edgewater arrived with a tea tray and cakes and Whitney rose to a seat on the settee opposite Kate. Kate watched her pour, a bit dumbfounded by her ladylike demeanor and her comfort with the task. Kate's eyes misted as she accepted a delicate china cup and realized how often, in years past, she'd dreamed of this very thing: Whitney in a fine parlor, pouring tea, dressed like a fine lady, glowing like a beloved wife. Whitney blushed under Kate's loving scrutiny, grateful that now she at last had a chance to thank Kate for all she'd been taught.

As they talked about the events of the past weeks, Garner watched, sipping his tea and tossing in a cogent quip from time to time. In his mind's eye he saw Rapture's vivid characters brought to life again and relived his compelling impressions of his time there. An odd warmth built inside him. He was genuinely glad to hear Uncle Ballard had survived a bout of influenza and that Uncle Julius and Uncle Ferrel Dobson were helping Uncle Harvey with his construction project. And he accepted Robbie Dedham's greetings to his "Uncle Townsend" with a strange constriction in his throat.

Twenty-one

It was past sunset when a housemaid ventured into the parlor to close the shutters and draw the brocades at the windows. Whitney started. "Oh—supper! Come, Aunt Kate, let me show you to—" She turned to Garner with a slight frown. "Did you mean what you said? Your room?"

"Put her in any room you like, Whitney." Garner laughed and raised a meaningful eyebrow. "Except yours."

Whitney blushed like a bride and dragged Kate with her from the parlor and up the grand stairs, explaining breathlessly about the house as they went. She installed Kate in a guest chamber done in fine green and golden brocade and sent Mercy to arrange for a fire and a hot bath. Then she hurried to her room and selected one of her own new dresses and a full change of undergarments for Kate to wear for dinner.

"How lovely." Kate touched the elegant lilac velvet and Cluny laces with hesitant fingers. "He bought you new clothes?"

Whitney nodded, chewing the inner corner of her mouth. "You don't think it was wrong . . . me taking them . . . do you? I honestly don't do much to earn my keep, and everybody gets so upset when I try to bargain anything."

"I expect they do." Kate bit her lip to keep from laughing at the images that conjured in her mind. Daniels trading precocity meeting staid Boston money.

"Honestly, he had to lock me up to make me take them."

"I expect he did." Kate put her hand over her mouth.

"But we struck a bargain finally." Whitney's fetching half-smile suggested plainly the nature of that bargain. "And I'm trying to be a proper wife to him. He's a good man, Aunt Kate."

Kate watched the womanly wistfulness about her niece and had to ask, "Is he . . . gentle with you, Whitney?"

"He is—" Whitney nodded, lowering her eyes as she added with a naughty twinkle—"when I want him to be."

It was Kate's turn to blush. But just then Mercy ushered in servants with firewood and fresh linen and kettles of hot water and there was no further time for talk. Kate was soon submerged in a tub of deliciously hot, scented water, soaking away the aches and strain of travel. Whitney perched on a nearby chair, watching Kate's rapturous expression and grinning.

"Isn't it wonderful? I had a bath the very first morning I was here, and at least every other day since. I remembered you talking about it and it is every bit as good as you said it was. In fact, everything is as good as you said it was. Everything except Garner's Iron Family."

When Kate raised her head to look, Whitney had a tart gleam in her eye. "Aunt Kate, you'll just have to ignore Garner's father. Ezra—that's Garner's grandpa—he says Byron just doesn't have any urges himself, so he doesn't understand them in other people. And Madeline, she's spoiled and contrary in the extreme. But old Ezra is quite a fellow. He's a distiller, or he was one. Now he's confined to a chair on wheels and he pinches the housemaids to keep life interesting . . . and sneaks rum to drink whenever he can."

Kate chuckled at Whitney's irreverent summary of her wealthy in-laws.

"Oh, you'd better hurry." Whitney pointed to the rose-scented soap and stood, smoothing her dress. "They'll be holding supper for us and we mustn't be too late." She turned to go and then turned back with a thought. "Oh, and please don't be too put off if Madeline has them serve lobster tonight. She did that to me once, hoping to put me off my feed. But I realized it's just like a big red crawfish, only there's a lot more meat on it." Her quixotic grin brought a bubble of a laugh to Kate's lips.

"Lobster." Kate recalled her own first encounter with the formidable delicacy, and savored Whitney's unshrinking pragmatism. "I'll be sure to remember."

* * *

Whitney and Kate entered the dining hall only a few minutes late, pausing in the doorway to brace for what would undoubtedly be a taxing encounter. Every eye in the room fell on Kate's womanly form, searching the curves beneath the pale lilac velvet, the luxuriant fullness of her dark, upswept hair, and the exposed satin of her breast. Whitney felt Kate's hand tighten on hers and sent her a reassuring smile as they moved forward into the half-tamed pride of Townsends.

Garner formally introduced Kate to Madeline, then to Ezra, who took her hand and sat noticeably straighter in his chair. Byron acknowledged her with an inhospitable grunt and waved them all to the table with what seemed an ill-placed comment on the exact number of forks set at each place. Whitney missed the meaningful look he turned to Kate as he said it . . . and missed the spark it struck in Kate's eyes as it hit.

Conversation was brisk during the meal, with two predictable abstentions: Madeline and Byron. Kate savored the delicious food visibly and, to Whitney's surprise, guessed correctly the region of origin, if not quite the proper vintage of each wine served. As each bit of Kate's refinement was revealed, Byron huddled a bit deeper in his chair at the head of the table. When Ezra recalled there was something familiar about the name Morrison, Kate was coaxed to reveal that her late husband's family had engaged in commerce in Allentown and had sat in the first state legislature in Pennsylvania. Byron harrumphed wordless disbelief and motioned for the final course.

Whitney bristled again at Byron's open disdain for her ladylike aunt, and took it upon herself to explain to Kate Byron's view on the criminal background and slovenly habits of frontier folk. By the time she got to infestations, muck, and immorality, Kate's eyes were flashing.

She took a final sip of her wine and laid her napkin gently beside her plate, complimenting in a restrained manner the choice of menu. Then she rose with great flair, and blatantly collected the five forks she'd refused to allow the servants to remove with the courses. She carried them to the head of the table with her eyes blazing.

"Your forks, sir." She held them before Byron's surprised face.

"I know you were concerned about them in my care. But I assure you, they're all here. *One . . ."* She began to drop them one by one, sharp tines downward, into Byron's unsuspecting lap.

"Ow!" He jolted protectively as the points jabbed through the broadcloth of his snug breeches and bounced off, clattering onto the floor around him. "Dammit—oww—what—"

"Three . . . four . . ."

"Stop it! This instan—"

". . . and five . . ." She finished with a flourish and a vengeful smile. She backed away as Byron gained his feet, cursing and blustering, and she turned to Whitney and Garner. "And will coffee and sherry be served in the parlor?"

Ezra was wheeled from the dining hall in such fits of laughter that Whitney was afraid he'd do himself damage. But by the time coffee and sherry were served in the west parlor, things were outwardly calm again. As Madeline poured, Byron stubbornly reappeared, looking and moving like Townsend granite. Townsends didn't quit, Garner intoned mentally, even when it made good sense to. He swallowed back a smile that was some part empathy.

In the excruciating moment when Byron had sat there in shock, with forks dropping—stabbing—into his lap, Garner had experienced a shocking oneness of feeling with his pompous, hard-nosed father. He knew exactly what it felt like to be whittled down to human size by a brazen, outrageous female. And having experienced it himself, he felt entitled to enjoy it when it happened to his unimpeachable sire.

He was still grinning as he unbuttoned his shirt that night in Whitney's bedchamber. "Your Aunt Kate," he murmured as he felt her impatient fingers sliding underneath his shirt from behind, "she's quite a woman."

"She is, isn't she?" Her laugh was wickedness itself. "I'll never forget the shock on your father's face, not as long as I live. He deserved every bit of it." When he just laughed, her fingers took a wicked turn as well, sliding around his waist, beneath the band of his breeches, caressing his waist and belly. "You know, I never realized how much Aunt Kate gave up to come to Rapture to take care of us. I don't think she ever got used to the way we did things there. To this day she can't bargain worth diddle."

"Can't bargain? You mean she uses money?" Garner managed to salvage that bit of reason as her tantalizing fingers slid down his taut belly beneath his breeches.

"I'm afraid so," she whispered, rubbing her bare breasts in erotic patterns against his back. "But don't let it get around. We Danielses do have our pride. Are you going to wear these clothes all night? Not that I mind, actually. I'm really rather fond of breeches."

"I've come to see if you've had any word from your agent concerning Blackstone Daniels." Garner seated himself in Henredon Parker's office the very next morning. Kate Morrison's fear that the prisoners had been marched to the capital for trial weighed heavily on his mind, and he was determined to have some news soon.

"No word at all, sir." The distinguished lawyer stroked his chin thoughtfully. "Is it just possible that he's been taken to Philadelphia with the rest of the whiskey prisoners?"

"With the rest?" Garner leaned forward sharply. "Then some have been taken to the capital for trial? If so, why have we heard nothing of it?"

"Boston newspapers are so parochial concerning news from the nation's capital—or anywhere else," Parker lamented. "We hear none of this stuff for weeks." He went to rifle through piles of papers on a nearby worktable, looking for something. "Ah-ha!" He pulled a worn newspaper from a stack and used his monocle to scan it. "My associate just returned from a stay in Philadelphia and brought me several papers." He quickly read two articles that pieced together a rather grim picture.

The "whiskey rebels" had been marched from Pittsburgh to Philadelphia and had arrived in the city on Christmas Day, to a great public celebration of their defeat. Speeches were made, President Washington made an appearance; it was quite an affair. And according to a later paper, charges were being vigorously pressed against the "heinous criminals and traitors" who had "threatened the nation's order and sovereignty."

"What do you think? Shall I send an inquiry to my friend Bartholomew Hayes in Philadelphia?" Parker asked.

Garner took a deep, unsettled breath. "Blackstone Daniels is a distiller, arrested for nonpayment of the tax, not treason. Why would they have taken him all the way to Philadelphia?" He saw Parker's shrug and felt his questioning look. "Still . . . if you have someone to spare . . . or could write your friend . . ."

Over the next two weeks Kate's controversial presence in the Townsend household was tolerated, though it was made clear that she was considered a serious strain on the boundaries of Garner's forty percent of things. Whitney tried to explain to Kate the Townsends' odd synthesis of business and family that allotted privilege and position based on ownership; forty percent belonged to Garner, forty to Byron, and ten percent each to Ezra and Madeline. Kate recoiled and declared it the most bizarre way of structuring a family she'd ever heard in her life. Whitney shrugged ruefully and remarked that Garner had found Rapture's expanded concept of family—relationship by alphabet—to be rather strange too.

Each day some new pique or insult was added to the enmity between Byron and Kate. He referred to her as "that female," and she had early on dubbed him "that beast." He refused to ever hear a single word she said, and in so doing ignored her warning that his teacup was sliding and about to upset. He jumped up with a scalded lap and ruined breeches and exited the parlor with Kate's laughter rasping his raw male pride. For her part, she bristled each time he appeared, and became absurdly independent, insisting on carrying her own bags, all at once, upstairs when they arrived. She watched in horror as one aged satchel bounced down the main stairs and ruptured, spilling her undergarments practically at Byron's feet in the center hall. He nudged the pile of worn muslin with an elegant shoe toe and turned a gentlemanly sneer up at her flaming face.

Not long after she arrived, Byron came home unexpectedly

one afternoon and caught her in his study, surveying his books and wondering about him. He steamed at the invasion of his private sanctum and accused her of pilfering. Abashed by the unthinkable straying of her thoughts, she hotly denied it. Her face was flushed and his was bronzed as he advanced on her, backing her toward the door. He called her an opportunist; she labeled him a pettifogging tyrant. And by the time they reached the door, they were inches apart, staring into each other's eyes and confused by each other's heat. Kate turned on her heel and flew down the hall on weakened knees. Byron slammed the door and wobbled to his desk with an unnerved snarl.

Despite Garner and Whitney's urgings to the contrary, Kate insisted on making inquiries with agents concerning more permanent accommodations: something modest to match the remnants of her inheritance and yet with a bit of flair to match her tastes. Whitney realized that Byron's ever-present resentment and pointed barbs were probably responsible, but was unable to think of a way to counter or alleviate them. The most she could do was insist on helping Kate review potential lodgings, and pray nothing suitable would be uncovered too soon.

But daily forays house-hunting would provide a perfect opportunity to implement her "deal" with Ezra, Whitney realized with true trader's instinct. She spoke with Ezra about it and he enthusiastically agreed. They combined forces to insist that he accompany Whitney and Kate on their first outing to look at properties, and Kate's sensible arguments were no match for Whitney's ebullience and Ezra's crusty charm. They waited until Garner and Byron had gone off to their offices and Madeline was safely tucked in the morning room with her stitchery, then secretively bundled Ezra into the carriage and had Benson and Nolan tie his wheeled chair on the back.

Inevitably, they found themselves in the south end of the warehouse district on a narrow, smelly street. A large darkened brick building with rags stuffed into broken windows loomed outside the windows. Whitney and Ezra exchanged wide-eyed looks of surprise. Imagine finding themselves passing the Townsend distillery! It would be unthinkable not to stop, since they were practically on the doorstep. . . .

They stood inside the street door of the distillery, staring at the sloughing whitewash on the walls, the frost-crusted windows, and the dank brick of the floor. Whitney noted that the rotting straw and wooden crates were gone and the unpleasant sour smell had diminished. But there was still an unmistakable air of decay about the place.

"I warned you it was in a state," Whitney reminded Ezra as she and Kate pushed him along the dim passage past the stacking rooms and toward the offices. His mutters of indignation were mercifully unintelligible. Rounding the corner near the distilling room, they came face-to-face with the master distiller in heated debate with . . . Garner.

Whitney smiled sweetly, swallowed hard, and tried valiantly to explain their presence as "just passing by" and thought they'd "stop in." His tightened features and narrowed eyes said he didn't believe a word of it.

"I know exactly what you're doing here," he charged, stalking closer and lowering his voice to a furious whisper before the master and workers. "You're meddling, interfering again. I'll not have it, Whitney."

"But, Garner, you're not a rum man," Whitney contradicted him quietly, "you don't even drink the stuff. If you're really, going to change things around here, you have to taste." Her liquid green gaze tugged at him over Ezra's huddled, petulant form. "And your grandpa's got the senses for it. He could teach you."

Garner stiffened. His eyes dropped to his grandfather's stubborn, nutlike face. Faded gray eyes met sharp gray-blue ones for the first time in many years. Ezra wouldn't ask, wouldn't even offer, but the desire was so clearly there.

Despite the fact that she wasn't permitted to stay, Whitney wore a decidedly pleased expression when she and Kate reached the carriage. "We'll have to get home early this afternoon in order to send the carriage back for Ezra and Garner. And we'll have to be sure to tell Madeline there'll be only four for supper." She smiled and explained cryptically: "Ezra's going to teach him about rum."

* * *

But Garner and Ezra arrived home in time for supper, eyes bright, faces ruddy, and obviously pleased. Apparently Ezra's instructional technique had moderated since his last bout of educational fervor. Both made it through supper, then managed a withdrawal to toddle quickly off to bed afterward. Whitney watched Garner strip his coat and shirt and fall facedown on the bed, and she ruffled his hair with a tingle of warmth in her chest and a rueful expression.

He awakened, hours later, to a room lit only by the golden glow of a fire and the awareness of his breeches inching downward over his buttocks. Soon he felt her warm presence at his side, then sliding onto his back like a heavy satin comforter. His mouth curled lazily as he imagined just which parts of her created which delicious sensations. She wriggled seductively over his back and buttocks, wakening, summoning him, and he suddenly recalled what had happened the last time she'd wakened him in such a manner.

He arched and turned forcefully, trying to dump her onto the bed as he went, but she braced above him and in the brief, sensual struggle she managed to slide between his legs, claiming instant victory. He lay on his back, her curvy body wedged between his legs, feeling her palms rising up his belly, swirling over his chest. Her hair was a glowing, tousled mane, her eyes glistened in the semidarkness.

He drew her up slowly, letting her slide purposefully against his roused and aching parts. Spreading and wrapping her about him, he made love to her like a man possessed, caressing and commanding every part of her.

She sighed sometime later, and snuggled against his damp body, relishing the sated splendor of his features, the dark crescents of his closed lashes. "It worked out well, didn't it, Ezra at the distillery?"

"Just like a woman." He sighed with a forced bit of exasperation. "Demanding homage to her intuitions."

"Distiller's intuitions, thank you. It did, didn't it?" she insisted, tracing his side with insistent fingers. His resultant shiver ran through her breasts as they pressed against him.

"It did . . . this time. But it can't continue," he declared with firmness.

"Oh, but it will," she declared just as firmly. "It's part of the bar—" She could have bitten her tongue.

"What?" He came to life, pushing up onto one elbow and staring at her, feeling his skin tightening all over. *"Bargain?* What bargain? Blessit, Whitney, I'll not have you dealing and interfering—what bargain?" She realized he was teetering on the brink of real anger.

"Well, it's not quite a bargain exactly. More like a nudge. Ezra liked you and he wanted so much to be part of the distillery again."

"So you arranged it." His jaw flexed as he pinned her with his gaze and watched her squirm. "Ezra gets to work at the distillery again and what do you get?" he demanded.

"Well, actually . . ." She swallowed hard, watching his eyes silvering above her. "It's you who gets it." Her voice went craven on her and dropped to a squeak. "Your grandpa's ten percent."

He twitched, his eyes narrowed furiously, and he sprang from the bed to pace violently back and forth. He stopped once, twice, running his hands through his hair with raw frustration, and then turned to stare at her in the firelight. She was sitting up in the bed with the sheet pressed against her breasts, her eyes great luminous pools of uncertainty that tugged at both his higher and lower impulses. She'd done it for him . . . she'd wheedled and bargained his grandfather's percentage so he'd be one step closer to controlling Townsend Companies.

"I don't understand," she said simply. "I thought you wanted it."

"I wanted to *earn* it." His arms flexed impotently. "Not to have it bartered for me by my wife!"

"Oh, but you did earn it, you and your urges." She came to her knees and inched forward on the bed.

"My *what?"* He stomped toward her, confusion mounting.

"Ezra said he always liked a man with urges. He says sometimes a man has to follow his urges in business as well as in a woman's bed. He thinks you'll make a good head of the companies. All I did was give things a little nudge." She bit her lip and watched him struggle with it visibly.

"Blessit, Whitney!" he roared, looking as if he were ready to explode. And after a losing struggle he did explode—straight at Whitney, knocking her back onto the bed on her back and pinning her there with his big, naked body. He was heaving, coiled, roused. "No more nudges, dammit!"

She watched the need billowing in him with a sense of relief and smiled. She slid her silky arms around his neck.

"You'll make a wonderful distiller."

Garner watched the devious flicker of desire rising in her and knew in his marrow that no edict would withstand her for long. She would interfere and wheedle and "nudge" and bargain until her dying day. It was one of the things he couldn't help loving about her. He eased against the softness of her sweet curves and gave himself over to her.

"The old boy says I have the senses for it."

"I could have told you that. You have a very keen nose." Her voice flowed over him like warm honey, stirring things inside him. He felt her seductive undulation. "And a marvelous tongue."

The next afternoon Ezra made another of what were to become daily treks to the Townsend distilleries, with Whitney's and Kate's assistance. Whitney watched the excitement in his face and the lively glow of his faded eyes with a deep sense of pleasure. Garner now had fifty percent, and a grandpa to boot. Her thick lashes lowered in concentration. Now all she had to do was figure out what prickly little Madeline wanted.

The Hancocks' ball was always the most celebrated event of the winter in Boston's elite society. There was heated discussion when the formal invitation arrived and Garner surprised everyone, especially Madeline, by suggestion that it would be an excellent opportunity for Madeline to be introduced into society for the first time. He pointed out that she'd had few social opportunities and would soon come of age. That unexpected bit of consideration put Madeline firmly on Garner's side for a change. And despite thinly veiled hints that certain members of the household and their "guests" would feel ill at ease and out of their depth, the invitation was accepted on behalf of the entire Townsend family and one lady guest.

A strong current of curiosity about Garner Townsend's new wife ran through the gathering as they arrived. Rumors of her beauty and background had circulated freely. None were disappointed when the pair was announced in the candlelit drawing room of the Hancock mansion that evening. Garner was splendid in his best black-velvet coat and evening breeches, his chest full of starched linen ruffles and his corded neck bound by an elegant gray cravat. But it was Whitney who captured their eyes.

She was gowned in a silk the color of precious jade, which was embroidered with a web of lacy gold thread. Both her high-waisted gown and her unusual burnished ginger hair shimmered in the warm candlelight, drawing attention to her curvy form and perfect skin. And when she felt the reassuring pressure of Garner's hand over hers, she eased so that her eyes began to sparkle and her smile cast an intriguing aura of woman and warmth about her.

Byron watched with a certain pique as Garner and Whitney were besieged by Boston's elite. He was further stung when Ezra, escorting Kate Morrison, drew more notice than he had. Then, when he watched numerous male heads turn to follow the striking Kate, he was seized by an unholy urge to bash every one of them. But he was unable to tear his eyes from her provocative form and the gentle sway of her skirts.

Pulling down his waistcoat firmly, he led Madeline out for her first dance, then hastily turned her over to the son of a business acquaintance. He followed Garner and Whitney and Kate about the first floor of the Hancock mansion like a brooding shadow and was appalled when an acquaintance led Kate out for a dance. With hawklike intensity his eyes followed her graceful steps, absorbed the impact of her lush smiles, and narrowed at the way everyone else seemed to be watching too. Had the woman no shame at all, displaying herself in that flimsy gown, inviting the attentions of strange men? As soon as the last strains died, he was in motion, set on a course to interdict her flagrant behavior.

"The next dance, Mrs. Morrison?" Byron planted himself before Kate with a heated bronze glow that forbade all answers but the one he sought.

She agreed with a demure nod, but a wary glint crept into her eye as he led her stiffly to the farthest corner of the floor. She saw the words working their way up his neck and into his stubborn jaw before his mouth opened.

"Give a care, Mrs. Morrison." His lips scarcely moved from his forced half-smile as he towered above her. It was an expression meant for onlookers, not for her. "You may not concern yourself with your own reputation, but there are others here who may suffer from your behavior."

"My behavior?" she murmured, indignation billowing as she realized he'd sought her out to reprimand her. "How dare you presume to censure my behavior, sir. Look to your own sad manners." She turned to go and he caught her arm to stay her.

"I presume, madame, because you are a guest in my home and here under my auspices. Your flaunting of yourself is a dread reflection upon myself and my family."

"And just how have I flaunted myself, sir?" she demanded with reined heat, turning to face him. "Just what have I done to outrage decent sensibilities?"

"Promenading and parading yourself all about," he charged.

"Walking." She steamed quietly. "I was *walking.*"

"Rushing onto the floor with the first man who casts an eye on you," he snarled.

"We were properly introduced, sir, by our host."

"Flaunting yourself . . . laughing openly and conversing in a loose and untoward manner—"

"L-loose—?" Kate sputtered, just managing to realize that every time she'd glimpsed him in the last hour, he'd been staring at her with the same dark intensity he wore now. She straightened and raised her chin defiantly. "You have taken pains to catalog my faults, Mr. Townsend. But I think fault, like beauty, often lies in the eye of the beholder. If watching me offends you so, then why do you apply yourself to it so strenuously?"

Byron twitched as if she'd slapped him. Why indeed . . . except that beneath his professed distaste lay an intensely personal interest? He had "applied himself" because she was beautiful and spirited and warm . . . too damned warm. And she had a way of making a man feel very much a man when she looked at him— dammit! His jaw turned to granite, and he released her arm only to take hold of her shoulders, ignoring her tugs of resistance. She was so warm and soft in his hands, and every time he met her eyes, they were littered with glowing sparks threatening to burst into true flame.

Kate felt the odd tenor of his arrogant stare: it was almost *proprietary.* She wriggled her shoulders discreetly, but was unable to pull free. More than his hands held her. There was a force, a potency in his handsome features, a dangerous heat in his gray eyes. The warmth of his hands seeped through the silk of her fitted sleeves and flowed toward her middle. It was the strangest sensation . . . all fluid and trickling . . . as her eyes focused on the bold sweep of his sometimes cynical mouth.

Half the couples on the dance floor were standing stock-still, waiting for the music to begin and watching the exchange between them. Byron held her captive only inches from his taut body, and something was certainly passing between them. Their faces were flushed; their eyes shone with an unmistakable luster. The music began, and a discreet cough and the reluctant motion of the dancers around them jolted them back to reality. Kate wrenched free at the very moment Byron would have withdrawn his hands in horror. Each flushed a deep, angry crimson, and turned the opposite direction and fled through the crowd.

In the cool privacy of the upper hallway, Kate sagged against a door frame and pressed icy hands to her burning face. Never in her life had she stared at a man like that . . . into his eyes . . . with that strange, hot, trickly feeling in the middle of her. The wretched beast—he'd made a bloody spectacle of her in front of half of Boston society!

It would have been little consolation to her, but downstairs Byron was in similar turmoil. A bloody debacle, he groaned internally, grabbing her, holding her bodily in front of half of his peers in the financial world! It was those damned eyes of hers. And the satiny skin. And the enticing way she swung her . . . he got near her and he began to feel things, stirrings he hadn't felt in twenty years. It was like something was uncoiling in him. D-dammit! By morning his respectable name would be on the lips of every tawdry gossip in the city, linked with *that female!*

Elsewhere, Whitney was actually enjoying her first grand evening in society. Powdered faces and rustling silks, perfumed hands and admiring winks, all ran together after a while. But it was an exceedingly pleasant blur with Garner always at her side. He led her into a country dance that proved remarkably like something she'd done in Rapture's rowdier celebrations, and squired her discreetly through *one* cup of wine punch. Thus, the rumors of her strange preferences in drink were summarily debunked, as were the whispers regarding her bizarre frontier upbringing. Anyone with two eyes could see she was a lady, bred to the bone.

Later in the evening Whitney excused herself with Kate to go to the ladies' rooms on the upper floor. Kate chose to remain a bit longer and, since Whitney was eager to rejoin Garner, she left Kate and retraced her steps toward the stairs. Pausing at an unexpected junction in the hallway, she chose the wrong path and soon found herself approaching the end of an empty hallway. Something caught her attention as she turned, and she slowed, senses alert. Voices were coming from a partly open door. She wouldn't have listened, except the hallway was very quiet and something seemed very familiar.

A moan. That's what it was. Whitney's cheeks pinked. It was the kind of moan she identified with physical pleasures, a hungry male sound. And on its heels came a very familiar female voice . . . with words that became increasingly audible.

"No, we don't have to go . . . not yet."

It was Madeline! And the full, husky quality to her voice widened Whitney's eyes. She was there, in what was probably a bedchamber . . . with a man who was moaning? Alarm galvanized her.

"Really, Madeline—" the fellow's voice was clearer—"if

someone were to come, you'd be—we'd both be compromised. Ohhhh . . . minx . . . you're much too young for such . . . umm . . ."

"I'm not too young," Madeline countered with a sultry whisper. "Do it again . . . please, Carter . . ."

Outside, Whitney vibrated with shock. Do *what* again? She strode into the room, slamming the door and startling the embraced couple. They stood, fully clothed, against a window seat on the far wall, arms about each other. Whitney nearly wilted with relief.

"Oh—*oh!*" Madeline reacted slowly to her presence, and the youngblood pushed Madeline behind him, set to take the brunt upon himself, muttering, "Good God!" Every nerve and muscle in the room froze as Whitney scrutinized the twosome. Hardly a ruffle disarranged, she observed frantically, trying to decipher the best course. There was probably no major harm done.

"Madeline, your grandfather is calling for you." She drew herself up and managed a remarkably level tone. "I suggest that we not keep him waiting." Her heart thudded expectantly as Madeline peered around the nattily dressed fellow, her eyes now crackling with displeasure.

The scarlet-faced young gentleman seized the chance Whitney was offering them and turned to take Madeline's hand. "Miss Townsend," he muttered with a pained nod, then gave her hand a sharp tug to send her on her way.

Madeline huffed and glared at him, then at Whitney, and lifted her skirts to sail out with her cheeks aflame. Whitney stayed only long enough to offer the fellow a bit of advice. "Madeline is very young. I suggest you listen to your own good sense in the future."

She caught up with Madeline in the main hallway and pulled her bodily into an elegant bedchamber. "What on earth did you think you were doing back there?"

"Kissing." Madeline jerked her arm from Whitney and huddled back, snapping like a cornered vixen. "He was kissing me. Surely *you* know about kissing—you and Cousin Garner do it often enough!"

"How do you . . ." Whitney reddened but refused to allow Madeline to distract her. "Garner and I are married; that's quite a different matter from stealing off to a secluded place with a man and allowing him to . . . to . . ."

"Kiss me," Madeline provided defiantly, crossing her arms. "I wanted to learn how it was done and so I got him to do it to me. And it was going splendidly until—how dare you barge in and embarrass me and ruin everything!"

"A great deal more might have been ruined if I hadn't come when I did," Whitney said, coming forward, eyes flashing. "One kiss leads to another, and several kisses lead to other things, things between men and women that you're not ready for. Things that would ruin your reputation and disgrace your family!"

"D-don't be absurd."

"Absurd, am I?" Whitney's eyes narrowed, and she wondered just how much proper little Madeline actually knew about a proper bargain between a man and a woman. "It starts with kisses, long, openmouthed kisses. Then everything gets very hot and his hands start to roam inside your dress, then under your skirts. If I'd come twenty minutes later, would I have found you buff naked and him sprawled over you on the bed?" Her thrust found its target, and Madeline's hazel eyes flickered briefly with uncertainty.

"And what would have been wrong with that?" Madeline asked defiantly, determined to conceal how Whitney's words had shaken her. "Do you know who he is? He's Carter Melton, probably the most eligible bachelor in Boston." She lifted her stubborn chin. "Who better to be 'compromised' by?"

Whitney's jaw dropped. Apparently Madeline had already considered the possible ramifications of her behavior, and embraced them. She wouldn't have minded being compromised and caught, she had decided, with a rich, handsome fellow who was coveted husband material.

"Why, you little Delilah!" Whitney was stunned by the sheer deviousness of it. Prickly little Madeline obviously harbored a few untapped desires beneath all that Townsend superiority. "You get an itch and are bound to have it scratched no matter who gets hurt in the process. Well, did you ever consider the pain your little plan might cause? The disgrace, the disruption of futures, the anger he'd feel toward you after you've forced him to violate his own judgment and exposed him to disgrace? He seemed a decent enough sort—maybe he has affections for someone else already. Did you ever once think about that?"

She was shouting, stalking Madeline furiously, her eyes ablaze. The girl tried to hold her ground, but Whitney's height advantage and outrage forced her back with a draining countenance.

"Let me tell you, Madeline Townsend, there are two kinds of women in this world." She shook a furious finger near Madeline's paling face. "Decent women and *Delilahs*. Delilahs have fleshly desires and pleasureful cravings just like men have. And those desires can make them do things they regret later. But let me tell you, just because you're a Delilah and have desires doesn't mean you have to act on them. You can choose not to. You don't have to tempt and betray a man to get what you want. You can choose to act decently and honorably. Because if you don't—if you choose your desires over the wisdom of your head and your heart—things go wrong. People get hurt."

She ground to a halt, shaking, her words rumbling in her head and in her heart. It was true. A woman might be born a Delilah, but she still had a choice as to whether or not to act like a Delilah. It struck her that she'd had that choice too. When bargaining Garner Townsend out of Rapture didn't work, she had *chosen* to plant herself in his bed. And that moment in his bed when he spoke of a proper bargain between them, she had chosen that as well.

Madeline stared at Whitney with wide and suddenly very girlish eyes. After that first flush of Townsend defiance, she was beginning to realize the full impact of her behavior. What if what Whitney said were true about kisses and where they led? She recalled the way Carter kept opening his mouth against hers, the curious hot flushes she'd felt, the furtive way his fingers had slid over her chest and dipped under. . . . She went perfectly ashen as Byron's face sprang up in her mind, glowering at her, denouncing her, branding her a tart and a disgrace to the Townsend name.

"You're not going to tell them, are you?" There was an uncharacteristic waver of anxiety in her voice.

That look and that question produced a heady, unexpected

rush in Whitney's blood. Her eyes began to glow as the trader in her heard the call and sprang to life. This was it, a voice inside her crowed deliriously, something little Madeline wanted. Her silence. Whitney took a deep breath and smiled a crafty smile. Everything had its price.

"Well, Madeline." She struck one of her subtler trading poses and looked little Madeline straight in her anxious hazel orbs. And she stopped dead. The girl was biting her lip, beginning to tremble visibly. She'd never seen Madeline like this—small and vulnerable, devoid of her usual arrogance and hauteur. She was acting like a naive young girl of sixteen. Perhaps somewhere inside that Iron Madeline persona there was a lonely young girl who'd been raised by Iron Townsend men to seem older, prouder than she really was.

Whitney took a step back, clasping her hands to still them. The trader's fires damped in her eyes as the ramifications of it all multiplied within her. The sight of Madeline's girlish anxiety and her own startling realization of moments ago somehow merged in her mind. Just because she knew what Madeline wanted didn't mean she had to strike the deal. Everything had its price, she'd been raised to believe, and her experience had proven it true. But was it possible that there were some things that just shouldn't be bargained or bought?

She turned toward the door and Madeline's voice halted her halfway. "Whitney . . . a-are you going to tell them?"

Whitney turned back to settle a thoughtful look on her. "You'd better find your grandpa and stay with him. I haven't decided yet."

Halfway down the wide main stairs, Whitney paused. She undoubtedly had found the key to Madeline's cooperation. Why was she so hesitant to use it? She bit her lip as she noticed Garner coming to fetch her with a loving smile on his handsome face.

Now she was a Delilah with a choice on her hands.

Late the next afternoon, when the family had recuperated enough to gather in the east parlor for tea, all were astonished to see Madeline offer her cherished dominion over the tea tray to Whitney. There wasn't a single drop of condescension in her tone or expression. Whitney paused, searching the girl's subdued manner and the rare and tenuous offer running beneath her words. It was an offer of acceptance, a very Townsend sort of apology, and a bit of a plea, all at the same time.

Everyone watched as they faced each other, and all witnessed the hallmark Daniels grin that was borne on Whitney's face. Madeline managed a wavery, unaccustomed smile that said she was grateful for Whitney's silence. But only Whitney understood the full ramifications of the decision she'd made. For the first time in her life, Whitney Daniels had walked away from a loaded bargain.

Twenty-two

Two days after the dance, boots stamped and scuffled on the marble floor and the muffled metallic rattle of blades in scabbards whispered through the center hall. Three soldiers, resplendent in blue coats and white breeches, eyed the polished elegance of the hall as they waited for their message to be delivered. Edgewater reappeared, showed them into the west parlor, and saw to it that a warming fire was laid.

Half an hour later, near sunset, Garner and Whitney returned from a walk on the common to find Garner's family, Kate, and the military envoy awaiting them. They paused in the doorway, hand in hand, their eyes bright and their faces polished from the cold. The precise military rise of the soldiers generated a ripple of expectation.

Byron rose with great dignity and introduced the captain and his juniors, attached to—

"Maryland Division," Garner provided, nodding tightly. His entire body tensed with expectation and, without looking, he knew the same was happening to Whitney. Her grasp on his hand was suddenly deathlike as he ushered her forward. "I confess, I am surprised to see the Maryland Division still active."

"Until the trials are finished and the danger of a resurgence is past, some troops are being kept on active duty, sir," the young captain intoned. "I am here to deliver this to you with the compliments of President Washington." He removed a sealed document from the official dispatch pouch his lieutenant carried and handed it to Garner with a smile that bespoke admiration.

Garner released Whitney's hand to take the parchment, then turned it over, noting the presidential seal set in crimson wax.

He tried to detach from the emotional tension the sight of it built inside him. Byron took two hurried strides toward him, then stopped for the sake of dignity.

"Well, don't just stand there," Byron said, fidgeting, eyeing the parchment eagerly. "Open it. God forbid you should keep the President waiting!"

Garner slid his thumb under the seal, then unfolded the parchment, knowing what he'd find inside. The script was bold and flowing, illuminated at key points with intricate scarlet and gold scrollwork. His eyes skimmed the lines, catching relevant phrases that might have come from his family's archives—"commendation," "highest honor," "service," and "gratitude." Five months earlier it would have been the answer to a fervent prayer, the key to his future. Now they were just words, prettily done on parchment.

"Well?" Byron drew nearer with compressed excitement. "What is it?" Garner held it out to him.

Confusion flickered through his aquiline features as he took it and began to read. At Ezra's prompting, he continued aloud: " ' . . . do hereby issue this Special Commendation to Major Garner Adams Townsend for his outstanding performance of duty in the expeditionary force of October, 1794, into the western counties of Pennsylvania.' " His voice increased in volume and excitement. " 'While in command of a force of militia, Major Townsend quelled uprisings of grievous treason and high crimes against the sovereignty of this nation, acquitting himself personally with bravery and highest honor. For such exemplary and distinguished service to his country, he has earned this Special Commendation and the irrevocable and undying gratitude of his commander, his government, and his countrymen. Signed . . . George Washington . . . President and Commander.' "

There was awed silence for a long while, then the captain came to attention, drawing his men erect with him to salute, though Garner was not in uniform. "Congratulations, Major Townsend, on this great honor. It is indeed a privilege; I understand there were precious few issued." The junior officer and sergeant offered their hands, and Byron rushed forward to grasp Garner's arm and shake his hand firmly.

"Damnable fine work . . . a Special Commendation!" Byron beamed. "Think how it will look in the *Gazette!* This calls for our best French brandy—Edgewater!"

In the flurry of admiration and questions that were unleashed, Garner remained silent, looking down at his hand, gripped tightly in his father's. All he could think was that it was the first time they had touched in years.

Whitney had moved to Kate's side and watched Garner's rigid back and telling silence as Byron read the commendation. Her eyes flew over his broad, responsible shoulders and his aristocratic features, and she was torn between a deep well of pride that his stubborn sense of honor and duty was at last being recognized, and a twinge of pain that it was secured at the cost of her father's freedom. But this honor meant a great deal to him and to his rightful place in the family. With that understanding and the painful remembrance of her pa's parting words to her, she pushed her personal conflicts aside.

When his gaze found her, she blinked back a trace of moistness in her eyes and sent him a proud grin. Garner stared at her stubborn smile and darkening eyes, reading fluently the pride and love she was determined to show, and the pain she was determined to hide. An empty feeling began to open in his middle, and he forced an approximation of pleasure onto his face as he accepted the long-awaited plaudits from the Townsends. Their praise was like the deep winter sun, dazzlingly bright but strangely devoid of warmth.

"Sir—there was yet another part to our mission," the captain recalled, producing a second document from the dispatch pouch.

" 'By the authority of the Federal Court of the United States,' " he skimmed, " 'Major Garner Adams Townsend is hereby subpoenaed to appear in the Federal Court in Philadelphia, beginning April First of this year, to give testimony as to activities and events pertinent to the examination of one Blackstone Daniels, on the charge of high treason against the duly constituted government of these United States.' I am instructed to return with confirmation of your appearance. The first of April, sir . . . will that be convenient?" Garner's smile faded abruptly as he stared dumbly at the paper the captain handed him.

"We'll make it convenient." Byron stepped in to assure the captain, sending his son a dark look. "Townsends have always extended themselves in service to their country. A trial for treason, you said?"

"One of the leaders of the rebellion, sir." The lean-faced captain turned warily back to Garner. "Apparently your work netted a prize, Major. Lord knows we can use one. Bradford's armed band escaped into the Ohio territory and Sheriff John Hamilton and the Reverend John Corbley, who were prominent among the rebellion's leaders, were both acquitted for lack of evidence and proper witnesses. They'll take no chances with this one. Your testimony is critical."

The captain stumbled to a halt, realizing Garner was staring past him, in the direction of his wife. Byron, oblivious of all but the throb of his exalted Townsend pride, interjected: "My son's testimony may be counted upon to see at least one of those wretched rebel traitors properly disposed of."

Whitney heard it all, the wording of the subpoena, the call to testimony, and Byron's crass response. But the sound of her father's name linked to a charge of "high treason" eclipsed all else in her mind.

She moved through an airless void to Garner's side, reaching for the summons with cold, clumsy fingers. His eyes on her were probing and uncertain as she read for herself. "One Blackstone Daniels" . . . "charge of high treason." Her eyes fixed on the fanciful script of her father's name, and the blood drained precipitously from her head. She swayed, and Garner's hands shot out to steady her. "Whitney—"

Every eye in the room was riveted on them as she raised luminous, pain-darkened eyes to him and he grasped her shoulders tightly. Tension thickened the air with every heartbeat.

"Treason . . ." Her voice was choked. "A trial for *treason?*" She saw Garner swallow hard, felt the tightening of his hands and the tension that radiated from his hard frame. When he remained silent, she looked to the captain and his men, who frowned confusion, then to Madeline and Aunt Kate. "B-but . . . they hang traitors," she sputtered, grasping Garner's sleeves and again searching for some denial in his stony features.

"Traitors deserve to hang," Byron declared, watching the tense exchange between Garner and Whitney and keening at the way his pride in the moment was being cheated by her unthinkable interference. "That's the price they pay for trying to destroy the forces of order and reason, for defying the constitutional authority of our nation."

Whitney heard no more. Her thoughts were suddenly lost in the bleak certainty of Garner's gaze. Her pa . . . on trial for his very life. Two or three years, Black had said, and he'd be free again. She'd come to Boston with Garner, believing it. She'd begun to make a new life here with him, believing it. She tore from Garner's hands and ran from the parlor.

"Whitney—" Garner lurched after her, jolting to a halt after two steps. He turned on Byron, trembling, and lunged at him, grabbing his coat front and shaking him. "You bastard. You miserable, cold-blooded bastard!"

"No—Garner—no!" Kate flew to grab Garner's arm as he grappled with his father. "You can't—he's your father. Think of Whitney—Garner—she needs you!"

The sound of Whitney's name and Kate's pleading face managed to penetrate Garner's fury. Only the sheerest margin of will kept him from unleashing the rage coiled in his muscles. He shoved free, heaving, and snarling, "Go ahead, put it in your damned *Gazette*. I've gotten a Special Commendation for hanging my wife's father."

He wheeled and ran after Whitney, and confusion broke loose. The soldiers made a shocked and hasty withdrawal. Byron quaked with humiliated fury under their covert glances and under Ezra and Kate's burning glares. He roared from the room, making straight for his study. Ezra blustered and demanded to be helped from the room and, for once, Madeline complied without a moment's demur.

Garner reached Whitney's door and stopped with his hand on the handle. His entire being was in raging turmoil. The pain in Whitney's face minutes before thundered through him again, overriding even his rage at his father and his damnable duty.

She'd stood with bittersweet pride in her face, giving him the support of her love in his wretched "triumph." And moments later she'd clung to him, dark-eyed, hurting, refusing to believe her father's peril, and his own cursed role in it.

Treason. Dear God. He closed his eyes as icy fingers of reality sank through him. How could he have known they'd twist his statements to accuse Blackstone Daniels of leading the rebellion and charge him with high treason? He thought back to Colonel Gaspar's grasping order: he wanted prisoners—evidence be damned. The courts would take care of that, he had sneered. Garner was only then beginning to realize the awful implications of those words.

The sight of the bruised trust in Whitney's eyes pierced him afresh. He wanted to go to her . . . to love and comfort her. But did he have the right? His hand tightened of its own will on the door handle.

Whitney stood by the window in the dim evening light, her arms wrapped tightly around her waist. The straight line of her back, the stark angle of her jaw, both spoke of her struggle to deal with the horrifying new reality. She turned as he came closer and the tumult in her face halted him. For a moment they searched each other in pained silence.

"Did you know?" she whispered.

Garner went hollow inside. He had asked her the same question once. And he'd believed the circumstances more than he'd believed the honesty of her heart. Now he could only pray she'd give him more credence than he had given her.

"No, Whitney, I didn't know." Every word was ground from his soul. "I arrested him for illegal distilling, nothing more. I had no idea they would charge him with treason. Believe me, I would never have taken him otherwise."

She stood, watching him, the conflict of her heart plain in her face. She wanted to believe him, the look said. But how could she? He was called to testify against her pa, to give evidence of his treason. Why would they call him to testify if he had nothing to say?

He read the thoughts, the doubts in her face, and had no defense against them except the ache her hurt caused in him. "I love you, Whitney."

"I love you, Garner," she whispered, motionless, suspended between loving and desperation. Her eyes filled with pain's delicate crystal. "And I love my pa too."

Garner nodded. His arms hung at his sides, feeling stripped and impotent. Their strength was incapable of protecting and sheltering her this time, for this time the greatest threat to her loving heart was him.

He turned on his heel and strode out. When he reached the center hall he blew, coatless, out into the frigid night air, letting it penetrate him and praying the numbing cold would blunt his pain.

The door to Byron's private study had scarcely quit vibrating from his violent entry when it was wrenched open again and slammed a second time. He started about, coiling for another round with Garner or Ezra. But it was Kate Morrison who stood just inside the door with her arms crossed. Her face was flushed and her hazel eyes simmered like molten copper and scorched just as surely.

"Just what the hell do—"

"You are without a doubt the most callous, unfeeling wretch ever birthed," she charged, uncoiling to stalk closer. "Have you no human feeling in you at all?"

"How dare you barge in here—" Byron shot at Kate, then launched his own defense. "I have every damned right in the world to be proud of my son's accomplishment, every right." His voice thickened as his gray gaze darkened. "I've waited years for this, to take my son's hand in a moment of triumph."

"Triumph?" Kate stared at him with that way she had of piercing his very skin. "That's what you call this? A *triumph?*" The depth of his arrogant self-absorption appalled her. "It's her father. Whitney's father, Black Daniels. Garner arrested him in Rapture and it's him that Garner is called to testify against."

His features hardened into turbulent bronze as he battled the heat and confusion boiling up visibly within him. "H-her father?"

"Yes, Whitney's father. It's Garner's *father-in-law* you so eagerly promised he would help dispose of." She could see her razor-edged charge found entry through his thick hide.

"Well, how the hell was I supposed to know?" he stormed, chagrined he hadn't investigated more fully the circumstances of his son's marriage, especially after hearing that Garner had arrested her father. Good Lord—a traitor. "I—I've never even heard the wretch's name before today!"

"Because you've never bothered to learn a thing about her, have you? Your own daughter-in-law. But then, why should you, when your own son is a perfect stranger to you?" Kate breached the outer perimeter of his defenses, invaded both his ire and his senses as she neared.

"You don't know or care that he loves Whitney—and that she loves him. And it probably doesn't mean a thing to you that having to testify against her father could tear him apart." With ferocity she chose a still sharper-edged thrust and delivered it with unerring aim. "You wouldn't understand, because you don't have the faintest idea what it's like to have feelings for someone."

Her accusations were only partly to blame for the tangle of heat and emotion rampaging through him. The friction of her hot gaze down his form brought his blood near the point of combustion. No woman had ever dared or abraded both his pride and his passions the way she did. He was trembling, assaulted by her on every level, roused. A shaft of elemental heat erupted from that tough core to rip through his senses and burn a swath all the way into his loins.

"Ezra was right about you." Kate's contempt rained sparks through him. "You haven't got any damned urges of your own, so you debase and belittle them in others."

"No damned urges?" He grabbed her shoulders and pulled her tight against him. "No urges, have I?" In half a heartbeat his hard mouth closed over hers, his hard arms clamped about her, and desire sprang to life against her stunned frame.

An outraged gasp parted her lips, and he took full advantage of it to penetrate her lush mouth, forcing her to recant her charges, daring her to deny this "urge." She pushed against the sides of his silk-lined coat, frantic to escape the feel of his mouth on hers, and the upwelling of her own desire to meet it. But her twisting only drew the vise of his arms tighter, thrust her harder against his focusing male heat.

She slowed, stunned by the billows of smoky desire that filled her senses, claimed by the heat uncoiling in her. Fluid sensations swirled through her body, burning, congealing in her womanly places. He felt the change in her, and his mouth softened, coaxing, commanding, even as her body softened against him, lush and luxuriant. A shudder signaled the completion of his arousal and he groaned, lifting his head to stare hungrily into her flushed face. Then he tasted her again and sent trembling hands down over the voluptuous contours of her waist and bottom.

"Oh, God, Kate—" He moaned, clasping her rounded bottom, pressing her hard against his swollen desire and shocking even himself with the natural, if involuntary, thrust of his hips against her. He couldn't remember ever wanting a woman the way he wanted Kate Morrison. And the mildly shocking way she rubbed her tantalizing breasts against his ribs, the way her tongue danced over his—she wanted him too.

Blood pounding, bodies aching, they stood entwined, kissing, pressing, until their knees weakened and he moved her back against the desk. He dragged his mouth lower to nuzzle the hollow of her throat and to explore the tantalizing swell of her breasts. His hands followed, feathering, caressing, luxuriating in the texture of her skin. She arched, offering, and his mouth followed where his hand led.

"Byron." Desire swirled up from the very ground of her being and curled through every part of her as the fullness of the sound blossomed erotically in her mouth. "Oh, Byron—"

The sound of his name on her lips brought his head up, and his lips poured over hers hotly as he probed the steamy depths of her desire, pushing her toward the melting point of surrender.

A strangled human sound at the door managed to register through the storm raging between them, and Byron lifted his head over Kate's shoulder to behold Madeline's huge eyes in the doorway. There was a swirl of skirts and the muffled smack of the door against its frame, and Byron jolted upright, panting and struggling to focus his eyes. His shock relayed through his hands on her body, and Kate opened her eyes, blinking, dazed. His arms slid from her and he staggered back.

Kate followed his eyes down her body to discover her bodice tucked to bare most of one breast. She groaned, tugging the fabric up to cover herself as she slid from the desktop onto legs that would scarcely support herself. He'd kissed her, her head swam dizzily, and touched her. She tried to swallow, to say something, but her throat was still in desire's paralyzing grip and her lips felt swollen and hot.

Byron stood, sharing her shock, still feeling the heat of her lush body against him and suffering the wild throb of arousal in his loins. He looked down his front to the blatant bulge in his breeches and felt an icy blast of humiliation. No damned urges, old Ezra had said.

The sight of her backing toward the door pulled him from his turmoil. In her luminous eyes he saw the same dismay, the same bewilderment, and the same lingering shimmer of desire. "K-Kate—"

The sound of her name somehow energized her, and she wheeled and fled the study, her face burning with shame. Byron watched her go, unsure whether he should stop her, or whether he even wanted to. He was quaking; hot currents of illicit desire still swirled through his chest, his loins.

Ezra be damned, he realized. He'd unleashed his urges on Kate Morrison because he bloody well wanted Kate Morrison! He groaned, sliding weakly into his chair. She was incorrigibly lovely, infuriatingly accomplished, defiantly female . . . and *hot*. And that heat had set him on fire, all of him: his pride, his passion . . . even his wretched conscience.

Kate's heart pounded madly as she leaned back against the door of her room. Never—not in her entire life—had she behaved with such shocking wantonness. Wriggling and moaning and thrusting herself against . . . against *Byron Townsend!* But the shock of who had aroused her was momentarily overshadowed by the strength of her passions themselves. She'd been on fire in her womanly places, burning, craving the feel of his body so much that she couldn't breathe or speak. She'd never felt such things before, certainly not in the five years she spent as handsome Clayton Morrison's wife. Dry husbandly pecks and even drier, dutiful submission were her lot on the nights philandering Clayton deigned to come home at all. But Byron Townsend made her feel hot and tingly and wet inside, filled her with all manner of shocking, undulating desires.

Her eyes widened in horror. Desires? *She* had desires? How could she; she was a *decent* woman!

The dim chiming of the great clock in the center hall indicated it was the wee hours of the morning, and Garner still hadn't returned. Twice Whitney had donned her heavy velvet robe to look for him, and now she ached with worry, consumed by the gnawing fear that he might not come back.

The bleakness of his expression when he left tortured her. She burned to recall her words, to purge the frightened accusations that had filled her mind and heart. In the chill of predawn, things seemed clearer, less charged with emotion. She should have listened, talked, or just held out her arms to him. With each lengthening minute her worries grew more feverish. Perhaps he wouldn't come to her bed even when he did come home. She picked up the branched candlestick and hurried across the hall to his room, finding it as empty and quiet as her own.

Both disappointed and relieved, she began to wander about his room, seeking his presence, trailing fingers over polished wood furnishings and rich, claret-red brocades. His big bed, his comfortable chair by the fire, his lap desk. The air held a faint, tantalizing trace of his musky scent, an aura she'd come to associate with his loving and with the intimacy of his body and habit. Her eyes filled and she blinked, turning to go. But her gaze caught on a small leather trunk sitting in the corner. Her heart beat erratically as she paused.

It was his military kit, the small trunk he'd had with him in Rapture. Drawn to it, she set the candles on the mantel and dragged it onto the rug before the cold hearth. Her fingers traced the tarnished brass fittings, the scuffed leather straps, the initials tooled into the side. Memory began to wash over her in waves . . . his glorious uniform, four soft shirts, his bellowing exasperation, gleaming buttons, his reluctant arousal . . . a proper bargain. They'd come through so much together. She massaged a faint ache in the middle of her breast.

The trunk was light, probably empty, she thought. But she worked the straps and latch and opened it anyway. In the golden candleglow she saw felt, wool felt, drab gray and familiar. And there were polished horn buttons, ones she'd helped Black Daniels make from the rack of the first stag she'd ever brought down.

Her coat. Her rough, ugly old coat. Her throat tightened fiercely. He hadn't burned it.

Through the painful squeezing around her heart she picked it up and brought it near her face, breathing deeply. Woodsmoke, and horses, and the musk of old leaves. It smelled like the forest, like her home. When her eyes opened, she strangled a cry. Deerskin. There in the trunk, beneath her old coat, was a pale tan patch of deerskin. She dropped the coat and snatched up her old breeches, rubbing the soft, worn leather against her cheek. He saved her breeches too.

Something glinted from the bottom of the trunk, and she reached for it, lifting a solitary gold button into the flickering light. A button bearing teeth marks. His button.

Her fingers closed around it as a terrible ache slammed through her. He'd saved it all: her coat, her breeches, the button she'd bitten that first day in Rapture. And without fully understanding why, she buried her face in her deerskin breeches and began to sob.

Garner found her just after daybreak, sitting on the cold floor of his unheated room. Thinking she wouldn't want to see him, he'd already decided to spend what was left of the night—and likely all future nights—in his own bed. And he'd gone straight to his own door.

He'd spent the evening and most of the night walking the streets and pacing the deserted Townsend offices, blaming himself for the painful sundering of the trust between them. After his last meeting with Henredon Parker, he'd known her father had probably been taken to Philadelphia. And Parker's Philadelphia newspapers hinted that the government was becoming increasingly desperate to fix blame for the revolt on someone. He hadn't told her any of it, convincing himself that it would only worry her.

Tonight, when she had asked him if he knew, he'd said no. It was true in one sense; he was as shocked as she was to learn Black Daniels was being tried for treason. And yet his denial carried a taint of dishonesty; he *had* known conditions were worsening, and he'd withheld that information from her. His desire to protect the tenderness between them and to keep her with him had eclipsed another basic need in loving, the need for honesty.

The simple truth was, he was terrified of losing her. All along, a cynical little maven of doom inside him had whispered that someday, something would come along, something she wanted more than she wanted him. That's just the way women were, experience had taught him, always on the lookout for a better deal, a more profitable bargain. And much as he protested that she was different, there was the inescapable evidence of her former betrayals to prove otherwise.

Someday something would come along, and in the depths of his being he must have recognized what that "something" would be. Twice before, when she betrayed him, it was for her father's sake. Now her father's very life was in peril, and he was the one responsible for it, even if he hadn't intended it to go so far. She had every reason to recoil from him, to withdraw her love, to declare the bargain and the love between them dead.

Garner was totally unprepared for the sight of her, sitting on the floor before the cold hearth with her eyes reddened and her face filled with a haunting blend of love and sadness. Then his eyes fell on his open trunk and her old coat and breeches, now clutched in her hands. His heart stopped and his muscles turned to stone.

"You—you didn't burn them," she whispered, her eyes shining with the sweet pain of loving. In the thundering silence she watched prisms of moisture form in his eyes and saw his fierce struggle to contain them.

"I could never destroy anything of yours, Whitney." It was a confession ripped from the very fabric of his soul, and one to which there were no exceptions.

It was true. Her eyes closed, releasing suspended tears, and she bit her lip. He loved her, he would never intentionally hurt her or those she loved. Then she rose, coming straight for him with open arms and a hungry heart.

"Oh, Garner—"

His corded strength and vitality engulfed her at the very moment her life-giving warmth and stubborn faith in him invaded his chilled heart. They stood, wrapped in each other's arms and in the resilient love they had forged in passion's hottest fires. She raised her tear-streaked face to him, reaching for his kiss. And he lowered his trembling lips to reclaim the precious prize of her love.

Their hands and bodies began to move, expressing that love, trusting it, clinging to it. They made love in Garner's cold bed, scarcely noticing the chilled air and icy sheets. And afterward, in the love-warmed cocoon of soft linen and down comforters, they clung tightly to each other.

"What do we do, Garner?" she murmured into his bare chest, somehow knowing his thoughts were the same as hers.

"I don't know." The Iron Townsend in him rebelled at such an admission, but he wouldn't lie to her again, not even by omission. "But we'll find some way to help him, I swear." Tears filled her eyes as he tilted her chin up to look at her. "I love you, my sweet Whiskey." She nodded and drank in the tender promise of his lips on hers.

"Garner, you arrested Pa for distilling and not paying the tax," she observed with amazing absence of resentment. "Then how did he come to be charged with treason?" She rose onto one elbow as mental wheels began to move behind her beguiling face.

It was the question Garner had dreaded. But he looked into the fathomless love in her sea-green eyes and told her the truth as he knew it, the whole truth and nothing but the truth. He spoke of Gaspar's prejudices and coercion, and admitted the blend of duty and anger that had driven him to arrest Black Daniels. Under her solemn look he talked of the "watermelon army's" frustration at having no supplies, no pay, and no enemy to fight, and of the futile search for the leaderless rebellion's "leaders." Then he revealed what he'd gleaned of the government's growing desperation to punish *somebody* for leading the "whiskey revolt" in order to politically and financially justify raising a largely unnecessary army.

"You mean they've got a cost on their hands," she said. The glint of outraged understanding stole into her gaze. "And they have to make some kind of profit out of it . . . to save their wretched pride."

"More like to save their political hides," he corrected her, a little awed by her uncanny capacity for getting right to the "ledger balance" at the bottom of any situation or person. With her unique frontier trader's philosophy, she managed to reduce the most complex human tangles to manageable terms of cost and profit, of need and supply. She was a true master of the fundamental economics of life itself. And heaven help him, he was beginning to see things in terms of "profits" and "price" and "bargains" himself.

"Then they want something, those federal boys," she declared with a dangerous glow and a faraway look in her eye. "And a fellow who wants something . . ."

"Whitney . . ." Garner watched the glow and saw her chin rise to a fateful and familiar angle. And he felt himself being drawn along, reading the alarming "bargaining" trend of her thoughts and realizing she was probably right . . . again. "Whitney!"

She turned to him with irresistible determination. "We can do it, we can help him, Garner, together." She read his odd expression as reluctance and added with a pure wriggle of her bare hip against his sensitive parts: "I can make it . . . worth your while."

Garner's first impulse was to correct the notion that he needed any such persuasion, but a second impulse quickly overtook him. And he very generously allowed her to "bargain" him into cooperating. After all, the Danielses did have their pride.

Twenty-three

By midmorning the Townsend household was spinning with the story of Whitney's father and Garner's role in his fate, and with Kate Morrison's announced intention of taking up respectable lodgings elsewhere that very day. Byron heard it from a very terse Edgewater and came charging out of his study to confront her. Madeline glowered at her disheveled uncle and informed him Kate was in her room, packing. He charged up the stairs and barged straight into Kate's room without so much as a knock.

"Just what in the hell do you think you're doing?" he demanded, slamming the door back on its hinges and spreading his feet determinedly

"I sh-should think that was obvious," Kate sputtered, stuffing the petticoat she'd been folding into the open valise on the bed and raising her chin. Her eyes widened on his crumpled, half-open shirt, the rings about his eyes, and the stubble on his face. He looked terrible, which pleased her in a vengeful sort of way. Apparently he hadn't slept a wink either.

"Running off," he charged.

"I cannot possibly stay here any longer, not after what happened," Kate said, flaming.

"Shocked, are you? Compromised? Well, it can't be anything I've done." He adroitly wielded her own words against her. "I don't have any urges, remember? Then it must be *your* urges you're running from."

Ignoring her outraged sputters, he stalked her, forcing her back toward the bed. A spear of excitement shot through him at the proximity of her reddened lips and flashing eyes. She darted for the door, but he caught her by the wrist as she opened it, and he reeled her back partway.

"S-sir! You forget yourself—" she rasped. wrenching her arm in his unyielding grip.

"Dammit, Kate Morrison, I'm just *remembering* myself," he growled. "And it's your damned fault. You made me think about things I haven't thought about in years—desire and pleasure, feeling and family." As she stilled and braced, he released one of her wrists to run a possessive hand over her cheek. "You're not going anywhere, Kate Morrison, not yet."

Kate shivered alarmingly under his taunting caress. "How dare you presume to give me orders," she said. Byron's light gray eyes glowed with an insufferable certainty that was somehow different from his usual arrogance.

"You made me remember." His voice lowered suggestively. "While I apparently made you *forget* . . . yourself . . . your niece. She'll want to know why you're running off, deserting her at so critical a time."

Kate reeled, stung sharply by his self-serving logic and utterly unable to refute it. Whitney—Lord, yes—she had forgotten all about poor Whitney! Horror at her unthinkable lapse melted her rigid posture. All she'd thought about was escaping . . . both Byron and her own Delilah desires.

Byron watched the fiery, independent Kate Morrison giving way to a softer, more vulnerable woman. And that strange, hollow feeling opened in the middle of him again. It was a wanting, a hunger for the closeness of her, for the pleasurable feel and taste of her, a need for sharing and completion of a sort he'd never really known.

He reached for her chin and tilted it up, searching her darkened eyes until his lips found hers. The contact was brief and full . . . and stunningly pleasurable. He tore himself away, battling back the urge to pull her fully into his arms.

"Unpack, Kate."

He turned on his heel and strode for the stairs. Kate stumbled back a few steps and sagged against the bedpost. He wasn't going to let her run. And he'd just served notice what would happen if she stayed. She slid her arms around her waist and suffered a dismaying shiver of anticipation.

Outside, Edgewater had thrown himself against one wall to keep Byron from seeing him as he left. He was gasping, blinking, shocked beyond words. Master Byron and—*that female.*

Garner and Whitney emerged from their rooms that afternoon to announce that they would be traveling to Philadelphia as soon as possible. Kate received the news with profound relief and instantly declared her intention of accompanying them, for Whitney's sake. Byron stood across from Kate at tea, glowering at her and declaring he intended to go as well. And Madeline refused to be left behind, not when her family might need her. Everyone stared at her in amazement, and she blushed for the first time in years.

Edgewater would have to go, of course, and Mercy and Benson. Ezra grumbled at having to stay in Boston, until Whitney pointed out that he wasn't being left *behind,* he was being left *in charge.* With that new perspective, his attitude improved markedly. In point of fact, the mood of the entire house seemed to have undergone a change for the better, in the way that bad news has of drawing people together.

Byron quickly engineered an invitation to use a business acquaintance's, former Senator Samuel Potter's, Philadelphia town house for a while. Garner's eyes narrowed on his arrogant father when the announcement was made. Byron Townsend never did anything without expecting a profit, and Garner was at a loss to explain what Byron thought he would gain by helping them. Then it struck him: Byron undoubtedly wanted to be there in person to minimize the damage done to the precious Townsend prestige when connection of the Daniels and Townsend families was revealed. Garner rolled his shoulders to dispel the tension collecting inside him. He was long past caring what icy, implacable Byron Townsend thought of him . . . or his marriage. But if the bastard said or did anything to hurt Whitney . . .

* * *

Black Daniels was being held in an old jail commandeered by the federals for the expressed purpose of providing maximum security for their dangerous rebel prisoners. Garner made inquiries immediately upon arrival in Philadelphia, and learned the accused men had been brought on a forced march from western Pennsylvania to occupy the grim premises. Only twenty or so of these unfortunates were actually being brought to trial. The others were gradually being released for lack of evidence, and were forced to find their own way home or to seek whatever sustenance could be found on Philadelphia's streets.

Under the half-truthful pretext of seeking legal assistance for Black, Garner left Whitney and Kate and the others to settle into the house and made his way through the bustling streets to the ramshackle prison. He stood across the street, staring at the soot-blackened brick, the barred and shuttered windows, and the surly slouch of the guards posted at the door. He was right to have come alone; he knew the dismal reputation of military prisons and braced for what he would find inside.

What Garner hadn't anticipated was the difficulty he would have getting in. He was stopped by the guards at the door and just managed to talk his way through, only to be stopped again by two more guards in the dim, sour-smelling interior. With his best sneer he demanded to see the superintendent of the facility immediately. The grizzled soldiers spat tobacco onto the rough wooden planks, precariously near his polished boots, and resentfully complied. He was led through a low passage and down a set of wooden steps to a dank wardroom that appeared to have been chiseled out of the stone foundation of the structure itself.

A squat little man with a crimped mouth and bilious eyes sat at a scarred table that was littered with food remains and papers. He looked up at Garner, who had to bend to avoid hitting the ceiling beams with his head, and barked, "Well, whadda ye want—" He trailed an eye down over Garner's gentlemanly attire and added, "Yer lordship?"

"I'm here to see a prisoner. Blackstone Daniels," Garner intoned quite reasonably.

"Don't nobody see nobody in here. Them's m'orders." The

fellow rose with a snarl even yellower than his eyes, and edged closer, squinting in the lantern light.

"I don't think you understand. I'm family, and I've come to see him on the matter of his legal defense," Garner asserted with determined calm.

"Don't care if you're King George hisself." The fellow stuck up a bristled chin, clearly enjoying the run of his power. "No vis'ters."

Their eyes locked in steely confrontation, and Garner was surprised to read an acquisitive glint in the superintendent's beady gaze. The Daniels axiom that nothing ever comes free rose in his mind. He felt beneath his coat for the small bag of coins in his pocket and drew them forth slowly. Watching the fellow's gaze fasten on them, he allowed the coins to trickle tantalizingly through his fingers, back and forth. Then to his surprise the fellow jolted back a step and raked a contemptuous glare over him.

"Put yer money away—less'n ye figure to buy yerself a room here wi' it," the superintendent growled. "We don' take no bribes."

Garner purpled with chagrin and wheeled, bumping his head on a beam on the way up the steps. When he reached the top, he found the street door blocked by a fracas of thrashing bodies and flailing limbs. The guards were apparently trying to evict some ragged wretch who didn't have enough sense left to leave. One of the four guards aimed a nasty kick at the fellow's ribs, and when he crumpled with a groan, they joined forces to shove him out onto the cold street. Garner stepped outside after him, scowling as his attention snagged on something about the fellow.

The prisoner was holding his sides and staggering to his feet in the cold air. The sight of Garner's elegant boots made him freeze in the middle of testing his bloodied mouth with his fingers. His gaze climbed that memorable footgear, raising his shaggy countenance to Garner.

Garner started. Overgrown brown hair, square, blocky features, tattered shirt, and half-rotted boots. The frame was thinner, much thinner, but the defiance in those piercing brown eyes was the very same.

"You!" Charlie Dunbar coiled and glowered and turned to spit blood from his bashed lips. Unfortunately, one of the soldiers at the door took his haphazard aim as a personal insult and another round of shoving ensued. Garner just managed to draw Charlie across the street and quickly found himself staring straight into the jaws of Dunbar wrath. "I shoulda known it was you." Charlie coiled and Garner tensed as they arched back, evaluating each other. "Come to spring me, have ye . . . to salve yer damned conscience?"

Garner was speechless at the conclusion Charlie had drawn from this bizarre coincidence, but had no inclination to set him straight just then. Charlie saw the deliberation in Garner's eyes and lifted a bloodied chin to what Garner recognized as a hard-trading angle.

"You gonna take me to Whit, or do I have to find her m'self?"

"Take you . . . to Whitney?"

"I promised Black if I got out first, I'd find her an' see what you done with her. He's still in an' I'm out, an' a Dunbar never goes back on his word. I figger ye owe me that." Charlie glanced meaningfully at his battered frame and filthy clothes. "An' maybe a coat."

That was it? A damned coat? Garner nearly staggered. No mayhem, no bloody outrage, no roiling lust for revenge? It took every bit of composure in him to draw himself up straight and say, "I'm not taking you anywhere looking like the wrath of God, Dunbar. How long has it been since you washed, or ate?"

It was an odd twosome that turned warily down the street and strode into a nearby tavern; no one was more cognizant of the fact than the two of them. Garner ordered food and the tavernman's best ale and sent the beer boy off with a few coins to find a warm coat and a large pair of shoes or boots, all under Charlie's suspicious glare.

"I tried to see her father," Garner revealed stiffly, watching Charlie put away the food as if he hadn't eaten in months and feeling strangely empty himself. "Didn't get very far, not even with a flash of coin."

Charlie quaffed a full pint of the golden ale and canted a pained look at Garner. "You ain't ever been in prison, have ye?"

"I suppose it shows," Garner retorted dryly.

"Money don't mean nothin' in prison, not to pris'ners nor to guards. Cain't eat it, nor wear it, and it won't keep ye—"

"Well, then, suppose you tell me just what the hell the fellow would want," Garner gritted out, chafing under Dunbar's "trader scorn." Hell, here he was, sitting in a smelly tavern being lectured on the arts of prison bribery by a man he'd kept chained to a tree for weeks on account of his rival lust for Whitney Daniels! Dunbar's wily grin was nothing short of astounding, in view of the circumstances.

"Food, Majur." He lifted his tankard and a hunk of the fried meat pie he was devouring. "A few good bottles, a bit o' decent food, maybe a good shirt or a pair o' boots."

"Dammit," Garner muttered nastily, shifting on his bench, "doesn't anybody just use plain money anymore?"

"Food can make a buck do things, Majur," Charlie taunted with ill-suppressed glee. "You forgot how well it works?" He chuckled wickedly at the redness of remembrance creeping into Garner's ears.

"I suppose I just amble in with a basket on my arm and offer the wretch a friendly snootful of rum?"

"Hell'sfire, Majur, you have forgot!" Charlie braced an arm on his thigh and cocked a look of grave disappointment at Garner. So much potential, that look said, and so little finesse. "That super'ntend'nt won't do squat for you nor me. What we need's a weepy female." His grin became deviltry itself. "Got any idears where we can get us one?"

Whitney hurried down the stairs in the front hall of the borrowed town house with Kate only steps behind her. Edgewater had brought word of Garner's return and she prayed he had some word of her father. She hurried across the parlor toward Garner, then stopped in her tracks as she caught sight of the shaggy, disheveled form planted in front of the nearby hearth. Her heart rose into her throat as Charlie Dunbar turned and leveled a searching brown gaze on her. With a strangled eruption of joy she launched herself first at Charlie, then at Garner, hugging and laughing, beaming girlish gratitude at Garner, who surely was responsible for freeing him.

When things calmed a bit, Kate gave Charlie a teary-eyed little hug herself, assuring him that Aunt Sarah was fine and that all Rapture missed him. Byron glowered through a tense introduction, but Madeline recoiled blatantly from Charlie's grimy hand, turning pointedly to tight-lipped Edgewater and demanding a cover cloth for a chair so that he wouldn't contaminate the furnishings.

Once seated, Charlie related the grim details of his incarceration and forced march to Philadelphia. He and Black had been together the whole way, until recent weeks, when outspoken Black had been moved from their communal cell to somewhere deeper in the prison. There was pride in the way he related Black's unquenchable spirit and beliefs, and the way he'd stood up for himself and the other prisoners repeatedly, even to his own peril. Black Daniels was a man to be reckoned with, Charlie observed with a hushed reverence. And it was clear to all that the federals were intent on reckoning with him.

Then Garner took Whitney's hands in his and stiffly related his failed bit of bargaining. Whitney smiled at him through teary eyes as the implications of it rumbled through her. Stubbornly eastern and aristocratic Garner had actually tried to bargain a bit to help her pa; the thought warmed her all the way to her toes.

"What was it you said we need, Dunbar?" Garner turned to Charlie and glowered at his insolent sprawl on the parlor furnishings.

Charlie tore his attention from haughty little Madeline's curvy form, and his woolly face creased with a wicked grin. "We need us a weepy female . . . and maybe a bit o' pie."

Charlie had to stay with them, at least until he got his strength back; Whitney insisted on it. Much as Garner disliked the idea, he found himself agreeing on the grounds that Charlie's knowledge of Black's circumstances might prove helpful. Madeline glared at Charlie as if he should be tarred for the mange, and withdrew in a huff. Byron muttered and went for his coat and then for a bit of air.

Benson and Edgewater and the house servants were assigned

the monumental task of rendering Charlie fit for human company. At no small cost to themselves they managed to bathe and decontaminate and shave him and by supper had stuffed his now-leaner body into a set of Garner's older clothes.

They wobbled down the stairs later, looking ashen and itchy. Charlie followed, grumbling that he'd been "done up like a sore thumb." But a Dunbar was nothing if not adaptable. Charlie was soon basking in Kate's and Whitney's compliments and looking for a bit of profit in being trussed up in fancy "gentleman" clothes. As they went in to dinner, he saw Madeline's head jerk as she averted her eyes, and he realized she'd been staring at him. By the time Garner and Whitney began to plan the deal that would get them in to see Black Daniels, Charlie's mind was already set on other bargains.

The next morning Charlie and Garner watched from across the street as Whitney and Kate carried large willow baskets, leaking delicious aromas, past the mesmerized front guards and into the shabby prison.

"I should never have let her go near that hellhole." Garner smacked a gloved fist into a gloved hand.

"Whit's a helluva trader, Majur." Charlie frowned, quelling his own misgivings. "She's got a trader's nerve. She could do a weepy-female bargain in her sleep." After a weighty silence he muttered, "An' if this don't work, we can alwuz make the bastard a fingers bargain."

There was no cause for worry. Inside, Kate was sniffling into her handkerchief, mostly from the overpowering reek of ammonia in the air, and one look at the premises had made Whitney's expression convincingly bleak. Her pa, she told the grizzled superintendent with an artful sniff, was all she and her aunt had left in the world.

"We know you're hard put to see to your many charges"—she forced a brave little smile—"and I told Aunt Kate you were bound to look after him as a man of integrity would do. But she's pining and sorrowful . . . afraid that with all your responsibilities he might become a burden. She insisted we bring food and plentiful libation, and soap and a razor, and a shirt."

The seductive smells of beef pastries and apple cobbler and

fresh-baked buns were curling through the wardroom, and through the paunchy superintendent himself. He looked into Whitney's sea-pool eyes and succumbed to their tidal pull.

"We shan't beleaguer you to see him, sir." Whitney put her arms around Kate, whose weeping had escalated judiciously. "We ask only that you tell him we long for him and suffer with him. And that you allow us to bring him a basket each day."

"Each day?" The superintendent quivered with anticipation; his mouth watered violently. Kate's sobbing increased and the fellow solicitously offered them a chair, and a small bend of the rules. "Wull, mebee we could let ye see 'im a spell."

"Oh, sir . . . oh, could we?"

Black was cleaned up a bit and hauled upstairs to a drier cell without being told why. He snarled and snorted and sheltered his dark-conditioned eyes against the lantern light, expecting some new torture or harangue. What he got was a glimpse of heaven. Whitney—his Whitney. His hunger-thinned frame quaked as she stood in the cell door, tears streaming down her lovely face. She rushed to his arms, and it was a long while before he could credit she was real and return her crushing hugs. At length he pushed her back to look at her, and the womanly glow of her brought tears to his eyes. A moment later he was setting her back, insisting he didn't want to spoil her pretty clothes.

"Does he take good care of you?" Black choked as she nodded and defiantly snuggled closer to lay her head on his dirty shoulder. Relief poured through him at the realization that his intuitions about the major's feelings toward Whitney were correct. "Your iron-arsed major, Whit . . . have you made it a proper bargain?"

"Yes, Pa," she whispered, "it's a true marriage bargain. And, Pa, he's helping me help you. He's getting you the best lawyer in Philadelphia, and he's helping me bring you good food and decent clothes. We're going to get you out of this somehow, Pa, my iron-arsed major and me."

From that day forward, Black Daniels became a preferred prisoner, lodged on the drier upper floor of the meager facility and given lantern light and modest exercise. Whitney and Kate came daily with willow baskets that thoughtfully contained two of

everything: two shirts, two pairs of boots, two pies, two bottles
of whiskey. It wasn't long before the daily boots and shirts became conspicuous on the guards outside the front doors. Black's
health and appearance improved daily and Whitney felt the
weight on her heart lifting with each visit.

Influence was what they needed now, Garner explained to
Whitney, Kate, and Charlie Dunbar. There was probably little
hope of actually eliminating the charges against Black, but there
might be hope of mitigating them. With time running short, Garner suggested they concentrate on those with direct influence on
the outcome of Black's trial: prosecutors, judges, certain elected
officials.

What did prosecutors want, Whitney wanted to know. Garner
thought about it. "In general, I suppose, they all want to be
judges." Well, what did judges want? "To be reelected, reap-
pointed, or maybe elected to Congress," Garner said, quoting
Ezra on the dismal state of the judiciary. And to do any of that,
they had to appear upstanding and virtuous and hardworking—at
least in the newspapers. They had to give speeches and shake
hands and listen to people—and have it reported in the papers.

Newspapers. It all kept coming back to newspapers and the
slippery, ill-defined commodity Garner labeled "public opinion." Everybody in government seemed to be either running
scared of it or panting after it like a randy swain.

"Gloriful Gabriel," Whitney sighed, "then what do newspapers want?"

Garner rubbed his chin. "To sell lots of newspapers, I suppose.
And to do that, they have to have stories people are eager to read.
And they want to be believed." He saw the trader's flame flicker
to life in Whitney's eyes as she stood up.

"Well, I've got something the newspapers want!"

Philadelphia's *General Advertiser* had run articles from various correspondents expressing criticism of the government's

military solution to what was primarily a regional and economic problem. And when they were visited by a sweet waif of a girl in homespun, whose father was wasting away in prison, they were eager to listen and to write vivid stories of the monstrous hardships the brave frontier folk endured during the heinous military occupation. Two other papers picked up the trend, running articles on the heartless federal juggernaut that prosecuted the Reverend John Corbley, whose wife and children had been massacred before his very eyes not long before, and on the pillage and plunder inflicted on the western residents by Washington's "watermelon army."

Garner paced nervously the first time Whitney gave such an interview, waiting on the street with Charlie, down the block from the newspaper offices. He was stunned to witness a dignified white-haired fellow escorting Whitney out, shaking his head woefully and wiping at his reddened eyes with a handkerchief. He turned to Charlie with a drooping jaw, and Charlie grinned.

"Whit alwuz could talk nineteen to the dozen."

But the amorphous beast of "public opinion" was not enough. They needed swifter and more specified opinion to be of real benefit to Black Daniels. Garner compiled a list of men in Congress and in the judiciary who were known to be sympathetic to western causes and whose influence might be great enough to affect Black's fate.

He first tried to make appointments, the ascribed procedure for access to public officialdom. Virtually nobody he wanted to see was "in." How their coats and hats had managed to make it to the coatracks of their outer offices without their owners was a mystery indeed. It was infuriating to him and to his sense of fairness.

"Blessit! How am I supposed to bar—*persuade* them if I can't even get in to see them?" he groaned, pacing the parlor under Whitney's, Kate's, and Charlie's troubled frowns.

"I can get you in to see them." Byron stepped inside the warm parlor, his face still flushed from the cold. He'd just arrived from a business meeting and heard Garner's angry complaint as he paused outside the door to remove his coat. Over and over in these last days, Kate's strong words to him had been echoing in his head: "He loves Whitney—and she loves him" and "Having to testify against her father could tear him apart."

The air charged around them as Garner faced his father, tightening visibly at the accusation of failure he heard in Byron's tone. "I neither need nor want your help . . . or interference."

"Dammit." Byron flamed. "You don't know politics—the way things work. I've dealt with it on a daily basis—"

Kate watched between them anxiously, reading in Byron's offer a tenuous step toward reconciliation with his son. In these last days she'd experienced an altogether different Byron Townsend, one whose covert looks grew ever more tender and whose brief touches grew ever more hungry. She'd watched him watching Garner with Whitney. And she'd seen long-denied feelings rising beneath his polished defenses of arrogance and privilege. Protectiveness toward that tender little core of developing emotion surged in her.

"Garner, how can you talk to your father that way?" She inserted herself between them, catching both in surprise. "He's offering to help both you and Blackstone—and you're letting your pigheadedness keep you from accepting the very help that might save Black."

"What's in it for him?" Garner growled defensively, surprised by Kate's intervention. "He never does anything without expecting a return."

"Maybe he's doing it because you're his son," Kate sputtered, "and because he cares what happens to you and Whitney."

"Or maybe because he's afraid of having his precious family name dragged through the mud," Garner charged, stalking closer to Byron, his eyes burning.

Kate backed a step, stunned by the depth of Garner's animosity and by the size of the gulf between father and son. She looked at Byron's stony features and read so clearly the turmoil and pain behind his hard exterior. How could anyone fail to see it?

"What does it matter why he does it?" she choked, feeling tears rising inexplicably. "If he's willing to help Blackstone, why can't that be enough?"

Garner caught sight of Whitney as she stepped forward, her shoulders rigid, her face pale and troubled. The sight of her prodded him to recall the trust between them, to recall his vow to do whatever was necessary to help her father. What was the matter with him? Only a fool would reject such help, even if it did come from his cold, calculating father. He made himself ease and turned to Kate, feeling like he'd just been snatched back from the edge of a precipice.

"As you say," he said, deferring to Kate's wisdom, then turned a sober look on Byron, "what difference does his motive make? We . . . accept your help willingly, sir."

"But not gratefully." Byron ripped his eyes from his son to stare at Kate. "Fair enough."

Kate turned and fled the parlor, and Byron excused himself a moment later as Whitney walked into Garner's arms. Byron stood in the hallway, his eyes burning dryly as Kate's defense of him rumbled about in his heart and mind. No one had ever defended him. He flew through the dining room and the kitchen, looking for her, then rushed up the stairs to her room.

She was sitting in a chair by the window, her face in her hands. In three long strides he was across the narrow room and pulling her startled form into his arms.

"Why did you do that, Kate?" His voice resonated through her.

"What difference does my motive make?"

"It makes all the difference in the world to me."

She stared up into his softening face and dared tell him the truth. "I know you wanted to help him—I've watched you. You're a hard man, Byron Townsend, but you're not made of iron. You really do care for him. I wanted you to have a chance with him."

"God." It really was a prayer at that moment. "In all my life no one's ever cared about how I felt, or cared what I wanted. Lord, Kate, you scare the hell out of me." He groaned, wrapping his arms tightly around her, savoring her softness and sinking into the warm liquid of her eyes. "But I want you, Kate Morrison, in every way it's possible to want a woman. And I won't be denied."

His mouth lowered over hers, and a moment later he felt the explosion of her response all through him. They came together joyfully, seeking and giving things neither had known before.

His hands moved hungrily over her waist and sought the hardening fullness of her breasts, claiming her passions and her heart. She pressed against him, reveling in his strength and giving her desires full rein. It was several minutes before Byron lifted his head and cleared it enough to recall the untimely interruption of their last such encounter. He lowered Kate's love-tousled form to the bed and reeled to the half-open door to close and latch it securely.

Whitney peeled herself from the far wall in the hallway, her eyes as big as saucers. She'd come to see if Kate was all right and found . . . Her knees wobbled as she let herself into the room she and Garner shared. The sight of Kate's loosened bodice, of her glistening eyes and full lips clung to her mind's sight. Aunt Kate . . . with *Byron*. Kissing and rubbing, acting like a pure Delilah. Proper Aunt Kate had a bit of Delilah in her? A giggle bubbled up from her stomach and grew into a laugh that carried the releasing sound of insight. If upstanding, elegant, and refined Aunt Kate had some Delilah in her, then probably all women had a trace of it in them somewhere.

Twenty-four

The next morning a peculiar alliance was formed in the borrowed Townsend quarters, a tripartite force of political acumen, righteous determination, and wily brute force. Over the next several days, Byron, Garner, and Charlie Dunbar made discreet forays into the political arena, targeting and contacting men of influence, from senators to justices to undersecretaries. Garner watched his father's smooth blend of charm and intimidation open doors to them that had been irrevocably closed to him alone.

Garner began to relax enough to study the style and delicacy of Byron's opening gambits, which were different for each man they encountered. It struck Garner that Byron seemed to know, or to quickly read, what each man valued, and that he worked that value to the hilt. Money was never mentioned, nor ever even implied in the subtle transactions under way. And the comparison with Whitney's policy of determining what a person wanted and dealing with him on that basis was inescapable. In the highest echelons of power, he realized, as in the very lowest, the mode of commerce was barter and bargain. A word of influence for a word of support; a vote was traded for a piece of information or a confidence. "Favor" proved the most liquid of all currencies.

There were times, however, that no amount of logic, persuasion, or outright flattery would prevail, and they were given polite ear, then ushered out. The first time it happened, Charlie tugged his waistcoat down and narrowed a hard look at the office door closing sharply behind them, snarling, "We shoulda made 'im a *fingers bargain.*"

Byron leveled a penetrating look on Charlie's wry blend of frontier simplicity and worldly grasp of the human condition.

"A fingers bargain? I believe I know that one, Dunbar." He met Charlie's wary gaze with a knowing smirk that turned into a startlingly wicked laugh.

"A *fingers bargain?*" Garner glared at their humor.

"It's the kind of a deal," Charlie drawled, "where you get what you want, an' th' other feller gets to keep 'is fingers."

With all of the new nation's capital already a boiling stew of political intrigue and influence, the "Townsend effort" didn't seem such a major ingredient. But in certain quarters its effects were quickly noted. The influence they conjured was indeed exerted, through legal channels and through less traceable avenues of personal contact. The subtle nature of the campaign diffused the identity of its source and, indeed, everyone from Secretary of State Randolph to Pennsylvania legislator and distiller spokesman Albert Gallatin was considered suspect.

Daily, the prosecutors assigned to Black Daniels's trial felt the trickling flow of pressure. And in the way political pressure has of rubbing some men wrong, the mounting push of influence entrenched their determination to deal harshly with the frontier rabble-rouser.

With only a few days until the trial, they sent for Garner Townsend. He arrived, under military escort, to find Oliver Gaspar closeted with the chief prosecutor, Mr. Everhart. The pretentious colonel wore his spotless military uniform and an oily smile that raised the temperature of Garner's blood on sight.

"Good to see you again, Major Townsend," Gaspar crooned, flicking a conspiratorial glance at the long-faced prosecutor. "Much has happened since our last meeting in Pittsburgh. I believe you are to be congratulated on a Special Commendation for your exemplary work."

"As are you, Colonel Gaspar." Prosecutor Everhart managed a humorless smile. "It is a privilege indeed to be able to enlist the testimony of two such accomplished men in this difficult case."

"The testimony of *two?*" Garner's brow raised.

"I shall be testifying at the trial," Gaspar announced.

Garner stared at him, absorbing the fact of his "Special Commendation." Gaspar had craved a commendation as much as Garner had, and had apparently invented himself a part in Black Daniels's capture to secure it. The warty little toad. When the prosecutor offered him a seat, Garner fought an overwhelming urge to stalk out, and made himself settle into a stuffed leather chair before the prosecutor's desk, beside Gaspar. He had to learn all he could.

"I am surprised to hear you will testify, Colonel, as surprised as I was to hear that Black Daniels was charged with treason. I recall distinctly arresting him on charges of distilling illegally and nonpayment of tax," Garner observed calmly. He watched the way Gaspar and Everhart looked at each other.

"This case has been beset from the start," Everhart explained. "The whiskey collected as evidence was somehow . . . lost. And your written deposition and other documents met a similar fate before they left Pittsburgh. Thus, we were vastly relieved when Colonel Gaspar came forward offering testimony to the fellow's treason."

Garner stiffened, his mind racing. The evidence against Black and Charlie Dunbar had been lost? So *that* was what prompted Charlie's release! Then, lacking lawful evidence, they'd been desperate enough for a scapegoat to accept Gaspar's greedy offer to fabricate a charge of treason!

"You may have seen recent articles in the papers," Everhart continued. "It is my duty to warn you, there has been other pressure, from numerous quarters. There are strong forces at work, attempting to block this trial. I don't doubt they might try to dissuade you."

Garner's shoulders squared as he looked the prosecutor in the eye. "I doubt they would concern themselves with me. I have nothing to tell. I arrested Black Daniels for distilling and possessing untaxed spirits, no more. I know nothing that would contribute to his conviction as a traitor."

It was a small pleasure, watching the long-featured Everhart turn waxen, and seeing Gaspar redden like a turnip.

"Flaunting the law, speaking openly against the taxing authority of the lawful government, encouraging others to resist lawful authority by non-payment of tax—" The froglike Gaspar came to the edge of his seat, glaring. "He's guilty, all right, and it's your duty to dispose of this vile threat to the nation's security!"

"It's my duty to speak the *truth*." Garner met Gaspar's ire with steely determination. "If I speak at all."

"*If* you sp—" Everhart pushed to his feet, his last bit of color draining from his face. He shot Gaspar a horrified look and the little colonel shoved to his feet. "You'll speak, all right. You're subpoenaed to testify. It's your duty."

"He's my father-in-law." Garner rose with full Townsend grace and leveled an icy stare at first one, then the other. "Surely you can't have forgotten, Colonel, you were present at my wedding. Black Daniels is my wife's father, and I'll not speak a word against him."

Gaspar puffed with sudden fury. "Dammit, Townsend, you will testify. We'll not be made out to be fools. They wanted a rebellion leader, and we found them one! Daniels is guilty as hell, and we intend to see him dance a gibbet for it—"

"And wrangle another empty commendation, Gaspar? Go to hell." Garner turned to the door and found his way blocked by Everhart.

"Oh, you'll testify, Townsend." Gaspar came after him, hissing. "Because if you don't, you'll find *yourself* on the docket. On the same charge, treason. And what jury wouldn't believe that you deliberately withheld testimony to save your wife's father from hanging? You'll be an officer who betrayed his duty and his country, for *personal* reasons." Every word drilled into Garner's mind. "And you'll dance the gibbet beside your wife's traitorous father."

Garner quivered with rage. They'd do it—they'd charge him, too, to secure their fortunes with the faceless but almighty "they" in the corridors of power. Whitney's father and husband, both hanged.

Gaspar's beady brown eyes raked Garner's handsome, gentlemanly form. They had him, Gaspar crowed privately; they had the almighty Major Townsend exactly where they wanted him. "On the other hand, Townsend, if you were to prove cooperative, who knows what rewards could lay in store for the courageous officer who brings to justice the mastermind of the whiskey insurrection?"

Garner's eyes became chips of flint, but he remained silent.

"You'll testify, Major." Gaspar smiled coldly and spoke to Everhart. "Ever the dutiful aristocrat, Major Townsend. Perhaps we ought to insure his safety. Perhaps provide him with a military escort until after the trial." Everhart nodded.

Whitney knew something was wrong the minute Garner walked through the parlor door, and she went immediately to his side. But he steadfastly refused to talk about it and withdrew to the small sitting room on the second floor to be alone awhile. It wasn't until she and Kate left to visit Black in prison, some minutes later, that she saw the soldiers posted by their front door and realized something terrible had occurred.

When she and Kate returned and the soldiers were still there, Whitney paused on the steps, reading in their presence an ominous new force in their lives. She found Garner pacing the sitting room, his face and mood dark.

"What's happened?" she asked, turning the special look on him that always pierced his armor.

"I was called to the prosecutor's office this morning. They intend to see Black hang." Something in the bleak way he said it weakened Whitney's knees.

"Well, we expected that, didn't we?" She tried to allay her own mounting fears, but his next words overwhelmed her determined bravery.

"They expect to do it with the help of my testimony."

"Your—" Whitney swayed under the impact of his words. "But you said you wouldn't testify if you could help it. You said . . ." The blood began to drain from her head, leaving her reeling. "The soldiers outside . . ." She began to understand.

"For my . . . protection." Garner's muffled sneer had a bitter edge that stopped her heart for a moment. They finally faced the reality both had denied these last weeks; Garner would take the stand to give word against her father's very life.

"Garner . . ." She grasped his sleeves and looked up into his face. Twice she swallowed back a plea as she searched his tight features. The third time it escaped her in a choked whisper. "Garner, please . . . please don't testify against my pa."

"God, Whitney—" The desperation, the beleaguered trust in her voice and face, sent a burning slash of pain through his chest. "Do you think I would if there were any other way? It's my damnable duty as a soldier; I've taken an oath, I have to testify. But I swear to you, I have nothing to say that can incriminate him for treason."

"Then why are they forcing you to testify?" She gasped a breath. "The soldiers—they *are* forcing you, aren't they?"

Garner's eyes became lidded as he clasped her shoulders with quaking hands. "I have to testify, Whitney. I've promised you I won't do anything to hurt Black. Please, Whitney, please trust me."

The traces of anguish in his voice were real, the darkness in his face compelling. Whitney trembled in his grasp, trying to withstand the maelstrom of pain and confusion that assailed her. What could she do to keep him from testifying? What did he want enough to keep him from testifying against her father?

She searched the dark centers of his gray-blue eyes and found in the turmoil of his soul a desperate need for her to believe and trust in him. He wanted her, she realized, wanted her love, wanted her to live with him as his wife. But did he want it enough to turn his back on his precious duty? Desperation spurred her savagely. He'd done it before, he'd said. Perhaps if the stakes were high enough, or dire enough, she could bargain . . .

But in those moments of decision, as she delved into the vulnerable depths of his eyes, she encountered his fathomless love, his unwavering trust in her, and the tender man who had saved her breeches and a button she'd bitten because he couldn't bring himself to destroy anything of hers. The sight stopped her breath, her heart, as his love spiraled through her, dragging across the strings of her soul, stirring the awarenesses and responses of the woman she'd become. She was a Delilah, but she always had a choice. Some things, she had come to realize, should never be bargained. To bargain with love was to lose it, no matter what else was gained.

"Oh, Garner—what can we do?" Tears burned down her cheeks and rose to fill her throat. She clamped her arms around his waist and buried her face in his chest.

"Trust me." Garner's eyes filled as he tightened protectively around her, feeling like his life had just been given back to him. "I love you, my sweet Whiskey. Please trust me."

Late that night, when Whitney had finally fallen asleep, Garner rose to walk the upstairs sitting room like a tortured ghost. Byron heard the rustling and the rhythmic creak of the floor and went to investigate. By nightfall the whole household had heard the outcome of Garner's visit with the prosecutors, and witnessed the soldiers' ominous watch at both front and rear doors.

"You needn't worry"—Garner felt his father's searching eyes on his back and assured him bitterly—"I'll do my duty . . . like a proper Townsend."

Byron shuddered privately as it struck. Garner still had little trust in him, even after the last two weeks. "And I'll do mine," Byron countered in a subdued voice. "There are still a few days. I'll see to what we started."

When Garner turned, their eyes met, testing and hesitant. But in that brief contact a promise was born. Garner eased and nodded mute gratitude, and Byron turned with heavy steps back to his bed.

The federal courthouse was packed—lobby, corridors, and courtroom—when they arrived that first day. They threaded their way through the noise and bustle in the marble-floored halls, and only a combination of Byron's imperial indignation and Garner's name on the list of witnesses secured them entry to the courtroom itself. Garner, resplendent in a newer version of his military uniform, ushered Whitney to a seat, while Byron escorted Kate and Madeline. Charlie, understandably court shy, chose to remain standing in the crowd just outside the open doors.

The huge, paneled room was ringed on three sides with a gal-

lery of seats on stepped levels. A large judicial bench and witness's platform sat on a raised dais on the main floor, and before
it huddled tables that were stacked with books and documents.
Black-robed lawyers were clumped in consultative knots here
and there, including Prosecutor Everhart, who spotted him and
cast a knowing smile in his direction. Garner tore his eyes away
and sought out Bartholomew Hayes, the lawyer friend of Henredon Parker's whom he'd engaged to see to Black's defense.
Hayes nodded to him and smiled reassuringly at Whitney.

Black was ushered in, wearing the sober brown woolen coat
and breeches Garner had provided, and he searched the gallery
for sight of Whitney and Kate. Kate whispered to Byron and he
whispered to Garner that Kate had something to give Black,
something she wanted him to wear. Kate opened her hand under
Garner's frown and in it was an aged bit of ribbon and a worn
badge of purple fabric made in the shape of a heart and embroidered with worn golden thread. Byron's jaw loosened as the
shape and style and age registered in his mind.

"The Badge of Military Merit?" he managed to say, looking
up at Kate and Whitney, who nodded soberly. "Good Lord."

Garner stared at it; the legendary badge, created by General
George Washington himself to acknowledge extraordinary bravery among his men during the War of Independence. It was the
one and only decoration ever awarded by the United States. And
Black Daniels had earned it.

"You take it to him." Kate thrust it into Whitney's hand, dabbing her eyes, and Garner helped Whitney down the stepped aisle
to the railing that separated the gallery from the courtroom floor.
As she embraced Black, Kate's hand tightened fiercely on Byron's arm. They watched as Whitney pinned it on Black's chest
and saw the way he drew himself up a bit straighter under its
weight. Kate could scarcely see them as they made their way
back up the steps to their seats.

The prosecution opened its case first thing the next morning,
calling as its first witness a fellow named Horace Nevin, a collector of revenue from western Maryland. Under pointed questioning, the fellow described the horrors perpetrated upon
himself and his family by mobs of excise-maddened farmer-

distillers—the tarring and feathering of his person, the burning of his barn, the terror of night riders trampling his crops. Hayes objected to the man's pitiful, rambling account as having nothing to do with the charges against Black Daniels, and was summarily silenced by Judge Peterson. Apparently the justice didn't feel that a little thing like a two-hundred-mile distance between the man's home and Black's known whereabouts had any bearing on the case.

Taxman Nevin was but the first of several witnesses with similar tales of woe caused by the lawless disregard of distillers for the sacred authority of government. It became clear, as Counselor Hayes frequently objected, that the whiskey insurrection itself, not Black Daniels, was on trial. And it became all the clearer that Judge Peterson was content to let it be so, for he consistently hammered down Hayes's objections and once threatened to have him removed from the courtroom if he continued the unthinkable disruptions of the legal process.

On the morning of the third day, Major Garner Townsend of the Ninth Maryland Militia was called to the stand. He rose in the charged, air-starved courtroom and made his way down the crowded aisle to the front to be sworn. When he placed his hand on the Bible and swore to tell the truth, the whole truth, Whitney's eyes blurred with tears.

Everhart came straight to the point; how did the major learn of Black Daniels's traitorous distilling operations and how did he apprehend the wretched "enemy of order?" Another Hayes objection was pounded down, and the jury drank it in with widening eyes.

"As to how I learned he distilled untaxed spirits, I simply pieced together information gleaned from the locals. And after searching the settlement and surrounding farmsteads, I led and sent out nightly patrols looking for the cache of whiskey. One night I found it."

"The whole truth, Major," Everhart prodded. "Who informed you that Black Daniels was the leader of the ring of distillers? Which of the 'locals'?"

Garner's eyes found Whitney's across the courtroom, and the

unflinching support in her gaze was his salvation. "I learned it from Whitney Daniels . . . his daughter."

"Then Black Daniels's own daughter informed you of his treasonous activities," Everhart concluded with a badgering air of triumph. "You are to be congratulated on your powers of persuasion, Major. I understand that shortly afterward you married that same Miss Daniels." Everhart pointed straight at Whitney. "Is that not so?" A shocked murmur passed through the court as necks craned and people stood to get a glimpse of her.

Garner bronzed with ire, but he fought to contain it. He had known his relationship with Whitney was likely to be exploited here, and had determined to deal with it factually. But the prosecutor's insinuating smirks and Gaspar's taunting leer from the gallery almost undermined his control. "It is true, I married her."

"She was shamed by her father's treasonous activities and determined to join the side of order. She came to you with evidence of his treasonous activities!" Everhart delivered the quick, savage conclusion straight into the jury's surprised faces.

"Why, you miserable wre—" Garner lurched partway over the railing at Everhart. Only a loud and opportune outburst of objections from Bartholomew Hayes saved him from being censured from the bench. The judge's harangue against the counsel for the defense permitted Garner a moment to recompose himself before Everhart turned to him again.

"Black Daniels is indeed your father-in-law. An incontrovertible fact. And did you arrest him before or after the nuptials?" Everhart strutted toward the jury, readying his final volley. "Answer please."

Garner's jaw twitched. "After."

"You arrested Black Daniels after you married his daughter. Remarkable, Major." He turned to the jury with a nastily jovial glint in his eye. "How many of us wish we might rid ourselves of troublesome in-laws so handily?" It pulled a muffled titter of amusement from the entire courtroom. Then he turned on Garner with his last gambit. "Why did you continue to pursue and arrest Black Daniels even after you had married his daughter?"

There it was, the question Garner had wrestled with these last weeks. He glanced at Whitney, at Black, and at his father, then stared hard at Everhart's covert glare of warning. And he gave the only answer possible.

"It was my duty . . . to uphold and enforce the law."

Everhart eased, and an unpleasant smile sliced his pasty countenance. "You found him with his gang of rebels, transporting kegs of untaxed whiskey, did you not? And you arrested him because it was clear to you he was guilty!"

"Of distilling whiskey without paying—" Garner tried to clarify, but his disclaimer was drowned out in Everhart's assault on the jury's senses.

"He arrested Black Daniels because he knew he was guilty. He knew Black Daniels for the vile, treasonous anarchist he is! And despite his shocking familial connection to the man, he did his duty to see this threat to order and decency removed from our nation's frontier. Now you must do your duty—" he lectured the jurors. "Declare Blackstone Daniels guilty as well, and see him duly punished!" He wheeled toward his table, declaring, "No more questions."

Counselor Hayes was permitted to cross-examine Garner, though he suffered numerous interruptions and objections that were always upheld by the judge. Garner's charged testimony was halted just prior to its emotional peak by an adjournment for dinner.

When they returned to court, the jury was lidded with wine and stuffed with food and disinclined to listen to anything seriously. The jurors perked up, however, when Garner described the battle that netted Black Daniels, then quickly settled back into torpor. Garner's vehement assertions that he'd not arrested Black Daniels on a charge of treason, only for his distilling activities, were met with a dangerous lack of interest. And he was dismissed.

Colonel Oliver Gaspar took the stand next, detailing his trip to Rapture and his "attendance" at the nuptials of Major Townsend and Black Daniels's daughter. The jurors revived a bit at that, and he began to speak directly to them, detailing his pride in the major's achievement, and his own encounters with the treacherous Black Daniels. He detailed incidents that occurred while Black Daniels was held in Pittsburgh. Carefully crafted, artfully related stories of how Black spoke out furiously against the government and tried to get his fellow prisoners to revolt against the soldiers. And by the end of the day, when the court was adjourned, it was Gaspar's dramatic renditions of Black's reputed statements about "bringing that whoring federal Babylon to its knees" that rang in the jury's ears.

Two witnesses to treason were all that was required under the law. The prosecution rested its case. Judge Peterson hammered the courtroom quiet and asked Counselor Hayes if he had anything to say before the jury retired to deliberate. Hayes was stunned; he had an entire defense to present, he stammered. The judge declared it was a waste of time, since the evidence already presented proved Black Daniels overwhelmingly guilty.

The packed courtroom broke into open chaos, newswriters shouting and shoving for the doors and howls of protest from the divided gallery. Hayes argued himself hoarse and threw himself into a nose-to-nose shouting match with the prosecutor, Everhart. The explosion of outrage convinced Peterson to reverse his opinion, and when order was restored, he grudgingly permitted Hayes time for two witnesses . . . no more.

A hush settled over the courtroom as Counselor Hayes reclaimed his composure and, in a move of pure desperation, called Mrs. Garner Townsend to the stand. Garner started and stared at her. Then, seeing the anguish in her eyes, he rose to allow her passage. It was so quiet, the rustle of Whitney's petticoats could be heard all through the room. She swore to tell the truth and was helped up the steps to the witness stand.

After verifying her identity as Garner's wife and Black's daughter, Hayes came straight to the point. "It has been alleged that you were responsible for informing Major Townsend of your father's illegal distilling operations. Did you tell him?"

"Yes."

A rash of murmuring swept the court, and Peterson pounded it down so they might continue. "And why," Hayes asked, "did you tell him about your father's illegal activity?"

Whitney fixed her eyes on Garner's face and bit her quivering lip. "I told him because . . . I was coming to love him . . . and I thought he should know." Her appealing face and guileless answer produced another current of emotion through the gallery.

"Did you tell him because you were ashamed of your father's so-called treasonous actions?"

"No!" She gripped the railing, her eyes shining with tears. "I'm not ashamed of my pa, or of anything he's done. It's true he didn't pay the tax. He believed it was wrong. But lots of people believe it's wrong, and you don't charge them with treason. My pa believes in the liberty he fought for in the War of Independence. He fought to help rid us of unfair English taxes, and to secure our God-given rights and liberties. He fought by George Washington's side in that war, and got the Badge of Merit for it. He loves this country and our people." Her voice clogged and as she paused, tears rolled down her fair cheeks. It was the most important bargain of her life, and she wept in earnest. "Blackstone Daniels would never betray the country that he shed his own blood to help build."

Hayes lent her his arm as she stepped down from the box, and she went straight to Black Daniels's arms, carrying the somber eyes of the courtroom with her. There was a long silence as they embraced, then Black pried her loose and sent her on to Garner, who stood by the gate in the railing. And the court watched as he embraced her wobbly form and held her tightly, oblivious of everything but his powerful need to comfort and protect her. The scope of the personal tragedy enacted before their eyes left no heart in the courtroom untouched.

Whitney's tears bore fruit; for the first time, the jury looked on Black Daniels with a bit of sympathy. And when he took the witness stand in his own behalf, every eye was riveted on his striking, weathered face and vibrant eyes . . . that were so like his daughter's. He answered Counselor Hayes's questions and used every opportunity to declare his loyalty to the young United States of America. And when asked about the decoration he wore, he told the story of how it had been earned, of comrades' lives saved in battle, of the double wound that almost took his life. Not a veteran there failed to understand the meaning of the small purple badge. And when he spoke of the tax, he spoke of the hard, often perilous life of the frontier and how unfairly the excise extorted funds from those least able to pay. It was a stunning defense of the principles of the whiskey revolt, combined with a humble admission of resistance to the tax itself. And it left the jury in a sober mood indeed as they were adjourned for the evening.

The summation came the next morning, the fourth day of the trial. And again Judge Peterson astounded Counselor Hayes and most of the spectators by dispensing with the defense's arguments altogether. He summed up the case in his own words, and charged the jury to bring back the only verdict possible in the face of such overwhelming evidence of guilt. The jury retired and the court settled in to wait.

Garner and Byron assured Whitney that all was not lost, but they exchanged worried glances over her head. Kate and Whitney and Madeline spoke in hushed tones, and when Whitney's eyes filled with tears, it was Madeline's arms that went around her, and Madeline's handkerchief that dried them.

The wait was tedious, as hour upon hour dragged by, but no one abandoned the high drama of the landmark trial for treason. Garner and Byron paced the aisle, stopping occasionally to speak with Black and Counselor Hayes. Midafternoon, they left the heated courtroom to fetch something to drink, and while they were gone, the jury began to file back in with the verdict.

Shock galvanized Whitney. She rose with her heart beating erratically, gripping the seat before her with icy hands. Madeline squeezed through the crowd, surging forward in the aisle to find Garner and Byron. It was all happening in a slow blur: the judge's return and his hammering for order, the question to the jury and the order to the defendant to rise and face his peers. And then it came.

Guilty.

The verdict pierced Whitney like a knife.

Pandemonium broke loose as people shoved against the front railing. Boos and cries of protest rang out, shoving and near violence erupted in some quarters between opponents and upholders of the federal machine that had wrought the verdict. Garner and Byron had to fight their way down the aisle toward the prisoner's docket, where Black stood trembling, hearing a sentence of death by hanging pronounced upon him.

Garner pushed through the teeming crowd, catching sight of

Whitney's ashen face and eyes that were now dark with pain and betrayal. Guilty. Her eyes poured into him. They would hang Whitney's beloved father, and it was his fault. She ripped her anguished gaze from him and began to move, quickly lost in the press and mayhem caused by other spectators. Garner was frantic to find her. He began to shove and push his way back up the crowded aisle.

Byron had seen it all, the desolation in her face, the pain in Garner's as they confronted each other. And for some reason, he'd felt the clashing forces of their fates and the desperate intensity of their love in the depths of his own being. They were hurting . . . they might not survive . . . unless . . . He shot into motion, jostling to intercept Garner.

"I have to find her—" Garner groaned, trying to shove his father aside. But Byron grabbed his arms fiercely and held him.

"No! Listen to me, Garner—there won't be much time! We've got to do something now!"

"She needs me—"

"No, dammit, Black needs you!" He shook the urgency into Garner's straining form. "You'll find her later. Think of Black— we have to find a way to save him. Come with me now!"

Something in Byron's tone reached Garner, and he eased in his father's grip. "Come where?"

"The President—he's the only chance Daniels has now."

Garner was stunned. *The President.* Washington could *pardon* Black! "Wait!" He yelled and turned, fighting his way back through the crowd and past the bailiffs to reach Black. He just managed to grab the purple patch of cloth pinned to Black's chest before the bailiffs dragged him away and shoved him through the railing gate.

Once in the comparative calm of the corridor, Byron ordered Charlie to escort the women home, and turned to Garner. The two set off through the crowd.

They strode along the streets, shoulders braced, booted legs covering ground, hearts pounding furiously.

"What are we going to do?" Garner rasped.

"Damned if I know," Byron growled. "Probably make him a deal of some kind—"

Twenty-five

A deal. The words beat in Garner's brain. A bargain. God. Dear God, help them. They were going to try to bargain the President of the United States into issuing a pardon to a convicted traitor. Garner's stomach pulled into a tight knot at the thought. It was a desperate move in a desperate cause. And somehow they'd have to do it—Black's life and his life with Whitney both depended on it.

President Washington had left his offices for the day, they were informed, and they trailed him to his residence, where soldiers and secretaries and servants blocked the way in successive waves. Byron's Townsend arrogance and almost invective use of "Townsend" and other powerful names badgered, bullied, and intimidated them through each ring of obstacles. And as they strode into Washington's study, Byron muttered to his son, "I got you here, it's up to you now."

Garner swallowed, staring at the large-boned man who sat behind the littered writing desk. The man was no smaller than the legend. And the eyes were no less piercing as they lifted from behind tin-rimmed spectacles. They fixed on Garner as he came forward, introducing himself and his father. And the President's lined and fleshy face registered a spark of recognition. "Townsend, I know the name. Boston, and the militia. What is this news you bear?"

"Urgent news, sir." Garner came to the point and to the edge of the table. "The trial of Blackstone Daniels has just ended in a verdict of guilty. It is a grave and terrible miscarriage of justice, sir, and we have come to appeal to you to do everything in your power to see the error is not compounded by the hanging of an innocent man."

"The whiskey trial?" Washington's eyes narrowed. "And what have you to do with such an undertaking?" But the light of understanding dawned as Garner explained his bizarre connections to the Black Daniels case and proceeded to explain in vivid terms how such connections came about. The President's jaw loosened and his spectacles were shed as he heard of a longing that became a bedding that became a forced wedding . . . and the capture of a major distiller. It was a remarkable story, a shocking disgrace that had ripened into both a true marriage and a family tragedy.

Garner paused for breath, realizing he'd rattled on for a quarter of an hour, nonstop. He read what Washington was about to say in his grave expression before he even spoke.

"It is a tale, indeed, Major Townsend, one that taxes both the heart and the mind. But it is one in which I have no part. The man is duly tried and condemned by a jury of his peers."

"Only with the most biased and unreasonable conduct of a federal judge," Byron interjected. "This was not justice, sir, but a fierce mockery of it!"

"The man is duly convicted." Washington rose and turned away toward the window. "Have you any idea how many forces are at work to tear down this fragile patchwork of order and government? The man is a confessed tax resister—"

Garner's hands clenched in frustration at his sides as he felt the tide turning, slipping away from him. That involuntary motion reminded him of a desperate bit of evidence. He raised and opened his hand to stare at the purple, heart-shaped patch that was mute testimony to Black Daniels's bravery and loyalty. He thrust it out to Washington, his eyes catching fire.

"And a patriot," Garner declared hoarsely.

In the prickling silence, Washington turned back with a furrowed brow. He took a step toward Garner, his eyes riveted on the purple heart. Then he took another step, and another. His voice lowered. "Where did you get that?"

"From the man you awarded it to . . . Blackstone Daniels." His voice carried the urgency of his pounding blood and racing heart. "He spent the winter with you at Valley Forge. And the following year took a double wound while saving a group of his fellow soldiers from certain death."

Washington's ruddy face seemed to gray. "If what you say is true . . . the faces of that bitter winter are etched in my soul. Who is this man—what is he like?"

"A man of medium height with dark hair and fiery hazel eyes and an odd dent in the tip of his nose. He's a born trader and leader and he talks—they say he can talk a dog down off a meat wagon!"

Washington raised a thick hand to halt Garner, and his eyes closed. In his mind, vivid images of ragged, frozen soldiers roiled up in him, as in the dreams that sometimes plagued him. And a face, hazy but flashing an indomitable grin, with a peculiar dent at the end of his nose seemed to come to him. And the fleeting impression of a bloody, barefoot swagger . . . in the snow.

"I would sell my soul for those men who suffered that winter with me." Washington's voice was choked. "But I cannot sell my country's. We must quell treason wherever it starts."

"But it was *not* treason!" Garner groaned with angry frustration at how close they'd come. "I arrested him for tax evasion, not treason. They've trumped up these charges and threatened me with the same if I refused to testify." He began to quiver with desperation. Damn! What did a man like Washington want? What would it take to bargain him? And that desperate half-prayer was answered from the old general's lips themselves.

"History must not record that we struggled to birth this nation only to let it die in infancy. And if I have a place in this history, it must be that I defended . . ."

History—a place in history! Washington was a man who had no desire unfilled in life except the desire to be remembered, credited to future generations. To leave a noble legacy was what he *wanted*. It was a desperate gamble; and if it worked, a paradise bargain.

"And how will history record a government so rattled and uncertain, so frightened of its own shadow that it rushes to convict and to hang innocent men, its own patriot sons, for speaking out as is their right under the Constitution? How long will this country last when judges deny lawful defense in the courts and direct verdicts to suit political winds? How will the generations judge a president who allows such a blatant miscarriage of justice to go forward?"

Garner saw the clouding of Washington's eyes, and knew with shocking insight that he was teetering on the edge. "And how will you sleep at night with Black Daniels's fate on your conscience? Will you be the first president to hang a man for treason, an innocent man, an old campaigner of yours?"

Garner moved around the desk and thrust the scrap of precious purple cloth into Washington's hand. They were of a height, eye to eye, searching for the future in each other's faces. "You are the first president. God willing, there will be many after you in this office. But let there be no one in years to come who is more dedicated to the principles of justice and truth than you. It can be your legacy, and yours alone. Your honesty told and retold for years to come. And it can start tomorrow, in the papers, then on people's lips and in their hearts. Proof of his loyalty lies in the palm of your hand, General. Blackstone Daniels deserves more from the country he fought to create. He deserves the justice and the liberty he shed his blood for . . . in your service."

Washington looked down at the faded badge of honor in his hand, its ripped ribbon, its worn gold embroidery. When his head rose there were prisms of moisture in his aging eyes. And there was a pardon in his heart.

Garner and Byron blew through the door of their lodgings, faces burnished with triumph. Kate and Madeline and Charlie came running from the parlor to meet them and were engulfed in delirious hugs.

"He's being pardoned!" Byron bellowed, scooping up Kate and swinging her around. "Garner's bargained Black a pardon!"

"Where's Whitney?" Garner boisterously grasped Charlie's shoulders and then Madeline's, craning his neck around them. "I want to be the one to—"

"She's gone, Garner." Madeline recovered enough to grasp

his sleeve. "She fled the courthouse—we thought she might have come here, but no one's seen her since."

Gone. It took a minute to register through the blood pounding in his head. The sight of her face when the verdict was read suddenly flooded his senses, and his head snapped toward the half-open front doors. She was out there somewhere, wandering.

Minutes later he was on horseback, racing through the streets of Philadelphia, searching for her. She knew almost nothing about the city—where would she go? Vivid scenes of her, devastated and defenseless as she drifted, spurred him hard. He should have reached her at the courthouse, asked her to trus— *Trust him?*

What reason would she have had to trust him, with her heart in pieces and her father bound for the noose? The thought rode him hard as he wove through the streets. But where would she go? He tried thinking as she would, she who loved whiskey and bargaining. . . . Bargaining. It burst in his brain like a rocket, and he spurred his horse, heading for the central market. She loved Boston's bawdy, bustling market. Perhaps the raucous sounds had drawn her there.

Threading his way through the crowded stalls and vendors' carts, he searched the hurly-burly for a patch of sea-green velvet, the coat that matched her eyes. And there she was, drifting with melancholy aimlessness among the rows of stands and carts, watching the people, absorbing the comfort of the brash spirit of bargaining all around her. Garner dismounted, calling her name, but the sound was swallowed up in the din of fishmongers and butchers shouting prices, grocers haggling over spices, and tinkers hawking their wares.

"Whitney!" She heard her name faintly and her head came up, searching the faces around her. He was bearing down on her, his face hot and glowing, his eyes burning strangely. "Whitney—" Instinctively, she backed away. She was totally unprepared to face him or to face the specter that now lay between them. Her pa . . . condemned to die.

"Whitney!" He watched her melt back into the crowd and hurried after her, knowing now just how much she was hurting. He gained on her with each panicky turn she made until he lunged, just managing to grasp one coat sleeve. "Blessit, Whitney, stop—I have to tell you—"

"No—" She tugged and struggled, backing as he advanced, jostling vendors and patrons aside bodily in the process. Didn't he understand that she had to be alone? That the sight of him was like a knife in her heart?

"Whitney—" He glimpsed the faces turning on them with escalating curiosity and groaned, "Come home with me. I have to tell you—"

"No—I can't go home with you. Please, let me be alone." His hold on her strengthened as he snagged her wrist itself, but she braced to resist being reeled closer.

"Listen to me, Whitney." Determination to reach her pushed him beyond caring who else might hear him. "Black's being pardoned. Do you hear me? *Pardoned!*"

Whitney froze, turning a pain-filled look on him. For a moment, all movement, all existence, came to a halt. "Wh-what?"

"I said, he's being pardoned. The President is reviewing the case and has promised to grant him *a full pardon.*" He took advantage of her shock to grab her other wrist, and the motion startled her back to her senses.

"Please, don't say that—"

"Blessit, Whitney, it's true. Byron got us in to see Washington, and I bargained a pardon for your father out of him—I swear it!" Only then, faced with the utter disbelief on her face, did he realize how improbable it must sound . . . how improbable it *was!* Staid, proper, Boston-bred Garner Townsend, bartering and dealing the President of the United States into pardoning an acknowledged whiskey rebel, one of the very men Washington had vowed to run to ground and rid the nation of?

That same instant, Whitney realized that upstanding, uncompromising Garner Townsend would never say it if it weren't true. In all their problems, in all their conflicts and cross-purposes, he had never lied to her. He would never lie to her. Her legs went weak as blood rushed up from her middle to burst against her skin. *"You?"* Rising hope choked her words. "But you're no trader. You don't know the first thing about it."

"Well, apparently I know enough about it to save your father from hanging."

Her jaw loosened; he was serious. "A real pardon—are you sure?"

"He'll be released as soon as the documents are drawn up, probably tomorrow." He watched the hope in her eyes being realized, and was seized by the urge to take her into his arms just as she was seized by a last spasm of doubt.

"But how could you possibly . . . *General Washington* . . . good Lord, Garner, what did you say to him?" She braced with stiffened arms.

"She still won't believe me!" he roared to the heavens and to any and everyone present in the motley audience they were collecting. Toothless old fishwives and fat, oily butchers, barelegged tars, and businessmen in silk hose and stock-wrapped collars all craned their necks to see. Garner released her and ran a hand back through his dark hair. His chin rose to a recognizable angle.

"Come home with me and I'll tell you . . . word for word." A wicked glint, a pure trader's light, leapt into his eyes.

"B-but—"

"You want to hear how I bargained your father a pardon? Well, you'll have to come home with me, Whitney Daniels Townsend." He began to stalk her, and as she backed away, their audience shifted to move with them. "You'll have to come home with me like a proper wife and quit making a spectacle of us in front of half of Philadelphia."

She stopped dead. "Quit making a spec—" Then the realization galvanized her; he was bargaining her . . . now . . . this very minute. Garner Townsend was bargaining her. He *had* bargained her pa a pardon, just as he said!

Joy burst inside her, raining hot sparks through her doubts, consuming them. She had them both now, it rang in her heart, Garner and her pa!

Tears rimmed her eyes as she met his and poured all the love and the gratitude of her extraordinary heart into them. And Garner distilled all the pride, the trust, the caring in him into the potent liquor of a whiskey-hot look. In that intimate exchange, both found the promise and the fulfillment of a life-giving love.

"I want a proper wife, wench." His voice deepened, woven richly with feeling. "But I want you even more. I've been responsible for all your heartaches, Whitney. But I swear, from now on, I'm going to be responsible for your joys. Come home with me and be my woman. You can wear breeches and bargain the servants and work at the distillery. And if you promise not to get my grandfather too drunk, you can drink whiskey whenever you want. And if you promise not to kick too hard or fight too dirty, I'll make you a paradise bargain . . . to last the rest of your life."

The onlookers held their breaths awaiting her reply.

"It's a deal!"

She launched herself into his arms, laughing, tears rolling, squeezing him. He plunged voraciously into the welcoming heat of her kiss, and enjoyed a foretaste of the paradise he'd just bargained.

Black Daniels was indeed pardoned and released the next day. Under the conditions of his pardon, he was never to distill liquor again within the boundaries of the United States, a condition he considered nearly as drastic as the alternative. He suggested he be allowed to speak with his old commander himself, maybe make old General George a proposition. Garner's volcanic wrath and Charlie's bone-jarring persuasion finally convinced him the terms of the pardon were more than adequate, and he graciously agreed to abide by them. He exited the prison a free man with a furrowed brow and a Daniels bit of calculation in eyes utterly undimmed by months of hardship. "Kaintuck," he told them on the way to the Townsends' temporary quarters. He'd heard quite a little bit about it from his fellow prisoners since his arrest. It was reputedly the place to be for a distiller: west of the long federal arm, good soil, good water, and next to a river for transport.

He arrived at the Townsends' lodgings to a joyous reunion with his daughter and sister-in-law and his new relations by marriage. Whitney hugged Black and Garner and Charlie, but when she came to Byron's stiff form, she paused. Her chin managed only a modest angle and her eyes glistened. "Thank you for all you've done." When she put out both hands to him and he took them, there was a bit of sniffing and throat-clearing in the parlor around them.

Edgewater marshaled a fine feast of celebration that evening, and at dinner Black rose to propose a toast of gratitude to Garner and Byron. Garner rose next to propose a toast to Byron's generous assistance and Charlie's ungrudging help. Then he turned to Whitney, and informed her that she had one more "weepy female" bargain to do . . . another trip to the newspapers to reveal the President's divinely guided wisdom and unerring sense of justice. It was an inherent part of the deal, letting everybody know the extent of the old general's greatness. She smiled and agreed.

When Byron rose, everything became quiet.

"It is late, but no less heartfelt. Welcome to our family, Whitney." He stood with both his glass and his proud chin raised. And at that moment all realized that was exactly what had happened in recent weeks. They had weathered adversity together, helped and supported each other . . . like a real family. Garner looked at Whitney and glimpsed her brash, unquenchable spirit and the generous, forgiving heart beneath it, and knew she was the cause. She'd brought her vitality, her life-giving warmth to his family as she had brought it to him. And he felt like the luckiest man on earth.

"To my son's marriage." When they'd all cleared their throats and drunk to that, he continued with a gallant tilt toward Kate. "And to our own upcoming nuptials."

The glasses were halfway to their lips before it sank in. He watched their surprise a bit smugly and clarified: "Kathryn and I will be wedded as soon as possible upon our return to Boston."

The only one in the room who was surprised was Garner; he was the lone member of the household who hadn't caught Kate and Byron in a compromising position. But Kate herself stared at Byron in shock. Crimson-faced, she rose to her feet, staring, then glaring at him. "How dare you make such assumptions, Byron Townsend. Without even speaking to me—*marry* you—

ooohhh!" She whirled and exited in a blaze of fury. Byron stared after her, then at the other men present.

"Don't know much about females, do you?" Black cocked an appraising eye at Byron, then broke into a wicked laugh. "You sure picked a tough one to learn on."

Byron looked for all the world like he was regretting his recent part in freeing Black Daniels, and, as he turned on his heel, he found little Madeline standing in his way, her arms crossed and her hazel eyes flashing.

"You'd better not botch this, Uncle Byron. I've got a chance for an aunt Kate and you'd better come through." Her eyes narrowed determinedly. "Or my ten percent goes to Cousin Garner."

Thus when Byron wheeled and went charging upstairs to Kate's room, it was with his love, his manly pride, and his business future all on the line. As the muffled sounds of a heated exchange wafted down the stairs, Black rose with a wicked grin and rubbed his chest, declaring he might have a walk after supper. Whitney and Charlie both offered to go with him, but he declined. He just wanted to savor the freedom, he said, and to think a bit.

Garner yawned broadly, mentioning what a full day it had been with a meaningful glance at Whitney, and soon they were climbing the stairs arm in arm. The sounds of contention from Kate's room had subsided, but below them in the hallway they heard little Madeline's most "Iron Townsend" sneer.

"Try that again and I swear—I'll bite!"

And they heard Charlie Dunbar laugh.

The fifth of May, exactly a month after Black Daniels's pardon, Kathryn Morrison and Byron Townsend were married in Boston before a select group of its political and financial elite. At the party that followed, Byron announced that his son, Garner, would be assuming the reins of Townsend Companies, and that after a suitably long honeymoon, he intended to run for Congress. At his side, Kate glowed with pride and love. And down the table from him, his son and daughter-in-law beamed, and old Ezra Townsend nodded moist-eyed approval.

Throughout the festive evening, Black and Ezra argued the

merits of various distilling methods and spirits, as had been their wont in recent days, and Madeline heatedly ignored Charlie Dunbar, who took it in stride and managed to console himself with the admiration of the other young ladies present. It was just as well, Charlie thought, watching little Madeline's seductive sway at the side of the handsome Carter Melton. He would just have to break her heart when he and Black took off for "the Kaintuck" soon anyway.

Later that evening, when the guests had left and the house was quiet, Garner and Whitney mounted the stairs to their room, very aware of each other physically. The knowledge of Kate and Byron's wedding night in progress nearby piqued their own desires. Whitney had Garner undo her laces and stood in the midst of the rug before the cold fireplace, peeling her elegant watered silk very slowly.

Garner's throat tightened as he watched the delectable, dark-tipped mounds of her breasts emerge, nestled above a snug and frilly corset. He latched the door and stood watching her provocative movements as she shed her petticoats, letting his eyes collect some of the heat radiating from her voluptuous body. His gait became an animal prowl as he approached and slowed, inching closer.

But when their bodies were a breath apart, he still hadn't touched her. Whitney's heart was thudding, her skin was warm and tingly with expectation as his hands raised and hovered over her bare shoulders, so close that she could feel their heat. That almost-touch began to glide over her, and she closed her eyes, feeling the heat of his hands sliding down over her bare arms, her half-bare breasts, and up over her throat and face. Stimulation and perception merged and she couldn't tell if he was touching her or if she imagined it . . . and knew it didn't matter. She rose onto tiptoe, her mouth parting, seeking.

She opened her eyes to find him moving back a pace, then another. Frowning, she swallowed against the desire gripping her throat, and she watched him sit in a nearby wing chair and throw one long, muscular leg casually over the arm.

"You know, I've been thinking." The huskiness of his voice betrayed arousal, but there was a very disciplined gleam in his eye that said it was mastered. "I'm a very lucky man. I've a beauty of a wife who's deliciously eager to please me in all respects but one." He let that sink in a moment and relished the becoming flush of confusion on Whitney's face. His expression became doleful indeed. "I'm a man whose wife won't spend his money, won't spend proper money at all." Whitney's jaw dropped and his expression became pure martyrdom. "It's a painful disgrace, shames me right down to the roots of my eastern business magnate's soul. So, I've decided to take the matter in hand, starting tonight."

Whitney turned to him fully, bemused by his gambit and feeling the smoke of frustration curling through her well-primed body. Her eyes widened as he pulled a leather pouch from his coat pocket and let its contents jingle against his lean fingers. Coins tinkled in the silence.

"I'm going to teach you to spend money, wench, in the most pleasant and memorable way possible. Tonight, if you want pleasures, you'll have to buy them."

Whitney gasped, and her jaw worked for a moment before the words issued forth: "Don't be . . . absurd."

Garner's grin was borrowed from the Daniels repertoire of wicked determination. "It's not absurd, it's only fair. *I* had to learn to bargain, *you* have to learn to spend money. It's really very simple; you tell me what you want and I tell you the price. You give me the money . . . and I give you . . . whatever you want." His long leg slid insolently from the chair arm, and he rose with seductive grace, savoring the way her eyes slid helplessly over his bulging breeches.

"Don't be ridiculous, Garner." She gave him a scorchingly seductive look and brushed pointedly against his front. But when his hands closed on her arms, he set her back firmly and thrust the bag of coins into her hands. She stared at it, then at him. He was serious.

She plunked the bag down firmly on the table and paced as far from him as the room allowed. *How dare he!*

He sank back into the chair with a very determined look and watched her pace and fume, wondering if he should have warmed her up a bit more before introducing the "lesson." She paused to glare at him and he shrugged. "Of course, if you can't . . ."

"There's nothing to spending money, Garner Townsend. Every half-wit and lowlife in Boston does it," she snapped, unaware she was abetting his logic. She stiffened as his taunting grin struck home. Every lowlife and half-wit did it . . . but *she* couldn't, that grin said. It was like waving a red shirt in front of a bull. She stalked to the table and snatched up the bag of coins with a growl, opening it with a jerk. Gold winked back at her in the dim light, gold coins of different sizes, marked with different denominations. She swallowed hard, feeling a strange tightness in her throat and a cottony feeling in her head.

She took a deep breath and pulled a large, mint-bright coin out, raising both it and her chin to Garner's twinkling gaze. Her voice was a dry rasp. "I want a kiss."

Garner was on his feet in a flash, coming toward her. "A fifty-dollar kiss? Wouldn't you rather start with something smaller?"

She huffed angrily and, with a black look at the twitching of his mouth, she delved into the pouch for something smaller. She came out with a smaller coin stamped with a "20" in the middle and demanded irritably, "Will this do? Twenty dollars, is it?"

"We'll have to work on your spendthrift ways after you've mastered the basics," he taunted tenderly, coming very close, nudging against her.

"Well, then, make it worth twenty dollars." She felt a strange rush of excitement in her that felt like power. And a heartbeat later, as he took her in his arms, she realized she knew this feeling. It was the same feeling she got the instant she struck a bargain!

Garner's mouth closed over hers; his tongue tantalized her lips in erotic circles, then slipped inside to stroke the sleek velvet walls of her mouth and the polished hardness of her teeth. She opened to him, sagging against his hardening body, feeling the familiar warming in her loins and the hunger of wanting in her stomach.

Then he straightened and backed a step, his eyes silver, his features sharpened with desire. His arms twitched to enfold her, his body burned wherever she had touched it. But he knew the outcome would be even sweeter if his Townsend determination held sway over his desires. And the ire that flamed briefly in her eyes tested his resolve sorely.

"Hold me," she demanded hoarsely, her breasts rising and falling faster.

"That's ten dollars, wench. And I suppose you'll be wanting another kiss with it . . . another twenty," he managed to add, sounding surprisingly calm.

"Blessit, Garner Townsend—" she flared, stomping a foot. The dormant Delilah in her was suddenly jarred awake. Garner had passions too, however he controlled them. She'd get what she wanted. She fished in the bag for ten- and twenty-dollar coins and pressed them into his palm. He dropped them into his pocket and drew her into his arms to plunge into the hot, wet honey of her mouth again. In the last second, as he held her tightly against his hardening frame, his body flexed, thrusting his swollen shaft against her involuntarily. When he pulled away, they were both breathing hard, both feeling molten currents of desire coiling through them.

"At these rates"—he grinned an exceedingly lecherous grin— "it's going to be a very costly night."

"How much is a touch?" She ignored his scandalous teasing.

"What kind of touch?" he asked thickly.

"Private. And long. And firm." Her voice was a sultry rasp as her hands came up to nudge her breasts free of her corset, demonstrating. "Here."

"Twenty . . . both hands." He could scarcely whisper, watching her lush nipples harden before his eyes as her fingers trailed across them. She reached into the pouch and, without looking, miraculously pulled forth a twenty-dollar gold piece. Flashing it before his gaze, she dropped it in his pocket. His hands closed firmly over her pale, satiny breasts and his fingers trapped her nipples, working them expertly. Her eyes closed and her head dropped back as she arched against that contact and sighed raggedly.

When his hands stilled on her, she opened her eyes, looking straight into his black-centered gaze. She put her hands on his wrists and dragged his palms down her sides, onto her buttocks as she rubbed erotically against his front. "Is this the same touch, or a different one?"

He managed to straighten only by not breathing and not thinking about the firm, silky mounds he was relinquishing. His entire body was on fire. Whatever had possessed him to attempt such madness? "Different."

She reached for another coin. "Touch me again."

He did touch her, kneading her smooth, rounded buttocks while suffering the glorious, self-inflicted torture of feeling her warm body against his arms. It took every ounce of determination he possessed to finally withdraw. He stood, trembling, afraid to move, as she picked up the bag of coins and swayed to the bed.

She slid across the soft linen and beckoned. "Take your clothes off. Slowly," she ordered, holding up another large gold piece, a fifty. He peeled his garments with obedient leisure, watching the fires of passion flickering through her as she hungrily searched the emerging mounds and angles of his body. She rubbed her legs over each other languidly and lay back on the bolsters. "Then kiss me all over."

"You do have expensive tastes, wench," he groaned, climbing onto the bed beside her. "Another fifty at least."

She pressed a coin into his palm and lay back, letting him do his work. He knelt beside her and began with a brief kiss on her lips and then her temples and ears and throat. By the time he reached her breasts, he began to throw in a few free nibbles. And by the time he reached her hipbones, he was stroking her with his tongue and his hands, sending trickles of fire under her skin. Then her thighs, her knees, her feet . . . and back up the inside of her thighs . . . he was consuming her.

Her body became a living flame under his attentions, undulating, flickering, hot, and glowing. It was heavenly torture, wave upon wave of pleasure too full, too wild for her to contain. And when he imbedded a final kiss in her thatch of gingery curls, on her most sensitive flesh, a hoarse moan ripped from her throat and vibrated through them both. Garner rose onto his knees, between her parted legs, staring down at her loveliness, her openness to loving, to him.

"Lesson over."

He lifted the pouch and poured the remaining coins onto her body, scattering them over her silky belly and soft breasts. She gasped as the cold metal showered her skin, but a moment later Garner's hot body slid over hers, too, trapping the hard gold coins between them. He kissed her hungrily and cradled her in his arms, joining their bodies with a series of strong, rhythmic thrusts.

They arched and trembled, giving, releasing, joined in passion, in will, and in love. Then, as the peak approached, everything slowed, and in the calescent heat they merged, becoming one. And when the raging tide in their blood subsided, they refused to part, lying wrapped in each other's arms, their legs entwined.

Sometime later Whitney wriggled contentedly and kissed his chest and his stubborn chin. "Did I do all right, for a shameful spendthrift?"

"You seem to have a great deal of natural talent for it." He tucked his chin to look at her with soft-eyed wonder.

"For spending your money or your passions?" she asked silkily. And he laughed, relaxing around her once again.

His face was so beautiful, she realized, with its fine straight nose and high cheekbones and graceful, expressive mouth. He made a very handsome man. Her thoughts began to drift and took a peculiar, womanly bend. He would probably make handsome children too . . .

"Garner?"

"Umm-hmmm?" He was drifting a bit.

"How much would you charge for . . . making a baby?"

She felt him start and felt the shaking of his body against her as laughter worked its way up through him. He drew back on his shoulder to look at her and turned her reddening face back to his.

"I won't charge for babies," he said, his eyes twinkling, "if you won t." He laughed again, pulling her against his chest in a tight hug. "You see the way it really works is . . . the good Lord lets us have babies on credit . . . and then we get to pay for them the rest of our lives."

Author's Note

I hope you enjoyed Whitney and Garner. The historical setting of this book is based in fact that sometimes reads stranger than fiction. The Whiskey Rebellion was a surprisingly bloodless uprising by largely poor and loyal frontier farmers. Beset by external enemies and fearful of internal factions, Washington and his cabinet believed "overaction" was preferable to "underaction" and determined, based on "intelligence" that was sometimes absurdly inaccurate, that a show of military force was imperative.

The "watermelon army" was hastily conscripted, ill-equipped, and populated largely by the East's landless poor. The brawling, uncivilized behavior of the troops was often an embarrassment to their "gentlemanly" corps of officers; George Washington himself was upset that in some places his men pillaged so that they "did not leave a plate, a spoon, a glass, or a knife" behind. As Garner Townsend illustrated, the very word "militia" became a term of contempt. In one instance, on the march west, the men of several units revolted, refusing to strike their tents for the day's march. Bewildered officers were forced to distribute an extra ration of whiskey and to give the men the day off to get drunk.

Some young gentlemen of fashion did agree to serve, but only in gentlemanly regiments (like mounted "dragoons") and argued endlessly over the style and color and "accoutrements" of uniforms. "Where egos and sartorial tastes went unsatisfied," historian Thomas P. Slaughter writes in his book, *The Whiskey Rebellion,* "refusal to serve or, in the case of draftees, purchase of substitutes were the choice alternatives for men of substance. Honor and ambition often supplanted patriotism as the highest priorities of both the resplendent dragoons riding west and those who petulantly stayed behind."

Of those rebels arrested and taken on the forced march to Philadelphia, only two were actually convicted of treason; both were pardoned by George Washington himself upon the pleas of men of substance. The trials themselves proved an embarrassment to the prosecutors, so many of the men were released due to lack of evidence and witnesses. Observers recorded that only the most flagrant of judicial prejudice and misconduct permitted the two convictions that were obtained.

Thus Garner and Whitney's situation, as wild as it might seem, could actually have happened. A girl, raised in the cashless society of the frontier, a gentlemanly officer, resplendent with gold buttons and burning with ambition . . . It is my own family background and loose connections to latter-day distillers ("moonshiners") that provided some of the color of Black Daniels's distilling operation . . . and the "old uncles." And it is a bit of my own philosophy that everything probably does have its price . . . but that there are some things that should never be bought, bargained, or sold.

ROMANCE FROM FERN MICHAELS

DEAR EMILY   (0-8217-4952-8, $5.99)

WISH LIST   (0-8217-5228-6, $6.99)

AND IN HARDCOVER:

VEGAS RICH   (1-57566-057-1, $25.00)

Available wherever paperbacks are sold, or order direct from the Publisher. Send cover price plus 50¢ per copy for mailing and handling Penguin USA, P.O. Box 999, c/o Dept. 17109, Bergenfield, NJ 07621. Residents of New York and Tennessee must include sales tax. DO NOT SEND CASH.

ROMANCE FROM JO BEVERLY

DANGEROUS JOY   (0-8217-5129-8, $5.99)

FORBIDDEN   (0-8217-4488-7, $4.99)

THE SHATTERED ROSE   (0-8217-5310-X, $5.99)

TEMPTING FORTUNE   (0-8217-4858-0, $4.99)